Traitor

Zeb Carter Series, Book 5

By

Ty Patterson

Copyright © 2019 by Ty Patterson

All rights reserved

Published by Three Aces Publishing

Visit the author site: http://www.typatterson.com

Books by Ty Patterson

Warriors Series Shorts

This is a series of novellas that link to the Warriors Series thrillers

Zulu Hour, Book 1
The Shadow, Book 2
The Man From Congo, Book 3
The Texan, Book 4
The Heavies, Book 5
The Cab Driver, Book 6
Warriors Series Shorts, Boxset I, Books 1-3
Warriors Series Shorts, Boxset II, Books 4-6

Gemini Series

Dividing Zero, Book 1
Defending Cain, Book 2
I Am Missing, Book 3
Wrecking Team, Book 4

Cade Stryker Series

The Last Gunfighter of Space, Book 1
The Thief Who Stole A Planet, Book 2

Warriors Series

The Warrior, Book 1
The Reluctant Warrior, Book 2
The Warrior Code, Book 3
The Warrior's Debt, Book 4
Flay, Book 5
Behind You, Book 6
Hunting You, Book 7
Zero, Book 8
Death Club, Book 9
Trigger Break, Book 10
Scorched Earth, Book 11
RUN!, Book 12
Warriors series Boxset, Books 1-4
Warriors series Boxset II, Books 5-8
Warriors series Boxset III, Books 1-8

Zeb Carter Series

Zeb Carter, Book 1
The Peace Killers, Book 2
Burn Rate, Book 3
Terror, Book 4
Traitor, Book 5
Zero Dark, Book 6

Sign up to Ty Patterson's mailing list and get *The Watcher*, a Zeb Carter novella, exclusive to newsletter subscribers. Join Ty Patterson's Facebook group of readers, at www.facebook.com/groups/324440917903074.

Check out Ty on Amazon, iTunes, Kobo, Nook and on his website www.typatterson.com.

Acknowledgments

No book is a single person's product. I am privileged that *Traitor* has benefited from the input of several great people.

Special thanks to Robert Gollberg for coming up with the name of *Hammish* and Gary Bristol for the name of *Amelia*.

I am grateful to Simon Alphonso, Jeanette Allsop, Paula Artlip, Matthew Bell, Gary Bristol, Sheldon Levy, Molly Birch, David T. Blake, Tracy Boulet, Patricia Burke, Mark Campbell, Allan Coulton, Tricia Cullerton, Linda Collins, Claire Forgacs, Mike Davis, Dave Davis, Sylvia Foster, Lyn Fox, Cathie Jones, Cary Lory Becker, Charlie Carrick, Pat Ellis, Dori Barrett, V. Elizabeth Perry, Ann Finn, Pete Bennett, Eric Blackburn, Margaret Harvey, David Hay, Jeane Jackson, Mary and Bob Kauffman, Jim Lambert, Shadine Mccallen, Debbie McNally, Suzanne Jackson Mickelson, Blanca Blake Nichols, Franca Parente, Heather Tudgey, Tricia Terry Pellman, Tania Reed, Wa Reedy, Colin Rochford, Jimmy Smith, Robin Eide Steffensen, Maria Stine, Don Waterman, Theresa and Brad Werths, Chuck Yarling, who are my beta readers and who helped shape my book, my launch team for supporting me, Donna Rich for her proofreading and Doreen Martens for her editing.

Dedications

To my family, for bending their lives to support me

Sometimes you have to pick the gun up to put the gun down

— Malcolm X

Chapter 1

Zeb Carter awoke suddenly.

One moment he was asleep in his room in Tripoli, Libya; the next, he was awake. He lay motionless, trying to work out what had roused him from his slumber.

His hotel was in Ben Ashour, a neighborhood south of downtown. It was a relatively more affluent district in the city, featuring several embassies and shopping opportunities.

Zeb was staying in an upscale hotel to go with his cover, that of Latif Wakil Misfud, an arms dealer.

He scanned the room without moving his eyes: Dim light seeping through the curtain covering the solitary window. Pale walls, cheap art mounted on them. A desk in a corner, a chair. A small passage that led to the bathroom.

Nope, there wasn't anyone else in the room.

He got up noiselessly and reached for his Glock near his bedside table. He had always trusted his instincts, his inner radar, and now, it was telling him there was danger. Close by.

He dressed swiftly. The custom-made plate armor over his upper body. Tee over jeans. Trainers on his feet. A jacket to cover the shoulder holster. It wasn't the attire Misfud would wear in public, but convenience was more important than cover.

His backpack was good to go, with his sat phone, spare mags, tablet computer and other equipment. He was inspecting it swiftly when it happened.

The room door exploded inwards. Two shapes appeared in the smoke and haze surrounding the entrance.

Combat suits. NVGs on their faces? These aren't friendlies.

Zeb reacted the instant his room was breached. This wasn't the time to freeze or panic. His training and experience took over. He moved on autopilot. Leapt towards the hallway and raced for the bathroom. At its entrance he paused for a fraction and looked back at the intruders.

Combat suits. Helmets.

One of them shot into his empty bed; the other checked out the room.

They came to kill.

The second man caught the flicker of movement as Zeb ducked out of the passage and shouted a warning, alerting his companion.

There could be more. Got to move, Zeb thought as he smashed the bathroom window, climbed onto the toilet seat and half-jumped, half-wriggled through the narrow opening.

He had planned for such a contingency. His room was on the third floor, and the bathroom window opened into a dark alley in which the hotel dumped its trash. Drainage pipes ran down the length of the building. He kicked out at the window sill and thrust forward. Reached out in the dark night, caught hold of one of them and yanked himself forward. Slid down a couple of inches before he gathered himself and climbed *up*.

Eight seconds from the breach, he was on the outside of the hotel, hugging its pipe, clinging to its wall.

Sheer, dumb luck had favored him. If the second man had fired around the room … he shrugged mentally as he reached with one hand and unholstered his Glock. Adrenaline filled him, sharpened his senses even as his mind raced.

Who are they? Do they know who I really am?

He shoved the questions to the back of his mind and waited.

The familiar grey fog took over him. It dulled the edges of the night. He was dimly aware of shapes in the alley. Trash bags and cans, thirty feet below. A rusting heap of a car abandoned by its owner years ago. A car's honk somewhere. A police cruiser's wail. Sights and sounds registered on him unconsciously, but the bathroom window became the center of his universe.

Muted murmuring came to him. He strained his ears but couldn't make out the language. He was thirty feet from the ground. Several trash bags lay below him, which he had arranged strategically for just such a moment.

A shadow crossed the window.

Zeb took a breath.

Another shadow.

A head poked out swiftly and withdrew.

More talking from inside.

A barrel extended.

Looks like an HK 416.

He couldn't be sure, however. Not that it mattered.

The weapon swung to the left and then to the right. *The shooter's looking out from within. Checking if I'm at the sides of the window. Or beneath it.*

As if on cue, the man thrust his head out cautiously and looked down, left and then right. He spoke to his companion and leaned out further.

Zeb acted.

Chapter 2

———∞∞∞———

Zeb threw himself down and sideways. He hurtled through the night, a human missile, his left-hand straightening with the Glock, right hand loose and empty.

He crashed into the leaning man.

Grabbed him by the shoulder with his free arm.

Fired his Glock blindly through the open window at the second shooter, triggering as fast as he could. Saw the intruder jerk and stagger back as rounds slammed into him.

He saw no more, because he was falling, dragging along with him the first shooter, who cried hoarsely, let go of his HK and flailed wildly.

A fraction of a second's flight that felt like minutes. Zeb maneuvered desperately and just in time to land on top of the intruder, who crashed into one of the trash bags.

One knee on the stranger's chest, another on the slippery plastic. He dug his Glock into the man's throat.

'Who are you?' he whispered harshly, in Arabic.

Looked up swiftly when the shooter groaned.

No heads peered out of the bathroom window, but the hotel was lighting up.

'I won't ask again,' he snarled and smashed the shooter's head on the spongy bag.

All he got was a long sigh.

Zeb swore and brought out his sat phone. He turned on its flashlight and inspected the fallen man.

He was dead.

Zeb felt beneath the man's head. Something hard and long, maybe a wooden frame in the trash bag.

That broke his neck.

He holstered his gun and took the man's picture. Searched the stranger, extracted his wallet and cell phone, and pocketed them.

He hurried out of the alley after one last glance at the hotel. He thought he could hear the distant wail of cruisers converging in front of the establishment.

Zeb turned right and joined al Jarabah Street, a main thoroughfare on which the hotel fronted. A bunch of onlookers in its porch, several police vehicles and suited hotel personnel gesticulating as they spoke with officers.

They'll be on the lookout for Latif Wakil Misfud. It was time for the arms dealer to disappear.

He walked away from the hotel, head bent, took a left after a mile, passed a Turkish restaurant, and entered the courtyard of an apartment block. It was fifteen floors high and was home to several government officials.

He used a key to open the wrought-iron door and entered a concrete lobby. No concierge service in the building. It didn't cater to that clientele.

He climbed swiftly to the fifth floor and headed to an apartment door at the far end of the hallway.

Put his ear to the door. No sounds from within.

Unlocked it, kicked it open and dropped to the ground, his Glock coming to his arm as if by magic.

No shots came his way from the dark interior.

He got to his feet, shut the door behind him and turned on the light. Living room. A few pieces of furniture, a thick layer of dust on them.

Zeb went to the bedroom, to the wardrobe, removed its back panel and extracted a box.

Passports of several countries, identity cards and wads of various currencies. He removed several bundles of Libyan dinars, Egyptian pounds, US dollars, and shoved them into his backpack. Inspected passports from those countries, and those too joined the notes in his go-bag.

He removed his clothing, changed into another pair of jeans. Kept his armor, threw on a shirt and replaced his jacket with another.

Saad Hadad Raahal. He practiced pronouncing his name in front of the bathroom mirror. Oilfield worker. *Lost my family in a terrorist attack. No one left in Libya.*

He inserted cheek pads to make his face look fleshier, inserted contacts in his eyes to make them look black, and threw more pieces of clothing into his backpack.

He wiped the apartment down and, forty-five minutes later, was back on the street. He flagged a cab. 'Gergaresh,' he told the driver, and gave him a hotel's address in the upscale neighborhood that overlooked the Mediterranean.

Half an hour later, he had checked into his room. He brought out his sat phone and sent a message to Beth and Meghan.

Who else knows my identity?

Chapter 3

Washington DC

'He escaped,' the voice said bitterly. 'You said you would send your best team. I am getting reports from Tripoli that both your men died. Zeb Carter is out there, alive.'

The speaker was tall, distinguished, his long, aquiline nose and greying hair adding to his air of importance. He rose from his desk at a knock on his study door. Opened it to usher in his butler, who laid out a tray on his desk and poured him a cup of Jamaican Blue Mountain coffee.

The man had flunkies, a security detail, and even though it was 4 am in DC, he was dressed for work. A pinstriped suit, a discreet tie and a US flag pin on his lapel. He looked like a senior politician. He *was* a senior politician, whose face and name were familiar not just to Americans but to millions around the world.

'He got lucky,' his caller responded wearily. 'In any case, we didn't expect to kill him in the first attempt. We know his track record; how good he is.'

'But he's out there,' the DC man protested.

'I will send another team. The Company,' he paused. 'I mean, the CIA—'

'I know who Company refers to.'

'Yeah, well, they'll be sending a team, too. All our allies—MI6, Mossad—everyone will join in the hunt. Zeb Carter is good, but he can't escape forever.'

'What about Clare?'

'Your sources didn't tell you? She has accepted the decision. She has no choice.'

'What about her team?' The politician ignored the pointed remark.

'They'll start hunting him too.'

'They haven't yet?'

'Nah. Give her time. I understand her position. He has led those agents for years. She has to give the kill order diplomatically.'

'Carter needs to die.'

'He will. But you need to back off. You're too close to this.'

'Carter is too close to everything,' the DC man said through gritted teeth.

'And he will be taken care of. But what you're doing, this call ... we discussed this. Back off. You are in the public eye. Everything you do and say is watched and commented on. You don't want a loose word to slip out of your mouth.'

'I know what I'm doing. I am using our agreed security protocol.'

'I'll take care of Carter.' Randy Spears, the caller, sighed and hung up. He rubbed his eyes and glanced at his watch. It would be 10 am in Tripoli. He punched a number on a burner phone and routed the call through several proxies.

His device was equipped with voice-altering software. It

also had a program that replaced key words with innocuous ones. Every person in the operation had such phones, which was why he was relaxed about the call he'd put in to the politician, even though he had made a show of security. *Anyone listening in wouldn't have heard Carter mentioned.*

'Bob,' he asked when a voice came on the line. 'You got any more intel?'

'Just, what I told you previously,' Robert Marin, former Delta commander and ShadowPoint operative, replied. 'Our shooters are dead. One body in the bedroom window, killed by Glock bullets. Another in the alley behind the hotel. Carter's bathroom window was broken. It looks like he and our shooter went through it. No idea how.'

'What do the police know?'

'Nothing. Our men carried no identification. Their prints and DNA are not in any system.'

'They were Europeans, right?'

'French assassins. We might have a problem, however. The second killer's wallet and phone are missing. Looks like Carter took them. ... Relax,' he said quickly when his caller stayed silent. 'They know nothing about us. I went through several cutouts to hire them. They got an advance payment and Carter's details. We are good.'

Spears nodded in the darkness of his room. Bob was right. 'Get another team. We need to nail Carter today.'

'I'll have to use our men. It's too short notice to get mercenaries. I've got a three-man team coming from Iran. They should be wheels-down any moment.'

'Use them. I'll get Carter's location from the Agency and send you the deets. We need to terminate him soon.'

He hung up, poured himself a drink despite the early hour,

and sipped it as his mind raced.

Spears was the CEO of ShadowPoint, a PMC, private military contractor, in Virginia. He had founded the outfit after leaving Delta Force, where he had been squadron commander. It was in the Special Forces that he had come across the DC man. The two had bonded quickly, had participated in several missions and had stayed in touch after leaving the Army.

Spears had founded his unit and started taking jobs from the Pentagon, using the contacts he had made.

The DC man pursued a career in politics and, with his media-friendly backstory and movie-star looks, reached dizzying heights in the corridors of power.

With him acting as benefactor and invisible string-puller, ShadowPoint became the largest PMC in the country. *In the world,* he corrected himself. With revenues of close to a billion dollars, the firm stuck to its core competencies. It provided skilled, experienced fighters and did nothing else. There were other military contractors, private security firms, larger than ShadowPoint, but all of them had diversified.

We fight. That's all we do, Spears mused. *That's why our clients come to us.*

It became the go-to agency for any mission the Pentagon, CIA or other agencies wanted to outsource. It had operations on all the continents and worked with the world's biggest militaries and corporations.

The outfit also became the DC man's private army.

A mutually beneficial relationship. Highly beneficial. I stopped worrying about my pension a long time ago, he thought, as he brewed coffee and looked around his luxurious house.

Their relationship worked not just because of their Special

Forces history. They had similar personalities. Both men had a hidden streak of ruthlessness and self-interest that they masked successfully. A moral code that most humans wouldn't identify with. They had psychopathic tendencies that served them well. Made them driven and ambitious.

More. I want more of what I have. Much more, Spears clicked his fingers and a wall-mounted TV turned on. *And he wants to become president.*

Which meant Zeb Carter had to die.

Chapter 4

─────ᴄᴇᴇᴏ─────

Tripoli

Zeb was up at 6 am the next day. A restful sleep in the night. No one had breached his hotel room; no masked figures had lain in wait in the bathroom.

He showered, dressed in a Tee and jeans and threw on an ill-fitting jacket that concealed his armor and his shoulder holster.

He watched the news while he brewed a drink in the coffeemaker. No reports of the attack on his hotel. It didn't surprise him. There were too many shootings and killings in the country for every one of them to be covered.

Libya was a country gripped by warring factions ever since Gadaffi was deposed. Shootings and killings were everyday occurrences and didn't receive special coverage.

We in the Western world decided to get rid of him. Didn't have a Plan B, and present-day Libya is what happened, Zeb snorted as he tasted his drink. It was bitter, strong and wouldn't kill him, he decided. He took a deep sip.

The Government of National Accord, GNA, the United

Nations–recognized administration, was based in Tripoli, but its grip over the city and the country was weak.

Over to the east was Hazim Kattan. He was a military leader who had been a general in Libya's Armed Forces. He had broken away, had taken battalions of soldiers with him and established an alternate government in the eastern city of Tobruk. He controlled that side of the country and vast swathes of southern Libya. He was at war with the internationally recognized government in Tripoli.

He's making a play for the capital and has sent his troops to battle against the government.

Then there were the numerous militia organizations led by warlords who were pursuing their own interests.

There was ISIL, too. The terrorist organization had been driven out of Libya, from their base in Sirte, after the GNA's military, supported by the US and its allies, attacked the city, killed and captured several terrorists, freed many hostages and ended ISIL's hold in Libya.

However, the terrorists had returned. They weren't as strong as they were before, but they were a potent force.

To add to the chaos in the country was the migrant crisis. The lack of a single, powerful government had led to the country becoming a gateway for African migrants, who attempted to cross the Mediterranean and seek a better future in Europe.

They came from war-torn countries from all parts of the continent. They even came from the East, from Syria, Saudi Arabia, Jordan, each one of them wanting to make a better future, a safer life for themselves and their families. Every one of them trusting pirates and gangs, who made tall promises of safe passage across the perilous stretch of sea and safe haven and opportunity in Europe.

Zeb wasn't in Libya for the migrant crisis or Hazim Kattan. He was after Nasir Fakhir Almasi, an ISIL leader who looked positioned to regroup the fallen terrorist organization and lead it.

Almasi was a charismatic leader whose fiery speeches had invigorated the group's followers. He was from a wealthy Syrian family, well-educated, and could speak the language of the street or carry out a highbrow debate with intellectuals.

He wasn't a mere preacher. He had bloodied his hands in Syria, where he had carried out several gruesome killings. He had killed Western journalists and broadcast the act live. He had tortured pregnant women and had beheaded several innocents.

He fled to Libya when Syria became too hot, and there, he started rebuilding the evil group.

His calls for the terrorists to rise again and create a caliphate were starting to be heard. Killers who had fled Syria, Iraq, Jordan and all the countries that ISIL had been defeated in started coming to Libya.

To Sirte, where Almasi was rumored to be based.

Nothing much was left of that city. It was dotted with wreckage, demolished and devastated buildings that had been destroyed in the Battle of Sirte.

It was a ghost town; its residents had long since fled, but that hollow shell of a city was now filling with terrorists again. Under Almasi's guidance, they resumed their suicide bombings and attacked government and public properties. They attacked oil wells and refineries, and terror returned to Libya and the neighboring countries.

The Western world reacted quickly. Secretive meetings

were held among MI6, Mossad, CIA, Pentagon, France's DGSE and several other covert outfits. They agreed Almasi had to be taken out. That decision made, every agency put forward its case for owning the mission. Every one of them had the operatives, the capabilities and the resources.

But only one got the unanimous vote.

The Agency.

Clare, its director, greenlighted the mission the moment she returned to DC. Zeb Carter was the automatic choice for the operation. It would require several months in-country. He was used to lone-wolf assignments; in fact, preferred them. It needed someone who could pass as a native. With his deeply tanned coloring and fluency in Arabic, with the right accent, he would blend in in Libya.

On top of that, he had the lethal skills.

Zeb drained his coffee, rinsed his mug and checked the wallet he had removed from the shooter the previous night. Libyan dinars, a couple of Benjamins. He fingered the US dollar notes. They were well-used. *Their presence doesn't prove anything. Many people in the country buy foreign currency on the black market.* There was no identification document. Nothing that said, *I am Joe Shooter. Contact Killers Inc in case I die.* He checked the shooter's phone and sighed when he saw it would require a thumbprint. *I should've unlocked it last night.* But he hadn't the time. Escape had been paramount. He removed its SIM and inserted it in a spare device he carried. The phone lit up and locked onto a local cell tower. *Now to see if anyone calls it.*

He pulled out his sat phone, frowned when he saw the *Message Not Delivered* notification on its screen. *Beth and*

Meg never got my text. He chewed his lip as he made a call. Got a dull tone. Disconnected and stared at the device.

That's weird. No signal. Satellite's down? Never happened before.

He connected his tablet computer to the hotel's WiFi and typed in a realtor's website. It was another means of communicating with his team, by posting queries and receiving responses about properties. Only he and his team knew what those messages meant. To anyone else, they would look like listing enquiries.

He sucked his breath sharply when the browser responded with an error message. The website was down. He tried another website, an online dating agency. Same result. He tried his phone again. Still no network. He went to his rarely used email account. Couldn't log in.

Zeb sat motionless for several moments as the implications sank in.

He had no means of communicating with his team. He could neither receive nor pass intel. His team couldn't warn him of threats.

I am cut off from them. He stared unseeingly out of the window.

Lone-wolf missions didn't mean an operative was truly alone. There was always a means of communicating with the command center. There were backups and fail-safes.

Not in my case, he thought bleakly.

He was all by himself. In a hostile country. Tracking the most dreaded terrorist in the world. While unknown enemies, who seemed to know his identity, hunted him.

Chapter 5

Zeb moved swiftly.

The tablet went into his backpack, the sat phone in his pocket. One last look around the room, a check in the bathroom, and ten minutes later he was out of his room.

As Saad Hadad Rahal, the oilman, he jammed the elevator button and stood back in the hallway. No one but him. It was a fancy hotel. Soft carpet. Dim lighting. Flowerpots. Bland art on the walls. It was a relatively safe haven compared to the one he had been attacked in. *This one's owners will have political connections. They'll have paid the cops and militia groups to stay away.* It was how Libya worked. Those who had juice were more comfortable.

He straightened his shoulders when the car arrived, creaking and groaning, and carried him to the lobby.

A second's pause to check out the interior of the lounge. A family in a corner, kids playing with a ball. An Arabic-looking couple at the reception desk. A suited man reading a newspaper. A security guard, yawning lustily in a corner. Outside, a line of cabs at the hotel's driveway. The doorman, in his uniform.

Nothing pinged Zeb's radar.

He walked out briskly and drew on his shades: Ray-Bans that had been customized, with stems that had been hollowed out to accommodate nano cameras that projected the rear view onto a small part of the inner lens. They were his eyes at the back.

No car swung out to follow him. No pedestrians appeared to show him any interest. He glanced at his watch and hurried.

The sat phone signal, the Realtor and dating website—he pushed all of those to the back of his mind. He couldn't afford to dwell on them.

He had an appointment with Abu Bakhtar, Nasir Fakhir Almasi's closest aide.

It had taken three months to secure the meeting. As Misfud, the arms dealer, Zeb had made himself known to various militia groups. He sold great product at better prices. He undercut every other weapons supplier in Tripoli, and whenever anyone asked him how he could afford his rates, he flashed his teeth and said, 'How much does one man need to live?'

Establishing himself and building up a reputation hadn't been easy. He had two covers. One was that of a respectable Syrian who had fled that country and was now arranging security and protection to Western visitors and businesses. He had a permit for the guns he carried and had often to mingle with mercenaries, whom he used as contractors.

His story for his illegal activities was simpler. He was a Syrian arms dealer who had moved out from his home country because it was no longer safe. He used to sell stolen weapons to the terrorist groups there and was establishing himself in Libya.

He set up warehouses in various neighborhoods in Tripoli. Paid off several officials and hired mercenaries to protect his precious goods, which had been arranged by Clare.

He haunted bars and hotels, talked to taxi drivers and hotel doormen. People in places that militia shooters and arms dealers were likely to haunt.

He had references: Well-known warlords who had handed themselves to the Western forces, their surrender a closely guarded secret. Bar owners and hotel managers in Syria who vouched for him and his generous spending. Corrupt police and snitches who whispered that he was the genuine deal.

He had people vouching for both his official legend and the weapons dealer one. He needed such extensive backstories because they would be checked. There were many times he had been followed in Tripoli, and the staff at the hotel where he stayed had been questioned.

He was arrested several times by the police and questioned. Each time, he had stuck to his official cover.

One time, he was captured in an alley and interrogated by masked gunmen. He stuck to his story and was released after a few hours.

The blows and punches he had suffered and the US dollars that had been stolen from him … that was a small price to pay to reinforce his legend.

Zeb's first sale was ten FIM-92s, shoulder-fired Stinger missiles, to a militia group that controlled a part of southern Tripoli. 'Sayyidi, please spread my name,' he told Muneer Rihab, the leader of the group. 'If I get another customer through your reference, I will give you a better price next time.'

Zeb's business grew slowly. He outpriced his competition, who often sent heavies to beat him up. He retaliated. Misfud was no pushover. He shot one weapons supplier, Gamali Haffez, in the shoulder, in broad daylight, as the man was stepping out of his car.

'Back off,' he snarled in Arabic as the Libyan bodyguards trained their guns on him. They didn't fire. It was a public place, and even though they were criminals and it was a lawless country, some rules had to be followed. 'This is a warning. Next time, my bullet will come from the shadows and you will be dead.'

He burned the warehouse of another arms dealer and broke the leg of a third. The message spread. Misfud was there to stay, and anyone who went against him had to prepare for a very rough ride.

Meanwhile, Zeb's business grew. AK47s, AR15s, grenade launchers, machine guns, shotguns, Stingers, there was nothing he couldn't procure.

'Baksheesh,' he used to smile slyly, when his customers asked how he procured his goods. 'Politicians, soldiers, everyone likes some baksheesh.'

In the midst of the continual conflict between the various militia groups and Kattan and the official government, no one noticed that Misfud's customers died quickly. An American drone strike here, a sniper attack there. None of their newly acquired weapons were ever recovered.

'Inshallah,' Zeb sighed and looked heavenwards whenever someone pointed out that his last customer was no more. 'Fate,' he would shake his head and then go about negotiating his next deal.

Zeb slipped into side streets, twisted and turned, stopped aimlessly several times. He hurried to Gergaresh Main Road when he was sure he wasn't being followed and flagged a taxi.

'Al Fatah Road,' he told the driver and gave him the name of the fancy hotel on the seafront.

The last few months, the clandestine meetings, the attacks on him, the lone-work mission, everything had built up to this moment.

Meeting Nasir Almasi's man.

Chapter 6

———∝∝∞———

Zeb entered the revolving glass door and slowed as he made a show of groping inside his backpack.

He looked around. Abu Bakhtar didn't know Rahal and was expecting to meet Misfud. *A meeting that we set up over the phone. But I hope he isn't aware of my Rahal disguise,* he thought grimly. *Given that attack on me, anything is possible.*

There, in that corner, was a sofa arrangement. It would give him a good view of the hotel's entrance, the elevators and the discreet exit behind the reception desk.

He placed his backpack on one seat, sprawled on another and gave a drink order to an attending server. He brought out his sat phone. Still no signal. Ignored the sudden gut-clench that brought. *Later. I'll worry about it later.*

He hadn't known it then, but Almasi had bought arms from him using various cutouts. Small deals for handguns, AK47s. *It looks like those were tests.* Because, then came the cautious reach-out, through a middle man. A Very Important Man in Tripoli wanted to meet Misfud.

Zeb pushed back. He didn't meet Very Important People unless they came to him in person.

The messenger said the MAN couldn't move in public. He was Very High Profile.

'It's not as if I can move about safely,' Zeb snorted. 'I guess your principal wants to buy arms? Who is he? Kattan himself?' He roared with laughter and slapped his thigh. Misfud had a reputation for joviality.

The messenger stiffened. 'Not him. Someone like him.'

'I don't meet like that,' Zeb told him. 'It could be a trap set by the Americans or the British.'

'It's not a trap. Sayyidi wants to meet and discuss a trade.'

'Well, your sayyidi can meet me himself instead of sending you.'

The elaborate dance went on over weeks and finally concluded when the messenger let slip who his boss was.

'No other dealer can provide what he wants,' the messenger said, nervously.

'What? He wants tanks? Predator drones?' Zeb chuckled. He was a laugh riot.

'Please meet him,' the middleman urged. 'You'll be the biggest dealer in Tripoli, with his business.'

'He is the most wanted man in the world. If I do business with him, it will paint a target on my back too.'

'Do you want to sell arms or not?'

'I want to stay alive.'

'Perhaps Latif Misfud is a coward,' the messenger scoffed. 'He's happy to deal with small-time groups but—'

'Alright, set it up,' Zeb growled. 'But it had better not be a trap; otherwise I will kill him myself.'

Zeb sipped his tea noisily and skimmed through the pages of an Arabic newspaper. 'Taken,' he said rudely to a hotel guest who was eyeing the empty seats next to him.

He was early. By design. *Gives me time to check out whether it is really Abu Bakhtar who shows up. And if he does, with how many heavies.* His Misfud disguise was in his backpack. Once the terrorist turned up, he would slip into the bathroom and return to the lobby as the arms dealer.

Bakhtar's a killer himself, he recalled from the files he had read on the man. He and Almasi grew up together in Syria and were at the forefront of ISIL's attacks against innocents. They had fled to Libya, like many other militants. But they were smarter than the average terrorist. They left with the terrorist group's wealth, bitcoin passwords, access to bank accounts and money men. That gave Almasi a start.

Meet Bakhtar. Find a way to get to the terrorist leader through his aide. Take him out.

He suppressed a sardonic smile. It sounded easy when laid out like that. Wait! Who was this?

Three men had entered the hotel. All of them Middle-Eastern looking. Short, cropped hair. Dark shirts, loose over their bodies, blue jeans, as if they were uniforms. Sneakers on their feet.

They stood in the lobby, spread out, as they scanned the hotel from right to left. Hands close to their bodies, not speaking, just their eyes moving.

Zeb looked at them over the top of his newspaper. His radar was pinging. The darkness inside him that he called *the beast* was growling.

Not average Libyans, for sure. Look at how they're positioned. Covering each other. Not in each other's firing line.

They couldn't be searching for him, however.
No one knows—
And then they looked at him.

Chapter 7

Dark eyes. That's all Zeb could make out as he met their gazes. He had put a curious expression on his face as he flipped the newspaper's page.

Even over the thirty feet separating him from the men, he could feel the impact of their looks. He ignored them and looked down, his lips moving silently as he read an article.

The reflection on the table's glass surface in front of him gave him a good view of the hotel lobby. Of the three men, who didn't say anything. *They don't need to. They are pros. A team. They can read each other.*

The darkness filled Zeb swiftly. He didn't know what it was. He called it *the beast* because it rose inside him in times of intense danger, brought a grey fog in his mind that blanked out everything except the scene of action. It sharpened his edges and turned him into a lethal killing machine.

As it did now, though an observer would see no difference. All they would see was an Arab man reading a newspaper.

The men spread out. Four feet between them. Seemingly looking at nothing. The one in the center brought out his phone and played with it. His left hand, Zeb noticed. *His right hand's close to his thigh. There's something at their waists.* Their shirts were flattening against something angular and hard. He could guess what those shapes were.

Zeb didn't move. His backpack was close to his right hand, its mouth open, but he wouldn't need anything from it. His Glock was in a quick-draw holster. Spare mags in his pockets.

He rustled the newspaper and swore at a news report. Frowned at the world and went back to watching the approaching men in the reflection.

Twenty feet. Still no attempt to draw their weapons.

Maybe they're Bakhtar's men. To take me to a rendezvous point. Problem is, they don't know Rahal.

Fifteen feet now.

A twitch in the man in the center. The slightest cocking of his head. His companions stiffened.

Attack was the best form of defense.

Chapter 8

Zeb acted.

His right leg kicked the table. Its top shattered from the impact. Crockery and shards of glass flew in the air towards the approaching shooters.

The hotel's lobby, which was his universe, faded. Other guests, the reception desk and the staff behind it, the security personnel, all became vague shapes.

Only the gunmen remained. In sharp relief. Reacting to his kick as they ducked from the flying projectiles, their hands dipping inside their shirts.

Zeb dived to his left. A brutal lunge that sent him sprawling and skidding on the polished floor. His right hand drew out his Glock in a smooth move. His arm straightened. His eye locked onto the sight, the barrel trained on the first shooter.

A moment to be sure that he wasn't drawing on innocents. There, that gleam of a gun, from beneath the shirt of the shooter he was aiming at.

Zeb compensated for his slide, his shooting arm straight and steady. A double tap that almost sounded like a single shot. Red bloomed on the gunman's chest. He staggered back, but Zeb was already focusing on the remaining shooters, who were breaking away, the one in the center dropping to the ground, the last one racing away.

A sharp crack. Center Man had unholstered and fired a hasty shot that bit into concrete, sent chips flying into Zeb's face and careening into the air.

Slow down. One deep breath. Shooting true was more important that shooting quick. Another shot from the gunman. From the corner of his eye, Zeb saw the third hostile spin around, his weapon rising.

He fired a long burst, left to right, low to high, some of the rounds whining aimlessly, but then the smack of a bullet on flesh. The middle shooter grimaced as a round caught him in the shoulder. The third man flinched and ducked but fired in return.

Zeb had moved the moment he had finished shooting. He slithered desperately on the floor, seeking cover behind a stone pillar, and got to his knees. Peeked around it, then quickly ducked back when another spray of shots came at him.

They're ducking behind the sofa where I was sitting.

Fast mag change. Another long burst to keep the men pinned behind the furniture. Another sneaked look. Yeah, they were still there, just their arms showing as they pumped their triggers, firing blindly.

Zeb risked a glance behind him. Hotel staff cowering behind the reception desk. Guests prone on the floor. Shouting and screaming. No cops, yet.

They'll come soon, he thought grimly, *if this doesn't end quickly.* What was that? A couple of vases to each side of the square pillar. Potted decorative plants.

He shot more rounds at the hostiles as an idea emerged.

Thought turned to action. He switched the Glock to his left hand. Grabbed one vase. It was heavy. It would require two hands.

Another glance at the shooters. A steady barrage from them now, rounds clipping the column and the air around it. *They're working to a plan. One of them will burst out in the open and open on me from an angle.*

He had to preempt that move.

He bit his gun between his teeth, bent down, caught hold of the vase with both hands and heaved with all his strength.

The makeshift missile went spinning in the air, bounced heavily on the sofa, which teetered on its legs. A shout from behind it.

Zeb threw the other potted plant, this time with better results. It landed just behind the sofa with a dull thud that suggested it had landed on flesh.

Another yell.

Zeb sprinted from behind the pillar and swung wide, firing rapidly as he raced across the open lobby, curling inwards until the couch's arms were in sight. Then a pair of legs. Two heads turning his way. More shouting as the gunmen started correcting their aim.

Zeb threw himself to the floor, went into a slide, both arms holding the Glock as he triggered round after round into the center of mass behind the seat. Felt a bullet whip over his head. Another feathered his hair, and then he was slamming into a side wall, but there was no more incoming fire.

He changed mags again and got up cautiously as the universe made itself known. Loud screaming. An alarm sounding somewhere. Guests running out of the hotel. Sirens in the distance.

Zeb approached the shooters carefully. The first man he had shot was dead, staring sightlessly at the ceiling. He searched the man swiftly, without taking his eyes away from the hostiles behind the sofa. Pocketed the man's phone and wallet.

Crabbed sideways to the remaining gunmen. One was twitching and gasped his last breath as Zeb neared. The second's face was bloody, his eyes closed.

Zeb kicked his leg. The man didn't stir.

Zeb reached out to his waist with his left hand just as the man exploded into action.

He propped himself on his elbow and twisted his upper body around, screaming as he started firing wildly.

Zeb lunged to the left as he double-tapped the shooter in the chest. He crashed into the wall but held his Glock steady. Ready to shoot, but this time, there was no need.

The hostile was dead.

Zeb bent down to snatch their phones and wallet. Paused when he noticed a tattoo peeking out from beneath a shooter's shirt. He pushed it up and sucked his breath sharply when he recognized the ink.

No time for this now, he told himself as he pulled out their phones and wallets and snapped a hasty picture of the ink, as well as their faces.

He looked up when he had finished. No one approaching him, but there was a hotel employee who was staring at him while speaking into a phone.

Time to go. Zeb raced towards the exit behind the reception desk. Women screamed as they flung themselves out of his way. Men stumbled back.

A small office. Its door opened into a hallway. More doors.

Sounds of clanking in the distance. Zeb followed them, opened a larger pair of doors and entered the kitchen.

'STAY BACK,' he yelled as he ran past ovens and lines of pots and pans and white-aproned staff. Through a pair of double doors, past a storage room—there, another door, which opened to the rear of the hotel, its loading area.

He scaled the brick wall at the side of the driveway. Dropped into the side yard of another office building. Vaulted over a bike, ran around a parking lot, leapt over the entrance barrier, past a pair of startled guards. And then he was down the street, forcing himself into a walk, joining a bunch of pedestrians who were unaware of the shooting in the hotel just a few hundred yards away.

Safe, he thought grimly, as he discreetly removed the padding from his cheeks and took out his contacts.

For now.

Chapter 9

——∞——

Zeb was in a dark, dusty café off Musheer market, two miles from the hotel.

He had cut through alleys and side streets, taken taxis and asked the drivers to go circuitously before he had ended up at the establishment. By then, he was sporting a new wig with greying hair in it and a pair of glasses that made him look older. The jacket stayed. It was needed to cover his Glock.

He looked out as he sipped his tea, steaming hot, sweet.

An open yard, an ornate clock tower behind it, and beyond, the Central Bank of Tripoli. Men crowded in the open, shouting, waving their hands, gesticulating furiously. The incongruous sight of wheelbarrows being navigated from the gathering, disappearing into alleys. Weapons in sight. AK47s on shoulders, Turkish and Italian automatic rifles. Every man sported a gun.

They're trading currency, Zeb thought, the sight distracting him from his problems for a moment. Cash was in short supply in the country. Lines of credit were almost impossible to get. That had given birth to the Musheer cash bazaar, where unlicensed currency traders bought and sold US dollars, euros,

British sterling and many others. The wheelbarrows were to cart away the stacks of cash, which were piled in bags.

Zeb had come to one of the safest places in Tripoli. Everyone knew of the cash market and also of the presence of heavily armed men who would protect their business.

None of those hunting me will come here and start a fight. That tattoo on that shooter's back: that was the SEAL Trident. Those men were SEALs?

Why would a SEAL team be hunting him? Or were they mercenaries or some black-ops team?

Anyone can get that image inked. That tatt doesn't prove anything, either way. For all I know, they could be from some Libyan militia outfit.

How did they find me?

No one knew about his Saad Hadad Rahal disguise. Not even Beth and Meg.

Was he followed from the previous night?

No, he was sure of that. He had taken extensive precautions. *Besides, they would have attacked me in my hotel room if they knew where I was.*

Was any of this related to the comms blackout he was experiencing?

But how?

Zeb went through everything again.

Those shooters in his hotel room the previous night, the way they had breached his room—those were professional killers. *As were the killers today. Pros. I acted first and fast. That's the only reason I'm alive today.*

He brought out the phones and wallets he had retrieved from the kill team. All the devices were fingerprint-locked. He removed the SIM from one and inserted it into the last remaining burner he had. *Let's see if anyone calls. I'm betting no one does. These guys knew what they were doing. Whoever sent them will know they're dead by now. Will they send another kill team?*

Yeah, he answered himself. *They will.*

Which circled him back to his unanswered question. *How did they find me?*

He ran through every move he had made, every interaction he had with other people. *Nope, there's no way anyone could have known of Rahal.*

The server came across and filled his glass at Zeb's nod. He was skinny, hard ribs and bones outlining the ragged Tee he wore. Dark circles under his eyes. *He's lost someone in the conflict. Or is an immigrant who's escaped war.* Libya was like that. There was no one untouched by killing.

Zeb took a sip, toyed with his sat phone idly. The currency market was still going strong. Wheelbarrows were brought and lugged away, heaving with weight. Shooters moved about threateningly, doing their job of keeping onlookers away.

It was warm inside the café. Grizzled old men talked with one another, nodded, laughed. Snatches of conversation came to him.

'Anyone can steal that money,' one worthy speculated.

'Ghaby!' *Fool.* His companion shook his head in resignation at his friend's comment. 'Those bundles can be tracked. They have GPS in them. That's how they do it in banks,' he said, showing off his knowledge.

Zeb stiffened. His hand, which was raising the cup to his lips, paused. Sound faded. *GPS! Of course. That's how they could track me.*

He looked beneath the table at his sneakers, which had

miniature, long-life trackers inserted in them. Standard accessories for every Agency operative when on a mission. It was how his team kept tabs on agents' locations. It was vital for providing logistics support.

Zeb shoved his chair back, swept the phones and wallets into his backpack, and shouldered it. Threw several bills on the table, including a generous tip, and shouldered past other patrons.

Once outside, he removed his shoes and socks and walked barefoot, swiftly. Eyes swiveling, checking out everyone within sight, hand close to his holstered Glock.

Second kill team had to be organized, which was why I wasn't attacked in my room.

There. An open-top vehicle filled with gunmen. Some militia outfit. The shooters' attention was on the bazaar, the vehicle's rear was facing him.

Zeb brushed past the spare wheel bolted to the rear door, pretended to stumble and swiftly stuffed the shoes behind the tire. He apologized profusely, bowing his head, when a gunman glared at him threateningly.

'Ana asef,' *I'm sorry*, he mumbled, weaving as if he was drunk, his hands raised in apology. He shuffled away, feeling the man's eyes on him until he turned a corner.

Now, everything fell into place. Why his phone remained silent. Why his team had gone dark on him.

Some hostile agency hacked into our system. They got hold of my GPS data and sent the kill teams. We got compromised, which is why Beth and Meghan went quiet. They shut down everything. It made sense. *There's no other reason they'd leave me in limbo. The breach must be serious. The Agency's never shut down its systems since it was formed.*

Relieved by the explanation, he strode forward confidently. And slipped on a plastic wrapper that was lying on the street. That fall saved his life.

Chapter 10

New York

'Yes, ma'am.' Meghan hung up and put her cell phone away. She blew a stray hair back from her forehead as she looked away into the distance.

'What's up?' Beth nudged her. 'Who was that?'

The elder twin swiveled her chair to face her sister. Seven of them in their office on Columbus Avenue, New York. Sunlight streaming in through the window. Blue sky high above. Air-con blowing cool air on the hot summer day. Normally, Broker would be practicing his golf putt on the small strip of green in the office, Roger and Bwana would be playing with the wall-mounted hoop, Bear and Chloe would be cuddled up on a sofa, and the twins would be at their screens.

It wasn't a normal day. It hadn't been for over twenty-four hours.

The Agency's systems and communication infrastructure had gone down the previous day and, despite their best attempts, couldn't be restored.

Sat phones, cell phones, landlines, their encrypted comms programs, nothing accessible or working.

They couldn't log into their databases or programs, because those had disappeared from their servers and machines. They couldn't make or receive calls. *No network* or *number out of service* was the message.

They had work and personal email accounts. Those had disappeared. Password reset attempts on the latter didn't work.

The sisters had improvised. They had run out to the nearest Best Buy and bought several SIM cards, which they then inserted into their phones. Now they had phone communication, but those numbers weren't secure and no one knew of those numbers but them.

'One thing at a time,' Meghan announced and went to her work on her screen.

In vain.

It was as if the databases, the algorithms, the entire operational and security setup had never existed.

Their machines were wiped clean. Their screens had bland, off-the-shelf, document processing and communications software that was used in billions of offices around the world, and nothing else.

Werner, their Artificial Intelligence program, on which they so heavily relied, had disappeared too.

The twins and Broker were the operatives who had designed the systems setup at the Agency. They had hit a brick wall.

They had tried to restore the systems through backups. Those backups and fail-safes had disappeared, too.

They called a little-known company in Virginia that provided a secure satellite comms network to the Agency and a few other black-ops outfits.

'The network's down,' that company said apologetically. 'We're working on it.'

On the second day, it still hadn't been operational.

Bewilderment turned to desperation and anxiety. 'Can't you hack and see what happened?' Bwana had asked the previous day.

'DON'T YOU GET IT?' Beth had yelled at him. 'THERE HAS TO BE SOMETHING FOR US TO HACK INTO. THERE'S NOTHING HERE. ZILCH. NADA.'

They brought in external consultants, who hammered away on their keyboards for hours and then left, helplessly.

They had then worked the phones. A call to Clare the previous day, but she was facing the same problems. The National Security Agency, with whom they collaborated extensively, had sent its experts. Same result.

'We have been attacked,' Broker said, voicing their concerns, late in the night. 'There can be no other explanation. Some hostile agency that has the expertise and resources to pull this off.'

'What about the satellite network?' Bwana asked, clutching at straws. 'That Virginia company got hacked too?'

'We have to assume that. They said their other client networks were up and running. Only ours went down.'

'Zeb is out there, in Libya.' Beth's voice trembled. 'We've no means of making contact.'

They had tried. There were emergency protocols. Websites through which they could communicate in case the sat phones were down. Those sites were inaccessible, too.

'He might call us,' Chloe offered, forlornly.

They shook their heads as one. 'He won't get through,'

Meghan replied. 'He doesn't know these new numbers we've got.'

And that was when fear had set in.

'Clare,' Meghan responded to Beth. 'She wants us in DC. Right away.'

Her sister's face brightened. 'Maybe she's got something for us.' She reached for her phone and ordered their Gulfstream to stand by.

An hour later, they were taking off from JFK. Seven of them, grim-faced, looking out of their windows, no one speaking.

Clare doesn't have good news, Meghan thought. *The way she sounded ... I've never heard her like that.*

Her belly clenched. Her nails dug into her palms.

How much worse would it get?

Chapter 11

Washington DC

The Agency's headquarters.

An anonymous-looking building on Sixteenth Street Northwest, in DC. Bland, carpeted hallways, people hunched over screens or speaking quietly on phones.

Clare's office, equally characterless. Cream-colored walls, no artwork, no personal touches. The White House, a few blocks away, just about visible through a street-facing window.

Meghan, leading the operatives, faltered when she saw the director.

She looks ... bad.

Their boss was always immaculately turned out, in business suits, dark hair neatly combed back, icy grey eyes sharply observing the world. Sometimes, a slight smile tugging at her lips.

To a casual observer, she looked the same. *Those wrinkles around her eyes. Those lines around her mouth. Doesn't look like she slept. And something about the way she's looking at us.*

Meghan's stomach roiled as she followed their boss's hand gesture and sat opposite her. Beth dropped into a chair to her left, Chloe to her right. The rest of the operatives ranged behind them. Bwana, Roger and Bear leaning against a wall. Meghan knew that without looking back; standard posture for them.

'What's happened to our systems, ma'am? Any update? We're crippled without them,' Beth burst out.

In reply, Clare hitched her chair forward, turned her laptop's screen towards them and pressed a button.

A video, initially blurry, then clear, sharp. A strange angle, as if the camera was at a height. A dimly lit room, tables covered with white linen, cutlery neatly arranged. All tables empty, except one in a corner.

Restaurant. Camera is ceiling-mounted. Probably an HD CCTV one. Meghan observed all this automatically, her focus on the two men at the occupied table. One man seated opposite the other, his back to them, obscuring the other person.

Time seemed to slow as she took in the details. *That hair, the shoulders, the way he sits.* The man leaned back, half-turned, threw his head back and laughed. She gasped. *That's Zeb.*

His movement had uncovered his companion for the camera. *And that's Jian Hsu.* A chair scraped next to her. Chloe, shifting in her seat as she hunched forward. Bwana growled something under his breath. Meghan didn't look at her friends. Her mouth was suddenly dry. *What's Zeb doing with him?*

The Chinese man was head of MSS, the Ministry of State Security, China's secretive intelligence agency. Some said he was the most powerful man in that country. *He took charge when we killed the previous head, Duan Shuren.*

Hsu was as mysterious as his predecessor, but all Western intelligence agencies agreed he was even more dangerous than Shuren. It was rumored that he had somehow found out Zeb was behind Shuren's killing and had directed MSS's agents to kill the American if they came across him.

Clare fiddled with the controls, and voices became audible. Zeb, still laughing, raising his hand disarmingly. *'No, not standard currency. Bitcoin. I want to be paid in cryptocurrency.'* He mentioned a sum.

What? Meghan's jaw dropped. She snapped a look at Chloe, Beth, then behind. Her friends were similarly shocked, their eyes riveted to the screen.

Hsu thought for a moment and then nodded. *'I could pay more. You know that—'*

'If you've studied me, you'll know I'm not motivated by money.'

'Then, why are you doing this?'

'Ping heng,' Zeb replied. Equilibrium, in Mandarin. *'Balance. My country cannot be the only superpower in the world. Your country is a suitable counterweight.'*

'Yet, you killed Duan Shuren.'

Zeb didn't respond for a long while. *'Shuren was out to destroy the world order. Harmony in the world requires powerful countries like ours to either work together or to act as a check on the other. China and the US will never be allies. But yeah, they can counteract each other. Ping heng.'*

It was Hsu's turn to fall silent. Both men had half-turned in their seats, giving a good view to the camera.

'Those are fancy words for what you are doing,' the Chinese man responded finally.

'I'm sure you've got a thick dossier on me. Your people

would have evaluated me. Let me guess ... all of them must have told you I can't be bribed. I work to my principles. I turn down Agency missions if I don't agree with them ...' He trailed off and then resumed. *'I know what I am doing and how that will be viewed by my country. I think it's important for your country and mine to coexist without escalating world tensions, and this is the only way. But, at the end of the day, your opinion does not matter. What's important is you accept what I am doing, make the payment and agree to our terms.'*

'Terms? What's he talking about?' Meghan didn't know she had spoken aloud until she felt Chloe's nails digging into her forearm. She bit her tongue and continued watching, the feeling of dread in her intensifying.

'And what if I leak this meeting to your people?'

Zeb laughed scornfully. *'Who will believe you? Those who know me are aware I am incapable of betrayal. They'll think this is a deep-fake video.*

'And if you do leak it,' he continued, *'remember what happened to your predecessor. I will find you and kill you.'*

'How do I know this isn't a trap?' Hsu demanded. *'This could be an elaborate setup for you to infiltrate my organization.'*

'You'll know whether it's a trap or not by what I pass on.'

Chloe squeezed Meghan's arm involuntarily, but the elder sister didn't respond. Her heart was beating so loudly she thought the whole room could hear. A bitter taste in her mouth. Dry lips that she tried to moisten with an equally dry tongue.

'What is this?' Beth looked at her.

'QUIET!' she hissed angrily and kept watching the screen.

'You could feed me false information. I know how this game is played. We play it in our sleep.'

'*It's your choice,*' Zeb said, shrugging. '*I have one of the highest security classifications in my country. I work very closely with MI6, Mossad, DGSE and many other Western intelligence agencies. I know where my country's agents are deployed. Who our double agents are. The kind of intelligence I could pass on to you ...*' He made a move to rise.

'*Wait,*' Hsu exclaimed. '*I need some proof. I can't believe that you set this meeting up without an ulterior motive.*'

'*Have you heard of the White Angel?*'

'*What's he doing?*' Beth gasped.

The White Angel program was a highly classified operation led by the CIA, aided by the Agency, to infiltrate MSS. They had succeeded and had turned one high-level Chinese operative, dubbed as the White Angel, who was passing on highly sensitive, valuable information.

The quality of his product was exceptional; the US and its allies had arrested several Chinese spies operating in the West and had shut down many corporate and military espionage operations.

Barely a handful of people in the US knew of the agent's identity. Zeb was one of them.

'*Is that a serious question?*' Hsu's eyes glittered. '*We knew you had a double agent in the MSS. We knew you had given him that fancy name. I've turned my agency inside-out trying to identify who that traitor is.*' Hsu's eyes glittered. '*Who is he?*'

'*Chung Ma.*'

'*NO!*'

Meghan jumped when Bear crashed his fist on the wall, but she didn't turn away. Clare sat motionless, expressionless, as the video rolled on.

'*Chung Ma?*' Hsu asked incredulously. '*My deputy director?*'

'*Yeah.*'

'*He was the first we looked at. He's clean. It cannot be him.*'

'*It is him.*'

'*I need more proof. I vetted him personally. I looked over his file, his records, I went through his life with a lens. There's no way he could be the leak.*'

Zeb reached into his jacket and withdrew what looked like a photograph. '*Is that enough?*'

The sick feeling in Meghan deepened. They couldn't see what Zeb had passed on, but she knew.

Chung Ma had met his handler a few times in various cities in the world. London, Paris, DC, New York. Each meeting had been videoed and photographed by the CIA. Insurance, in case the Chinese spy developed second thoughts.

It must be one of those photographs, she thought numbly as Hsu studied the image in silence, frowned and then sighed and sagged back in his chair.

'*There are more photographs. Recordings,*' Zeb said. '*You need more proof, I can provide them.*'

'*I'll kill him.*' Hsu's hands trembled as he returned the photograph. '*I'll torture him personally. I'll—*'

'*You'll do nothing of the sort. Use him to pass misinformation, or low-level intel that you don't mind losing.*'

Jian Hsu drank from his glass of water and controlled his anger. '*I'm still not convinced about you.*'

'*The quality of my intel will. This is the start.*'

'*You'll become a pariah if this comes out. Your government will want to kill you. You'll have no friends.*'

'*I'm aware of that. I've given this a lot of thought. That's why I need the money. Not to live a life of luxury, but to keep myself safe.*'

'*What'll you tell your boss? Your friends? You've worked with them a long time. How will they react?*'

'*That's not your problem,*' Zeb said roughly, voice hardening.

Hsu nodded slowly. '*If I find this is a setup—*'

'*I know. You'll send your agents after me. What's new? I'm already on your hit list.*' Zeb's voice hardened. '*You need to be more worried. You know the damage I can do. If you betray me, your government will need a new MSS head.*'

'Ping heng.' Hsu smiled briefly. '*Balance. You check me, I check you, meanwhile we help each other. Send me your bitcoin wallet details. I'll—*'

Zeb reached for a paper towel and scribbled rapidly on it. '*You'll get another intel drop once you pay. I'll send you protocols for passing intel. Secure comms details. No,*' he stopped the Chinese man, who was reaching for a pen. '*I know how to reach you.*'

'*Stay alive, stay safe,*' Jian Hsu called out to his departing back. For one moment, the camera captured Zeb fully from the front, and then the video ended.

Silence in the office. Harsh breathing. Broken by Beth, voice trembling. 'What does it mean? The video?'

No one replied.

Meghan wiped her palms on her jeans. She swallowed when she felt bile rising in her. She reached out for a glass of water and drank blindly, uncaring that several drops spilled down her chin.

'MA'AM?' Beth yelled, her face red, the hint of tears in her eyes.

Clare didn't move, a thousand-yard stare in her eyes.

'SIS?'

'It's obvious,' Meghan forced the words from her lips, hearing herself sound distant, remote.

'Zeb turned. He's become a traitor.'

Chapter 12

Tripoli

Zeb was in an alley leading out of Musheer market when he slipped.

His right foot gave way. He slid a foot and felt the bullet whiz through the air above his head.

Shooter!

He threw himself to the ground, rolling desperately to where the alley ended and sidewalk began. Caught sight of two gunmen behind him, their weapons raised, racing towards him.

No time to fire back. Stone chips showered his face as another round hit the ground in front of his face. He shoved to the side with his left hand and left leg. Evasive maneuver. Someone screamed. People started fleeing when they saw the killers approaching.

Busy street beyond the pavement. Cars, motorcycles, a few trucks. Another *phat* as a round peppered more stone and dirt on him. That one came closer.

Twenty feet separated him from the approaching shooters.

Both bearded, tanned skins, dark hair. AR-15s or AK47s in their hands. He couldn't gather more details because … escape and survival were more important.

One last look at the street. He drew a deep breath. The beast coiled and tensed.

With a loud roar, he powered off from the ground, hands and legs acting like a spring. He flew a few feet sideways and slammed into the approaching motorcycle rider he had targeted.

Horns blared, drivers cursed, brakes squealed as he and the rider went crashing to the ground.

'Sorry!' he shouted, grabbed the Libyan by his shoulder and shoved him away. Caught hold of his helmet, which was rolling on the ground. Ignored the flare of pain in his left leg where it had smashed into the vehicle.

A car overtook from the left, its driver leaning out, swearing savagely and shouting. *Gives me cover. Those gunmen are right there, waiting for it to cross. No one near them. They're confident, as if they know no one will approach them or call the police. And they're right.*

It was Libya. The innocent tended to mind their own business.

Zeb moved swiftly, with controlled haste, aware of the threat but not giving in to panic or blind action. *Key's in the bike.* He fitted the helmet over his head. Looked over at the driver, who was propping himself up, rubbing a shoulder, dazed by his fall.

'Ana asef,' he said again. Hauled the bike upright, mounted it, revved and raced down the Souq al-Turk, turning his helmeted head to look at the gunmen as they receded into the distance, their eyes tracking him until he turned a left and disappeared from view.

He didn't drive far. The bike's owner would call the police. Those shooters might have connections. The cops would make an effort to find him.

He drew the bike to Druj Mosque, a block away from Musheer market. Parked it among other vehicles. Left a wad of US bills inside the helmet, which he hung over the mirror. He checked his left, right, and six. No one paying him any attention.

He went to the mosque's entrance, ran his eyes swiftly over the footwear left outside. Picked a pair of sneakers that fit surprisingly well.

Next stop was a small clothing shop. Two minutes later, he was out, sporting a black shirt, dark trousers, a red-and-white checked shemagh that he draped loosely over his neck, covering the lower part of his face. Shades over his eyes. The glasses were gone, but the grey wig remained. The jacket, too, but he had turned it inside-out and it was now sporting a grey color.

Ten minutes since I escaped from the market. He hurried back to the currency bazaar. *Will the gunmen still be there? How did they know it was me? I'd removed my shoes by then. No GPS tracker on me. Unless they had triangulated me at the café and were waiting at the alley.*

But that still didn't explain how they knew who to look for at the currency bazaar. Or who they were.

Which meant he had to ask them, if they were still around.

He hurried back, keeping his backpack close, right hand gripping its strap, keeping it close to his weapon.

A shortcut through a side street, past grocery-shopping women, school kids who were ogling candy and sweets, and then the alley through which he had escaped.

He slowed.

A bunch of police vehicles. People milling around, talking, craning over shoulders, cell phones out, snapping pictures and videos to post on social media.

Zeb elbowed his way through. 'What happened?' he asked a bystander.

'Shooting,' the man shrugged, as if it was commonplace.

They were shooting at me, Zeb thought. *So, why's the crowd still here?*

He got his answer when he reached the front of the throng. Two bodies on the ground. He recognized them immediately: the gunmen who'd been firing at him.

Who killed them?

'What happened, sayyidi?' he asked ingratiatingly, to the nearest police officer.

The man looked at him, turned sideways, hawked and spat. 'These men were shooting at someone. That person got away. Unfortunately for these dogs,' he nodded at the bodies, 'a police vehicle was passing the street. I was in it.'

'You engaged them?'

The man puffed out his chest. 'I and my brave men. We asked these men to surrender, but they fired on us.' He pointed to a cruiser that was riddled with holes. 'We jumped out, took cover, and shot back. Stupid men. They had no chance against Tripoli's police force.'

'Thank you, sayyidi. It is people like you who keep our city safe.'

The police officer straightened his shoulders and brushed invisible lint off his uniform as he basked in the praise.

'Who were they?' Zeb asked him.

'We don't know,' the Libyan growled. 'There's nothing to

identify them. Their phones are locked. Must be from some militia group.'

'What about the man they were firing at?'

'He stole a bike and got away. No one got a look at him. Must be from a rival group. That's what most of the killings in Tripoli are about.'

Zeb watched as policemen loaded the bodies into an ambulance and then dispersed the crowd.

Another dead-end, he thought bitterly.

But at least I got out alive.

Chapter 13

Traitor!

The word hung heavy in the air in Clare's office. No one moved for several moments, until a loud crash broke the silence.

Meghan jumped, startled. Turned around to see Bwana had hurled a chair at the wall. Rage and fury on his face, fists bunched, biceps threatening to tear his Tee's sleeves.

'Zeb is no traitor,' he growled. 'That video's fake.'

'It's not fake,' Clare responded. She was calm, but … *there's something in her voice. Resignation. She's accepted that she was betrayed.* Meghan looked at her boss, searching for more clues, but the director had regained her control. The grey eyes were fathomless. No expression on her face, but for a nerve twitching on her temple.

'Zeb Carter is incapable of selling out,' Broker snarled. Bear murmured in support. Beth got to her feet and ranged by her friends. 'Yeah,' she shouted, her face red with anger. 'Someone's playing us.'

Clare ran her eyes over them, studying them, finally resting on Meghan.

'What do *you* think?'

'She thinks like us!' Beth leaned forward and smacked her palm on her boss's desk. 'This is bullshit. None of us believe that video. We know Zeb better than we know ourselves. He has a code. Betraying his country is not in it. He can never—'

'Beth.'

'—sell us out,' the younger sister carried on, ignoring Meghan. 'Ma'am, how can you even believe that? After all that he's done for you, for his country, how can—'

'BETH!'

Meghan raised her voice to silence her sister. Nothing but heavy breathing and the shifting of bodies in the room. *Don't let it be true. Don't let it be true. Don't let it be true.* The refrain ran in her mind like faint background music. She felt both hot and cold, heated from the inside, perspiring on the outside.

'Meghan?'

'You shut down the systems?' She swallowed several times before she could speak. Hid her hands beneath the desk and clasped them to stop them shaking.

'Yes,' Clare acknowledged. 'I had to.'

Roger swore. He surged forward. 'You didn't think of telling us? Zeb's out there, alone, without help, no backup. What must he be thinking?'

'That video—'

'IT'S FAKE. DON'T YOU GET IT? WE'RE BEING MANIPULATED.'

'It's not fake,' Clare replied, unperturbed by her operatives' palpable anger.

'You checked it out?' Meghan asked. *What does she know that she isn't telling us?*

'Yeah.'

'MEG!' Beth whirled on her. 'WHY'RE YOU EVEN BELIEVING HER?'

'You pulled the plug on everything after you were convinced?' Meghan asked robotically, ignoring her sister, heart pounding so hard that it could burst out of her chest.

'Yes.'

Zeb, what did you do? Was her first thought. Then came the arguments. It couldn't be true. *Clare must be mistaken. Deep-fake videos are so good these days, anyone can be duped. Even the Agency.* The questions, the doubts swirled in her mind until Beth caught her shoulder and shook her.

'YOU BELIEVE HER?'

Beth's tear-streaked face. Trembling lips. Wide eyes. Splotches of color on her cheeks. Her friends, their faces twisted in anger, behind her sister.

'Let's hear Clare out,' Meghan said with difficulty. That rushing in her head, it was her blood, furiously making its way through her veins and arteries, filling her with noise, trying in vain to silence her thoughts.

'You can't be serious.' Chloe, voice strained.

'Chloe, please … let's hear the full story,' Meghan pleaded. 'I don't want to believe this, either. I too think Zeb is incapable of betrayal. But I want to know why Clare believes.'

When no operative protested, Clare began: 'You remember when Zeb was in China?'

'Yeah. Last autumn,' Beth replied, stiffly. 'He was undercover, gathering intel on Jian Hsu.'

'You were in constant communication with him?'

'No. That's not how it works when any of us are in hostile country. Comms are only for emergencies.'

'But you were tracking his GPS. You knew where he was at any time.'

It came to Meghan suddenly. She felt like she was punched in the gut.

'Not really,' Beth licked her lips and looked at her for support. 'There was one time he disappeared. He went off-grid.'

'Would that be an afternoon in October?'

'We would have to look it up.'

'That recording is from the Happy Jack, in Kowloon. A restaurant frequented by MSS and Chinese government officials.'

That was when Zeb went offline, Meghan thought numbly.

'The time stamp matches his GPS log,' Clare confirmed a moment later. 'He met Hsu. You heard what he proposed. Several experts have looked at this video. All of them say it's untampered. Genuine.'

'It's true,' she said heavily, when no one responded.

Broker roused at that. 'You seem to be enjoying this,' he countered bitterly. 'To find Zeb a traitor.'

'ENOUGH!' Clare sprang from her chair and towered over the desk. 'ZEB WAS OUR LEAD AGENT, BUT HE WAS MORE THAN THAT. HE WAS MY FRIEND. YOU MIGHT KNOW HIM FROM HIS SPECIAL FORCES DAYS, BUT I'VE KNOWN HIM FOR JUST AS LONG. DON'T YOU DARE ACCUSE ME OF ENJOYMENT.

'You have no idea what I and the Agency have been going through ever since this video came to light,' she continued, quietly, and took her seat.

'I've carried out every check on this video,' she said, cutting off Meghan, who looked about to speak. 'I backtracked Zeb's movements. Checked his comms records. Spent hours brooding and wondering and thinking and cursing and swearing and disbelieving,' she snorted savagely. 'It comes back to this. The video is true. More importantly—'she held a finger up when Beth opened her mouth— 'Zeb never briefed me about this meeting. Did he tell you?'

'No,' Meghan replied with difficulty. 'He had a lot of intel on Hsu, but no meeting.'

'He might be setting a trap for the Chinese,' Bear said. 'We all know how Zeb is. He plays his cards close to his chest.'

'I considered that. Then three other events fell into place when I got this video. You know the offshore accounts we have?'

Meghan nodded, half-listening. That rushing noise her blood was making was growing louder. She knew where Clare was going.

'Look at this,' Clare turned the laptop around, played with the keys, faced the screen back towards them and pressed *play*.

Another video. A bank's locker. Barred gate. An array of security boxes to each side of a small, central table. One man pocketing various documents and transferring bundles of cash into a backpack.

Zeb.

'That's from our offshore account in the Bahamas. A month after Zeb returned from Hong Kong. Any of you know he had been there?'

Beth shook her head reluctantly. They didn't track GPS when operatives were on downtime.

'That was when he was on vacation. But he told me he was going to Brazil.'

That's what he told us, too. Meghan bit her lip. *All of us have access to the offshore accounts. They're to be used in emergencies. There was no such crisis then. No need for Zeb to empty that locker.*

'We lost an undercover agent in April. Shaming Chia was working in their Ministry of National Defense. He was a high-ranking Chinese national and had been feeding vital information to us on their war readiness, nuclear subs. He was arrested in the middle of the month and hasn't been seen again.'

'Why do you think Zeb is responsible?' Beth flashed.

'Because his last report to us was that he'd been given up. By one of our own, whom Hsu was running personally.'

'Did he mention Zeb by name?'

'He didn't need to. There could be only one agent the MSS chief was handling himself.'

'WAS ZEB NAMED?' Beth yelled.

'No.' Clare didn't react to the hostility directed at her. 'There was no doubt, however, who Shaming Chia implicated. There's only one US agent the MSS wants to desperately kill. Or turn. Zeb. He betrayed both, Chung Ma and Shaming Chia.'

She's right. Meghan wanted to jam her fingers in her ears. Wished her mind would stop making logical conclusions. Wished she was anywhere else but in that office.

'Then this, the clincher.' Clare pulled up another file. 'Zeb sent it to me the day before yesterday.'

Meghan tensed when she heard Zeb's voice on the audio clip.

'Ma'am, I could have called you and told you what I am about to say, but I didn't. You'll know why in a second. I have started working with Jian Hsu.'

She moaned, clapped a hand over her mouth and sank in her chair.

'I won't explain because you won't understand. Maybe one day you will, but I doubt it.' A pause. *'I know what this will do to you, to the Agency and my friends. I know what this means to me. What will happen next. I am sorry.'*

'Voice analysis confirmed it's him,' Clare said dully, when the clip ended. 'There's no sign of duress or coercion. No keywords that'll warn us he's been forced to say that. He recorded that voluntarily.'

Beth's face crumpled. She turned blindly, buried her head in Meghan's shoulder and sobbed.

Broker shifted on his feet, his face dark like thunder. Roger and Bwana were looking into the distance. Chloe, pale-faced, hugging Bear.

We were the best black-ops outfit in the country, Meghan thought dazedly. *Now, what are we?*

'What did he mean by that last line?' she choked out. 'That he knows what will happen next.'

Her world crumbled at Clare's next words.

'There's a kill order on Zeb Carter.'

Chapter 14

Tripoli

Zeb lay for a moment, blinking, immediately aware of his surroundings.

Early morning. The third day since the first attack on him, in his hotel room. Sounds of traffic outside. An aircraft droning high above.

The previous day's events came back to him. The attack in the hotel where he was supposed to meet Abu Bakhtar. A meeting that never happened because those gunmen turned up. His escape to Musheer market, where he was attacked again.

He yawned, stretched and looked over his surroundings. He had slipped away from the market when he found that the killers in the bazaar had been shot by the police. He had found a bombed-out house a mile away, behind the city's bus station in Gergaresh.

He had only his clothing and his backpack on him.
That's enough.

He washed and showered in the bathroom that still worked

and went to a street-side vendor and ordered a hot tea.

As the sun rose over Tripoli, he considered what he would do next. It was a very short list.

Complete the mission.

Stay alive, he added sardonically. *And if possible, try to find out who's behind me.*

He went to a restaurant on Jamal Abdulnasser Street and tucked into a breakfast of almonds and pancakes and washed them down with another cup of tea.

The street had come alive by the time he finished. Stores had opened, shoppers were out and about. Zeb paid, donned his shades and peered out from inside the shade of the eatery. No hostiles. His radar didn't ping.

He went to an electronics outlet and bought several phones and SIM cards. Paid in cash. The clerk didn't twitch an eyebrow.

In the shadow of an awning, he tried Meghan. *Number disconnected* was the automated response. Same result for Beth. He called the other operatives and grimaced when no attempt got through. He then dialed the office number and hung up in disgust when the call didn't go through.

They must have changed numbers as well. He wasn't unduly worried. *Beth and Meg will find a way to make contact as soon as they've got our systems up and running. Nothing that I can do from here except wait for them.*

He didn't notice a passing vehicle slow down suddenly as its driver and passenger and looked at him.

He didn't see them turn back for a second look.

That was his first mistake.

He was engrossed in another call, to a store in Fashloum. 'I've got a package for delivery,' he said.

'What kind is it?' the owner replied.

'Heavy.'

'We didn't order anything heavy.'

'It has your address and number on it,' Zeb insisted.

'Okay, bring it. But it had better be for us.'

Zeb hung up. Making contact with Abu Bakhtar involved an elaborate protocol. He had to be vetted physically, his identity confirmed in person before he was sent to the next security check.

If I had met him in the hotel, all this wouldn't have been necessary, he reflected.

He flagged a passing taxi and climbed into it.

'Fashloum,' the told the driver.

Zeb didn't notice the vehicle fall in behind them. That was his second mistake.

Chapter 15

New York

'A kill order?' Beth shrieked. 'WHAT? HOW CAN YOU DO THAT?'

'It's beyond my control,' Clare said wearily. 'I got that video in my email a week back. Then Catlyn, Catlyn Feder, director of the CIA, called me and said she, too, had received it. As had Mike Hoosier, DNI, director of national intelligence. Several other agency heads had gotten it as well. I bought time to verify the video, but when I reported that it was genuine, gave them Zeb's call, the decision was no longer in my hands.'

'YOU COULD HAVE SAID IT WAS FAKE!' Beth yelled, tears streaming down her face. Meghan put an arm around her shoulder and drew her back to her chair.

'Does it look like I am liking any of this?' their boss replied, her face pale, shoulders slumped in defeat. 'And, Beth, you know I couldn't do that.'

'What happened then?' Bwana asked coldly.

'You know how termination orders work. I have briefed you on them. They aren't taken lightly. Killing our own or an ally's operative isn't a decision we take often or arrive at quickly.'

She took a deep breath and continued. 'An emergency meeting was called. The deputy heads of all the agencies that report to the DNI. Twenty attendees in that meeting. CIA, Coast Guard Intelligence, NSA, Naval Intelligence, all the intelligence bodies in the country were represented. Along with me and a few other black-ops agencies. Twenty-one attendees, if you include the DNI himself. It was brutal. Our existence was questioned. A second meeting was summoned last week. That was when the kill order was issued.'

'Don't say it.' Clare held her hand up when Meghan made to speak. 'I did everything I could … I told the other directors that we could bring Zeb in. I cited his record, everything he had done for the country. He deserved a hearing and a trial, I said. But I was overruled. That video, his confession and the loss of that Chinese agent, those were damning. There were some agencies who wanted to see us shut down. This was the opportunity for them.'

'What happens now?' Chloe asked tautly.

'It's already happened,' Clare replied sadly. 'Kill teams are out, hunting Zeb. They—'

She stopped when Bear crashed his fist into the wall. The skin over his knuckles split, blood streamed down his wrist, but he didn't look at it. If fury had a face, it was his … and that of every other operative in Clare's office.

'Any agency that can spare agents … some of them work with PMCs. They are out there. They have Zeb's details. They have everything we have on him,' their boss said.

'What about us?' Broker asked woodenly.

'I have a meeting with President Morgan and Daniel

Klouse, the National Security Advisor. They will decide what will happen to the Agency. As for you … you all have a choice. You can stay back or join the hunt.'

And kill Zeb. She didn't say the words, but they hung in the air.

Meghan rose from her bed thinking of that. She couldn't sleep. Two am. The events of the previous day ran through her mind over and over again. They had raged at Clare, shouted and threatened and shed tears, but she had been implacable. A decision had been taken. She had no hand in it. She had no choice but to shut down the Agency until Zeb was dealt with.

It's not her fault. What else could she do? Even now, Meghan found it hard to come to terms with it. Zeb, a traitor? Their friend. The man who had recruited them. Who had been her and Beth's mentor. A man of few words, who filled a room just by his presence. Who had saved their lives on numerous missions. Who put country and honor first.

How could he be a traitor?

Disbelief, anger, sense of loss, bitterness, feeling adrift … the emotions swamped her again, and in the solitariness of her room Meghan Petersen broke down and cried; deep, heaving sobs, tears not just for herself but for Beth and for the rest of her friends, because they were broken and she didn't know how they could get back.

How do we go on from here?

She tossed the question around and around but got no answers. Finally, she freshened up and made her way to the office. Reached for her Glock when she spotted the glow from a computer monitor. The way she was feeling, she fully intended to shoot first and ask questions later.

A head in front of a monitor. Earphones wrapped around. Watching Zeb's video with Jian Hsu.

Beth. *She couldn't sleep either.*

Her sister's head turned when Meghan approached. Tear tracks down her face. She reached out blindly to hug her elder twin.

'I kept playing it over and over again.' Voice muffled; face buried in Meghan's shoulder. She lifted her head up, her green eyes teary. 'I feel adrift. The last time I felt like this was way back when, at college.'

And at that Meghan pulled her close and held Beth tight. *That was when she was shot in the head. Active shooter, in college in Wyoming. We lost Dad in that incident.*

Beth had lost a large part of her memory at that time and never regained it. Meghan had been at her side continually, had helped her rehabilitate. Had filled in the gaps in her memory, had made her whole again.

Remembering those dark months brought a lump to her throat, and as she watched Zeb laugh on the screen, Meghan broke down again and the two of them rocked together, trying to comfort each other. They stayed like that while the dark night beyond the glass-fronted windows of their office lightened, and rays of light appeared and lit their office. Their friends came down but none of them joined the twins, because each one of them had dark circles under their eyes; they moved about listlessly because, what was in store for them?

Zeb's death.

'Mossad, MI6, DGSE, they will join too,' Claire had said the previous day. 'Because Zeb knows too much about all of them.'

'Avichai Levin will never act like that,' Beth had replied

fiercely, referring to the Israeli agency's director. 'Zeb saved his life. He saved Israel!'

'He has no choice,' their boss said, sadly. 'I spoke to him, as well as the other agency heads. They have to act; however reluctant they are.'

Broker sat at a desk next to them, turned on his screen and watched the video too. The coffee mug in his hand trembled and the drink sloshed over his jeans. He cursed at his clumsiness, but Meghan knew it was because he, too, was adrift. She looked around to see her friends in similar states, similarly preoccupied.

Beth's fingers flew over the keyboard and a news site came up. *She's checking for reports from Tripoli. Any announcements of death.*

The day dragged on leadenly, with none of them discussing the elephant in the room. Whether they would join the hunt for their friend.

Meghan didn't know what prompted her. She opened their security consulting company's website. It was still up, because the firm, while a front for their covert operations, was a genuine one and had real clients. They advised executive boards on personnel and perimeter security and had several listed companies as their customers.

It was no different from other corporate websites. It listed their credentials, experience, a few customer quotes. An *About Us* section that had all their names, photographs and bios.

She sucked in her breath sharply when that page loaded. Zeb's photograph was there, but on it was a large, black **X**.

She turned blindly towards Beth, who looked defiant. A distant memory and a conversation surfaced.

'We need to have a system,' Beth had said slyly. 'For when you'll turn traitor, and to warn you we're coming after you.'

'Why would you warn me in those circumstances?' Zeb had countered.

'Oh,' she punched him in the shoulder, 'for old times' sake. For the times we have had. It's the only warning you'll get.'

'I couldn't help myself,' Beth said brokenly when Meghan looked askance at her. 'I know he betrayed us ...'—she waved her hands helplessly— 'but he was also our friend.'

Bwana came up and took in the web page. His jaw muscles flexed. He stood silent for several moments and then nodded shortly.

'Zeb deserves that much warning,' he said.

Meghan gripped his forearm and squeezed. She didn't tell her friends that she had been planning to do just that if Beth hadn't preempted her.

Zeb was our mentor. And now, we will have to kill him.

A chill swept through her when Bwana's words sank in, and when she looked at the other operatives, their hardened jaws confirmed it.

They were, first and foremost, their country's best covert agency. They would deal with traitors in their midst.

They would kill their friend, Zeb Carter.

Chapter 16

Tripoli

The storekeeper in Fashloum, a swarthy man with an apron around his waist, looked at Zeb critically.

He compared the man in front of him to a photograph in his hand. He nodded to an assistant, who patted Zeb down.

'He's got guns,' the flunky squeaked.

'Of course, I have weapons, you fool,' Zeb, in his Latif Wakil Misfud disguise, replied contemptuously. 'I am an arms dealer. I am a wanted man. I need them for my protection.'

'No guns,' the shopkeeper said firmly. 'Not if you are going to the next level. They will be safe here. You can collect them when you return.'

'But—'

'Choice is yours. I don't know who you are meeting and I don't want to know. But my instructions were clear. You will go through without any guns.'

Zeb made a show of sighing. He reached into his jacket and brought out his Glock. He reached down one ankle and removed his spare gun. Unstrapped his Benchmade from his other leg. The assistant went bug-eyed. He fingered the weapons gingerly, as if they would bite him.

'Mahmoud, put them away,' his boss said with exasperation, 'and take him to the other place.'

The clerk gathered the weapons and went into a backroom. He returned with a piece of cloth, which he tied over Zeb's eyes.

'Come,' he beckoned.

'This isn't how I have met—'

'I don't want to know,' the storekeeper cut him off brusquely. 'I have got my orders. This is how it will be.'

I might be heading to my death, Zeb reflected, as he climbed into a vehicle with Mahmoud's assistance.

The clerk drove for half an hour, twisting and turning through the city traffic. He cursed and pounded his horn as he overtook and cut lanes, and when he came to a jarring stop, Zeb let out a sigh of relief.

Mahmoud grabbed him by the collar and shoved him inside what felt like a dark, empty space. An industrial warehouse, he realized, when his blindfold was removed.

'Hey!' he shouted when the assistant headed back to his vehicle, but the man didn't turn around. He drove away with tires squealing and disappeared out of sight.

Zeb turned back to the building. Dust in the air. Crates wrapped in plastic in a far corner. Concrete floor that was marked and chipped. He tensed when he heard footsteps from behind the crates.

'Face the door,' a voice shouted.

He obeyed.

'Raise your hands.'

He raised them.

He felt men coming close to him. The stink of sweat and cigarettes. Rough hands moved over him, searching his body.

'No guns.' A man grunted and spun him around.

Zeb stumbled, regained his balance and looked at four masked men. Balaclava masks over their heads. Belgian-made FN FALs held in their hands.

'Why didn't you meet Abu Bakhtar yesterday?' the man in the center shouted.

'Because there was an attack in that hotel,' Zeb replied angrily. *Give them attitude.* Everyone knew Misfud was an arrogant man. He wouldn't be cowed by a show of force.

'LIES,' the man yelled. 'We know you weren't there.'

Misfud wasn't. Saad Hadad Rahal was.

'You're not the only ones who have sources. Besides, do you realize it was all over the news? I didn't think it was safe to continue with the meeting after the shooting.'

'You could have called and left a message.'

I was busy surviving.

'Enough,' he snapped. 'Does Bakhtar and his boss want the weapons? I have them. But there are many buyers. I don't want to waste time if you aren't interested.'

'We need to see them.'

'I need to see the money.'

The man, who seemed to be the leader, nodded and another stepped forward. He removed a backpack from his shoulder and tipped it to the floor. Bundles of currency fell to the floor. US dollars, British sterling, euros … all used, wrapped in thick wads with rubber bands. Zeb picked one, riffled through the notes, removed one and held it to the light.

'They're genuine,' the first speaker boasted.

'They'd better be,' he retorted.

He tossed the bundle back at the gunmen. 'How do I know you are from Abu Bakhtar?'

The shooters looked at one another. One of them chuckled, the others laughed.

'Look at him,' the leader said. 'He's got balls. We can kill him, but is he scared? No, he wants to know who we are.'

More chuckles and sniggers, which faded when he pulled out his phone, dialed a number, spoke briefly in it and held it to Zeb.

'Speak,' he ordered.

'I don't like delays,' a voice came on.

Abu Bakhtar! Zeb recognized the whispery voice from the single call he'd had earlier with the man. *When I was working my way into the terrorist group.* 'I don't like them, either,' he snapped. 'If that hotel had been safer, we wouldn't be having this discussion.'

'Show my men the goods. If they are genuine, we will proceed.'

'I thought I would be dealing with the man himself.'

'Thinking such thoughts isn't healthy for you.'

'I always deal direct,' Zeb insisted. 'You know my reputation.'

I didn't expect to meet Almasi in the first attempt. But I have to put on a show.

'I decide who you will or will not meet.'

'And I decide who I should sell to. Have you got any other dealers for Javelin missiles?' he taunted, knowing that he had cornered the supply for the sought-after weapons.

'Let my men inspect what you're offering,' Bakhtar said finally. 'Then, we'll decide.'

Yes! Zeb fist-pumped inwardly. 'Tomorrow. Six pm. I will

tell your men where to come.'

He returned the phone to the leader. 'Give me a contact number. I will tell you where to come tomorrow.'

'That's not what—'

'You heard my call,' he said coldly. 'Do you want to go against your boss?'

The gunmen stood uncertainly for a moment, but clearly didn't want to buck Abu Bakhtar. The leader snarled, spat out a number and wagged his finger in warning. 'If there is any trap—'

'Don't be late.' Zeb turned his back on them and walked out of the warehouse.

This is Ben Ashour. He recognized the neighborhood in the southern part of the city. *My arms cache is to the west, near Gharghour.*

He heard a vehicle starting in the distance, turned back inside, raced through the empty warehouse and reached its rear. Through a broken window he saw a Jeep turn around a corner. *There go the gunmen. They must have come earlier, stayed hidden, checked me out as Mahmoud brought me in. They came out of hiding only when they were sure there was no trap.*

Good tradecraft. It's what I would do.

Which reminded him. He had an arms consignment to sell to the world's most wanted terrorist.

Chapter 17

It took two hours for Zeb to reach his destination in the west of the city. He backtracked, took circular routes, often doubled up, but saw no sign of pursuit.

The light was fading by the time he reached the fruit and vegetable market on the outskirts of the city. Long rows of stalls. Women, men and children shopping, under the light of naked bulbs and street lights. Their country, their city, might be at war, but life went on in Tripoli, its citizens a hardy lot.

Zeb snaked through the dwindling customers, who would disappear as soon as the market closed in another half hour. Already, a few stalls were putting away their baskets and pulling down their awnings.

He went to the back of the bazaar, where the warehouses were. A long, concrete building with shutters at regular intervals. Signboards above each entrance stating which wholesaler or retailer owned the storage space.

Zeb went to the middle one. 'Wa alaikum salaam,' he greeted a shopkeeper. Unlocked the shutter, rolled it up just enough for him to slip through and closed it behind him.

He felt the wall to the left, reached down and turned off an alarm. He then stood in the darkness, unmoving.

The smell of decaying produce. Voices from outside. He snapped on a light when he was sure he was alone. Baskets of rotting fruit and vegetables mounted high on a plastic sheet draped on the floor.

The decaying state was deliberate. He went out of his way to buy decaying goods and stored them in the warehouse. The strong smell was one of his defenses. There were others, not visible to an intruder. The alarm, barely visible CCTV cameras, and when he went to the rear of the warehouse, the final one.

The wall looked like the end of the storage space. Dirty white, smudged and soiled, marked by years of use.

Zeb went to the right corner and placed his palm against it, a foot above the ground.

The wall slid up soundlessly to reveal a smaller storage space. It was five feet deep and ran the width of his warehouse.

It was immaculately clean. Well-lit. Cases arranged in the sides and at the back. He opened the nearest one. M4 carbines, MK 18s, HK 416s, FN SCARs, grenade launchers, grenades, ammo, knives, bayonets—there were enough weapons to wage a small war.

Which is what the militia groups and the terror-ists are doing, he thought grimly. He went to the rear wall and opened another box. Four Javelins in them. The best, battle-tested, shoulder-fired anti-tank weapons, coveted by insurgents the world over.

Each missile had a GPS transponder embedded in its stock. That's how he located all his sold weapons, retrieved and destroyed them.

He closed the crate and pushed it back against the wall.

Scratched his cheek as he figured his next move. He would need to move the box to another location for the terrorists' inspection the next day.

There's no way I am bringing them here.

He turned off the lights, reset the alarm and locked the shutter behind him. It was fully dark. The market was deserted. Scattered street lights did little to dispel the gloom. An empty truck to his left, parked in front of another shutter. Another vehicle to his right, farther away.

This weapons cache of his had no mercenaries protecting it. *Don't want anyone near the Javelins.*

He took a step forward when he heard it.

A squelch, as if someone had stepped on rotting vegetables.

He wasn't alone.

Chapter 18

<hr>

Ten pm. A time when most good citizens were at home. A time for the police and emergency services to be out and about.

And the militia groups and terrorists, he thought as he sidestepped quickly and pressed against a dark wall of the building. His clothing was grey or dark and blended with the background.

This is a residential area. It isn't a high-profile neighborhood for the militia groups to operate in. The terrorists, they operated by different rules, however. *No rules for them.*

Zeb didn't know when he had drawn his Glock. It was there in his right hand. Polymer frame and Tenifered steel, just thirty-four components, making the weapon one of the most popular and deadliest handguns in the world.

He waited, letting the beast rise inside and fill him.

Directly in front was the market. An open space now. A rough square, hundred feet by hundred feet. One dark building, a warehouse, to the right. Another warehouse beyond it. An alley in between, from where the sound had come.

His building bordered the end of the neighborhood, beyond which was residential construction.

No movement that he could detect. The vehicles to his left and right were empty. He was sure of that.

Nevertheless, he went to the one to his left. Moving swiftly, hugging the wall, crouching wherever the dark background lightened.

He reached the truck. Rose cautiously and checked the interior. No driver, no passenger. He went to the rear. The loading area was empty, too.

He was heading to the front of the truck when he heard another squelch.

He dropped to the ground immediately, lined his Glock and waited.

I took precautions, but I could have been followed.

Three shadows emerged from the alley. Visible because he was hugging the ground, and it gave him a vantage point. The intruders were backlit by the glow of the night sky.

They moved quietly, quickly, spread apart. Those glints just in front of them, those shapes—they were weapons.

The beast growled. It had had enough of being attacked by shooters. It wanted revenge.

Wait, he told himself. *Let them show their hand.*

That moment came quickly enough, when they went to his shutter and bent close to it.

Thermal imaging? They must have seen me enter. They didn't see me leave? Maybe not, because the gunmen straightened and seemed to confer briefly.

Lots of foot and vehicular traffic when the market closed. They must have lost sight of the warehouse.

And then, one of them turned. Yelped in surprise when he looked in Zeb's direction.

What? They can see me?

They leapt away, making distance, and one weapon fired.

NVGs. They've got them. Zeb was rolling on the ground even as the thought registered. Going beneath the truck, between its wheels, as more rounds struck the ground where he had been lying.

He still had the vantage point, lying prone in the dirty yard, while they were outlined clearly, and he let loose a cutting burst, left to right; another one, right to left, as he scrambled back quickly.

A snapped look behind him. Nope, no threat there.

One shooter lay on the ground. Another was dropping down, hugging a warehouse wall. The third was sprinting to the left, trying to seek cover.

Zeb cut down on him, even as their weapons opened up, bullets clanging against the truck, whining away into the night sky.

Ignore the one on the right. The left dude's the danger. Because once he got away in the night, he could creep up on you.

He trained his sights on the fleeing shooter, who seemed to realize his predicament and was zigging and zagging, firing blindly in Zeb's direction.

He stumbled when Zeb's round got him in the leg. He tried to rise but fell down when Zeb emptied his magazine in him.

The round burned the side of Zeb's head. *The remaining gunman!* He was scrabbling forward furiously, his gun ahead of him, firing burst after burst beneath the truck.

Zeb rolled away evasively from beneath the vehicle. One look at the vehicle gave him the idea. Caught hold of the driver door handle, swung himself up, levered himself up with his legs, and he was on the roof, clambering over its surface, all within a couple of seconds—not enough time for the shooter to escape, even though he must have sensed his move. And there he was, desperately turning on his back and raising his rifle, when Zeb pumped a magazine into him, head to toe, reloaded fast and emptied more rounds into him and turned at the two other dark shapes and shot them again for good measure.

Silence returned to the market. Distant shouts from some building.

Zeb dropped to the ground. Breathing easily. A thin breeze drying the sweat on the back of his neck. The beast still roaring inside, tightening his nerves, giving him a fine edge.

He crab-walked sideways at the most distant shooter because he still was the biggest threat, given his position. Approached him wide and from behind. No movement.

Zeb turned him over with a leg.

The shooter's helmet was smashed. Blood streamed from his throat. His trouser legs looked slick with more blood.

He wasn't a threat.

He similarly approached the shooter in the center. He was alive. Just about.

Zeb kicked his gun away, patted him swiftly and removed his handgun and a knife.

Need to check the third gunman.

He picked up the dying man's rifle. A HK416. Mag full. *He must've reloaded before I shot him.*

Went to the body lying near the warehouse, rifle outstretched to anticipate any sudden moves. It wasn't needed; the man was dead.

Zeb ran back to the dying shooter.

'Who are you?' he asked urgently. He repeated his question in Arabic.

The man blinked slowly as if it was an effort.

'Why are you after me?' Zeb hissed.

'Sie … sind … list.'

'What? What did you say?'

The gunman shuddered, his breath rasped, and he went still.

Zeb checked his pulse. His breath. The man was dead.

He sat back on his haunches, his head reeling.

Sie sind list. Was that German? I am list? That didn't make sense. How about: I am on a list?

Huh, what was that about? What list was he on?

Inspiration struck him. He searched the man again quickly and found a phone. He took a moment to inspect it. Yeah, one of those smart phones that needed a fingerprint.

Was the shooter right-handed? Yes, he was.

He grabbed the man's right palm and pressed the index finger to the phone. Didn't work. Tried other fingers. Nope. Returned to the index finger and tried several positions.

Fingerprint scanners on modern phones use electrical conductance in the human body to read patterns. The charge diminishes and ultimately disappears when a person dies. Zeb was counting on the shooter's body still holding some charge.

He hit the jackpot after several more tries, when the screen suddenly glowed to life. He scrambled through the controls quickly and turned off the fingerprint reader. Entered a different access code. Sighed in relief when the device accepted his changes.

He went through the call records. Not a single incoming or outgoing call.

Burner phone? Or did the shooter delete all records before the operation? *We do that.* And if the gunmen did the same, it spoke of high-level tradecraft.

No number in the phone's directory. No messages, either, no communication via any app.

That was a setback. He pocketed the phone and searched the other shooters for their devices. There, he ran out of luck. Those bodies were dead too long for their devices to be unlocked.

He snapped pictures of the gunmen and checked out the alley from which they had arrived. No getaway vehicle there. Its shadowy length ran for a distance and joined a bigger street that had more traffic.

Zeb returned to the market and wiped his prints off the shooters' weapons. He shouldered his backpack, which had fallen during the firefight, checked that he was leaving no trace behind, and left.

He had survived yet another attack. But he was no wiser as to who was hunting him. He shelved the problem. He had a bigger one.

Find a suitable rendezvous for Abu Bakhtar and his weapons inspection.

Chapter 19

Washington DC

'Carter's still alive,' the politician fumed quietly. 'That video, that recording and that Chinese double-agent's statement was enough to convince every agency in the country. There's a wide kill-order on him. And still, he's alive.' He was in a fancy hotel in the capital, expected shortly to give a speech to party donors. He nodded and smiled to a guest and turned away to get more privacy.

He wasn't worried about lip-readers or eavesdroppers. No one was close to him, and everyone in the lobby knew better than to approach him.

His security people were augmented by ShadowPoint. They had screened all visitors and had kept reporters and media personnel away from the event. His presentation wouldn't get reported ... *unless it gets leaked,* he thought, grimacing. Which was always a risk. However, he didn't plan to say anything that the president wouldn't approve. It was a routine event, one of those where he pressed the flesh and made contributors and supporters feel important.

Spears had advised him to keep a low profile, given their activities in Libya, however the politician had turned down his suggestion. *I need to be visible, raise my profile.* He would be doing more events as it got closer to his presidential run announcement.

'Yeah, I know,' the ShadowPoint director replied. 'He killed some good men of ours. He also survived an attack from a German team yesterday night. They were given the job by one of our black-ops outfits.'

'The BND didn't send them?'

'Nope. The killers just happened to be German. Mercenaries are international. You'll find killers for hire from all continents.

'He's going to cause trouble. I know it. He—'

'He will die soon. Mossad, MI6, CIA, my outfit, we are all hunting him. The Europeans, too. His run of luck can't last for long. Besides, I've got a few cards up my sleeve.'

'Like?'

'I have circulated his details to the Libyan police and the armed forces. His photographs, the disguises he's most likely to use. He may survive a few more attempts; he won't live through every one of them. I have more killers I can send, but I'll hold back and see what these other teams do.'

'Did you hear? Clare has shut down the Agency's systems. For all practical purposes, it's not operating. I never liked her. Thinks too much of herself. She broke the news to the rest of the operatives a couple of days back.'

'Are they joining in the hunt?'

'They haven't said yet. But they have no choice.'

'Bugging her office wasn't a great idea.'

'We've discussed this before,' the politician flared. 'You

guaranteed that the equipment is untraceable.'

'It is. However, she'll find the taps, if she hasn't already. She'll see that it's military grade. That limits its sources.'

'But she can't circle back to you, can she?'

'No. There are several agencies who use that equipment, and not just in the US, either.'

'In that case, let her stew. I told you. I want her to know she's bugged. That she knows everything is being listened to. I have always wanted to put her in her place. This operation is where she and Carter get their comeuppance. I want you to continue applying pressure on her. Use your contacts. I will do that at my end, too. Discreetly.' His voice sharpened and lowered even further. 'What's the update on Almasi?'

'Don't speak his name,' Spears grated. 'You're in a public place.' He took a breath. 'He's still around. Carter hasn't reached him yet.'

'Do you think we should get word to him?'

'That's the last resort. That should happen only if Carter escapes these attempts.'

'What about the meeting with Kattan's people?'

'That's been arranged. Will brief you as soon as it goes down. After that, we'll meet government officials. And then, when everything's in place, you'll meet Prime Minister Rayhan Sabbagh himself and make the announcement.'

'What do you mean, when everything's in place?' the politician growled. 'My meeting with the PM is already penciled in.'

'Bob and I will take care of it,' Spears assured him. 'Everything will go as planned.'

The DC man hung up. He finger-combed his hair as he thought furiously. *Randy's never let me down. Bob's on the ground in Tripoli. He's very good.*

Robert Marin was the CEO of Saharol. He was a high-profile business executive based in Tripoli, from where he ran the business.

The firm was American-owned with interests in oil and energy. It had a widely respected executive board that had deep knowledge of the oil markets. That board reported to Bob Marin.

Saharol started by buying several small North African oil companies. It came to Libya, flashed cash and quickly established itself as the largest foreign oil player in the country. Heck, in the world. It was a billion-dollar, privately held corporation that owned distribution companies and retailers, and bankrolled refineries—and that was only what it did on the surface.

It embedded itself in the political and military world. Several high-ranking politicians and generals were in its pockets. It was everywhere. Not a single Libyan was unaware of Saharol.

The politician had come up with the idea for the firm once he knew the extent of Libya's oil reserves and the state of the country. Close to seventy percent of its economy was dependent on the country's huge oil reserves.

Libya's National Oil Company, NOC, owned everything. The oil fields, the refineries, the distribution networks, the storage and also the marketing and sale of oil.

However, the reality was that Kattan had grabbed control of the eastern oilfields and distribution facilities. ISIL, under the leadership of Almasi, was in Sirte and attacked NOC's facilities almost daily.

Then there were the smaller militia groups. In a country

riddled with multiparty fighting, each group wanted a stake in the oil. They used their control over the network to either extract financial and political concessions, or to strike against the government.

The result was that NOC's hold over Libya's oil suffered, and the country's economic standing suffered. The living conditions of its people were affected, and that spurred unrest and crime and attracted militia groups. It was a vicious cycle.

The DC man recognized as an opportunity what everyone else saw as a threat.

With ShadowPoint on his side, he could offer protection to NOC's oil from Kattan, ISIL and the militia groups. Being an American company with extensive political connections back home, it could act as a lobbying front for NOC and Libya in Washington DC.

In return, he wanted a share in NOC's business. Not of the joint venture or partnership kind. No, the politician thought big.

He wanted Saharol to have an equity partnership in NOC.

A minor one, because the Libyan populace would never accept a foreign shareholder in their state-owned business. It had to be kept secret for just that reason. Or if it leaked, explained away in marketing-speak.

Even a small shareholding in NOC was worth billions. *And I'm getting there.*

The politicians were coming around to the idea of having Saharol on their side. The American firm had already extracted several concessions from DC for Libya. Having an American shareholder who knew the oil industry and knew politicians around the world just made life easier for NOC. Fact.

The Libyan military was accepting, too. It was stretched

thin in fighting Kattan, ISIL and the militia groups. It saw value in having Saharol as an ally. It didn't question the numerous operators that the American firm brought into the country.

Of course, no one knew that the politician was the founder of Saharol.

No one other than Randy Spears and Bob Marin, who had to know because they had stakes too, much smaller than the politician's, in the company.

Appointing Marin as the CEO had been Spears's idea once the politician floated the oil company idea past him.

'He's one of my best people,' the ShadowPoint CEO said. 'He's come up from being a foot soldier to running teams, missions, and is now my COO. He's got a great business head, knows Libya very well. He will be a good appointee.'

The politician interviewed Marin and found that he was very capable. Sure, Saharol was an oil company, and the COO's experience had been in managing a military contracting firm, but at that level of leadership, it was his deal-making skills, financial acumen, strategic vision, and ability to deal with board-level, public- and private-sector stakeholders that mattered, and he had all of those.

They made a big show of announcing Marin as the new CEO. Spears sent out a press release stating ShadowPoint would miss Marin and wished him success in his new role.

No one asked any questions when, after Marin joined the oil firm, Saharol appointed ShadowPoint as its security partner. These deals always happened in the corporate world. The old-boys' network at play.

The politician and his partners hid their ownership in a complex maze of offshore, shell and shadow companies around the world. Spears bribed, blackmailed or killed the handful of officials in various countries who had helped set up the complex ownership arrangement.

They also made it look like there was no single individual person behind the oil company. They carefully promoted the story that its investors, banks and private equity firms, had come up with the idea for Saharol.

It was the perfect setup.

The politician visited Libya often in his official capacity, and no one raised eyebrows when he met Bob Marin publicly each time. Or when he endorsed Saharol.

It was entirely normal for Spears and Marin to meet and for them to have an open communications channel.

The politician openly mentioned Saharol's name in this meeting, in that speech to Wall Street, that charity dinner in DC.

He said it was a testament to American entrepreneurship. The company had foresight and thought beyond mere profits. It contributed to Libyan society.

The politician said it was a company he admired and fully supported ... not in any manner that created a conflict of interest, mind you. He played strictly by the book.

The media, in Libya and back home as well, lapped it up. A fast-rising American politician and an American company that committed itself to the North African country.

Many column inches of stories were written, and hours of video were devoted to the politician.

It enhanced his story.

None of them, he snorted to himself, *know who our backers are.*

Saharol needed funds when he had started it. And that's when he had his next brainwave.

Let's not go there, he told himself. Those people and his deal with them were so secretive that he didn't allow himself to think of it in public places.

Without them, I wouldn't have gotten this far. He straightened his tie and turned to his waiting people and flashed a smile.

Oil and money were behind his every move. Those would catapult him to the highest office in the country.

As long as Carter was dealt with swiftly.

Chapter 20

⊸⊸⊸

Tripoli

Zeb was five thousand miles away from the politician, in his hotel room in the Libyan capital. He, too, was on his phone, but unlike the DC man, his call wasn't successful.

Still no signal. He shook his head and tossed the sat phone on the bed. He looked out of the hotel window for a moment. Bright sunlight. His body ached: bruises from the gunfight in the fruit and vegetable market the previous night.

Which reminded him. He went to his backpack and drew out his tablet. Checked his email, the realtor website. Everything still down. He checked the dead shooter's phone. No incoming calls during the night. He scrolled through the call log and directory. Nothing had happened in the night to restore their history.

An idea struck him. He opened a maps application and tried to backtrack the shooter's movement. No luck.

He was preparing to fling the device away when its photo app beckoned him. He opened the gallery of images.

And went cold when he saw the five images.

The first was of himself, Zeb Carter. The second of him in his Misfud disguise. The third was a close likeness of Rahal. The remaining were alternative disguises. Cheek pads here, nose job there, different contact lenses, hair shading.

I could have gone with any of those two looks. My natural look and Misfud; the shooters had to have those if there was some hack into the Agency's system. But how did they get the Rahal pic? And the two others?

He swiped through the images quickly, noticing that they were all against a neutral background. Not surveillance shots. *My pic must be from one of my files, but the rest are computer-generated.*

His fingers froze over the keyboard.

Someone else has the photo program.

It was a cutting-edge algorithm written by Beth and Meghan that could generate hundreds of photographs of how a person might look disguised. The application took in a candidate's original images as a starting data set and then created variations by altering one or many features. Nose, cheeks, eyebrows, contact lens colors, eyebrow shapes, hair styling.

It had a high degree of accuracy, and once the NSA got hold of the program, it tweaked it further.

No one but we, the NSA, and a few other agencies have access to that program. We don't share it with allies. In fact, we integrated it with Werner.

Was it a US agency hunting him?

No, he shook his head firmly. Why would they do that? This had to be some hostile agency … though it beat him why that shooter in the fruit market spoke in German. And what about that list he mentioned?

Zeb could call Dieter Reinhard, the head of BND,

Germany's Federal Intelligence Service. They were friends. *Dieter will tell me if he knows.*

But that would mean Zeb would blow his cover in Libya. Nope. Not worth it. He would wait for Beth and Meghan to make contact. Meanwhile, he had a rendezvous to arrange.

He started rising and then sat down again. He didn't know what impulse prompted him, but he found himself typing the security firm's website.

That came up. He frowned momentarily and then his brow cleared.

Of course. It's a commercial organization. No known link to the Agency. Why would anyone hack it?

He idly perused through various pages. All of them worked. *About Us* had their photographs. He grinned at Beth's image, so formal. *She's never like that.* Then his smile faded when he noticed the black cross over his picture.

That couldn't be right.

He refreshed the page.

No question about it. There was a heavy **X** over his photograph.

He sat still, taking it in. A memory from way back came to him.

'They should have killed him,' Beth snorted and tossed the newspaper onto the table.

They were in the twins' favorite café, a few minutes from their Columbus Avenue office. Beth, Meghan and Zeb. A coffee break on a lovely spring day in the world's greatest city. No mission to occupy them currently. It was refreshing to just push back and relax with the sisters. They had this energy about them, a confidence, effervescent spirit that lifted everyone who interacted with them.

We got lucky when they joined us, Zeb reflected as he picked up the paper Beth had tossed and read the article she was referring to.

A CIA traitor, a Russian mole who had been leaking critical intel for years, had fled to Eastern Europe after he had been identified. However, the German BND had traced him, captured him and had sent him back to the US to face trial.

'Traitors,' the younger sister said as she emptied her drink and waved in the air for a refill. 'They don't deserve to enjoy prison time.'

'You.' She narrowed her green eyes at Zeb and stabbed the air with a manicured finger, grinning. 'If you betray our country, don't expect any mercy from us. We're not going to handcuff you, babysit you on a flight back from wherever you've fled to.'

'Danged right,' Meghan backed her up. 'Double tap between the eyes. That's what you get.'

'However,' Beth tossed her hair back, 'because you've been a good friend after all, we'll give you a warning.'

'A warning to Zeb?' Meghan asked, perplexed.

'Yeah. He did mentor us, after all. We can't forget that, can we, sis?'

'Nope, you're right. What kind of warning, though?'

'Lemme think.' Beth slurped her drink and wiped her lips. 'Got it. We'll cross out his photograph on our website. There you go,' she wagged her finger at him. 'You see a X on yourself, you know we're coming for you. You can run, but you can't hide,' she chortled.

Zeb stared at the web page. He blinked, looked away and turned back to the screen. He wasn't mistaken. That cross was still there. Beth's laugh and comments were still fresh in his mind.

His fingers trembled. His legs felt heavy. He could hear his own breathing, hard, harsh. A bead of sweat rolled down his face from his forehead, but he felt cold inside. A dull roaring in his ears. It was his blood pounding in his body. A darkness in the room because his vision had dimmed.

Traitor. He couldn't even form the word fully in his mind. *My friends are coming after me.*

And Zeb Carter, one of the most lethal covert US operatives, shuddered and shivered in his hotel room in Libya, where he was on yet another mission for his country.

Chapter 21

⚬⚬⚬

Bob Marin checked himself in the mirror. Slim, lean-faced, clean-shaven, blond buzzcut. He was in a dark, well-fitted suit. He nodded once. He looked like a businessman out to make deals.

He signaled to his security team and climbed into an armored SUV. His motorcade drove to a private airfield on the outskirts of Tripoli, where he boarded a Saharol Lear jet.

Three hours later, his retinue made its way to a heavily guarded office building in Tobruk. The soldiers at the gates checked his credentials, spoke into a phone and raised the barrier.

'Mr. Marin,' a suited aide greeted him in accented English. 'Welcome to the Libyan People's Government. General Kattan is waiting for you, sir.'

Marin followed the man to a bank of elevators, entered a car that took them to the highest floor. Plush carpets, art on walls, sculptures placed on stools. Kattan's office wasn't a palace, but it wasn't a bureaucratic office, either.

He's as powerful, or even more, than Prime Minister Sabbagh. No reason for him to stint on his building.

'Bob!' The general rose from behind an ornate desk when the aide showed the American in. Kattan was in full dress uniform, arrays of medals across his chest. He was dark-haired, with a full, neatly trimmed mustache and warm, dark eyes.

Marin wasn't taken in by his friendly appearance. *He's killed thousands of Libyans in his pursuit for power,* he thought.

Kattan shook his hand firmly. 'Come, let's sit there,' he said, gesturing towards a velvet-covered sofa.

The two men made small talk as another aide entered and served them dates and hot coffee.

'I've been through your file,' the general said once their refreshments had been cleared. 'My people have made a set of recommendations.' He snapped his fingers and a waiting flunky brought him a slim folder.

'We will not oppose Saharol's *relationship* with NOC,' he said, smiling thinly. He was one of the few who knew what exactly that relationship meant. *And he's got demands, or else he'll make it public that an American firm has a stake in NOC. He'll campaign against Saharol. He's popular and he can turn the people against us.* Marin didn't allow his thoughts to show on his face. He smiled encouragingly, as if the Libyan was his closest friend.

His years in ShadowPoint running black ops, and then in Libya heading Saharol, had trained him. He could cut deals with terrorists as well as with Fortune 100 CEOs.

'But,' Kattan carried on, 'we want something in return. The Libyan people need to benefit from this relationship.'

Marin skimmed swiftly through the contents of the folder. The list was as he expected. It started off with small items. Saharol had to invest in the country. In schools, hospitals, infrastructure, drinking water. Then the bigger demands appeared. Funding for the Libyan People's Army, weapons.

'How you do that,' the general waved his hand carelessly, 'is up to you.'

Marin stopped at the last item on the list.

'A speech at the United Nations General Assembly?' He raised his head, shocked. 'Every two years?'

'The Libyan people should have a voice,' Kattan thundered as if he was at a public event. 'The world should know the atrocities committed by the Tripoli government. The General Assembly is the only way for us to be heard.'

'But, sir—'

'That's non-negotiable. Saharol has connections in Washington DC. You meet world leaders. I am sure this won't be difficult for you.'

The man thinks big, Marin thought swiftly. *Speaking at that forum will put him on the world stage. It will have the official government on the backfoot. He's smart. On the one hand, he's waging a war on the ground. On the other hand, he's pulling the right political strings. If he speaks there and makes a compelling case, world opinion might swing in his favor. The Western and Middle East countries might think he's a better option than Sabbagh. I could be sitting with the future Libyan country head.*

Kattan's ambitions weren't a surprise to Marin. He and Spears had anticipated every possible move in the elaborate game of chess they were playing in Libya. One of those was Kattan and his Libyan People's Army being the official government of the country.

If that happens, NOC will be under his control, and in Libya, oil is the real prize every politician or militia leader wants.

Setting up a speech at the United Nations General Assembly, UNGA, wasn't impossible. *The politician can arrange that.* But it would not do to give in easily to Kattan's demands.

'Even we don't have those kinds of connections,' he said. 'What if I arranged for you to meet President Morgan?'

The general's eyes glimmered. Marin had him. President Morgan was widely respected in the Middle East for breaking through the Israel-Palestine conflict. His solution had been revolutionary, had attracted widespread criticism as well, but *had* delivered peace. Nobel Peace Prizes had been jointly conferred on the Palestinian President and Israel's Prime Minister. It was rumored that the Nobel committee had wished to include President Morgan in the honor, but he had declined.

A meeting with him is as good as addressing UNGA. If not better.

'I will need to think about that.' Kattan leaned back and stroked his mustache. But Marin knew what he would come back with.

He'll say, hell, yeah!

'What about the weapons?' the general prompted.

He wants F16s, anti-tank missiles, the latest weaponry that we share only with our allies. Not gonna happen.

'I'll see what I can do,' Marin said delicately. 'I think those items will take much more time. Lobbying, politicians to please, you know how it goes in DC,' he shrugged. 'But I don't think we should hold back on signing this for those weapons. Your commitment to this deal will go a long way with DC politicians, sir. I will take care of everything else once you sign.'

The general nodded almost imperceptibly at his words.

Gotcha, Marin thought. *He knows what I am referring to.*

Hundreds of millions of dollars would be deposited in Kattan's offshore accounts once the deal was signed. That was his payout. Baksheesh. Not many transactions in Libya happened without bribes. Especially of this magnitude.

'I understand,' Kattan said. 'Why don't we meet in a week's time? Have the paperwork ready.'

Marin suppressed his impulse to fist-pump in delight.

'By then, you'll be able to come back to me with some dates for meeting President Morgan?'

'I sure will, sir.' The American couldn't resist grinning.

He sent a simple message to Spears and the politician when he was back in his vehicle.

One job done.

We'll have to give him some weapons, he mused, as Tobruk flashed past his windows. Not what he wants, of course.

It was vital that Libya remained in the grip of a conflict between various groups. It wouldn't do for the entire country to unite under a single government and leader and for peace to return.

Otherwise, there wouldn't be a need for Saharol to offer protection to NOC.

His phone buzzed. A congratulatory message from an anonymous number. It was from Spears. The politician wouldn't reply. Security protocol had to be maintained.

Marin allowed himself a satisfied smile when he boarded the Lear jet. Just a small one, because there were two more parties to be convinced.

The first was Rayhan Sabbagh's people. He expected that negotiation to be tough but was sure he could win them over.

We have already sent out unofficial feelers and they seem to be cautiously interested. But will want to strike a hard bargain and not give the impression that they need us.

After that, Nasir Fakhir Almasi, the ISIL leader.

That negotiation would be the hardest.

Which reminded him. Zeb Carter was still out there and alive.

Hopefully, not for long. Now, even the police are looking for him.

Chapter 22

---⟨⟩---

New York

Meghan felt she was drifting in an alien world. It had been two days since Clare broke the news.

Two days since our lives changed, she thought listlessly as she lay on her bed. Very early in the morning of the second day. Pitch-dark outside. Another sleepless night for her, tossing and turning as she tried to come to grips with the new reality.

She felt adrift, aimless. She came to the office during the day, spent hours poring over the video, running it through every program she could get hold of. The results were the same.

The video, the phone call, they were all genuine.

Zeb Carter was a traitor.

Beth refused to believe it. Meghan didn't want to believe it, but she could not disbelieve the evidence in front of them.

Broker, Bwana, Bear, Chloe, Roger, they all were reduced to zombies. Hollow-eyed, pale-faced. If anyone was to attack them then, they—some of the most lethal operatives in the world—would go down without much resistance.

Meghan raised her head, punched her pillow, turned it over for the cooler side and settled down. Closed her eyes and willed herself to sleep, but that damned video played again in her mind.

Zeb throwing his head back, laughing. A side profile of his face, his eyes smiling. Jian Hsu laughing with him.

How could he do that? Why did he do—

She sat up suddenly.

Wait. That video … no. She shook her head. She wasn't going to allow herself to do down that path. *Clare checked that video with all the experts. We verified it as well. There was nothing wrong with that CCTV recording.*

But the thought that had struck her didn't disappear. She turned and stared at the numerals on the bedside clock. Three am. Watched the hands move painfully slowly. They didn't hypnotize her to sleep.

She swore and rose. Changed into a pair of jeans and a sweatshirt. Jammed her feet into a pair of sneakers and grabbed her backpack.

The thought refused to leave her. Her mind jumped ahead immediately, considering the possibilities. Her chest started pounding as she entered the elevator, went down to the office and seated herself at her screen.

She wiped her clammy palms on her thighs and hesitated for a moment.

Let it be. Let it be. Let it be. Let it be.

Let what be? She argued with herself.

Let that thought, my idea, let it be true.

She closed her eyes, uttered a silent prayer, opened them and brought up the video. Swallowed and hit play.

Heart thudding so loudly that it was a wonder the world

couldn't hear it.

The clip started. Zeb's back to the camera. Jian Hsu, face not visible, seated opposite.

Zeb threw his head back and laughed, showing himself partially, exposing the Chinese man.

Meghan's gut clenched. Her nails dug into her palms; her breath caught. She let the video run to its end and then played it again.

And then again.

Ran it until she memorized it to the smallest detail, until every move the two men made was imprinted on her mind and every muscle tic, every facial expression, every aspect of the restaurant was burned into her brain.

Only then did she push back her chair and go to the kitchen. She brewed herself a cup of coffee. Spilled it because her fingers were shaking so badly and that thing inside her— she didn't know if it was hope or fear.

Let it not be dashed. Let it not be dashed. Let it not be dashed.

Let not what be dashed? That voice in her head said wearily.

Hope, she said. *Let it not be dashed.*

And she went to the window and drank deeply, but for once the Jamaican Blue Mountain coffee didn't calm her down. She remained at the window, not seeing, remembering the video, ruthlessly punching down any thought until 6 am arrived and she fished out her cell phone and made a call.

'We need to meet, ma'am,' she told her boss, who answered immediately.

'When?'

'Right away.'

Chapter 23

Washington DC

'Don't settle down,' she told Beth, the other operatives, when they came down an hour later. 'We're going to DC.'

'Why?' her sister asked.

'Clare's called us.'

'Has she found anything?'

'She didn't say.'

'Perhaps that video is fake,' Beth said, and Meghan's heart almost broke at the look of hope on her sister's face, the wan eyes, the pale skin.

'Last time she called us,' Broker said tightly, 'it wasn't to deliver good news.'

They ranged out of the office without a word and climbed into two SUVs. Meghan driving one, Bear driving another. No bad jokes from Roger, no sarcasm from Bwana, no small talk from Bear or Chloe.

This isn't how we used to be, she thought.

But nothing was, not since Clare's bombshell.

They touched down at Reagan National Airport at 10 am. Hired two cabs and sped towards the Agency's office. A sudden, freakish thunderstorm opened the heavens up and poured their watery contents down on the capital, making everything grey and dull and wet.

But Meghan didn't notice. Didn't register when she got soaked as she raced from the cab to the Agency's office.

She was wired so tight that she jumped at the slightest noise. Her sister looked at her curiously but didn't make any comment.

Let it not be dashed. Let me be right. Please let me be right.

She punched the button for the elevator. Swore when it took an eternity to arrive.

'You're alright?' Chloe side-looked at her, wiping away raindrops from her face.

She nodded but didn't say a word. Turned her body slightly away because she didn't want to give away her nervousness.

Led the way to Clare's office. Clare raised her head when they entered.

'Ma'am,' Meghan began, then saw the sheet of paper her boss held towards them, read what was on it.

My office is bugged.

'We've decided,' Meghan continued smoothly, jabbing her sister in the ribs to ger her to catch on. 'We're going to Libya. To hunt Zeb.'

Please let them not contradict me. Them. Her friends, who, thankfully, echoed her words. Broker gave her a speculative look, but that's all he did.

'Great. That's the right move. Put personal relationships behind you.' **TAKE MY CUE,** Clare scribbled and held it up to them. 'Zeb's a traitor and needs to be dealt with, just like any other. When are you going?'

'Today. You know where he is?'

'Nope. None of our systems are running. In any case, I am sure he suspects something and will have gone off-grid. However, you know the disguises he will use. He shouldn't be hard to find.'

'How many other teams are after him?'

'Several. Look.' Their boss glanced at her watch. 'I need to grab a bite. There's a place nearby.' And with that she swept out of her office, looked back once to check that her operatives were following, handed out several umbrellas and proceeded to Fifteenth Street, to a restaurant where she commandeered a table big enough for all of them, seated herself and gestured at them to follow suit.

'I discovered it the day I told you about Zeb,' she said without preamble.

It. The bug, Meghan thought.

'Military grade. Used by the Pentagon. Used by us as well as several agencies. No way to trace who planted it. I checked the security camera logs but couldn't find anything. They've probably been tampered with.'

She rubbed the bridge of her nose and closed her eyes momentarily.

She looks exhausted. I've never seen her like this.

'Who could it be?' Bwana frowned. 'Bugging your office … that takes some doing.'

'I don't know. It could be any agency. It could be under the orders of the DNI. Maybe he wants to make sure we don't help Zeb in any way. You wanted to meet?' The last directed at Meghan.

'Yes, ma'am.' Her left hand beneath the table, fingers crossed, palms suddenly sweaty. She was conscious of her friends looking at her in surprise. *They thought Clare called for this meeting.*

Meghan brought out her screen and arranged it so that everyone could view it. Pulled up the video.

'We've seen that,' Bear said tightly. 'I don't want to see it again.'

She ignored him and played it.

Paused it after Zeb had laughed and reared back in his chair.

Looked at her boss, held her breath. *Let me be right. Please. Dear God.*

'Zeb doesn't laugh,' she said, her voice trembling with hope, with wanting to be right, wanting so badly for her world to be restored to normal.

Her eyes focused only on Clare, who sat still, motionless, her grey eyes still cool despite the tiredness evident on her face.

Her boss didn't move. Long, interminable moments while she didn't say a word. Meghan started feeling deflated. Hope started leaking out of her. Greyness returned. The rain outside reflected how she felt. Cold. Drowning. Her shoulders drooped. Her head bowed.

'Yes, he doesn't laugh.'

She thought she hadn't heard right. She looked up. Something in her boss's eyes. *Tears*, Meghan thought. *Tears in her eyes.*

The words were still sinking in. Her mind was still processing it when Beth gasped. She snatched the screen, reset the video and played it again. Stopped it at the laugh. Stared at the screen, then at her sister.

That look. Meghan knew she would never forget that expression on Beth's face for as long as she lived. Joy. Belief.

A loud crash. Silence fell in the restaurant. Every eye turned on them, on Bwana, who had punched a neighboring table so hard that the flimsy wood had splintered.

'**I KNEW IT!**' he said and glowered at a server who dared to head their way.

'It's alright,' Clare told the restaurant manager, who was hovering at a distance, uncertainty on his face. 'We'll pay for the damage.'

'He doesn't laugh like that. The smile never reaches his eyes. Not with others. That happens only with us. That isn't him. I didn't spot it immediately. I should have. It struck me at night. I played the video a million times. Didn't tell anyone. Was hoping you would confirm.'

Meghan knew the words were spilling out of her, was aware of Broker fist-pumping, Roger thumping Bear on the back, Beth gripping her shoulder so hard that it hurt. But she had eyes only for Clare, who was nodding, those tears still in her eyes. Meghan didn't know she was crying herself until Chloe held her, wiped her cheeks with her fingers, hugged her tight and then let go. She must have been bawling, because her friends whispered something in her hair and kissed her head, but none of their words registered.

All that mattered was that the earth had righted itself and it was still raining and it was still dull and grey outside, but it felt like it was sunlight and spring and flowers and bees and the heavenly smell of fresh baking.

'The video is fake, as is the one in the offshore bank,' Clare said. Her hands trembled when she said it.

Meghan reached out and held it, and her boss smiled for

the first time, blinked rapidly, cleared her throat, and withdrew her hand.

'I don't know who sent them,' she said briskly, anticipating Meghan's question. Gone were the exhaustion and the tears. The director of the Agency, one of the most powerful people in the country, was back. 'No one knows. They were sent from an anonymous account. I had to report them officially, even though many others had gotten it ...' she trailed off.

Meghan nodded. Standard operating protocol when incriminating evidence on one's own agent was found.

'It's so good ... only someone who knows Zeb really well could have spotted that laughter thing. No, don't feel that.' She reached out and grasped Meghan's wrist. 'I know what you're thinking. That you should have spotted it earlier. On the first day itself. Thing is, it took me a while, too. Several days.'

'Who sent it?' Meghan nodded her head in thanks. *But I still feel small. Beth, I, the others, we work with Zeb. We've been on missions. We know everything about one another. Moles. Birthmarks. Habits. I should have seen through that video the first time she played it.*

'Meghan?' Clare brought her attention back.

'Yes, ma'am, I'm listening.'

'I was saying, I don't know who sent it. It came ten days ago, through an email account that seems to have been set up just for that purpose. To my work email. I traced that email, but it's one of those free accounts anyone can set up. Time stamp says sender was on the West Coast, but that doesn't mean anything. The other recipients got similar time stamps.'

Because many of those email providers have their servers there.

'I pulled a few strings, called a few people at the provider.

They couldn't offer any help.'

She probably invoked National Security and spoke to the CEO himself, who must have jumped at her bidding. Meghan knew how her boss worked.

'Dead-end,' Clare waved her hand. 'It's as good as any deep-fake video our best people can come up with.'

'There aren't many agencies around the world who can do that,' Broker mused. He hitched his chair forward, raised his fingers to attract the server's attention and placed orders for everyone.

'Iran, the Chinese, Mossad, MI6, BND, DGSE, the North Koreans, India, South Africa, a few others. It had to be a state-owned agency, because of the tech and the people needed.'

'Yeah,' Clare agreed, 'and many of those organizations are friendly to us.'

'Not China's MSS or Iran's IRGC,' Bear said grimly. The Islamic Revolutionary Guard Corps was a powerful branch of Iran's Armed Forces. It ostensibly protected Iran's political system. Over the years, it had grown so powerful, with covert operations around the world, that the US had declared it a terrorist organization. 'Zeb's still on their hit list.'

Clare nodded approvingly, broke off when their drinks arrived, waited for the server to depart and raised her mug to sip. 'Correct. We should not discount one of our own agencies who have turned hostile to us. There are several who want us shut down. Who think we are too powerful. Who don't like the access I have.'

Clare's access to the president, Meghan mused. She picked her cup up and momentarily closed her eyes in bliss as the warm drink went down her throat and heated her insides.

'I bet there are many of them,' Bwana growled. 'They're

envious of our funding, the way we operate—'

'And our track record,' Roger chimed in.

'Yeah, all of that. Those bugs are why I didn't tell you that day. I had to play it like I accepted the video,' Clare said. 'I am still moving carefully Talking to people whom I trust fully. But because we no longer have an operating agency, the going is slow.'

'Will we come back, ma'am?' Meghan asked her.

Their director's grey eyes sharpened. The tired lines around Clare's eyes disappeared. Her lips firmed.

'Meg,' she replied. 'We never went away.'

She smiled when Beth whispered a loud *yessss* and clenched her fist.

'I was confident one of you would spot that video,' the director continued. 'It was just a matter of time.'

'This video is fake and that offshore account, too,' Roger frowned. 'But what about that Chinese agent? Shaming Chia. Didn't he say Zeb exposed him?'

'No, he said one of our own betrayed him. We assumed it was Zeb because of these videos.'

'Ma'am,' Meghan leaned forward urgently, 'what about Zeb's call?'

'That call is genuine.'

Meghan's jaw dropped. She stared at her boss and then at her friends, who were similarly shocked.

Clare chuckled at their expressions. 'Zeb recorded that call several years back and gave it to me for safekeeping.'

'Why?'

'He thought there might come a time when we had to declare him a traitor. That way, he could cozy up to hostile agencies.'

Which means … Meghan worked through the implications in her mind. 'Someone stole that recording?'

'Not just that,' Clare said grimly. 'They hacked into our system. They might be the same people who planted that bug. That was another reason I had to shut down our systems.'

'And they're so good that we didn't detect their presence.'

'Yeah. Something troubling you, Beth?'

'Ma'am, I thought you said the president closed us down.'

'Nope. He doesn't know any of this. I have a briefing meeting with him and Daniel, later today.'

'The National Security Advisor knows? What does he think?'

'Daniel?' Clare snorted. 'He said I was a fool to even think Zeb could turn traitor. I told him that wasn't what I was thinking. Yeah, he knows. And he too thinks this is either the act of someone domestic or a hostile agency.'

'If it's domestic,' Meghan said slowly, 'everyone in that kill order meeting is suspect. Chances are higher that it's one of our own who's behind this. A foreign agency … there's just too much stacked against them to make this work. Bugging your office, hacking—sure, they could do all that. But, someone in-country, who has the security clearances, they have a better chance.'

Their boss sighed, rotated her shoulders wearily. 'You're right. That's what I've been thinking too. Twenty attendees in that meeting, excluding me. It could be any of them, or someone from their agencies. Heck, even the PMCs they use could have a hand. Which is why my investigation is slow.'

'What about the kill teams?' Meghan asked, cold gripping her again. 'You said CIA, our other agencies, had sent assassins.'

'That is true. Once the kill order was given, the agencies acted. There are shooters in Tripoli right now, hunting Zeb. And because someone has hacked our systems, chances are high they have the disguise program too.'

Meghan reared back. Someone gasped. Bwana swore. She didn't look at her friends.

'They know what Zeb looks like and how he might alter his appearance.'

Silence over their table.

'What about Mossad, BND and MI6?' Meghan asked, her head spinning with the revelations.

Clare's face softened. 'I lied to you about that,' she lifted a hand apologetically. 'The bug.'

She had to, because whoever planted it was listening.

'Alex,' Clare said, referring to Sir Alex Thompson, the head of MI6, 'snorted in that way he has when I told him about the evidence. Dieter from the BND grunted and said I fit the dumb American stereotype if I believed that about Zeb. Neither of them trusted the videos. They rejected them outright.'

'And Levin?' Beth honest-to-goodness giggled in delight.

'Avichai,' Clare's eyes sparkled. 'He listened silently. Said he would call me back and hung up. Called me an hour later. He said he summoned Carmen and Dalia to his office.'

Two of the best Mossad operatives. Our friends. Their faces popped up in Meghan's mind as she nodded, listening to her boss.

'He told them about Zeb and about the kill order. He ordered them to go to Tripoli and terminate him. He says Carmen looked at him for a long while and then told him to go see a psychiatrist. They walked out of his office. And then Avichai let loose. He called me names. Me, one of his closest allies. He said I should take a hard look at myself and decide if I am worthy to head the Agency. He didn't think I deserved to be, not if I thought Zeb had turned.'

Bear guffawed while Broker thumped the table in delight. Meghan joined in their laughter, and then it faded. *Sir Alex, Dieter Reinhard, Avichai, Carmen and Dalia, all of them disbelieved that video. They had faith in Zeb. But I ...* she turned her head away as her face flushed in shame.

'STOP!' Clare grabbed her wrist and squeezed hard. 'Meghan, I know how your mind works. DON'T FEEL GUILTY. I know all of you. None of you believed it. I am sure the last few days have been hell on you. But I will also stake my life that not once did any one of you ever entertain the thought that Zeb was a traitor.'

'Why didn't I react like them, then? Beth, Broker, the others, all of them furiously denounced the evidence. I listened. I—' Meghan whispered, her eyes brimming with tears.

'Meghan, you're one of the smartest people I know. But sometimes you are too smart to see the obvious.'

'What's that?' she sniffed.

'Emotional distance,' Clare explained. 'Y'all are so close to Zeb that when I presented the evidence, you went into shock. That rational mind of yours, Meghan, went into overdrive. But it wasn't working at full capacity.'

And when Clare laid it out like that, Meghan knew her boss was right, and it was as if a weight had been lifted from her mind. She shook her head, angry for not working it out for herself, sniffed, and then her face crumpled and she snatched a table napkin and cried into it. Embarrassed at her show of emotion, she rushed to the bathroom.

She leaned against the sink and sobbed till she had let out

everything inside that had been bottled and wound tight. She bent down to wash her face, dried herself with a towel and saw that Beth was there, leaning against the door, smiling, her eyes watery too.

'You're an idiot,' her younger sister said.

'Yeah, I know.' Meghan hugged her and for a few seconds it was just them, just like it had been when they had to rebuild their lives after Wyoming.

She was back to her normal self when they walked back to join Clare and her friends. Five feet ten inches of smarts and menace, green eyes and brown hair, a ready smile and whip-smooth gun action. Unquestionably loyal to her team.

Yes, Meghan Petersen was back, but then her step faltered when she thought of Zeb.

'Something you should know,' Clare resumed. 'It might not be relevant. Alex, Dieter and Avichai have not sent any teams. But they've made it look like their killers are out there.'

'They know about the bug?' Meghan asked.

'I didn't tell them, but I am sure they suspect we have been compromised in some way. That's the only way something like this could be pulled off.'

'Zeb. What do we know of him?' Meghan asked, almost fearfully.

Clare straightened and lowered her voice. 'He's been attacked a few times; I know that much. You heard about the shooting in a Tripoli hotel?'

Meghan paled. She thought back. 'Yeah, there was some mention in the news. Gunmen firing inside a fancy place.' Her eyes widened. 'Zeb?'

'He got away, from the descriptions I have. Remember, he was setting up a meeting with Abu Bakhtar?'

'Yeah. That's the last we know from him.'

'One man matching one of Zeb's disguises escaped. Shooters are dead. No identities on them. There was another attack in a hotel room. Not much description there, but I'm guessing the killers were targeting Zeb. And then, day before yesterday, a gun battle in a fruit market in Tripoli.'

'The weapons!' Meghan said.

'Yes, last known location of the Javelins. Last known to *us*, going by the GPS data we had.'

'Zeb survived?'

'Looks like it,' Clare replied. 'The shooters were German contractors. No, not BND people,' she said quickly, to forestall any questions. 'I did some digging. It looks like one of the black-ops outfits'—she mentioned a name— 'outsourced to them. I haven't found out who the shooters were in the previous attacks. It doesn't look like any other agency knows ... but they could be playing cagey. Tripoli, right now, is thick with assassins. CIA, these PMCs, NSA, and ...' She licked her lips.

'And?'

'I've heard the police have his details, too. They too are looking for him.'

'Ma'am,' Beth said worriedly, 'he'll have tried to make contact. He would have failed. He knows nothing of all this.'

'Yeah.'

Should I tell her? Meghan thought for a moment. *Heck, if I don't trust Clare, we might as well lie down, roll over and wait for the world to end.*

'Beth warned him,' she said.

'I know,' the director replied. 'I saw what you had done. I would have done the same in your position,' she smiled.

'Warned him?' Broker exclaimed. 'How?'

'Website. Photo. **X**,' the younger sister explained quickly.

'He thinks we're hunting him.' Roger frowned.

'Yes,' Clare agreed and looked at them searchingly. 'How do you think he'll react when you come across him?'

He'll think we're hostile. Meghan gnawed at her lip. *But this is Zeb. He's not some random agent.*

'He won't shoot at us,' she said with a deep certainty, immutable conviction.

'Yes,' Beth nodded. The other operatives grunted in assent. 'Zeb mentored us. He trained us. He's saved all our lives countless times. Zeb will not raise his gun on us. He won't hurt us.'

'Zeb Carter will take our bullets.' Bear's jaw flexed. 'But he won't fire at us.'

'That's my take as well,' their boss said. She straightened, all business. 'Twin-pronged approach. I will work the ropes here. See who might be responsible for the evidence.'

'And the bugs,' Meghan reminded her. 'We need to trace those down.'

'Leave that angle to me. Like I said, I will pull threads here, in DC and the Pentagon. See what unravels. But I have a feeling my going will be slow. There are too many people, too many agencies involved. Y'all find Zeb. Keep him safe from these other shooters. I'll declare that you're the Agency's kill team. See who reacts and how.'

'And we work from Zeb's end,' Meghan said. 'See if he's learned anything. Work out who benefits from this. China and Iran are the obvious suspects. They have enough reason to terminate Zeb. But maybe they're red herrings. This could be a false-flag operation to incriminate them. However, all possibilities need to be checked out.'

'There's one problem,' Beth said, frowning. 'We'll be working with our hands tied. We don't have Werner. Our programs are down—'

'Don't be so sure of that.' Clare's smile was like the breaking of the dawn. She brought out a sheet of paper and scribbled an IP address on it. 'Backups that no one knows of. In the cloud, with no link to me, the Agency or any of you. However—'

'We have to be careful. Nothing that will give us away.' Meghan saw where she was going. 'We get Werner back,' she said impatiently when she noticed her sister's expression at their boss's warning, 'we can run algos for connections.'

Clare looked at them in surprise. 'Why are y'all still here? Go get Zeb. Bring him back safe.'

The sisters spent several hours installing their systems on new servers and cloaking those so that detecting what they really were and what they contained was near-impossible.

They ran screening programs, sniffers that went looking for viruses, back holes, worms, anything that could be planted by hackers. They fussed over Werner, double- and triple-checked that the AI, the heart of their operations, was intact, untampered with, and fully functioning.

It was. The versions Clare had backed up had been before any hack.

They installed new firewalls, security checkpoints and intrusion detectors, refreshed their log-ins and access controls, and then declared they were back in business.

A loud cheer greeted that announcement.

Late that night, their Gulfstream climbed into the air again, this time from JFK, heading to Tripoli.

Meghan grinned involuntarily when she surveyed her friends.

The operatives looked younger, as if a weight had been taken off their shoulders. Bwana and Roger were back to their wise-ass selves. Bear and Chloe were huddled close. Broker was nodding to music on his headphones, and Beth was rubbing her toes on her seat's leather. *Her thing whenever she's on the aircraft.*

Her smile faded when she turned away from them and looked at the disappearing city from the window.

They had left Wyoming after their lives had been upturned in the active shooter incident. They set up a business in Boston. *It was very successful, profitable, but that didn't feel like us. We didn't feel engaged.*

They had returned to their home state on vacation, and then, they had been attacked by a Mexican cartel.

Zeb, vacationing alone, had intervened and saved them. As he protected them, they learned more of the tall, brown-haired man who spoke little, moved easily and had hidden, lethal talents.

We pleaded with him to let us join the Agency. She smiled at the memory. *He didn't budge. We batted our eyelashes. Mistake. He's never moved on from the death of his wife.*

They did everything they could to convince him, but Zeb remain unmoved. The Agency, he explained, was a small team. Former Special Forces operatives, ex-military. There was no room for civilians.

We'll make room for ourselves. We'll be useful, they had protested. He turned them down and left for New York after ensuring they were safe.

We crashed into his New York office one day, she

remembered, her grin returning. *We went after Broker. We convinced him that we would be valuable. He did the heavy lifting for us. He persuaded Zeb, and that's how we joined the Agency. Zeb made us who we are today.*

She glanced at her sister, who seemed to sense her thoughts and winked in understanding.

And now, he's out there, she thought, her smile fading again. *In one of the most hostile cities in the world. Hunted by agencies he thought were friends. He thinks we have turned on him.*

Hang tight, Zeb, she whispered in the night. *We didn't desert you. We're coming.*

Chapter 24

———— ∝∞∝ ————

Tripoli

Zeb sat in his room for a long time, staring blindly at the **X**.

Is that what they think? That I've betrayed them? Is that why all these people are hunting me?

What other reason could there be? Now, what that German shooter said made sense. He was on a kill list.

And my people, my friends, are coming for me.

He shivered again, even though his room was warm. His fingers shook, and his pulse beat fast and hard. His cheeks were wet when he touched his face.

You're crying, the beast hissed, finding a voice for the first time in all the years that it had been inside him. *Why are you crying?*

Zeb had no answer.

You've cried only for your family. For your wife and son.

They're my family now, he replied.

It was true. He had drifted, zombie-like, for years after their deaths. He had become a mercenary, taking on jobs from contacts in the Pentagon and the CIA. A brutal warlord in

Somalia. A dictator in Asia. A drug cartel boss in Colombia. A rescue mission for American soldiers captured by the Taliban in Afghanistan. Zeb went on high-risk missions that few dared to take. He didn't fear dying and would have welcomed it. But he survived.

And then, Clare contacted him and asked him to help her build the Agency.

Broker. Bwana. Roger. Bear. Chloe. Beth. Meg. They became much more than friends. They brought him back to life. Especially the twins. They battered down his walls. They demolished his isolation. Zeb didn't become an extrovert. But he had learned to smile and laugh again. Not with everyone. Just with them.

He still didn't fear death. He still would give up his life. Only now, it would be for the Petersens and the rest of his friends.

You have to take them out, the beast hissed. *They are your enemy now.*

Zeb trembled. Beth and Meg were his enemy? Broker? The rest of them?

Of course, they are, the beast insisted. *They are coming to kill you.*

Zeb moved as if he was drugged. He closed down the website. Shut down his screen.

Let them come, he replied.

Set up an ambush, the beast cackled.

No.

What do you mean, no?

I will not stop them.

The beast roared in anger. *They are after your life.*

I know.

Then—

I can't, I won't raise my gun against them.

I have saved your life thousands of times, the beast raged. *I have made you faster, stronger, I have given you the edge that made the difference between living and dying. I can't help you if you willingly decide to die.*

I know.

What kind of man are you?

Zeb couldn't answer that. He got to his feet slowly. Swaying as if he was weak. His vision was still dark. He shook his head drunkenly to clear it. The dimness started to fade, slowly.

A glint on the bed. His Glock. He picked it up and with shaking fingers, attempted to holster it. Failed on the first attempt, his hands were twitching so badly. It went home on the second try. He ran a forefinger over its steel blindly.

I will stand down if they show up. If they shoot me ... He tried to summon anger. He tried to make himself bitter, but he couldn't. He felt only emptiness inside him.

It's not them, the logical part of his brain said, fighting through the mist of shock and despair. *Someone turned them against me.*

I hope they tell me who it was. And why they think I am a traitor. Before they shoot me.

He drew on his ill-fitting jacket.

Where are you going, now? the beast asked in surprise.

I have to show the Javelins to Abu Bakhtar.

After all this?

Yes.

Because that's who he was. It was what made him.

Zeb Carter didn't give up on a mission. Not even if his own friends were gunning for him.

He wouldn't, even now. Not until he was dead.

Chapter 25

———⌘———

Washington DC

Clare took her security vehicle to the most famous address in the world. She composed herself as she sat in the back. A small smile on her lips as she recalled the meeting with her operatives.

I knew Beth or Meg would come through. They would spot the discrepancy.

Her cheer faded as the Capitol's dome became visible in the distance, to her left.

Her agency was under attack, and chances were it was someone within US intelligence. Jiang Hsu or Siavash Mostofi, the IRGC head, had the capability or the resources. *But would they run an operation of this scale? Tap my offices?*

No. She shook her head. *They wouldn't risk our retaliation if they were found out.* They were more likely to send assassins after the Agency. Which they had done several times.

She was certain there was a traitor within the US intelligence or military community. And it wasn't Zeb.

She straightened as the car approached the White House's

entrance at the back, away from the public's prying eyes.

After clearing security, she followed an aide, who tapped on a door and opened it to usher her inside the Oval Office.

'Clare.' President Morgan flashed his trademark grin and clasped her hand warmly. Some said his craggy good looks, sense of humor and smile were all that had won him his second term.

She knew better. She had come to know him in his first term. She had gotten closer to him during the Israel-Palestine resolution. The president saw through complex problems easily. He could sift through noise and identify core issues. He had a knack for bringing partisan people together, knocking down their walls and getting them to see the common good. But, most of all, he could see the bigger picture. And it often involved a global view.

He was a staunch supporter of the Agency. He believed there had to be one covert outfit that acted independent of the military and intelligence establishment. He had trusted Clare to deliver, and she had never let him down.

She greeted him warmly, even though she was nervous inside. This was unlike any other meeting. She had extracted one concession from the DNI: that she should be the one to break the news about Zeb's video and betrayal to the president.

He might not believe me. All other agencies are convinced Zeb is a betrayer. I have nothing to back me up but my gut instinct and Zeb's personality. That might not be enough for him.

'You know, Daniel,' the president chuckled, as the second man in the room came forward and hugged her.

She hadn't known he would be here. *Maybe,* she thought hopefully, *this will go better than I expected.* The National

Security Advisor was not just on her side; he was a close friend. In the back-stabbing, power-hungry circles of DC, such a relationship was to be treasured. *Or, maybe not,* she told herself. *He could be here to soften whatever blow the president delivers.*

'Sir,' she began when pleasantries had been taken care of and coffees had been served. 'I have some bad news.'

President Morgan stopped smiling. He made a give-it-to-me motion with his hand.

'You need to see this, sir.' She brought out her screen and turned it to face the president and Klouse. She pressed the play button and let the first video roll.

The most powerful man in the world was expressionless as Zeb discussed his arrangement with Jian Hsu. *He knows Zeb. He has met him a few times. He likes him. How will he react now?*

The president's face gave her no clue as she played the next video, that of her operative withdrawing money from the offshore account. She played Zeb's call finally and waited for him to respond.

'Where was that second clip?'

'In the Bahamas, sir.' She didn't elaborate. He didn't need to know all details. He had to have deniability.

'This isn't new to me,' the president said, finally. 'I have had people trooping in to tell me we have a leak at the highest level. That one of our assets has betrayed us. Catlyn mentioned Zeb by name.'

Catlyn Feder. The video went to her. But Mike, the DNI, promised me no one but me would break the news to the president, Clare thought, taken aback.

This is DC, she reminded herself. *Did you really expect*

him or the other agency heads to keep their word?

'Mike said he knew who the traitor was,' President Morgan said, watching her shrewdly, giving nothing away by way of body language or expression. 'He was investigating further, however, and would tell me the name once he was sure.'

So, he too came running to the president. Her nails dug into her palm in sudden anger at his duplicity.

'Lizzie, Paul, Lester, Luis, they all said they had heard of a betrayal. Someone of ours who was conspiring with the Chinese.'

Secretary of Homeland Security Elizabeth Kahn; Secretary of State Paul Vaughan; Secretary of Defense Lester McClellan; and Secretary of Treasury Luis Newman. *Looks like the entire cabinet came to him.*

But how did they know? Clare shook her head imperceptibly as the answer came to her immediately. *All of them are part of the daily security and intelligence briefings. There's no mention of Zeb or any leak in those, but people talk. Besides, many of the intelligence agencies are in their departments. I should have realized; this could not be contained.*

'Only Catlyn mentioned his name?' Clare asked, as professionally as she could.

'Yes.'

'Did she or the DNI say anything else?'

'No.'

'I will hand in my resignation, sir. Today.' *They outmaneuvered me, she thought dully. I thought I had the president's trust and could convince him. But I have no option, now.*

President Morgan looked astonished.

'Why would you do that?'

'Sir, Zeb, that video, your entire cabinet believes he's a

traitor. There's a kill order …' she trailed off. *Why is he looking surprised?* Did she dare to hope?

'What do *you* think?'

'Zeb Carter would sooner shoot himself than betray us,' she said emphatically.

'Then why would you resign?'

'Sir, but these others—'

The president smiled and the Oval Office lit up. He waved his hand dismissively and made a mocking sound.

Did the Leader of the Free World say "pshaw"?

'Clare. You think I don't know what other intelligence agencies think of the Agency? Many of them have come to me in the past. They said y'all should be part of them. You think I listened to them?

'You and your team have completed every mission you took up. Every single one. That's a success rate no other outfit has come close to. You have taken down terrorists, threats to national security, Mafia cartels … I have met Zeb myself. I think I am a good judge of people.'

She nodded unconsciously. That was a characteristic President Morgan was famous for. He read people instantly and accurately.

'I know Zeb isn't a traitor. But, just to be double sure, I called Daniel. You know the history we have.'

She nodded again, this time looking at the National Security Advisor, who gave her a discreet thumbs-up. The NSA and the president went all the way back to college. Theirs was not just a professional relationship. They were very close friends as well.

'You know what he said?'

Clare waited expectantly.

'He said, "Mr. President, don't be an ass."' He chuckled and shook his head in disbelief.

His grin faded when he saw her expression. 'No more talk of resignation. I know Zeb has been set up. Who do you think's behind it?'

'We don't know, sir,' she confessed honestly. A deep relief swept over her and she felt a little faint, drawing a concerned look from the president, who was sitting on a couch opposite her. Klouse leaned against the Resolute Desk, a gift from Queen Victoria to President Rutherford Hayes. It was made from timbers of the exploration ship, HMS Resolute. It was sturdy. Had stood the test of time.

Like his trust in me, she thought. She blinked rapidly and cleared her throat.

'I can imagine what you've been through these last few days,' the president said gently.

'Thank you, sir. I … what this means to me … I can't even begin to say.'

'There's nothing to say, Clare. You and your team have served our country for so long and so well … my believing in you is the very least I can do.'

'Thank you, sir.' She bent her head for a moment, and when she raised it, her composure had returned.

'Jian Hsu is an obvious suspect, sir. Iran, too.'

The president nodded. He was aware of that country's activities.

'However, sir, we cannot ignore that the perpetrators might be closer. Someone in our country.'

He turned grim; eyes flinty. 'I was discussing just that with Daniel before you arrived. Any suspects?'

'No, sir. When something like this happens, there's a

meeting of agency heads. Their deputies, actually,' she chose her words carefully. The president wasn't part of any kill-order decision and he wasn't supposed to know about them.

He surprised her. 'I am aware of the termination order on Zeb. People tell me things.' He smiled briefly at her.

'Yes, sir. That's why I asked if Catlyn or Mike had mentioned anything more. Every attendee in that room is a suspect. The agency heads are on that list, too. Everyone who came to you. All of them are powerful, have access to resources.'

'What about motive?' Klouse broke his silence.

'We don't know. But then, why would China or Iran go to these lengths? They know that discrediting the Agency does not mean much in the grand scheme of things. Another outfit will come up in our place. Even killing Zeb will not make a huge difference.'

'You think this is personal?' the president asked.

'I don't know, sir. There's something else, sir.'

She looked at him and then at Klouse. 'My office has been bugged. Ever since these videos came to light.'

The president was stunned. The NSA reared back as if he had been struck.

'Military-grade devices, sir. Used by all the outfits in that meeting. Some of our allies use them too. Untraceable. I don't know who planted them. Someone hacked into our systems too, altered the security camera footage. I have shut down everything, sir. I had no choice.'

'They want you to know they are listening to you,' Klouse said savagely.

'Yes.'

'My God,' the president whispered. 'This is—'

He straightened his shoulders and narrowed his eyes. 'What do you want from me?'

'Sir, you need to announce that you are thinking about the Agency's future.'

'But … I get it. You want to see how everyone reacts to that.'

'Yes, sir. If we are lucky, someone might incriminate themselves. But I don't think it will be that easy.'

'I'll get to that. Discreetly. Speak about it to small groups of people. What else can I do?'

'Nothing, sir, for now.'

'Where's Zeb?'

'In Libya, sir. He was hunting Almasi before this exploded.'

'Where's he now?'

'We don't know, sir.' She opened her mouth, thought better, closed it.

'What?' the president demanded.

'We know he's been attacked a few times, sir.' She swallowed. 'Kill teams, after that order. He's survived. We know that much. But now, even the Libyan police are after him.'

President Morgan paled.

'This gets worse,' Klouse whispered savagely.

'I can call Rayhan Sabbagh,' the president suggested, worry on his face.

'No, sir. That will give away that we know Zeb's implicated.'

'We can't leave him like that!'

'My team is on their way to Tripoli, sir. They will find him. Keep him safe.' She caught his and Klouse's eyes. 'I told them, in my office, that they should shoot him on sight. They are the Agency's kill team.'

The president's face darkened. He opened his mouth

angrily and then his expression faded. 'That was for the bene-fit of the listeners?'

'Yes, sir. Daniel, it would help if you repeat that. When-ever you speak with those meeting attendees, their bosses and the cabinet.'

'I will,' Klouse said.

She kept quiet as the president fell silent. She knew what he was thinking. Someone in his cabinet or an agency head could be responsible.

He stirred after several moments. 'We are confronted with several challenges. Deep inequality in many sections of soci-ety. The rise of terrorism. Racism. We are becoming polarized as a country. On top of that, climate change ...' He gestured at Klouse, who came forward and sat next to her.

'If a foreign agency is behind this,' he said, studying them, 'they are a threat to us. Deal with them appropriately.'

That's an order, Clare thought and got a confirming nod from Klouse.

'However, if it's someone of our own,' the president continued, 'I know each and every one of my appointees well. As well as this job allows. I rely on their professional judg-ment and expect their personal conduct to withstand scrutiny. None of them seem like candidates to betray us. I am sure, despite your constraints, despite the situation and in spite of the pronouncement I will make regarding the Agency, you will get to the bottom of this.'

Clare nodded.

The president's face hardened. 'If it turns out our people are responsible, they are traitors. They have worked to desta-bilize our intelligence apparatus. However, I am not sure if our country is ready for them to be exposed.'

'Find them, Clare,' he said sternly. 'Find out who's responsible. And then deal with them.'

He means no arrest. No public trial. The kind of termination my team is expert at.

'Yes, sir.'

'And above all'—he got to his feet and clasped her hand—'get Zeb back. Alive.'

Chapter 26

Tripoli

Zeb was unaware that his boss had met the president.

He had gotten out of his room, zombie-like. He had checked out his six and his periphery more than once, but he knew he was perfunctory.

Why does it matter anymore? Everyone knows how I look. His lips twisted as he put on his shades. He didn't see any guns pointing his way. Not that they'd show themselves. It was a normal Tripoli afternoon. Traffic. Military vehicles and pedestrians.

He looked up the nearest vehicle rental firm near him. There was one a fifteen-minute walk away. He set out and tried to get into the zone.

If people are hunting me, let them. He shrugged. He could not be looking over his shoulder continually. He was in his Misfud disguise because there would be no time to change before the rendezvous. The arms dealer was known to the police … *and also to the kill teams,* he thought sardonically. *My team—* No, he wouldn't go there. He wouldn't think about them and what they were thinking about him and the bitterness and anger they might be harboring. *It doesn't matter anymore. Once they come, they'll find me.* He was sure they would locate him. They were the best trackers in the world.

You're proud of them, the beast wondered. *Despite their coming after you.*

Yes, he replied and forced himself to stop thinking of his friends.

'How much?' he asked the burly shopkeeper. *Hassan's Rentals,* said the sign outside. A converted garage behind the Albaara Hospital. The front had a shutter, which was rolled open. A window to one side that looked into a small office.

Hassan had risen from behind his desk as Zeb entered and sauntered around, inspecting the various vehicles. All of them vans. White, black, grey, standard colors. Rolling doors to the side to load and unload. A driver and passenger seat at the front.

'One thousand dollars a day.' Hassan checked out his visitor. Rather loose jacket, jeans and shirt that was straining over his belly.

He thinks I look prosperous. 'That's too much,' Zeb replied. 'I can get this same type of vehicle for way less, just five minutes away.'

'Abdul's place?' Hassan snorted contemptuously. 'His vans will break down when you just sit in it. My vehicles are fully serviced, well-maintained. Full tank. All papers complete. Legal. No customer complains when they rent from Hassan.'

They haggled and came down to a hundred dollars a day. Zeb knew he was overpaying, but he was running out of time. Besides, the vehicles did look in good condition.

The white van had caught his eye, but at the last minute, he chose a black one. *Fits my mood,* he thought darkly.

'Latif Wakil Misfud,' he said, giving Hassan his details, a driving license, one of his fake addresses and numbers.

He set out, driving to the fruit and vegetable market. Parked as close to the warehouse he could get. The place was busy, and he was confident no shooter would try their luck there, not now. Escape would be slow. Slow enough for them to be captured.

'Sayyidi, can I borrow your trolley?' he asked a vendor, who waved assent without looking at him.

Zeb rolled the two-wheeler to his storage. Looked around carefully. No one was paying attention to him. Took a deep breath and rolled up the shutter. Stepped inside quickly and reached inside his jacket.

Stillness. The smell of rotting produce. He was alone.

He went deep inside, to the rear wall. Raised the false one and inspected his weapons. They were undisturbed.

The Agency knows where this cache is. Why haven't they sent anyone to recover it? Or, are my friends waiting for me? Watching me?

He shrugged. He could not let anyone dictate his movement.

He loaded the Javelin crate with difficulty onto the two-wheeler. Grabbed a few more weapons and pieces of equipment and put them alongside the missiles. Closed down the fake wall and exited the warehouse.

Ten minutes later, he was on his way. To Abu Sittah, on the east side of the city. A bombed-out factory that he had identified during one of his many recon runs.

The building was in the midst of an industrial area that

had been destroyed. Once, it had housed small workshops, carpentry shops, metal workers. A bombing by ISIL had killed several innocents in a nearby residential area. In retaliation, the Libyan Army had pounded the industrial area until only the husks of buildings were left.

Suits me fine.

He opened the crate and brought out two minia-ture, wireless-enabled security cameras. He mounted them discreetly at the entrance of the building. Planted a MiFi, mobile hotspot device, turned it on and connected the cameras to it. He removed a burner phone from the crate, set it up so that the camera feed transmitted to it. The last step was to relay the video stream to his phone. He removed his device from his jacket, fingered through the settings until he got two video links.

He grunted in satisfaction, grabbed more gear from the crate, and set up another pair of cameras at the rear of the warehouse.

Job done, he wheeled out of the warehouse and went to the last building at its industrial park.

Rusting iron pillars propped up a metal roof that had holes in several places. Sunlight streamed through those gaps and dimly lit the cavernous interior.

The building had been some kind of storage area. Concrete floor, racks to the sides, open and empty space at the center. But the best part of it was just the single, narrow rear exit, which had a secure door.

Zeb inspected the place. It hadn't changed since the last time he had checked it out.

He heaved the Javelins inside the building and placed the container in the center. Opened it and attached several remote-controlled explosives to its interior. Closed it, locked it, and adjusted its location so that it was visible from the outside.

He then went down the approach route and planted explosives along the sides. Attached remote detonators to them and set them to fire from his phone. Those were his backups.

He drove his van to the rear and hid it inside yet another empty building.

Then he made his call to the storekeeper in Fashloum.

Chapter 27

⎯⎯⎯∞⎯⎯⎯

The first vehicle came two hours later, as the afternoon turned to dusk. Light and visibility was still good.

The industrial area lay still, buildings creaking, loose cables whipping against metal somewhere in the distance.

Zeb watched as armed, masked men climbed out of their open-topped ride and stood ready, waiting.

In front of the building he had rigged with the cameras.

They spread out at an unheard command and went inside. Two more vehicles came up, bristling with men. The last one was another open-top, but the middle one was an SUV of some kind, and no one stepped out of it.

Zeb zoomed the video feed and tried to see inside the middle vehicle, but couldn't. Dark windows, sunlight glinting off the windscreen. Was Abu Bakhtar inside? The storekeeper had taken his instructions, had written down the rendezvous point, and had asked him to stand by.

He had returned and said his party would meet Zeb in two hours.

That's my party, Zeb thought. *Unless they are some of the shooters gunning for me.* Despite the grimness inside him, the numb feeling that came over him whenever he thought of his friends, he couldn't help grinning. *Lots of folks looking for me.*

One of the gunmen from inside came running to the middle vehicle. He spoke rapidly, gesticulating. The others joined him. The third vehicle emptied and its occupants crowded around. Ten shooters, Zeb counted, including the drivers. But no one stepped out of the vehicle in the center. The masked driver spoke through a rolled-down window.

Zeb dialed the Fashloum storekeeper's number. 'Connect me to your party,' he ordered.

'That isn't how—'

'Tell your party, if they don't speak to me, the deal will not happen.'

The man breathed noisily and then said, 'Wait.' He returned ten minutes later. 'They say they're waiting for you. Is this a trap?'

'I know they're there. You think I would lead them to the goods just like that? Latif Wakil Misfud is no fool,' he said scornfully. 'Put them on the line. Right now.'

The storekeeper disappeared, returned. He fumbled with something, and then a harsh voice came through. He's put two phones together, Zeb figured.

'You're playing games with us,' the voice hissed. On his camera, Zeb could see that the driver in the middle vehicle was holding a phone to his ear.

'No,' he replied. 'Just being careful.'

'CAREFUL?' the driver shouted. 'Do you know the risk we have taken to get here?'

'I know. I can see you. I had to be sure it was you.'

The driver removed the phone from his ear. Stared at it. Looked around. Said something to the gunmen, who immediately whirled, their guns rising to face an unseen enemy.

'Relax,' Zeb sneered. 'I saw you arrive a long time back. I saw your men enter the building. if I wanted to kill all of you, I could.' His voice sharpened. 'Is the main man with you? I don't deal with anyone else.'

'He is here.'

'I need proof.'

The driver leaned back. The phone disappeared in the darkness of his SUV.

'I don't like playing games.' Abu Bakhtar's distinctive voice. *It could be anyone else, mimicking it. But that's a risk I have to take.* Arranging such a rendezvous wasn't straightforward.

'Games are the only way I have managed to stay alive. And have the biggest arms business,' Zeb boasted. 'Tell your men to come to the last building at the back. It also has an open entrance. I am waiting there.'

Bakhtar fell silent and then snarled, 'If that turns out to be a dummy location—'

'Why don't you find out?' Zeb taunted him. 'It's just five minutes from where you are,' and he hung up.

It was important to maintain the upper hand. To run the show. He raced to the side of the building and hid behind a crate. Raised his HK 416, scoped it so that the container leapt up in his sights.

He was one man against at least ten deadly killers. Just his HK with him. *I won't survive a fire-fight with them. Hopefully it won't come to that.*

And then he was in the zone, the grey fog rolling inside his mind, blanking out every irrelevant detail, and the beast stirred and started filling him, sharpening him.

Thank you, he said, not knowing if the beast could hear.

How could I leave you? it growled back. *I live with you. I die with you.*

The sounds of vehicles came through. Shadows crossed the wall.

And then four gunmen entered the building.

Chapter 28

———⊗∞⊗———

Two of them drifted to the left and right, one remained at the entrance, and the last one approached the crate.

The men at the far end checked out the building swiftly. Neither spotted Zeb, who was hiding beneath a tarp, behind empty boxes.

Sloppy work. They should have checked out the entire industrial area before sending Abu Bakhtar. The shoddy tradecraft gave him hope. *They're desperate for the missiles. They want to do a deal.* That meant he just might get to meet Almasi in person.

And what then?

Zeb didn't know how he would take out the ISIL leader. He hadn't thought that far ahead.

'This is locked, sayyidi,' the man at the crate called out.

'No one here,' another gunman shouted.

I hope that dude doesn't try to force that box open.

'You are wrong,' Zeb said and stood up from behind his hiding place.

Four men snapped towards him, their guns trained on him.

Zeb raised his hands in the air, HK in one of them, and

stepped out, aware that any mistake would kill him.

He walked out carefully and came to the center. Faced the front, aware that he was in full view of the vehicles at the front. More shooters lined the entrance, all of them peering in, all of them with rifles to their shoulders.

'I don't speak to you,' he told the gunmen when one of them opened his mouth. 'I only speak to your sayyidi.'

'HE WANTS TO SPEAK TO SAYYIDI,' the shooter yelled and then swiftly searched Zeb. Took the HK and tossed it to the floor. Removed the Glock and threw it down. Looked at the Benchmade that he retrieved from the thigh holster and showed it to the other shooters. They nodded in approval. It was a good weapon.

He exclaimed in surprise when he saw the camera footage running on Zeb's phone, and the gunmen huddled over it briefly.

Zeb stood silently, watching impassively, until one of the men gave the all-clear.

Doors opened and slammed shut. Two gunmen spilled out of the middle vehicle and a third man climbed out. Ordinary height. Dark eyes. No other feature visible, because he was masked and wearing a dark robe from shoulder to ankle. He, too, was carrying a weapon. A Sig Sauer Rattler, a mini rifle.

'You are Misfud,' he whispered when he came near.

'And you are?' Zeb asked insolently. He was surrounded by terrorists, but he showed no fear. Latif Wakil Misfud was used to dealing with the most dreaded criminals in the world.

The speaker removed his mask and handed it to a nearby shooter. He wore spectacles, a neatly trimmed mustache and beard, short-cropped hair, and would have jelled in a room full of accountants.

He just happens to be the second most wanted terrorist in the world.

'Was all that necessary?' Abu Bakhtar jabbed a thumb behind his shoulder.

'It's how I stay alive.'

'Is that what I think it is?' The terrorist leader pointed to the crate on the floor.

'Yes.'

'What's to stop us from shooting you and taking it away?' A half-sneer. *But he means it.*

'Try unlocking it.'

One of the gunmen bent to the crate and fiddled with the clasps. They didn't budge. He peered closer. 'They require a fingerprint,' he announced.

'Your prints?' the ISIL number two asked.

Zeb nodded.

'We can kill you and use your fingers to unlock it.'

Zeb bent to the case. The shooters sprang back and trained their weapons on him. He ignored them and pressed his thumbs against the clasps. They clicked open.

'Now, ask them to open it. Slowly.'

Two shooters opened the lid and— 'The inside is lined with explosives!'

'I press a button on my phone … boom!' Zeb smirked. 'Everyone in a fifty-foot radius dies. You, too,' he told Abu Bakhtar pointedly.

A murmur swept across the terrorists. Their fingers tightened on their weapons. The leader quieted them with a hand gesture. His face, expressionless.

'Your phones are with us,' he said.

'Okay. Kill me and see what happens,' Zeb challenged

him. 'You think I wouldn't have planned for that? Everyone underestimates Latif Wakil Misfud, until it's too late. But don't believe me. Go ahead. Shoot me. Then you'd better get away fast, because that baby's going to explode and you don't want to be near it. Of course, once it does, bye-bye Javelins. Now, you decide. Is getting those missiles important, or killing me? Because you can't have both.'

Seconds ticked by as Abu Bakhtar's eyes bored into Zeb. Finally, he nodded once. 'I came to do a deal. I will honor it.'

Honor and ISIL! Zeb bit his lip to stop an incredulous laugh.

He removed one missile carefully and gave it to the leader. 'It's heavy,' he warned.

The ISIL man grunted at its weight as his eyes examined the weapon swiftly. Other gunmen came near, stroked it and fingered it.

'You know how to fire it?' Zeb asked.

Abu Bakhtar nodded.

They must have gotten their hands on some, trained their people, and then they ran out of missiles.

'Four is not enough,' the leader said, handing over the weapon to his men. 'I need twenty.'

'I can get you two hundred if you want,' Zeb said carelessly, 'but they'll cost you. A million dollars for each unit.'

The leader didn't react.

I had quoted the price earlier. They know what to expect. Still, I expect some haggling.

'You can deliver twenty?'

'Yes, I just told you.'

'How quickly?'

'A week, ten days.'

A chill raced through him. *What are they planning? Maybe attack the Tripoli government. Or, take over NOC's facilities.*

In any case, a resurgent ISIL was a deadly threat to the world. *I have to take him and Almasi out. Quickly. And let Beth and Meg know what they want.*

And then he remembered his friends were no longer on his side.

'How do we know these work?' Abu Bakhtar cut into his thoughts.

'You don't,' Zeb told him bluntly. 'You might have heard how I work. I don't deal with middlemen. No assistants. If I risk my life to sell my goods, I expect my buyers to do the same. I will demonstrate that these fire. In front of your sayy-idi. And then you can take these with you. After you have paid me.'

The leader's nostrils flared. 'You deal with me. Only me.'

'Then we don't have a deal,' Zeb replied coolly. He took back the missile from a gunman's unresisting hands, placed it back in the box and locked it.

'Nasir—' he began

'DON'T TAKE HIS NAME.'

'He needs to be here,' Zeb said, showing no fear at the aggression of terrorists. *They can shoot me to pieces. But that timer in that box will get them as well.* 'I conveyed my terms to your people. Everyone in the market knows my reputation. I don't make exceptions for anyone. You can try finding another seller,' he gibed. 'I am sure someone can provide you with four immediately, and then fifty.'

'We'll take these with us,' Abu Bakhtar said angrily. 'Then make arrangements for the others. For which, *he* will come.'

'No. And in any case, did you notice anything about these

missiles? Do you see the command launch unit or the tube assembly? These missiles cannot be fired without those. Bring the money. Bring *him*. I will show that these fire. And then you can take them.'

Abu Bakhtar's face darkened. He breathed harshly. 'You, Misfud, you're just a small weapons dealer,' he grated. 'You don't know who you are dealing with. You are in no position to make demands.'

'Abu Bakhtar,' Zeb ripped back. 'While you and him were running away from American drones and rockets, I was still selling weapons to all fighters in Syria. I built up a business here and have become the most reputed weapons dealer in this region. Do *you* know who you are dealing with? If you think you can just shoot me here and get away with it, think again.'

The leader's eyes glittered. A nerve on his cheek twitched.

'Very well,' he grated, after long moments during which his men didn't move. 'I will come back with him. But we want all twenty weapons. And they need to work.'

'Twenty-one, sayyidi,' one shooter said. His voice trembled when Abu Bakhtar looked at him savagely. 'The one that will be fired, we cannot use it again,' he explained hastily.

'He's correct,' the leader turned back to Zeb.

'I said I can get two hundred. I will tell you when they are ready.'

'Don't take too long, Misfud,' the ISIL man said and whirled on his feet to depart.

'Wait,' Zeb told him. 'You leave my way. I set this rendezvous up. It's my job to make sure you leave safely. Let me check that the exit is secure.'

He walked past the terrorists to the entrance. *I do want them to leave safely.* The industrial area was out of the way and the chances of anyone else being there was low. *But I have shooters after me,* he thought grimly. He didn't want to take any chances.

He went past the three vehicles and turned another building's corner.

He was lucky. The bullet whizzed past his face by a few inches.

Chapter 29

———— ∞∞∞ ————

One SUV blocking the dusty track that was the exit route. Six gunmen running towards him. Dark clothing.

Zeb saw nothing more as he dived back. *Are they after me or after Abu Bakhtar?*

Me, he thought, bitterly, racing back to the building. *If they were after the terrorist, there would be military presence, armored vehicles, drones.*

'Gunmen,' he told Abu Bakhtar rapidly. 'Six of them that I could see. Give me my phones, my guns, everything,' he snatched them from one of the terrorists. He brought up an app on his phone and pressed a button. An explosion rocked in the distance.

Movement!

He threw himself against Abu Bakhtar and brought him to the ground. Lunged for his HK and fired a spray at the gunman, who had turned the corner. A hundred yards away, but the weapon was still effective and the shooter fell to the ground and crawled behind the building, out of sight.

'This is a trap,' Aby Bakhtar shouted.

'SHUT UP!' Zeb roared at him. 'If it was, why do you

think I just saved your life? Someone must have seen you. Get back in your vehicles. Drive through those rear walls. They will break. I checked them. turn left immediately, go straight and then turn right and you will come to the bigger road. That was from where you turned in. You can get away from there. MOVE!'

Zeb had acted so swiftly, so surely that Abu Bakhtar and his men were still not comprehending what was happening. Their reactions were slow.

'GO!' Zeb shoved the leader towards his vehicle. 'Take him away,' he snarled at his men. 'I will deal with this. I will call you when everything is set up.'

'He's right, sayyidi,' one terrorist said and hustled the leader away.

Zeb didn't pay them any more attention. *Those shooters, they aren't Meg or Beth or any of my friends.* That was the first thing he had noticed and why he had no qualms about setting off the explosives.

Cold rage filled him. The beast filled his blood. If he was to die at the hands of strangers, it would be while shooting.

ISIL's vehicles started behind him as he brushed past the side of the empty building to his left. To the front was where the track bent and disappeared out of view. Where those men were. Some of them might have died in the explosion.

He knew why they hadn't appeared yet. *That dude who crawled back ... he saw the ISIL men. He couldn't have recognized them. Too far, and he was moving too quickly. Besides, the terrorists weren't brandishing their evil flag.*

No, he's huddling with his survivors, working out a plan of attack, because they are assuming all those men are with me and they are outnumbered.

Zeb climbed into the empty building through a broken window. He knew the industrial park very well. He had scouted it, had learned every structure's location, entry and exit points.

A loud crash in the distance. *That's Abu Bakhtar, escaping.* He shook his head bitterly. He didn't think the day would come when he had to save the terrorist's life. *But it's for the bigger prize. I will kill him and Almasi,* he vowed.

He ran down the concrete wall of the building. On the other side was the track where the shooters were located. There, that was another window. It would open squarely in the middle of the route.

He bit his lip in thought. The shooters could be either to the left or to the right. All of them could be alive, or just a few.

Zeb checked his weapons. His HK, a full mag in it, that he had inserted on his way. Glock back in its holster. Phone and knife. But no wire camera, no surveillance device with which he could check the outside.

He took a deep breath. There was no way he was going to leave the industrial area without finding out who these gunmen were.

Which meant …

He dived through the window into the track.

Chapter 30

⎯⎯⎯⎯ ⨯⨯⨯ ⎯⎯⎯⎯

Zeb landed six feet away, just off the center of the track.

SUV to his left, in the distance.

Four shooters to his right, two bodies on the ground.

Split-second views. Images imprinting on his retina, his HK coming up even as his brain was decoding them.

The gunmen were fast, very fast.

They dived away, spreading out, offering less of a target. A gun chattered. Dirt splattered Zeb's face as he fired back, catching one shooter in the chest.

Zeb rolled, kept rolling, zigging and zagging as randomly as he could on the hard ground, keeping up a continuous stream of fire, his HK moving, sweeping the air, his hands moving with blurring speed as they replaced another empty magazine.

He had the advantage of surprise. It was infinitesimal, but the hostiles were already three down. Four down, as another shooter went down in his burst. There was no need to aim. Just sweep the air above the ground. He was down and had the slightest edge.

And then a round burned his left shoulder. He bit back an

oath. It throbbed and the fiery pain would come. But the fog in his mind, the adrenaline in him, blanked it out for now.

Two surviving shooters. On the left side of the track. One on his knees, taking a sniper position, the other firing rapidly at Zeb, all his rounds going wide.

'GRENADE BENEATH YOU!' Zeb yelled in warning. *Do they speak English?*

The gunmen stopped immediately. They aimed their guns at him, he at them. Standoff. *But it's two of them against one of me.*

The beast tensed. It made him curl his fingers against the trigger. He knew his own shooting well enough to know he wouldn't miss at that range. *How good are they?*

He saw the calculation on their faces. He didn't recognize them. Westerners for sure. That tanned skin and those light eyes were a giveaway. *They don't know if I am bluffing. They're remembering the explosion.*

'THERE *IS* AN EXPLOSIVE. RIGHT BENEATH YOU. PRESSURE SENSITIVE,' he warned.

He saw it in their eyes. *I said 'grenade' the first time. 'Explosive' the second time. They think I'm bluffing.*

Kneeling Man's face gave it away. *He's going to shoot.*

Zeb double-tapped him just as the shooter fired, the gunman's rounds thudding somewhere into concrete.

Standing Man flung himself away, his gun chattering rapidly, and then he fell heavily when Zeb shot him in the chest.

A loud sound.

That's my heart. It was thudding so hard it was a wonder no one came to investigate.

Zeb dropped his head to the ground, rested his forehead on

dirt and breathed deeply. Dust particles swirled in the air. The smell of earth surrounded him.

How the hell did I survive that?

It looked like luck was still on his side. Now, the throbbing in his shoulder returned. He twisted his head and squinted at it. His jacket was torn and the edges around the wound were turning red. He fingered it gingerly.

Nope, round didn't go inside. Scraped some skin and flesh. It looked like he would live.

Something crawled. An ant scurrying away, blissfully unconcerned about the gun battle that had just taken place.

Zeb got to his feet with a grunt. Slapped another magazine in his HK and checked the fallen men. Five of them beyond talking, of whom two were barely recognizable. *Those two died in the explosion.*

He looked down at Kneeling Man. *You should have shot me. Your guess was right. There wasn't a grenade.*

Standing Man's eyes flickered when he approached and then turned empty as his breath left him.

Zeb crouched and searched him. Found dollars in his wallet and a business card. *Daryll Coates. Oil Consultant.* Zeb recognized the company name. It was a CIA front. *We worked with their agents a few times.* One time they had been presenting themselves from that outfit.

His eyes turned bleak; his face hardened.

CIA. It was getting more personal.

He took photographs of the dead men, hesitated when he remembered there was no one he could send them to, but continued. Good tradecraft had to be maintained.

He searched the other men and found similar cards, all of them affiliated with the same firm. And when he went back to Coates's body, he found his own pictures on the man's cell phones. Prominent among those were the Misfud disguise.

How did they locate me?

The missiles. No other way. They were tracking them.

Which meant the killers would have to check in. But Coates's phone had no history of calls or messages. Its directory was empty. He couldn't unlock the other agents' phones.

Why didn't anyone attack me earlier? When I was with the missiles? At the market or driving them around?

The answer came to him immediately.

It took time to get a kill team in position, and since he was always on the move, the circumstances were even more complicated.

He thought about moving the bodies.

Nah. Let the CIA find them. Let them know killing me isn't going to be easy.

He checked the men again. Coates seemed to be a couple of sizes larger than Zeb. He bent over the body and stripped the man of his shirt, tossed his own jacket away and wore the dead agent's garment. It fit. Loosely.

Which is okay. It'll hide my shoulder holster.

He returned to the missiles. Brought his van around to the building and inside it. Loaded the box with difficulty, cursing and swearing as his shoulder protested.

First stop, a shop that sells aluminum foil.

Chapter 31

Zeb didn't have the energy to bargain with the store owner in Fashloum. He paid the asking price for the sheets of aluminum foil and disappeared inside the van.

He shut the door behind him and wrapped the sheets around the crate. It was hard work and he moved clumsily because of his shoulder. By the time he was done, he was perspiring, his shirt sticking to him.

When he was finished, a rudimentary Faraday cage surrounded the missiles. That would block the GPS signals from being transmitted.

Hope it works, he thought as he inspected his work. *It'll have to, otherwise all those shooters will find me immediately.*

He climbed out of the van and stopped short when a bottle of water was thrust at him.

'Drink,' the store owner said in Arabic, his bushy eyebrows almost reaching his hairline. 'I heard you moving around inside.'

Zeb took a gulp of water and swallowed. *Did I curse in English?*

No, he reassured himself. When he was undercover in

another country, he made himself think in the local language, if he knew it. That way, fewer mistakes were made.

'You should have asked. I could have helped you,' the shopkeeper said.

'Shukran,' Zeb thanked him. He returned the bottle, waved at the man and drove away.

Back to the fruit market, which was closing down. It was still the safest place to stow the Javelins.

Whoever is tracking the missiles will think I moved them out. They won't imagine I will return them to the same place.

Or so he hoped.

He borrowed the trolley from the same vendor, loaded his crate and placed it back in its hide.

'Are you alright?' the vendor asked when he returned the two-wheeler. 'You're sweating a lot.'

'Lot of loading and unloading work,' Zeb told him honestly.

'How else would we sell our produce?' The man laughed and thumped him on the shoulder. The left one.

Zeb bit his tongue to keep from shouting in pain as fire raced from his joint and spread through his body. He stumbled away from the man and rested against his van once he was out of sight.

Took several harsh breaths and, when his pulse had returned to normal, climbed inside.

He left the van outside Hassan's Rentals, the keys inside. Grabbed his backpack and went searching for a pharmacy. There were several, since Albaara Hospital was close by.

Zeb bought dressings, bottles of water and painkillers.

Hotels won't be safe anymore, he thought. I can't risk them. All these killers may have circulated my images.

He thought of his predicament as he wolfed down his

dinner at a brightly lit restaurant. Couscous, followed by a slice of kunafa, a dessert. The fact he might be killed any day soon was no reason to stop enjoying his food.

He would have to sleep in the street. No other choice. Find a quiet place, spend the night and see what he could come up with in the morning.

A child laughed at a nearby table. A woman shushed him. Zeb looked at them, nodding when the mother caught his eye and smiled apologetically.

The memories returned suddenly, punching through his carefully erected walls. His wife, son, on a vacation in Turkey. Laughing at him. *No, don't go there.* He turned away when the father looked at him quizzically. Blinked rapidly. Noticed that his hand was trembling as he drank water.

And then they went away. The memories. Back to wherever they had come from.

Zeb finished his meal, paid for it, and circled the restaurant. At the rear was a water tap attached to the wall, overlooking a yard. It was fenced by a concrete wall and surrounded by other commercial establishments.

I can climb over those, however.

Night. Tripoli moved slower as office-goers went home, shops closed and families went back to prepare for the next day.

The lights of the hospital burned bright. He could hear ambulances wail as they brought patients for care.

He found the hulk of a car a couple of streets away from it. It looked bombed-out. No wheels. No doors. A row of houses a little beyond. Little better than shanties. Concrete walls, some kind of roof. Drapes for the holes in the walls which constituted windows.

He heard murmuring from one dwelling, laughter from another as he went past them and inspected the vehicle's remains.

Its seats were still in good condition, which was what mattered. It was in a dark part of the street, which was important too. And it was in Fashloum, which was as good a base for him as any.

Zeb went back to the restaurant, which had closed by then. Scaled the walls when he didn't see any signs of a security camera. Went to the rear and stripped his clothing. He washed himself quickly, tended to his wound, which was still burning but not bleeding anymore. Dressed it, put his clothes back on, and returned to the car.

He lay on its seat, adjusted his legs. Uncomfortable, but he could manage.

Thinking time.

Why had he been declared a traitor? He thought hard but found no answer.

Who was behind that decision?

Clare?

He knew his boss. He had worked with her for years. Trust was an understatement for what they had.

If she had turned against him, there had to be a good reason. A very good one.

Some kind of evidence that she can't dispute. Which was genuine.

There's no such evidence. I have never betrayed my country.

But it can be fabricated.

Yeah, he acknowledged. That was entirely possible. And with the technology intelligence agencies had, it wasn't impossible to manufacture false proof.

But it had to be so good that even Clare was fooled.

That led to the most important question: Who was behind it?

He nearly laughed.

Who? I have no shortage of enemies. But two stood out.

China's MSS and Iran's IRGC. He had brutally attacked both of them in previous missions and drastically reduced their operating capabilities.

But why now?

Why would they wait so long? *As it is, their agents are ordered to capture me, failing which, kill me.*

And how do they benefit by declaring me a traitor?

They hope other agencies will kill me.

That made no sense, however. Both those agencies, their heads, Jian Hsu and Siavash Mostofi, were driven by vengeance. They would want Zeb killed by their own people. Sure, they would be happy if he was dead by anyone's hands. *But they'd prefer their own people shot me. Besides*, another thought struck him, *they will want to capture me.*

He sat up straight. Winced when his shoulder shot needles of pain through his body. Ignored it. Was he onto something here?

Hsu and Mostofi ... they will want to torture me. Extract everything, I know. Only then will they kill me.

My dying by the CIA's hands or other outfits, it won't give them intel.

Who then, if not the MSS or IRGC?

And why now? Why in Libya?

He drifted off to sleep when no answers came to him.

The scream woke him up.

Chapter 32

The beast filled him instantly. His Glock appeared in his hand without conscious thought.

Zeb sat up straight, alert. Dawn. It registered on him unconsciously. No gunmen looming inside his car, or outside.

Another scream ripped the morning.

He climbed out cautiously. Looked right. The street was empty. Left side, too.

He headed in the direction of the sound. Now he heard shouting. Yelling. A woman's voice from the second house. She cried out again. Fear and anger in her voice.

'DON'T,' she said in Arabic.

And then she came into view, coming from between two houses. Dragged by two armed men into the street. Kicking and screaming, biting, clawing.

One man slapped her viciously, and she fell down. The other got hold of her hair and pulled her up. She shouted hoarsely, the desperate cry twisting Zeb's guts.

Don't get involved. You've got a mission.

'PLEASE STOP,' she cried helplessly. 'LET ME GO.'

The men didn't listen to her. A vehicle entered the street.

Slowed. Zeb stepped back towards his car. *There's help.*

'Put her inside,' the driver leaned out.

That's not help. He could make out one more person on the passenger side. *There could be more in the back.*

'HELP!' the woman shouted again. She sobbed and stumbled. One thug swore, punched her in her side.

'GET UP, BITCH. COME WITH US.'

Zeb wasn't aware he had drawn closer until one of the men looked at him. 'Mind your own business,' the goon snarled.

The woman shrieked.

You heard him, the dispassionate voice inside him said. *Not your problem.*

No one else on the street. *Everyone's scared of them. Hiding inside.*

And what about you? the beast asked. *What kind of man are you?*

'Let her go,' Zeb said. Voice calm. Glock behind him. 'Don't take her.'

The men took two more steps to the waiting vehicle before his words registered on them.

One of them, the man who had warned him, turned his head incredulously to look at Zeb.

'You heard him, Younus. He's telling us to let her go.'

His companion, Younus, snapped a glance at Zeb, spat, and laughed. He twisted the woman's hair in his hand and pulled her viciously.

'A do-gooder, Mashal,' he said, smirking. 'He's one of those.'

Mashal, the first speaker, snapped his fingers insultingly at Zeb. 'Go away, *friend,*' he said sarcastically.

'Leave her alone,' Zeb told them.

They are to the left of the vehicle. Fifteen feet away. Both the driver and passenger are leaning out. Both seem armed, but they're watching. Carelessly. Looks like no one else in the vehicle.

Younus jerked in anger. He shoved the woman towards Mashal, who caught her and slapped her across the face.

Zeb's insides tightened. Everything sharpened and slowed down. The woman crying, turning her tear-streaked face at him as the thug pulled her by the hair. The tightening of her dress against her ... *she's pregnant!*

'We told you,' Younus growled. 'Mind your business. This woman's our property.'

He took a step in Zeb's direction. 'Some people never learn.'

'People don't belong to others. No one owns a person. Let her go.'

'You won't listen, will you?' The thug's face twisted in anger. He reached for his rifle.

That was the last mistake he made.

Zeb's gun hand rose to shoulder height. Eye to sight. Sight to Younus's forehead. He hesitated. He didn't want to kill. *Let them give up the woman and escape in that vehicle.*

The gunman showed no signs of hesitation. 'He's got a gun!' he bellowed and brought his weapon up. He was leveling it when Zeb's first round got him in the shoulder and sent him staggering back. He managed to loose a few wild shots and then went down when a second round destroyed his face.

All in a second, during which Mashal had shouted in rage, shoved the woman away and was reaching for his gun.

Zeb chopped him down. No mercy. No second thoughts. No second chances. He stood to the side of the street, alone, tall, coldness inside him, fury turned to white-hot resolve.

Small things registered. The weight of spare magazines in his pocket. The woman crawling away desperately to safety. Her crying for help, but no one emerging from any house. A plume of smoke from the shooter's getaway vehicle. The exhaust. The orange in the sky as the sun rose yet again to cast its light on humans who never seemed to learn.

The passenger diving out of the vehicle, snapping three fast rounds at Zeb, all of them missing because he was moving too fast. That, combined with the vehicle's drift, made him inaccurate.

Zeb's first shot missed. His second caught the man in the belly and his third in his face, when the thug reared up.

Zeb stood like a pillar, only his arms moving, sweeping in a controlled arc, his left coming up automatically to replace the magazine in his Glock, the gun moving a few inches, triggering to shatter the vehicle's windscreen, even as the driver engaged the reverse gear and attempted to escape.

There was no give in Zeb. He kept firing until the windscreen was reduced to giant starburst patterns, and through them, he saw the driver slumped over the wheel. The vehicle yawed and climbed over the pavement and shuddered to a halt as it crashed into a house.

And only then did his arm lower. He turned to the woman, who had gotten to her feet. He wondered why she wasn't looking at him. She was still facing the shooters' vehicle, her fingers pointing at it, her mouth opening ... and then something smashed into him.

Zeb fell to his knees, the force of the blow turning him around so that he too was facing the car, and then he saw a fifth gunman had emerged from the back of the vehicle and was triggering rapidly. The edges of Zeb's vision were turning dark, and that orange in the sky was becoming purple. He didn't know why, but it wasn't important. With the last of his strength, he lifted his Glock, which felt like a block of concrete, fired unconsciously, felt himself jerk from another blow. And then he was falling, and the last sound he heard was the thunder of shots.

Chapter 33

Tripoli

'Yes, that's him,' the hotel manager told Beth.

Meghan stood to a side and watched the lobby. They had arrived the previous night and checked into a hotel in the heart of the city, next to the German embassy.

She and Beth had put Werner to work on the flight. They had got the AI program to look into everyone who had attended the kill meeting. And their bosses. And then, they had included the entire cabinet, when Clare had texted them with a brief summary of her meeting with the president.

Those are lot of people to dig into, she thought, as she checked out the other residents in the hotel's lounge. Business travelers, many of them in suits. Many Arabs which wasn't unusual considering they were in Libya. A couple of families. None of them paying the Agency operatives any attention, though Bear and Bwana cut imposing figures.

'Latif Wakil Misfud,' the manager said. 'That was who he checked in as. Gunmen tried to kill him, but he escaped from the window. The police came later and said he was an arms dealer. They said it might be some militia group behind the attack. It happens,' he said, shrugging as if to say, *this is Tripoli. A warzone.*

That was six days back, Meghan thought when her sister thanked the manager. They knew Zeb had stayed in that hotel, but confirmation helped.

The next steps were to trace his movement, see whether they could pin him down to any neighborhood.

Checking out the Javelins' GPS would be easier. If the missiles had moved, then Zeb was responsible. *But our copy of Werner doesn't have data on all the locations.*

She donned her shades and led her friends out. Bear got behind the wheel of the Range Rover that they had hired. Seven of them in one vehicle, a tight fit. But there was no way they were going to be split up.

'The other hotel?' Bear asked.

'Yeah,' she replied.

The manager of the hotel on Al Fatah Road was brusque. 'It's a busy time,' he said. 'We are hosting a big conference. Lot of international delegates.'

'That attack that happened in your hotel, five days ago,' Beth gave him her business card that stated she was from the US State Department.

They had decided they would present themselves as US officials, tracking down Latif Wakil Misfud. That would make it easier to ask questions. Meghan pushed her shades up her forehead, over her hair.

'Yes, yes, I gave my statement to the police,' the manager said irritably. His expression didn't change when Beth discreetly slid over a bundle of US dollars. 'I've got CCTV camera footage, if you want to see,' he said, and led them to a small office when Beth nodded.

He instructed one of his men to pull up the feed. 'Ahmed will help you,' he said and left them.

The hotel employee didn't ask any questions. If his manager had okayed the request, that was good enough for him. His fingers flew over his keyboard as he opened up a file, clicked on a video and pressed *play.*

The hotel's lobby. Guests at the check-in desk. A few lounging on various couches.

'That's him,' Ahmed pointed to a solitary figure in a corner. Heavyset. Loose jacket.

That's Zeb, Meghan nodded imperceptibly when Chloe looked at her. *That's one of the disguises Werner came up with for him.*

They watched silently as the Arab-looking man sat alone, flicking through a newspaper. Arrogance in his demeanor. He seemed to snap something at another guest who had approached the couch.

He wants the seat to himself, Meghan figured out. *He's there to meet someone?*

'Watch this,' Ahmed told them.

Three men appeared in the frame. Dark-haired, dark-eyed, spread out. They looked around the hotel lobby and seemed to freeze when they saw Zeb.

'They recognize him,' Bear muttered when they traded glances and headed towards the seated man.

And then Zeb exploded.

Meghan had seen him in action thousands of times. She had accompanied him on missions. She knew he could burst to explosive movement just like that. Watching him now still gave her goosebumps.

She watched the scene unfold as he kicked the glass table at them and dived for cover as the firefight began.

It lasted for less than five minutes, at the end of which the three men lay motionless and Zeb fled from the hotel.

'I was returning from the bathroom when I heard the shooting,' Ahmed said. 'I hid behind a pillar and watched it. That man,' he tapped Zeb's figure on the screen, 'He was like lightning. I was amazed someone of his age could move that fast.'

That's because he isn't as old as he appears in that disguise, Meghan thought but held back her words. 'Did the police identify him?'

'The police?' Ahmed made a rude sound. 'In Tripoli? The only thing they do is collect baksheesh.'

'What about those dead men?'

'Militia members. Some kind of gang shootout, that's what they told us.'

'Can we have a copy of that?'

'Yes,' Ahmed duplicated the video and saved it on a flash drive. 'Boss said you could take it.'

Next stop, the Musheer cash market. Meghan, Beth and Chloe interviewed several shopkeepers, showed them various Zeb disguises, until one skinny server responded.

'Him.' He pointed a bony finger at one of the photographs. 'I remember him. He left me a big baksheesh.' He looked around fearfully, as if the proprietor might overhear and demand the return of the tip.

'Where did he go?' Beth asked. 'Did you see?'

'No. It was a busy day. I was with other customers.'

'When was this?'

'Four days back. There was a shooting, too. That's why I remember.'

'Shooting? Where?' Broker rumbled.

The server glanced at him and slid away to gesture at one of the exits. 'There. Two men shot at someone, but he escaped on a bike.' He grinned, his face turning youthful. 'I heard it was like a movie. This man came running out of the market, dived in the air and crashed into the rider, sat on the bike and got away. There are so many guns here'—he nodded at the square where currency was being traded— 'but shooting is very rare.'

'Did they catch that person?' Meghan asked tightly.

'No. But the police shot those killers.'

She tipped the server heftily for his help and walked out. Looked for a moment at the transactions being made. Several gunmen turned around to stare at them, but no one made a threatening move.

Bwana joined her. 'No cameras,' he said quietly.

'I noticed. Even if there were, you can bet they wouldn't be operational. Those gangsters couldn't run such an operation if they were being watched.'

'That was Zeb?'

'Yeah,' she replied, knowing Bwana was referring to the escaped man. 'Who else,' she chuckled, 'would perform a Hollywood stunt?'

They checked out the fruit and vegetable market next. The warehouse where the missiles were stored. Meghan eyed its door without going close. GPS said that's where they were last stored.

'Should we try to open it?' Bear bought a bunch of bananas, peeled one off and bit into it.

'Nah,' Chloe said dismissively. 'He might have rigged it with explosives.'

They asked around again. One vendor said someone had borrowed his trolley. He looked like one of the men in the photographs, but he couldn't be sure.

'Have you seen this place? So many people,' he yelled over the din in the market. 'How can I remember everyone?'

Meghan looked at her sister's dejected face. Saw the drooping shoulders of her friends. Knew what they were thinking.

Sure, we've now got an idea of his movements. But we're no closer to finding him.

Give it time, another part of her argued. *We've been here less than twenty-four hours.*

Babe, in that much time he could already have been attacked several times.

Chloe came up with the idea. 'We're behind him in this hunt. We need to get ahead. Think like him.'

'How do we do that?' Beth asked.

'Find out if any shootings have occurred in the last day.'

Chapter 34

A fan was whirling lazily on the white ceiling when Zeb opened his eyes.

He stared at it, puzzled, and then everything came back to him. The woman. The shooting.

He looked around. He was in a small room, on a bed. A window on which a curtain fluttered. A chair on which were his possessions. Coat, shirt, body-armor, gun, magazines ...

He got up suddenly and the sheet covering him fell away. He was bare-chested, just his jeans on him. Something white on the periphery of his vision. A white bandage on his left shoulder. He felt his head and winced. Some kind of wound on his right temple. Stitches.

A bullet grazed me? Is that what knocked me out?

He remembered another blow and glanced down. Saw the angry coloring on his chest.

Body armor stopped that round.

Who had brought him here? The woman? This was her house?

He went to the window, but all he saw was a narrow alley down below and the wall of another building some distance away. He tried to crane his head out, but there was no view.

He was putting on his damaged shirt when she came into the room.

'Sayyidi, you're awake!' she exclaimed in Arabic. 'You should rest ... What is it?' she asked when he stared at her wrist.

'Your watch, the time,' he mumbled.

'This is the next day, sayyidi,' she chuckled. 'You slept for more than twenty-four hours. That's why I said, you need more rest.'

I lost a day. He sagged on the bed. *I've got to make the missile arrangements.* He got up suddenly, felt weak and sat down again.

'Sit back, lie on the pillows,' she said firmly. 'Whatever you have to do can wait.'

'Who are you, sayyidati?' he asked. 'Where are we?'

She brought him a glass of water and took it back when he drained it.

'I'm Amelia Karman. You saved my life.' She looked at him searchingly.

He sized her up. Dark, curly hair that fell over her shoulders. Brown eyes. Curvy lips. Average height. The patterned dress she wore did little to conceal her belly bump.

Amelia doesn't sound like an Arabic name.

She laughed when she saw his expression. 'I am hundred percent Libyan, sayyidi. My name ... my father was always fascinated with airplanes and pilots. He used to read a lot about them. When I was born, he named me after the American pilot, Amelia. He said I would be brave like her.'

''Who were those men?'

She leaned over him and inspected his temple. Checked

out the shoulder dressing. And only then she met his eyes.

'They were militia, associated with Hazim Kattan. You know of him?'

Zeb nodded. 'Why were they after you?'

She looked at his Glock and body armor for a long while, as if wondering how much she should reveal.

'They wanted to take me away.'

'I saw that. Why?'

She looked down, her fingers twisting uneasily.

'You heard what they said. They think I'm their property,' she said bitterly.

He watched her as her face worked in emotion. Bitterness and rage. 'I'm sorry, sayyidi,' she said finally. 'You saved my life. You deserve to know.'

'I am a nurse in the Albaara Hospital. They found me there and decided to take me away.'

Zeb didn't say anything. *This isn't easy for her. Let her tell it her way.*

Her fingers bunched the dress over her stomach, loosened and smoothed the fabric. She looked at him. Her eyes skittered away. She moistened her lips and sighed.

'They raped me,' she said, looking into the distance. 'Four months ago. They were raiding houses at night in that neighborhood. They suspected someone had informed on them to the police.

'They used to hide in bombed-out houses around the hospital. Everyone knew they belonged to Kattan's group. Those five, in that vehicle yesterday.' She shuddered. 'They used to come out in the daytime. Ride in that vehicle with guns, as if they owned us. Threatened whoever got in their way. Slapped women. Attacked men. Even in traffic, if they thought someone had cut them off, they would overtake, stop that vehicle and beat that man up.'

'No one said anything to the police?'

'Police?' she scoffed. 'They take money from everyone and do nothing.'

If that was routine behavior from those thugs, why did they kill her father?

'The police did go after them one day.' She seemed to read his mind. 'This was after Kattan raided an oil facility just outside the city. We knew these men had gone early in the morning and returned late at night. Everyone in the area gossiped about them. And then, the police came the next day, questioning everyone about these men. We said, no, we hadn't seen them. What else could we say?'

'The police found them in one house. There was lots of shooting. Those men escaped and didn't return.

'And then they returned. One night. They burst into houses. Beat men and women. Even children. I was returning from the hospital when I heard them in our house. My father was shouting at them, that he didn't inform. They didn't believe him. They found papers in the house that identified him.' She took a shuddering breath.

'He was a police clerk. That was enough for them. They beat him so badly ... he tried telling them that he didn't inform. That he wasn't an officer. He was just a clerk. They didn't listen. And when I entered the house ...'

Zeb could imagine what had happened. His insides tightened.

'They raped me in front of him. Five of them, taking turns. No one came to help. And when they finished, they shot him.'

Emotionless voice, expressionless face. Thousand-yard

look in her eyes. Looking away from him towards a wall.

Minutes ticked. She didn't move. Neither did he. And then she took another breath and faced him.

'What is it, sayyidi?' she asked, immediately concerned when she saw something in his eyes.

That's what those terrorists did to my wife. But it was worse. Much worse than what happened to her. No, she doesn't need to know that. I can't burden her with that.

'Nothing,' he said simply.

'The police came,' she continued after a while. 'They knew who they were, but never found them. My father ...' her voice cracked. 'They gave me his pension. That's all they did. I left my father's house. Rented another place and lived there. I still worked at the hospital. What else could I do? My life had ended.'

'Then I found this happened,' she caressed her belly. 'I wanted to end it,' her face twisted and tears shimmered in her eyes. 'I went to some people. You know the law here?' she asked bitterly. 'No abortion even if the woman is raped. That's how this country treats women.'

'I made peace. No, that isn't correct,' she shook her head. 'I will never ...' she broke off. 'But what happened isn't the baby's fault. I will keep my child.'

'Then, last week, one of them saw me in the hospital. I don't know why he was there. Maybe someone from the Kattan militia was shot or was being treated. I fled and didn't return that day. He wasn't there the next day. But I think they investigated and came for me. That's when you showed up.'

'No one came to help me but you. And I don't even know you.'

'What happened yesterday? There was a fifth man.'

'You don't remember?' she asked, surprised.

'No.'

'You killed him. You kept shooting as you fell and some of those bullets must have hit him. I dragged you away when it was finished.'

'Sayyidati, most people would have run away when the shooting started. You put yourself at risk in helping me.'

Her cheeks bloomed with color, but she looked at him steadily. 'You saved my life, sayyidi. It's the least I can do. And please call me by my name. Amelia. I am proud of it.'

'You should be. Your father named you well. What is this place?'

'We are in Ben Ashour.'

She capitulated when he kept looking at her. 'It's my boyfriend's apartment.'

'How did you get me here?'

'I called him. He came immediately.'

'What about the police?'

'He *is* the police.'

Zeb froze. 'He's a police officer?'

'Yes,' she smiled, her eyes lighting up. 'Don't worry. He won't mention you. He said he will report that some other militia person shot those men.'

'Sayyidi,' she insisted when he looked at his gun. 'You have to trust me. I know Hammish. He will not do anything to put you in danger.'

'Where is he?'

'Duty. He will be back in the evening.'

There are teams looking for me. I can't bring trouble on them.

He sat on the bed and considered his options. He was sure

his friends would have joined the hunt too. *They'll find me faster than anyone else.*

'I am in danger,' he told her. 'I can't stay here.'

'We guessed that. Those …'—she pointed at his gun, body armor and magazines— 'those are not what an ordinary Libyan carries. And then, that wound in your shoulder and that bruise on your ribs. I have treated enough gunshot wounds to know what they are.'

'I could be a killer.'

'I know you are.'

Chapter 35

Washington DC

'I won't be meeting any Chinese representative,' President Morgan told his Oval Office visitors.

Paul Vaughan, the secretary of state, nodded. 'We understand, sir.'

'There's more, Paul. We need to convey a strong message. We don't like what's happening in Hong Kong. They need to show restraint. Besides, there's the matter of that telecoms company. I don't want that firm to trade in our country or in our allies'.'

'What are you planning, sir?' Lester McClellan asked. 'Lian Huang, their first vice-premier, is in the country with several officials. He wishes to meet you.'

The president smiled as he surveyed his cabinet. Luis Newman, Lizzie Kahn, Marshall Stewart, they were all there.

'You will meet them. Y'all decide how many of you go, but I think, Paul, Lester, Lizzie and Luis, the four of you should be there.'

'Agreed, sir.' The secretary of state nodded. 'We'll meet

them in my office, in the Truman Office.'

'No, Paul. Meet them at their embassy.'

'But, sir—'

'That's how unhappy I am. That's the message I want them to receive.'

'I don't think they can miss it,' Kahn smiled wryly. 'Gentlemen.' She got up. 'Let's get going. We have a date to keep.'

'Lizzie, just a moment,' the president stopped her. He leaned against the Resolute desk and surveyed his team. 'Y'all know about the Agency? The developments there?'

'Yes, sir,' came a chorus.

'I don't think there's been a resolution yet.' Diplomatic-speak to say the traitor hadn't been terminated yet.

Heads nodded. The cabinet members received the security briefings. They knew what was happening in Libya.

'I have decided to wind up the Agency,' he announced. 'I have not decided what to do with Clare. I will let her decide. If she wants another role in the government, I'll find one for her. Or, if she chooses to retire ...' he shrugged. 'The choice is hers. She has served the country well, and the least we can do is to let her decide the manner of her exit.'

'I think that's the right decision, sir,' Catlyn Feder agreed. 'The Agency was untenable, given that their agent turned traitor.'

'When will you be telling her, sir?' Mike Hoosier asked.

'Today, right after you folks leave,' the president said, grinning.

'Let's not keep you waiting, then, sir.' Lizzie got up again and led the rest of the cabinet out of the Oval Office.

President Morgan was returning to his seat when the door opened and Catlyn Feder came back in.

'A second, sir?'

'What is it?'

'I know what everyone's saying about Clare and the Agency. I have met her a few times and have nothing but respect for her. I don't know this agent, Carter, but from the reports I have read, it doesn't seem likely he would betray us. How sure are we those videos are genuine, sir?'

The president eyed her speculatively. 'You've seen the intelligence community's reports, Lizzie. They are confident Carter is a traitor. You know something none of us don't?'

'No, sir. It's just that I go with my hunches, and whenever I meet Clare, I come away with the impression she's rock solid. Salt-of-the-earth kind of person. I wouldn't want her to go out under a shadow.'

'There won't be any shadow, Lizzie,' the president said firmly. 'I share your impressions of her. She will retire with respect, if that's how she chooses to leave.'

'Thank you, sir.'

'She's the only one who stood up for you,' the president said while briefing Clare an hour later. Just the two of them in the Oval Office. No aides.

'I think highly of her, too,' the Agency director replied.

'But she's still a suspect?'

'Yes, sir. After all, as secretary of homeland, she's got the resources to pull off such an operation.'

'I don't know whom to trust,' the president confessed. 'I sit in these meetings and all I think of is whether the person opposite me could be responsible.'

'My team's in Tripoli, now, sir. Hopefully they will hook up with Zeb soon and we can progress.'

'Any news of him?'

Clare hesitated. 'There was a shooting in the city yesterday, sir. Some members of Kattan's gang were shot by a rival militia.'

'Zeb?'

'I don't know, sir. The police were on the scene quickly, but the descriptions don't fit.'

'Kattan is not involved, is he?'

'Not that we know of.'

'You know of our policy in Libya.'

'Yes, sir. Support Rayhan Sabbagh, the prime minister, but also have a backchannel to Hazim Kattan.'

'Yeah. We need to tread delicately. We have commercial interests there. Several American companies are invested in their oil industry. They are an arms buyer.' He lowered his voice. 'Any luck with the tappings?'

'No, sir,' she said, grimacing. 'The problem is, if I make a move, I'll show my hand. I am hoping Zeb's people make faster progress.'

'I'm hoping Zeb stays alive,' the president replied grimly.

The politician couldn't believe his luck. The president had given him the perfect opportunity. *Does he realize this is what I wanted?* He suppressed a chuckle.

He wasn't alone. He and his cabinet members were being driven to the Chinese embassy in two armored vehicles.

He leaned back expansively, crossed his legs and watched Washington DC go by. Vehicles got out of the way of the motorcade, the overhead chopper drew attention, and several tourists snapped their cameras, thinking it was the president on the move.

When I am president, he thought, *the motorcade will be longer and noisier.*

He changed his expression quickly and adopted a professional mask when he noticed a fellow secretary looking at him curiously. Everyone knew of his presidential ambitions; heck, even the president knew. But whenever anyone brought it up, he laughed it off.

'I've a lot to achieve in my role,' he would say, smiling disparagingly. 'Running for president? I've not given it any thought.'

The vehicles turned in to the Chinese Embassy and were swept through. A bowing aide greeted them and led them down a carpeted corridor. He opened a pair of double doors with a flourish and bowed to the hosts inside.

Lian Huang, the first vice-premier, greeted them in impeccable English, shook hands with them.

'My friends,' he said when small talk had been made and beverages had been served. 'How can we improve our countries' relationship?'

The politician was exhausted after ninety minutes of political to-ing and fro-ing and delicate negotiations. Both sides had hard lines they wouldn't cross. Yet, both countries wanted to do more business with each other. It wasn't good for either's economy, or for the world's for that matter, for the two most powerful countries in the world to be at an impasse.

'Bathroom break.' He flashed his handsome smile when another round of beverages was served.

An aide showed him to the discreetly marked door. The politician entered it, stood at the sink and washed his hands.

He didn't turn around when the door opened behind him.

A Chinese man entered, checked out the facility and joined him.

'Carter's still alive,' Jian Hsu told him.

Chapter 36

'No one's here. This bathroom is not monitored,' the MSS head hissed. 'I've told my people not to allow anyone in until I exit.'

'Good to meet you, Jian.' The politician smiled warmly. He meant it. He and the Chinese had exchanged innocuous-looking messages to set this meeting up.

Hsu shook his hand, smiled briefly, and then turned serious. 'It would have been better if Carter was dead. He escaped a CIA hit team two days ago. He has survived every attack on him.'

'I know. Spears and Marin lost some good men in the first three attacks. But his luck will run out. Tripoli is literally crawling with people looking to shoot him. Heck, even his friends have turned against him and are in-country right now. I think it's they who will find and kill him. They know how he works, how he thinks. They can anticipate every move.'

'Yes, I heard about that.' Hsu grim face relaxed slightly. 'I have my sources.' A small smile played on his lips when he saw the politician's surprise. 'I heard of their arrival in Tripoli. I agree with you. All these other teams are good and they have the various disguises, but the Agency operatives have the edge.'

'What about Kattan?' He lowered his voice and moved closer to the politician.

'He's on our side. He wants a load of arms; I can wrangle that through DC. But he also wants hundreds of millions of dollars. For himself.'

'Is there any way you can use Saharol's funds for that?'

'Some of it, but not all.'

'Let me know how much you'll need on top,' Hsu said as casually as if he were discussing the weather.

The politician studied him as the Chinese man washed his hands.

It was the MSS head who had sought him out, when he and other cabinet members had been visiting that country.

By then, the politician had established Saharol and had appointed Marin as its head. Hsu had been waiting in his hotel room one night.

The politician didn't know how the man had evaded the tight security, or the hotel's cameras, but there he was.

'Jian Hsu?' the politician had asked, surprised. 'I wasn't expecting you, here.'

In reply, the Chinese man tossed an envelope on the bed.

'What's that?'

'Look inside.'

The politician ripped it open. His face greyed and his belly lurched when he saw its contents. He collapsed on the bed as he scanned the documents.

Details of the shell corporations behind Saharol, with one difference. These proved that he was behind the oil company.

Extensive records of his visits to various offshore havens. Those movements would further tie his connection to the oil company.

That wasn't all. There was evidence that Saharol had bribed Libyan politicians.

And then the clincher.

A photograph of him and Spears emerging from an office.

The picture was grainy but clear enough to identify the two men. The politician swallowed as he recognized the location: a bank in the Bahamas where the two had opened an account for Saharol.

'It's not a crime to own a company,' he said weakly.

'You are President Morgan's cabinet member,' Hsu sneered. 'It is illegal for you to be on company boards.'

'But I am not on its board!'

'You think anyone's going to believe that when they see what's in that envelope? Besides, Saharol uses bribes to win contracts. I know how the anti-corruption laws in your country work.'

The politician sat silently, his mind racing, as he gathered his thoughts. He had been in the special forces. He had seen combat. He had overcome setbacks in his life. He would navigate this, too.

Except that Jian Hsu wasn't a setback.

'I want a partnership,' the MSS head announced. 'With you.'

The politician's jaw dropped. 'With me?'

'What do you want to achieve with Saharol?'

'Saharol?' he asked dumbly.

'Yeah, the oil company,' Hsu said impatiently. 'What are your ambitions?'

The politician stared at him, wondering how much he should reveal.

'I can destroy you,' the MSS head said softly. 'If I leak these, you're finished. Not just finished; you'll face criminal charges.'

The politician moistened his lips. He sat straighter. What did he have to lose? 'I want to strike a deal with NOC.'

Hsu rocked back in surprise. 'The Libyan oil company? What kind of deal?'

'I want Saharol to be a shareholder.'

'No. It will never happen. The Libyans will never allow it.'

'They will'—the politician smiled smugly as he regained his poise— 'if the conditions are right.'

'What conditions?'

'If Kattan and ISIL continue to be a threat and keep attacking NOC's facilities.'

'They have been doing that for some time.'

'What if the US government didn't go all-out to support the Libyan government. What if it also established a relationship with Kattan?'

Hsu's lips pursed. His eyes turned distant. He was thinking rapidly.

'And what if,' the politician said so softly that the Chinese man had to lean forward to hear him, 'we didn't go all-out to destroy ISIL, either, and in fact strengthened it by giving it weapons.'

A light blazed in Hsu's eyes. 'Saharol steps in. Offers protection and lobbying. It's already got ShadowPoint, the world's largest military contractor, as its security consultant.' His lips curled in a thin smile. 'The way you think, so twisted, you should be the head of your intelligence agencies,' he said in admiration.

There was no judgment in his voice at what the politician had outlined. No recrimination at the mention of helping the terrorist outfit.

'An agency head has limited powers,' the politician scoffed. 'Limited growth.'

'You want to run for president,' the visitor nodded. 'I had heard rumors. I will help you. You need funds to make this happen. Sure, Saharol is a profitable company, but it needs more. You, yourself, will need a bankroll for your presidential bid.'

'I can do this—'

'This isn't a negotiation,' Hsu said in a steely voice. His eyes were cold, hard.

The politician sized him up. *Do I have any leverage against him?*

Nope, he didn't.

He had always thought quickly on his feet. Throughout his career, he had made snap decisions and they had never been wrong.

He considered his options swiftly. He was sure Hsu would expose him if he didn't cooperate. The MSS head had a reputation for cold-blooded calculation and ruthlessness that was often discussed in DC.

A high-profile arrest, followed by a very public trial and then prison, he thought. That was what he was facing if the Chinese man revealed the contents of the envelope.

The other alternative was to work with Hsu. In reality, the Chinese man was representing his government. China invested enormously in several African countries. He knew what the bigger play was, with Hsu's proposition. *If I go with him, China will be part-owner of one of the largest oil companies in the world. It can influence oil production and prices. It will have a hold on the world's energy market.*

But, do I want to face prison? Do I want my ambitions to die?

He came to a decision. 'We have a deal,' he said, thrusting out his hand and shaking Hsu's. He flashed his megawatt grin, thinking he would sure as heck try to find any dirt he could on Hsu. He could box the Chinese man.

He never got that because the two met rarely, and when they did, it was at an international conference, at the Chinese embassy, at various neutral places where it was impossible to record the MSS man or conduct any surveillance on him.

He told Spears and Marin, of course. The three men not only trusted one another; they had history. While his relationship with Spears went back longer, the politician had quickly grown to like Marin.

His partners were unhappy initially but had to go along because Hsu could destroy all of them. Spears tried his best to get something on Hsu, but the Chinese man was too wily.

Over time, their desire for kompromat dimmed and then died out. Hsu provided the accelerant for their plans.

The MSS head arranged for Chinese-owned venture capital firms and investment banks to pour money into Saharol. No one else in the political, intelligence or business community knew that those companies were MSS fronts.

Those investments made the Chinese agency the fourth shareholder in Saharol.

With that war chest, Saharol bought out competition in the Middle East, other oil companies that could be a threat. Hsu deployed the MSS's considerable resources to help Marin in cajoling, coaxing or killing reluctant Libyan officials.

The politician kept waiting for Hsu's demands for all the help he rendered. *MSS's stake won't be enough to satisfy him. He'll want more.*

But those demands never came, and as time passed, the politician realized what Hsu wanted. A much bigger play than mere money.

He wants to own me when I become president.

The politician was confident that with MSS's backing he could win the most powerful job in the world. The Russians had already proven how elections could be manipulated. The MSS under Hsu had pushed the boundary further.

As time passed, the politician found he had no qualms about having a foreign master. *So what?* He shrugged. Throughout history, presidents and prime ministers across the Western world had either been owned by or were loyal to vested interests.

No, with Hsu and Spears on his side, he had a golden ticket, and there was no way he was going to jump off the ride.

Things had been progressing smoothly until he and Spears learned that the Agency had deployed Carter to Libya to kill Almasi.

That couldn't be allowed to happen. It would upturn the delicate state of play in Libya that was tilting in their favor.

And that was when Hsu played his master-stroke.

'He and the Agency need to be destroyed once and for all,' he said savagely, when he and the politician met at the sidelines of a United Nations conference. 'Leave it to me.'

'But—'

'I have tried to kill Carter for a long time. Do you know what he did to Duan Shuren?'

The politician knew that the previous MSS director had

been killed in spectacular fashion and that China had accused the US of carrying out the assassination. However, he didn't know of the details, and he listened in silent amazement as Hsu briefed him.

'Carter,' he breathed. 'He pulled it off.'

'Yes,' the Chinese man hissed. 'He damaged us severely. It took a long while for us to recover. He must be destroyed, and I know just how.'

Hsu came up with the deep-fake videos and the politician got Spears to leak them anonymously. When the politician told him that Shaming Chia was a double agent, run by the CIA, he got the Chinese spy to write his last report, which implicated Carter.

And then, he made Chia disappear.

The MSS man even arranged for his best operatives to break into the Agency's headquarters and bug Clare's office with equipment that Spears provided.

He hacked into the Agency's system and tapped into a rich vein of intel, which included the disguise program as well as Carter's recorded call to Clare.

They now had ears on Clare; they could monitor everything the Agency did, and once they heard her order her team to kill Carter, everything had fallen into place.

Except that the American operative escaped every attack on him.

'He's got more than nine lives,' Hsu said bitterly, in the Embassy's bathroom. 'Everyone's looking for him, and yet he gets away.'

'We haven't played one card,' the politician replied, scratching his jaw. 'We haven't told Almasi about him.'

'Has Carter made contact with ISIL?'

'We don't know,' the politician confessed. 'Some missiles aren't in their warehouse. It doesn't look like he sold them to the terrorists, because they would have used them by now.'

'He took them and hid them somewhere else,' Hsu said confidently. 'I can guess how he works. Those missiles are his trump card. As long as he has them, he's in play with Almasi.'

'You really think he'll continue his mission?'

'I know Carter better than you do. He will never give up. All I need is where the other missiles are. He will go to them eventually, and we'll be waiting.'

'Other agencies might anticipate that. Their teams might—'

'Yes, and I am confident that his former friends will get to him. But I am not taking any chances. I will deploy my people.'

'You can't send Chinese agents to Libya,' the politician said, horrified. 'That might raise questions.'

'Who said I would use Chinese operatives?' Hsu smirked. 'We have a network of contract killers. Some of the best in the world.'

He glanced at his watch. 'We've been here long enough. You get Sabbagh and Almasi on our side. I will deal with Carter. Wait here for some time. Leave after ten minutes. My people will make sure no one asks you any questions.'

And with that, Hsu left the politician in the Chinese Embassy's bathroom.

Chapter 37

Tripoli

Amelia shrugged when Zeb gaped at her words. "The way you acted, how you shot them, it told me enough. You are some kind of agent. Like in the movies.'

'I—'

'Look under your coat.'

He looked. His backpack beneath it. The remains of his disguise next to it.

He whirled on her. *My Misfud look's come off.*

'Who are you?' she asked quietly.

'You opened my bag?'

'No.'

'Why not?'

'Sayyidi, I don't know what you think of us Libyans … we are not all hungry and desperate for American dollars. Yes, I couldn't help noticing those bundles when I emptied your pockets and removed your wallet. I don't know what's in your bag. More weapons? Money? Why should it concern me?

'All I know is, you aren't what you looked like yesterday.

You are younger. You look Libyan, but are you?'

Zeb could pass as a Middle-Easterner in most countries because of his deep tan, brown eyes and fluency in Arabic. He could speak the language in various accents, and that had stood him in good stead in several missions.

'You aren't scared?'

'What do I have to be scared of, sayyidi?' her lips twisted in a small smile. 'That you too will rape me? After saving me?'

He felt embarrassed. *Nice. Why don't you put your other foot in your mouth too,* he told himself.

I can't tell her who I really am.

Why not?

She might tell the police.

You fool, her boyfriend's a police officer. He could have arrested you by now. Questioned you about the disguise and the weapons.

She might talk to others. Her co-workers. Hammish might, as well. There are killers out there. My friends are hunting me. They could hear about me.

'Sayyidi?' Amelia asked. Her hand went to her belly and stroked it. A reflex action that drew his eyes and made his inward resistance disappear.

If his hunters found out he was in this apartment, so be it. If he was to die here, it would be wearing his own name.

'Zeb Carter,' he said. 'I am Zebadiah Carter.'

Her hand stilled. Something flickered in her eyes and then a smile broke on her face, like a sun dawning.

'Zebadiah Carter,' she repeated. 'That wasn't so difficult, was it? American?'

'Yes.'

'Sayyidi, you speak my language so well.'

He didn't reply.

'An agent? A spy?'

He didn't reply.

'Sayyidi, you are safe. If you are a spy, I know it will be hard for you to trust me or Hammish … but please believe me. YOU. ARE. SAFE. HERE.' She enunciated slowly. 'I don't care who you are, Zeb Carter. I don't know why you are in my country. But for you, I and my unborn, we would be dead. There's nothing Hammish and I can't do to repay that.'

'I need to leave,' he said.

'You will,' she said firmly, 'but not now. You are still weak. You need to rest,' and she pushed him unresistingly to the bed.

It was night when Zeb woke up. Dark outside the window. The beast was quiet; his radar didn't ping.

Why am I sleeping so much? It's not as if my injuries are serious.

He knew the answer. He had been in continual action since those shooters had crashed into his hotel room six days ago. Adrenaline, nerves and training had helped him survive. But his body had given way finally. The sleep was its way of regrouping.

A murmuring from outside drew his attention.

He got to his feet and crept to the door. A dimly lit hallway. A room. Door closed but for a narrow crack of light coming through its sides. Voices from inside.

'Carter.'

He stopped when he heard his name mentioned.

A male voice.

Hammish?

He moved slowly and peered through the narrow opening. A bed.

A man sitting on it, his side to Zeb. Beard, short-cropped hair. In police uniform.

That must be him. Returned from duty.

Amelia was standing in front of him, visible through the crack, her hand on his shoulder.

'I know his name,' she said, her voice low. 'He told me.'

'He's wanted by the police. I recognized him when you brought him here. I rechecked when I went to the office. It's him.'

Zeb bit his lip and listened.

'He's an American. His details were circulated to all of us, all police stations in the country. Someone from the American side will come to collect him. If he resists, we have been asked to shoot him.'

'Hammish Wahab,' Amelia's voice hardened. 'Have you reported him already?'

'No, honey,' he clutched her hand and gripped it. 'I kept his description vague in my initial report. I have not mentioned you, either. We agreed on that. But I am worried. I falsified the shooting report.'

'What will happen, will happen,' she said firmly. 'Don't forget. I wouldn't be here if it wasn't for him.'

'We don't know what he has done. Why his people want him arrested.'

'We don't need to know. LISTEN TO ME,' she whispered fiercely. 'IF I FIND YOU HAVE REPORTED HIM, THAT'S THE END OF US. DO YOU HEAR ME?'

He kissed her hand in reply and then her forehead. 'I would never do that. It's just that I am worried. Every day he's with us, the danger increases. My officers, you know they have a habit of dropping in unannounced. Our neighbors might hear something when you and I are at work.'

She placed her palm over his mouth and stopped him. 'He won't stay for days. He wanted to go today, but I convinced him to rest. We'll deal with anything that happens. We always have.'

Zeb crept away when she straightened. He climbed into the bed and pretended to sleep. He heard footsteps approach, his door open, and felt eyes on him. The door clicked shut and the steps faded away, but still, he didn't move.

Chapter 38

Amelia Kamran woke up at 6 am the next day. She emerged from the bathroom, kissed Hammish on the cheek as he went to freshen up. She dressed for work swiftly and went to the small kitchen to prepare breakfast.

She was washing up in the sink when she saw the empty plate, dishes and cutlery in the drying stand.

She went to the dining room. The table was clean.

It looked like their guest had eaten the dinner she had laid out at night and had washed up afterwards.

She looked down the hallway towards his bedroom. Door closed. She didn't have the heart to wake him up so early.

She went back to the kitchen and finished her preparation. Hammish and she had a quiet breakfast. Cozy, intimate, just the two of them, before they went out in the world.

'What?' her boyfriend asked when he noticed her smile.

'Will it be like this every day?'

'Better,' he said. 'The moment you marry me.'

'You'll get bored of me, soon. I will become bigger with the baby—'

He leaned across the table and kissed her. 'You'll become

bigger with *our* baby.'

Her eyes filled with tears. 'You never think about—'

'No,' he said fiercely, 'and neither should you. It is *our* baby. You should never, ever think of those men and what happened.'

'I don't deserve you.'

'I know,' he said loftily.

They finished, washed up, and as she was drying her hands, she cocked her head to the spare bedroom. 'Let me check if he's awake.'

Amelia knocked once on the door. Got no reply. She knocked again. The same result.

She pushed the door open a crack. 'Sayyidi?' she called out.

No reply.

She pushed it wide. A gasp escaped her. The bed was empty. No one in the room.

'HAMMISH!' she yelled.

'He's gone,' she said when he came running.

'When?'

'How do I know?' she flared, then raised a hand limply in apology.

Something on the chair drew her attention. A sheet of paper.

It's best this way.

Just that one line, in Arabic, in neat handwriting.

She showed it to Hammish, tears prickling her eyes.

'Do you think he heard us last night?'

Her boyfriend shook his head dumbly. He didn't know.

'I didn't get to thank him,' he said, sitting heavily on the bed. His hand reached out blindly, fell on the pillow and felt something under it. He upturned it and drew his breath sharply when he saw the thick bundle of currency.

'Dollars,' he replied, wonderingly. He hefted it and gave it to Amelia with trembling fingers.

'There's another note,' she said.

She reached over him, smoothed it out, sat next to him and read it.

Those men are dead, but they might have friends. They might come back. Someone might remember you dragged me away. It won't take long for them to find Hammish's apartment.

Take that money. Make a new start for yourselves. A new life for the three of you.

Amelia wondered why the words were blurring and then realized she was crying. Somehow, she knew they would never see her savior again. She turned blindly and sobbed in Hammish's shoulder.

'Someone who writes like this, leaves us this,' she hiccuped, 'you really think he can be bad?'

He stroked her hair silently.

She straightened after a long while and dried her face. Smiled wondrously when the baby kicked, and held Hammish's hand to her belly.

'If it's a boy, I know what his name will be,' she said.

'Zebadiah.'

Chapter 39

Zeb was at the fruit and vegetable market. He was wearing a dirty apron over a shirt and jeans, a cap over his head and chewing on gum.

He pushed a wheelbarrow stuffed with produce that, to any onlooker, made him look like a vendor or a vendor's assistant.

He checked out the entire market, his eyes moving ceaselessly. Nothing alarmed him.

He went to his warehouse, opened it quickly and ducked underneath the shutter. Wrinkled his nose at the smell and turned on the lights. Went to the rear and opened the fake wall.

The Faraday cage was there, the Javelins crate underneath it. He opened the box. Yeah, the missiles were there.

He contemplated them for a moment. His friends knew the location of the warehouse. Other intelligence agencies would know it, too.

It wasn't safe for him to come to this location anymore.

I need to move them, he thought. *And the other missiles too.*

He had boasted to Abu Bakhtar that he could get two hundred missiles. In reality, he had only twenty-five. The remaining were scattered in different locations around the city. *I'll have to retrieve them too, if they're still there.*

Which was a high-risk recon mission, because there could be shooters at every location.

On top of that, the police, he thought bleakly.

But there was no other option.

Not if he wanted to complete his mission.

And that wasn't in doubt.

It was who he was.

Hammish Wahab arrived at his police station in Al Dahra carrying his lunch box. He greeted other officers, cracked a joke, and went to his desk.

He had consoled Amelia as much as he could and had hidden the roll of cash in the bathroom before he left. They needed to talk in the evening.

Carter had made a valid point in his note. Kattan's people could find them easily if they were determined.

'Wahab,' his superior called out as soon as he had setteled at his desk.

'Yes, sayyidi?'

'Any progress on that shooting?'

'I have made more enquiries, sayyidi. I have now got a description for the shooter. I will finish my initial report today, sayyidi.'

'Did you identify the killer?'

'No, sayyidi, but the with the description I have, I am sure someone will know who it is.'

'Get onto it, then. I am getting a lot of heat for it.'

'It's just militia members, sayyidi, shooting each other up.'

'Just do it.'

'Yes, sayyidi.' *Promotion time,* Wahab thought bitterly. No one was really interested in who killed those men. All his boss wanted to show was a solved case. It didn't matter if the wrong people were implicated and arrested. A tick in the box was all that mattered for the higher-ups.

In a fit of fury, Wahab finished his report. He mentioned how Carter had shot the men, described him, but didn't mention his name. He opened the *wanted* report that the Americans had sent. Yes, his description matched their picture.

He submitted the report and went for his tea break. The first sip of the hot beverage brought sanity back. He swore, apologized to the other officers and rushed back to his desk.

He logged into his computer and prayed that no one had read his report. Otherwise Amelia would never forgive him. *How could I be so stupid,* he berated himself. *Carter saved her life.*

He clicked on the file and sent a silent, thankful prayer when he saw no one had read the report yet. He edited it, removed any resemblance to Carter. Made out the shooter to be a swarthy Libyan who had escaped the scene after the killing. Double-checked everything, and only then did he resubmit his report.

Thank Allah, he thought gratefully. He went back to his tea and went to a window. They were high up on the sixth floor, and he could see the city through gaps between other buildings.

Somewhere out there was the man who had saved Amelia.

Haz saaedaan, he wished Carter luck and raised his cup in a silent toast.

'You are back?' Hassan asked Zeb when he entered the man's rental outfit. 'My vehicle was good, no?'

'It was, Hassan. I need it again. Is it available?'

'You are lucky, brother,' Hassan clapped him on his shoulder. 'It came back a few hours ago from another job. I just finished washing and cleaning it.'

Zeb checked out the van. Yeah, it was the same one and smelled clean and looked shiny.

'I don't need anything else from you,' Hassan waved dismissively when he brought out his driving license. 'You're already in my system. Misfud, correct?'

'Yes.' He was back in the arms dealer's disguise. 'Is there any place where I can buy hardware? Tools?'

'Go down the road, brother. Left and then another left at the red light. You will pass paint shops, tools, anything you want, on your left.'

Hassan gave him a contract to sign and then Zeb was rolling out of the store. He adjusted his mirrors, checked that his Glock was loaded and drove down the street.

The hardware shops were where Hassan said they would be. He bought several rolls of aluminum foil and loaded them into his van.

He threaded through traffic-laden streets, driving to the west of the city until he came to Al Nasr Street, and followed it until he came to the junction of Al Jamahirriyah Street.

He turned into a narrow alley at the junction, which opened into a courtyard. A storefront, locked up. A couple of old men sitting under a tree, idly gossiping. A woman hanging her washing from an apartment, high above, opposite.

No one looked at him. There were other commercial establishments in the yard, and there was a reasonable amount of foot and vehicular traffic.

Zeb backed the van to the store's entrance. Jumped out and

opened the shop.

It was full of old furniture, and at the back, underneath a pile of broken chairs, was another crate, similar to the one in the fruit and vegetable market.

He unlocked it. Four Javelins inside. *No one's been here.*

He closed the box and pushed it across the floor, grunting with effort, and loaded it with difficulty into the back of the van.

Closed the shop and entered the vehicle. He shut its doors and tore out a large sheet of foil. He wrapped it around the crate, sealed it with tape and shoved the box in a corner.

He wiped his hands on his trousers and stood back, breathing hard.

I'll have to store them in the van. Maybe, sleep in it too.

Nowhere else was safe.

The next storage is in Ghargour, deep southwest in the city.

He wondered when he would come across another team of shooters. Or his friends.

He didn't have to wait long.

Chapter 40

———— ∞∞∞ ————

Werner was happy to be back. Nope, scratch that. Werner was ecstatic to be back, like singing-from-the-rooftops, breaking-into-a-jig-on-the-street happy.

Those days when the twins were away because Clare had shut down the operation … whew! They were some of the nightmarish days. It had missed their soft touch, their commands, their cussing and swearing and jokes and their quiet moments.

Hell, yeah, it was good to be back. It had reassured the twins that, no, it, the current version, hadn't been hacked. It had run self-determining checks and then looked over the remaining programs. Clean. It stayed vigilant, however, and got to work.

The missiles. One lot of them, the crate in the fruit and vegetable market, had been moved three days ago to Abu Sittah. Their GPS signals indicated they had been there for a while. They'd then shifted briefly to Fashloum, and then they had disappeared. Their signals had dropped off, just like that.

Werner scratched its head, rubbed its jaw. There was no reason for that to happen. The transmitters were fail-proof.

The only way they would stop working was if they were removed and destroyed.

Removing them required specialist expertise, since they were embedded in the base of the Javelins.

Zeb or someone else could have blocked out their signal. Yes, that must be it. Werner nodded sagely and checked the other locations.

Whoa! That other crate, the one near Al Jamahirriyah Street, its signal had disappeared too. Several hours ago. Which meant Zeb or John or Jane Doe had gotten to the Javelins.

Werner quickly checked the other locations that it knew of. Missiles still there.

Is Zeb heading to them? Why?

It slapped its forehead in disgust. The why was obvious. If it was Zeb who was concealing the GPS signals, then he was moving them to another location. *He knows those warehouses are the weak points. Traps can be set up for him.*

He was preparing to warn the twins when another report came to him that made him gasp.

Werner had hacked into other intelligence databases, those of the CIA, NSA, other black-ops agencies. It had done that the moment it became operational. It had official channels with several of those systems and was quietly, very quietly, eavesdropping on them. It had wormed its way in, in such a manner that no one at those outfits could detect it.

Someone hacked into the Agency's system? Werner would show them how the world's best AI did it.

CIA team killed in a shootout in Tripoli.

Werner read the details in a nanosecond. Six shooters killed in an abandoned industrial area. All of them hunting Zeb Carter.

Werner scanned the dead men's faces. Heaved a sigh of relief when it saw none of them were his friend.

That occurred three days ago. It placed the location of the shooting … in Abu Sittah! *That's where one set of Javelins had been for a considerable time.*

It looked like it was Zeb who had moved them and had then been attacked by the CIA men. *They too are tracking the missiles.*

Werner got up to warn the twins and then sat up again when another byte pinged it.

Werner hadn't just wormed its way into various US agencies. It had slipped into the Libyan police system, smirking all the way. One of the easiest hacks it had performed.

What was this? A description fitting Zeb? In a police report in Tripoli? Filed just that day?

Werner trawled the system. Nope, no such report.

It frowned. Why did that pesky byte mention that report, then?

It drummed its fingers, closed its eyes and thought rapidly. All this, in less time than mere mortals took to formulate a thought. It was an AI program, after all. World's best.

Its forehead cleared. It went back to the byte. It contained that report. One man shot down five others. Description fit Zeb, but the police officer filing it had named no names. The dead men were part of Kattan's militia. The shooter downing them was suspected to be of a rival militia group.

Why, then, did he fit Zeb's description?

And why wasn't the report available in the police system?

And then, Werner found it. The police officer had deleted the report almost immediately. But Werner, the greatest artificial intelligence program in the universe, had captured a snapshot of that report before it had been erased.

It patted itself on the back and readied for the praise the twins would shower on it.

But, wait. It needed to find some more information before it alerted them.

Hammish Wahab: that was the officer's name. Getting his address was a matter of snapping its fingers and putting its prodigious powers to use.

There. Everything ready.

Now, to ship out the information.

It pinged the sisters' screens.

'MEG!' Beth squealed, 'Werner's got something.'

And the best artificial intelligence program in the galaxy leaned back, put its feet up on the table and basked in their joy.

Chapter 41

'Javelins moved to Abu Sittah, three days ago,' Meghan broke it down swiftly to her friends, who were jammed in their Range Rover.

Bear driving, face grim. Eyes narrowed. Hands loosely gripping the wheel, ready for explosive action.

'What's there?' Broker asked from the back.

'Industrial area. Bombed out. Abandoned.'

'Why—'

'Let her finish,' Chloe interrupted him.

'We don't know why the missiles were moved there,' Meghan continued. 'But some time later, there was a gunfight there.'

A gasp. A curse. Bear sounded the horn in anger and overtook a slow-moving truck. He leaned out of the window and spat out a string of swears.

'Six men dead. Identified as CIA shooters.'

'Positively?' Bwana asked tautly.

'One hundred percent. Here,' she passed her phone around. 'Those are their photographs. See for yourself.'

'Zeb?' Broker asked. Meaning, was it their friend who shot those men?

'Yeah, that's what Beth and I are assuming. He moved those missiles. Those killers attacked him. He finished them and escaped.'

'Why there?'

'No traffic in that area.' Roger chewed his gum furiously. 'No passersby. No one lives there, if it's abandoned. Perfect site for a rendezvous with ISIL.'

Meghan nodded. She looked at her friends and saw it on their faces.

'He's still going ahead with the mission,' Bwana whispered.

'What else is he to do?' Beth said bitterly. 'He thinks we are after him, too.'

Another moment of silence while they digested what Meghan had revealed.

'Where are we going now?' Chloe stirred.

'That's not the end of what—'

'Wait. Back up a moment,' Broker cut in. 'This happened three days ago. Why did Werner find out only now?'

'Because their case handler filed the report only today,' Meghan replied. 'They probably had to verify the identi-fies, cross-check, etc.'

'Zeb's alive!' Beth exclaimed, punching Bear on the shoulder, causing him to swerve.

'Yes,' Meghan said, unable to suppress her grin. 'Werner found more. Two days back, there was another shooting in which a few of Kattan's men were killed. Their killer escaped. The Libyan police filed a report. It described Zeb as the shooter.'

'Why would he engage with Kattan's people?' Bear frowned. 'They were his thugs?'

'Yeah,' Meghan confirmed. 'And as to why, that's what

we are going to find out. From the police officer who filed the report.'

'He retracted the report,' Beth burst out, almost quivering in excitement. 'And he, too, filed the report just today. And there's the Javelins.'

She briefed them in detail on everything that Werner had found out, by the end of which they knew more.

But they couldn't figure out the Kattan involvement, nor could they work out where Zeb was.

They didn't confront Hammish Wahab at his police station. They checked out the multifloor office he worked in. They got Werner to dig into the officer's details. Smart, young, on the rise, clean, no charges of corruption or any such rumors, was what the AI returned with.

'A clean officer in Libya will find life difficult,' Beth mused.

They were parked opposite the police station's entrance, on the other side of the street.

Bwana, Roger and Bear were at a street-food vendor's stall, wolfing down chicken legs and rolls. Broker was in the vehicle with the twins and Chloe, peering over their shoulders, reading what Werner had spat out.

'Why did he take back that report?' he thought aloud.

'Werner can't read his mind,' Beth gibed. 'Not yet.'

Meghan turned her snort into a cough. *Beth's back to her snarky self. All we need now is to find Zeb,* she thought. *And she'll be complete. We all will be.*

She thought back to the shootings, placed them on a map of the city in her mind. The CIA incident was to the east, the Kattan one was near a hospital, which was down south. The first crate of Javelins was in the center of the city, the second was to the west.

She gave up. Werner was keeping an eye on the other missile location that it knew of, and it looked like they were still in their storage places.

We can split up and wait for him to go there. It looks like he's moving them to some other place. But he can anticipate that. He knows we might head there. Other kill teams, too.

No, she decided. It was best they question Wahab.

Zeb retrieved the third crate, which was on the outskirts of the Tripoli National Park.

It was located in a school building, long since abandoned.

It had been a primary school once, filled with the laughter and complaints of children. Now, birds, rodents and night animals made it their home.

He reconned the area before entering the school compound, wary of snipers or hidden threats. He didn't find any.

The absence of hostiles or his friends worried him.

If I was them, I would lie in wait at one of these locations.

He pondered this as he observed the building. The collapsed roof. The dirty, crumbling walls. A crater in the front yard. A gerbil darted as he watched. From somewhere above, a bird scolded him for intruding in its space.

He entered the yard, when he was sure there was no threat. He headed to the janitor's storage room and kicked down its unlocked door.

The crate was there, hidden behind brooms and mops and underneath cans of paint, one of which had burst in the heat and spread its contents over the box.

Zeb fingered the yellow pigment. It was dry. He eyed the

film of dust on the sides of the box. *Doesn't look like anyone's touched it.*

He went back to his van and backed it as close as he could get. Maneuvering the container was difficult, and by the time he had shoved it inside the vehicle, his shirt was soaked with sweat and the bandage on his shoulder had reddened.

He covered the box with foil and rested against the van's side.

Drained a bottle of water and wiped his mouth when the bird, which had continued to reprimand him, finally fell silent and flew away in a flurry of wings.

Exhaustion fled him. The beast awoke.

He wasn't alone.

Chapter 42

———⊶⊷⊶———

The school was L-shaped, the long leg facing the yard, the shorter one to its right. Rows of classrooms running down the two legs, gaping holes where once had been doors and windows. A concrete walkway fifteen feet wide, with steps at several places that led to the yard.

The janitor's room was at the intersection of the two legs, the van parked at an angle.

Zeb scanned his clothing swiftly. Perspiration-soaked dark shirt, sleeves rolled to his elbows. Body armor underneath. Jeans. Vibram-soled boots.

He drew his Glock and got to his belly. Crawled underneath the vehicle and peered out. His HK was in the cab, but there was no time to get it.

The entrance to the yard, once a road, was now a dirty track. Pebbled, muddied, with thick undergrowth. Beyond the school had been a residential area. It was deserted, too, but not visible from here. The slope in the approach road cut it off from view. All he could see was the sky.

The sounds of traffic could be heard faintly, from the Sharia Abu Hridah road.

No other sounds, however.

Was he mistaken?

That bird could have flown away for hundreds of other reasons.

His gut told him otherwise, as did the beast. His radar was pinging slowly.

He tried to remember what was behind the school. More bomb craters and thick undergrowth that continued for a long while and merged into the start of the national forest.

Entry that way was difficult. Too many dried leaves and twigs to make a stealthy approach.

He came to a decision. He'd had enough of being pinned down.

He crawled back slowly, used the vehicle as cover to climb onto the walkway. Darted into the nearest classroom, holding his breath.

No bullet came in his direction.

If there's someone out there, they aren't in position, yet.

That didn't feel like his friends. They would use drones. They would surround me. *And then*, his lips tightened, his eyes bleak, *would they chop me down without warning or would they get me to surrender?*

Stop thinking about them.

A rear window in the classroom. Its door creaked as he pushed it open cautiously. He held his breath and looked out. No one there, but the undergrowth that he remembered.

He climbed out swiftly, dropped to the ground and ran down the short leg. Bellied down again and peered around the corner.

Stillness. Unnatural quiet.

He would have to circle the yard, keeping to the undergrowth. That was the only way he could get to the mouth of the road and see who was there.

He started. Crawling swiftly, picking hard, twig-free ground to move on, Glock between his teeth, blinking hard, frequently to dislodge sweat from his eyelids. Checking his six often.

A shadow.

Zeb threw himself to his left as the silhouette resolved into a dark-clothing shooter facing the school, startled eyes behind transparent goggles as they registered his approach.

The gunman turned, but his surprise slowed him, and Zeb's two rounds slammed into his neck and head.

More birds flew into the air at the reports. The killer's body thrashed and then went still. Zeb checked the horizon. No one appeared.

He was safe from the rear. The large crate behind him had loose mud that would give away any hostile's approach.

He crabbed towards the fallen man. Caucasian. *Don't know him.* His eyes lingered on the shooter's weapon. A FN SCAR-H. Scope on top of it. That was a special forces assault rifle.

Many other countries use them, he told himself. *Mercenaries, too.* The weapon, by itself, was no clue to the shooter's identity.

He was reaching to grab it when a radio squawked thrice. There—it was Velcro-ed to the dead man's combat shirt.

Some sort of military contractors, Zeb decided. Operatives from the US agencies would use better comms equipment. *We use earbuds, bone mics at the Agency.*

But what did three squawks mean?

Are you okay? Did you get him? Squawk back?

He removed the radio and squawked twice back, hoping that meant *I'm okay.*

No other sounds.

Did I fool them?

There was only one way of finding out.

He holstered his Glock, picked up the SCAR, checked that it had a full mag, removed spares from the shooter's belt and proceeded.

More stealthy crawling.

There would be at least one more shooter. Possibly two more. Maybe five.

If this was an Agency operation, we would go with three or four.

He slowed down as he neared another curve while he circled the front yard and was approaching the road.

A faint sound.

He froze and cocked his head.

That sounded like … he looked up in the sky and dread filled him.

A drone was in the air.

Chapter 43

───❦───

Hammish Wahab never left the police station.

'I thought these officers patrolled the city,' Beth said, blowing hair out of her face in exasperation.

'He's an officer,' Meghan reminded her. 'Not a beat cop.'

The seven of them had split up. Bwana and Roger up ahead, watching a side exit through which police vehicles emerged. Bear and Chloe down the road, keeping an eye on a delivery entrance. The sisters and Broker in the Range Rover, opposite the main entrance.

Werner updated a screen inside their ride with alerts.

'Nothing on the twenty,' Beth grumbled beneath her breath.

The twenty people at the kill meeting on whom Werner was running background checks.

'Nothing on the cabinet, either,' Broker rumbled.

'You think it would be that easy?' Meghan uncapped a bottle of water, took a few swallows. 'They hacked us, made those videos. They would have taken precautions. Nothing in their backstories or movement that could implicate them.'

Werner had hacked into several hotels' reservation systems

but hadn't found anyone resembling Zeb. That by itself wasn't conclusive, because many Tripoli hotels didn't need photo identity and took cash.

'He could be anywhere.' Beth wiped a bead of sweat from her forehead.

'Or he could be under attack, right now,' Meghan snapped. 'Quit whining.'

Her sister didn't respond. Her eyes involuntarily went to the screen. Werner would alert them instantly if any gun battle was reported. Their AI remained silent.

'That's him?' Broker leaned forward, gestured with his chin as a young man emerged from the main entrance, in police uniform

'Yeah,' Meghan exclaimed. 'He's early. Four pm. Normally he leaves around seven.'

Wahab was early. He was worried about Amelia. He knew she was a worrier and would be thinking of the shootout, of Carter and of him.

He had decided to surprise her by going early. He could have called and checked on her, but she usually slept that time of the day.

He stopped his vehicle at a bakery, unaware of the Range Rover beside him.

He bought a chocolate cake, Amelia's favorite, not know-ing that seven pairs of eyes were watching him.

He went back to his ride, checked his phone for any missed calls, and proceeded home.

He parked in the building's lot, nodded to the security guard, greeted a few other residents as he went to his apartment.

He opened the door silently and entered. Checked the

bedroom. Yes, she was asleep. He smiled at her sight; the curve of her belly apparent beneath the sheet over her. A curl of hair fell over her face and stirred with every breath she took.

He placed the cake in the kitchen and went to the living room. Sat on a couch with a sigh and rubbed his eyes wearily.

They had to make a decision soon. Should they stay in the city or flee? Carter was right about one thing: if Kattan's men were determined, they would find him.

Wahab knew many police officers and beat cops were corrupt. *All the way up, right to the ministers,* he thought sourly. They took bribes from Kattan, from other militia groups, from businesses, from anyone who wanted information or a blind eye turned.

There were rumors that even ISIL had paid off a few cops.

Wahab didn't take any bribes, and that caused a lot of resentment among his fellow officers. There were barbed comments directed at him. Barely concealed anger at his honesty. *They fear I will snitch on them to our bosses.*

He snorted. Their bosses were equally dishonest. What good would his snitching do?

But his straight-and-narrow approach made life hard. He got assigned the most difficult and dangerous cases. The late shifts. The most challenging neighborhoods.

It's a matter of time before some cops go to that shootout scene and question the other residents. They'll then know of Amelia's involvement and work out what happened.

We have to leave, he decided. There was no way he was going to risk his girlfriend's life nor that of their unborn child.

He knew he was at odds with the majority of society. Many Libyan males would renounce a girlfriend who had been raped and was pregnant as a result.

I am not like them. And when he saw Amelia approach from the bedroom, felt her kiss, he was glad he wasn't.

'Carter was right,' he said after they had drunk tea and eaten the cake he had brought.

'You'll be leaving everything behind,' she told him. 'You have a career here. You have made something of yourself.'

'You have a career, too.'

'I am a nurse. I can get a job anywhere in the world. But you—'

The knock on the door silenced them.

Amelia looked at him, puzzled. He shook his head. No, he wasn't expecting any visitors. It wasn't uncommon for some of his fellow officers to drop in unannounced, but their knocks were more boisterous. This felt business-like.

Sudden dread filled him. Had his bosses found out the truth about the shootout? Was it Kattan's men on the other side of the door?

But he hid that from Amelia and went to the door. He wished he had his service revolver on him, but it was too late now as he looked through the eyehole and saw no one.

He was turning away, shrugging, when the knock sounded again.

He opened the door and stared.

Two women. An inch or two taller than him. Brown-haired, green-eyed, deeply tanned. Looking identical. *Twins*, he thought dimly. Behind them, another woman, petite. Four men at the rear.

He hadn't seen them before and he was sure they weren't from the police. While there were a few women officers, the country didn't have any black ones.

Wahab's eyes fell away from the giant at the back who was

watching him impassively. He eyed the bearded man. He, too, was huge.

These visitors weren't Kattan's people, either. Those people would have come shooting.

'Yes?' he asked as confidently as he could.

One of the twins pinned him with her gaze.

'Who was that man in your report?'

Chapter 44

That man was trying to survive, several miles away.

Does it have rear cameras? Zeb wondered as the drone stayed still in the air, its nose facing the school. He checked his front, his six. No one was creeping on him stealthily.

Does the pilot require line of sight? The ones they used at the Agency were highly sophisticated, packed with cutting-edge tech, and didn't require visual contact.

Did these killers have access to that kind of gear?

Irrelevant for the moment. He had to act. There could be any number of killers out there who might be coming for him.

Zeb brought the SCAR to his shoulder, thanked the pilot for keeping the drone stationary, and fired long bursts at it. No need to aim. One sweep, left to right, another, in the opposite direction, and the airborne vehicle shattered and crashed to the ground.

They'll now know their man is dead. They might guess my rough location. They will try to flank me.

Zeb moved immediately. There was nowhere to hide, but there was one place where he could get the high ground.

The school's roof.

He bent double and ran backwards, assault rifle ready. Turned back every now and then to check his rear.

He slowed when he reached the building's sidewall. Peered around it cautiously. Clear.

He went to the back of the school, climbed onto a classroom window. Stood to his full height and lunged up for the beam that ran the length of the roof.

The building was constructed simply. A basic four-wall structure whose interior was partitioned to form the classrooms. A flat roof on top, not high from the ground, parapet running around it.

He heaved himself up, kicked his legs in the air to gain momentum, got an arm across the top of the parapet and pulled himself up.

He fell onto the roof, his eyes scanning rapidly, automatically.

Muddy. Patches of moss where rain water had collected and dried. Branches and leaves scattered from the nearby trees.

No other human.

The parapet was about three feet high. Not enough cover for him to stand straight. He crawled swiftly to the front and raised his head cautiously.

Front yard. The drive through which he had arrived. The slope behind.

And there, two figures crouching, one of them reaching for something on his back.

Rocket launcher!

The gunmen seemed to have guessed his location, one of them pointing to where he was.

They can see my head.

Zeb ran through his options. Panic wasn't one of them. He was at one end of the school, on top of the short leg. His van was some distance away, to his right.

He could shoot the men, but did he have enough time? Even as he watched, Rocket Man inserted a missile in his tube.

A reckless plan came to him. High risk. *What choice do I have?* All he could hope was that they aimed for his side of the school.

Timing was important. He stood to his full height. Rocket Man brought the launcher to his shoulder. His companion seemed to be instructing him.

Zeb took a few paces to his left, where the leg's side parapet was.

He brought the SCAR up. The second shooter leaned towards Rocket Man urgently.

Zeb broke into a run towards the van.

Simultaneously, he started firing at the two men.

Five.

Four.

Three.

He leapt over the parapet, launching himself into the air, going sideways, shooting burst after burst, spraying and definitely praying, changing magazines in midair, seeing the first shooter break away, try to crawl. It looked like Zeb's rounds found him, because he fell back. There was a flash from Rocket Man's shoulder, who had triggered even before he could correct his aim, the distinctive *whump* of the missile as it left the tube, and barely a second later the crashing explosion as it smashed into the school where Zeb had been. But he was no longer there.

Rocket Man falling away, his hands thrown up, was Zeb's

last sight as he fell to the ground and the rise of the drive hid the shooters from view.

He groaned as he landed on his left shoulder. Gritted his teeth against the searing fire that tore through him. Checked that the van was unharmed.

It was.

He kept rolling as the building behind him collapsed. The ground shuddered as concrete and timber and steel were reduced to rubble and dust. Something fell, some distance away. He blinked, clearing his eyes of sweat. A window frame.

Move!

He stumbled to his feet and ran unevenly to the right of the approach road, keeping low and circling wide until the shooters came into view.

Both of them lay sprawled on the ground. Rocket Man on his side, the other gunman on his back.

Zeb approached them cautiously, angling through the side. He could chop them down even if they made a sudden move.

Rocket Man's hand twitched. His body shuddered. His breath, stertorious. Part of his head had been blown away, and as Zeb neared, his body fell still.

The second shooter was no danger. His eyes stared sightlessly at the sky; there was blood and torn flesh at the base of his neck.

Zeb crouched, feeling weary. He wiped sweat from his forehead and ran his tongue over dry lips.

The top of the school was visible from where he was. The long leg intact, but a major part of the small one was missing.

Check these men. They might have backup.

Both men were tanned. They could be of Mediterranean origin. Or Middle Eastern, or someone like Zeb, deeply tanned

Caucasians.

No identification of any kind on them. Their backpacks held food, water, currency of various denominations, nothing that said who they were. Their phones were encrypted. He recognized their make. *Used by special ops and intelligence outfits around the world. The SCARs, their body armor, the launcher ...* Zeb was sure the dead men weren't mercenaries.

Their vehicle must be somewhere in those houses. He looked at the empty houses some distance away. *Were they already watching the building? Saw my van approach and decided to attack me?*

No, that didn't make sense. There had been enough opportunity for them to fire at him if they had already been in wait.

They probably rolled in when I was inside. Saw my van and thought they had hit the jackpot. The rocket launcher was a good move. But they should have fired as soon as I was on the roof. Before I showed myself.

All that mattered was that he had survived yet another attack.

As long as I keep escaping until I get Almasi.

After that, it wouldn't matter. Sure, he would try to stay alive and find out who had put him in this position, but if his friends found him ... *that will be the end.*

He winced when his shoulder reminded him he was far from peak condition. The wetness down his face, that was blood from Amelia's stitches. His left leg, heck, his entire left side was throbbing from the awkward landing.

He picked up the men's phones and limped back to his van.

Stopped when a savage thought entered his mind.

He returned to the fallen men. Dug into their backpacks until he found a waterproof marker.

He emptied a backpack and placed it on Rocket Launcher's chest.

He scribbled a message on it.

Keep Trying.

Chapter 45

───❦───

'Which man?' Wahab stammered deliberately, trying to buy time, trying to figure out who the visitors were.

'The man you described in that shooting,' the other sister said impatiently. They spoke Arabic. Fluently. With the correct accent. *Who were they!'*

'Shooting?' he asked dumbly.

The first sister leaned in; eyes fierce. 'Don't waste our time, Hammish Wahab. We know about the report that you wrote. Beth?'

Her sister brought up her phone, turned it around for Wahab to see the screen. His eyes widened; he turned cold when he recognized it.

'I ... deleted ... that,' he stuttered. 'How did you get it?'

'You wouldn't understand,' the first speaker said dismissively. 'Who is he?'

'And, where is he?' the woman named Beth asked.

The two giants at the back shifted. The black man cracked a knuckle, the sound loud in the empty apartment.

'Let's take this inside,' the older man with them suggested.

The twins brushed past Wahab without a word; the others followed.

'But—' he protested, but they were in, and the last man, who looked like he had stepped off the cover of a magazine, shut the door behind him.

'Talking is good for the soul,' he said helpfully and sprawled in a chair as if he owned the apartment.

'Wahab?' the twin who wasn't Beth drew his attention. 'What happened in that shooting? Who is that man and where is he?'

A key in the door silenced them. It opened. Amelia, in her nurse's uniform. Blinking at them, puzzled, her hair in ringlets falling over her face.

'Hammish?' she asked him, 'Who are these people?'

'Who are you?' Beth demanded, and then her face and tone softened when her sister glared at her. 'We want to know about the report Hammish filed. You are …?'

'Amelia,' she said proudly, 'Amelia Karman, Hammish's girlfriend.'

'Girlfriend,' Beth's sister exclaimed. She traded glances with her twin and whispered something that Beth shook her head at.

'Yes. Who are you?'

'My name is Meghan Petersen,' the first speaker announced. 'Beth, my sister,' she nodded at her twin. 'Chloe,' she chinned at the third woman. 'Broker, that old man,' for which she got a sarcastic *thanks*. 'Roger,' the one with the looks; 'Bear,' the beard; 'Bwana,' the black man.

Wahab tried to take everyone in, but as usual Amelia was quicker. 'You speak Arabic just like him. As if you belong in this country,' she said. 'Are you American too?'

'He was here?' Meghan asked, her face urgent.

'They may be his enemies,' Wahab tried to warn his girl-friend. 'Remember that notice?'

'Enemies?' Bwana asked softly and Wahab shivered at the cold look on his face. 'No, we are his friends.'

'Hammish, Amelia,' Meghan asked impatiently. 'WHAT HAPPENED? WHERE IS HE?'

Wahab looked at his girlfriend. He was reluctant to reveal anything more. He could see the question in her eyes as her lips mouthed, *What report?*

Amelia turned away from him when he felt shame turn his face red.

'I will make tea,' she said abruptly. It was her way of composing herself.

No small talk while she was away. Wahab stood awkwardly as if it was he who was the stranger, while his visitors sat comfortably. There was tension in the air, but not hostile.

'He said his name was Zeb Carter,' Amelia said on her return. She poured steaming tea in cups and shook her head when Beth and Meghan rose to help.

'He told his name?' Chloe, who hadn't spoken till then, asked.

'Yes, sayyidati. But not immediately.' She sighed when she saw their expressions. Patted Wahab's hand. 'They *are* his friends,' she reassured him. 'I can sense it.' She turned back to their visitors. 'I should start from the beginning.'

'Always the best way,' Roger grinned lazily.

'Oh, stop it,' Amelia's cheeks dimpled. 'I know your kind. That smile—'

'Amelia!' Meghan stopped her.

'Sorry,' she sobered. 'Your friend, Zeb Carter, saved me from being raped.'

Chapter 46

⸺◦∞◦⸺

Travis Klapper was worried. He was sipping his coffee in the Art House's restaurant, near the prime minister's office.

He was dressed casually. Blue Tee over jeans, sneakers, shades rucked up to his hair. He looked like any Western tourist in the city.

Klapper was CIA. He was a case officer in the Special Operations Group, SOG, within the agency's Special Activities Center.

SOG's officers carried out paramilitary operations in countries wherever the US had interests. Neutralizing threats was one of those operations. Such as terminating a traitor like Zeb Carter.

Klapper checked his watch again and then his encrypted phone. He should have heard from Domingo, Cuban and Rolff. They were good men, former DEVGRU officers. He had dispatched them to the school site to keep watch in case Carter turned up.

Their orders were simple: Check in every few hours. Kill the traitor in case he turned up. The hunt had become more urgent, ever since Carter had escaped the attack in the industrial area.

Coates and his team were good men, Klapper thought bleakly. He had wondered how the traitor had survived an ambush by six men until he had inspected the site himself.

Carter had planted explosives on the approach road and had then used the element of surprise to dispatch the remaining.

They told me he was good. They didn't tell me he was this good, Klapper thought sourly.

He had never questioned the orders when they had trickled down to him. He had accepted unquestioningly the kill order on the Agency operative.

He had two teams in Tripoli, and when the first team failed, he had activated the second one.

Domingo should have checked in by now.

He decided to give it another hour and smiled absently at the server who refilled his cup.

He'd heard rumors that there were several kill teams in the city, all of them looking for Carter, and not one of them had found him.

Some did, he thought bitterly, and paid the price.

He swallowed his coffee savagely, threw a few bills on the table and stood up.

There was nothing he could do other than wait. He hoped Domingo would call soon with some good news. He wanted a win, something to overcome the previous failure.

But that uneasy feeling in his belly told him his second team had failed, too.

Zeb drove back to the city center, sticking to the main routes. He merged into a fat train of traffic as it snaked its way to the commercial and government districts.

Where to stay for the night? His van was riding low with the weight of the three crates. He had to recover three more.

He could park in quiet streets and sleep in the van until he set up the rendezvous with the terrorists.

Will that be safe anymore?

No, he thought, shaking his head. *Even the police are looking for me.* All it needed was one alert beat officer to take one good look at him and he would have to go on the run again.

I don't want to shoot any police. They aren't my enemies.

You killed CIA officers.

Yeah, and what choice did I have? His inner voice didn't reply. The only sounds were the hum of tires on concrete, honks from other vehicles.

Safer to check into a hotel. One of those that accepts cash.

Or, he could go to Amelia and Wahab's place. *They won't turn me down.* He was sure of that.

He pondered that for a minute. The nurse could tend to his dressing, and some of her home-cooked food would go down very well.

No.

He couldn't put them in danger. He couldn't bring assassins to their door.

They had enough problems of their own, and for all he knew, they might have left the city with the money he had left them.

He headed to Ras Hassan, to a seedy hotel he knew in the neighborhood. It had one advantage: Its parking lot was walled and gated.

Meghan listened to Amelia's story in silence.

That sounds just like Zeb, she thought.

'What disguise was he wearing when you saw him first?' She brought out her phone and turned the screen towards the nurse. 'Was it any of these?'

'That one.' Amelia pointed to one photograph.

'Misfud.' Meghan looked at her friends. 'He was in that getup.'

'Who are you? Who is he?' Wahab shifted uneasily on his chair. Their visitors were relaxed, sitting as if they felt at home, but he sensed the latent menace in them.

Those men, Bear and Bwana … they looked like they could do a lot of damage if they wished to.

'We are with the US State Department,' Meghan lied smoothly. 'Zeb is an American agent on the trail of terrorists in this country.'

A good lie had to have some elements of truth. It made the story believable, and there was less chance of a goofup if it had to be repeated.

'Why is he wanted by you, then?'

'For his own safety.'

'His identity was leaked,' Beth interjected. 'Bad people are looking for him.'

Wahab frowned. He wasn't a fool. He had some idea of how such operations were conducted. 'You can call him, can't you? You must have some way of contacting him.'

'He thinks we are hunting him, too.' Meghan replied. Which was true.

Wahab's lips compressed. None of this made any sense to him. He opened his mouth when his girlfriend interrupted.

'Hammish,' she warned him.

He subsided. He knew that tone of voice. He would rather walk over a bed of hot coals than face Amelia's ire.

'Did he say where he would go?' Meghan asked.

'No,' the nurse shook her head. 'He didn't say anything at all. He was gone in the morning—'

'What?' Broker demanded when she broke away.

'Sayyidi, do you know where this shooting occurred? Have you seen the place?'

'No,' Meghan admitted.

'Come, we will show you.'

'Amelia!' Wahab remonstrated. 'It isn't safe to go back there.'

'Between you and Zeb's friends,' she tossed her head back, 'I can't think of a safer place.'

'Can't you see it?' she pleaded when the police officer remained seated. 'Look at them. You can feel their desperation, can't you?'

Wahab looked, unwillingly, and even he had to admit there was an air of quiet urgency around the visitors. Beth, who it seemed was the younger sister, was tapping her chair. A vein throbbed on the black man's forehead.

They looked calm, focused, but the officer knew those were masks.

'We owe him,' he said, finally, meeting Meghan's eyes.

'We understand,' the elder sister replied. Something flickered in her eyes. 'He's like that. There are many who are alive because of him.'

And many are dead too, Wahab felt like saying, but he didn't because he was sure Carter had killed only those who deserved to die.

'Let's go.' He got up and went to the door. Held it open, but Amelia blocked their visitors' exit.

'You will keep him safe?' she asked them.

'If we find him,' Meghan replied.

Chapter 47

It was dark by the time Klapper reached the school site.

He parked his ride near an empty house and walked swiftly towards the building.

Even through the gloom he could make out the destruction that had occurred. One part of it was missing, there was debris on the ground ... and that stench.

He had been around enough dead people to recognize what it was.

His heart sank when he saw the two shadows on the ground. Used the flashlight on his phone to check the dead men. Swore when he recognized Cuban, and the other man, with his face ripped off, looked like Domingo.

Their bodies were cold. It looked like they had been dead for a few hours. Shot, judging by the wounds on them.

The missile launcher lay to the side. Now he knew what had damaged the school.

Where was Rolff? And had Carter escaped, or did his body lie in the rubble?

He hoped for the latter, but his gut told him otherwise. *He couldn't have killed my men if he was dead too.*

He strode towards the building, checking out each block of concrete, each dark shadow on the ground. There was the drone, destroyed, but no more bodies.

Half an hour later, he wiped sweat from his face and leaned against a wall to catch his breath.

Neither Rolff nor Carter were inside the school. He started searching in circles, going around the school, each wider than the previous one, and there … that was Rolff.

He too was shot.

Klapper was a case officer. He hadn't killed anyone in his career, and in fact had never resorted to violence, even though he had firearms training and knew basic self-defense.

Nevertheless, he thought he could kill Carter with his bare hands if the man had been standing in front of him.

Nine men. He killed nine of my best men.

And then a chill swept through him.

All nine of those officers had been from the military. Klapper had read their files. They were highly competent, experienced operatives. And Carter had put them down.

What chance would I have against him?

He snapped pictures of Rolff, of the destroyed building and of the battle scene. Went back to Domingo and Cuban and then halted, his breath leaving him, when he noticed the message Carter had left.

'This is where I was dragged,' Amelia's voice faltered as she pointed to the row of houses and the street in front of them. 'That,' she nodded to one residence, 'is my father's place. No,' she said when she saw Meghan's look. 'They grabbed me when I was leaving the hospital and brought me through here. As if they wanted to show the power they had over me.'

Wahab took her hand and held it tightly as his girlfriend walked them through the incident.

'Where was their vehicle?' Bear asked.

There was no traffic on the street that time of the night. Lights shone from a few houses, voices in a couple of them, but no one outside. No one, but them.

'There,' Amelia gestured. 'It came around that bend and waited there.'

'And Zeb?' Meghan asked, looking around. 'Where did he come from?'

'Down there.' The nurse waved. She hesitated. 'I returned'—she looked apologetically at her boyfriend when he turned to her swiftly— 'for no reason … just to see.'

'There was no need,' Wahab told her fiercely.

'I know. But it was something I had to do. Zeb Carter.' She turned to Meghan. 'I don't know … I am not sure, but I think he was sleeping in that car.' She pointed to the wrecked hulk lying some distance away. 'There's nowhere else he could have been. I don't think he was just walking down the street when those men caught me.'

Wahab stood with her in silence, and the two of them watched as their visitors checked out the street, looked at the houses, the alley through which Amelia had been dragged, and then, finally, inspected the wreckage.

Bwana and Bear returned to the center of the street, appearing to be replaying the shootout in their minds.

'It's possible,' they told Meghan.

She nodded and turned to Wahab and Amelia. 'It's just like him.'

'But why would he sleep there?' the officer asked, puzzled.

'Because he's hunted by everyone,' Beth replied bitterly. 'There's no place safe for him.'

Chapter 48

Tripoli Paradise.

The sign on top of the hotel was in pink neon. The *e* didn't light up and some of the letters flickered intermittently.

The outside of the hotel didn't look like a welcoming haven. A concrete driveway that linked to a narrow alley flanked by residential buildings. A small front yard, a dried-out pond and a fountain that wasn't working.

The parking lot was behind the hotel, entered through a metal gate at the side.

Zeb parked in the driveway and went inside, his backpack slung over his shoulder. He knew he looked rough and smelled of sweat and exhaustion. He got a wide berth and side glances from other patrons as he went to the reception desk.

'For one night,' he told the clerk, eyeing the room tariffs on a wall-mounted board. He peeled off a couple of hundred-dollar bills and slid them across. 'A quiet room on the ground floor.'

'Name?' the clerk asked.

Zeb hesitated. He was running out of aliases, and the way he was feeling, he was finding it difficult to come up with a made-up identity.

'Latif Wakil Misfud,' he said.

That would be the first name the kill teams would look for.

Let them. Doesn't look like this hotel is wired to any central booking system. They will have to come down in person to ask about me. I will have an escape route lined up if they do.

He knew it wasn't as easy as that. He knew he wasn't thinking properly. But weariness had caught up with him.

He took the room key, parked the van in the parking lot, well away from other vehicles, and went to his room.

It was clean, warm and comfortable.

White sheets on a firm bed, with that freshly laundered smell. Good-sized bathroom with a shower that actually worked and pumped out strong jets of water.

A single, large window that looked out to the parking lot. The sash could be opened easily if he had to make a quick getaway.

The hotel wasn't the heaven it promised, but given the way he was feeling, the room came close.

He stood under the shower for long moments, letting his tiredness drain away. Returned to the room freshened and, for a brief moment, wondering where his friends were and what they were up to.

They were in the Range Rover, heading back to Wahab's apartment to drop off the Libyans.

'Zeb gave you good advice,' Meghan said, hugging the nurse in parting. 'You should leave the city.'

'We will. Will you let us know if you find him?'

'No. We won't contact you again. It's safer for you.' Her tone softened at Amelia's crestfallen face. 'If you see nothing in the papers, you'll know he's still out there.'

'They may not report his capture or death.'

'They won't, but they can't hide a shooting. You'll know he's involved when there's no description … but it won't come to that. We will find him first.'

I hope, she mentally crossed her fingers.

'What?' she asked, on returning to their ride and seeing her sister's face.

Beth turned her screen around silently.

An alert from Werner, which was monitoring other agencies.

CIA team killed a few hours ago.

Meghan read the report swiftly, her heart thumping. Klapper, a case officer, had filed it. Not much detail to it, other than the number of officers dead, three, and the location.

'That's where another crate was,' she breathed.

'He's alive,' Beth's face glowed. 'He survived the attack.'

'We can't be sure it's him,' Broker cautioned.

'You didn't see the last part of that report,' Meghan told him and showed him the screen. 'Read that line.'

'Keep Trying,' Bwana read out aloud for everyone's benefit. 'That was the message left on one of the shooters.'

'Zeb.' Chloe thumped Bear's shoulder in delight. 'No one else would leave such a message.'

'That's where the third set of missiles was,' Meghan typed rapidly on her screen. 'GPS signal gone,' she said without looking up. 'Sometime before Klapper's report.'

'He's moving them,' Bwana rumbled.

'Yeah.' They were looking to backtrail him but were always a day or two behind. But with this shooting, the trail wasn't that cold.

'Where could he go?' she wondered, frowning. 'He's got three boxes of Javelins with him.'

'We don't know that,' Beth objected. 'He could have hidden them somewhere else. And he could have retrieved the others, too.'

'No,' Roger said confidently. 'The missiles will be with him. Remember, he knows he's on the run. He knows we or any other kill team could be watching the missile sites. He'll retrieve them and keep them.'

'Agreed.' Bear nodded. 'So, where could he be?'

'Werner—' Broker started.

'Has been looking for a while. Hacking into hotels, rental apartments.' Meghan expelled breath in frustration. 'Problem is, this is Tripoli. It's not as if many properties are hooked into the internet. Even if they were, the network's sketchy.'

'A million people in the city,' Broker thought out loud. 'He could be anywhere.'

Meghan jerked her head up. Stared at him for a moment. Something he said … she fired several commands at Werner. 'Hide in a crowd. That's what he keeps telling us.'

'You're searching for?' Beth leaned over her shoulder.

'For hotels near the city center that take cash. Don't require identity documents. Which have parking lots. Werner's already returned results …' she trailed off.

Meghan brought up a map program, laid out the addresses on them and turned to her friends, her eyes shining.

'Let's find Zeb.'

Chapter 49

'Yeah, the meeting's tomorrow.' Bob Marin tucked his cell between his neck and shoulder and poured himself a drink.

He went to the window and looked out at Tripoli's nightscape from his high-rise apartment in the city.

'You heard that Carter killed CIA officers?' Spears asked him.

'Yes. I have a good team, ready to deploy.'

'No. Let's hold back. There are so many teams hunting him. The Agency's operatives are there as well. Besides, our mutual friend has decided to step in. He's got contractors that he's going to use. Carter's nearing his end.'

Marin nodded silently. He knew the mutual friend was Jian Hsu. The Saharol CEO was clued in to the relationship with the Chinese spymaster. He had to know. *I am the front-man,* he mused as he swirled the whiskey in his mouth and savored its taste.

'Tomorrow's meeting—' Spears reminded him.

'Is with Sabbagh's people,' Marin completed the thought. 'It will be tough. There's no knowing what they will ask.'

'The mood music so far?'

'Has been warm. They want what we bring to the table but don't want to look eager.'

'Good luck for tomorrow.'

'We don't need luck. All we need is for Zeb Carter to die soon. Preferably, tonight.'

Zeb Carter wasn't ready to die. Not at the hands of other agency killers.

Refreshed by his shower, he unpacked his gear and laid out several items on the bed.

Two tiny cameras that could be hooked wirelessly to any system. A lump of play dough, white in color. Button cells.

He inserted the alkaline batteries into the cameras, went to his tablet computer and set them up to the hotel's WiFi system.

He went outside his room, yawned loudly and scratched at his chest. Just another tired resident.

No one in the hallway. .

He looked at the ceiling. Lights at regular intervals throughout its length. No cameras. The nearest lamp was about ten feet away from the top of his door.

He stretched to his full height and raised his hand. Yeah, he could touch the ceiling.

He went inside his room, pocketed the cameras and the play dough and returned. Rolled a small ball of the malleable material and jammed it tight against the base of the ceiling light. He then inserted one camera inside it and molded the dough around it and smoothed the edges until it looked like ducting material from a distance. He attached the second camera to another light in the opposite direction.

He checked his screen. The camera feeds were on his device. A few minor adjustments and he had eyes outside his door.

All I need is some kind of alarm, he thought, *whenever someone stops outside my door.*

He didn't have any alarms. The cameras would have to suffice.

He turned off the light, lay down on his bed and prepared to sleep.

Tomorrow, he would retrieve the remaining missiles and then work on finding a suitable demonstration area for the terrorists.

So long as I survive more attacks.

The absence of his friends worried him.

They should have tracked me by now. They got my last GPS position at the Musheer Market, but they also know where the missiles are. It wouldn't have been hard to locate him.

Maybe I shouldn't have used Misfud's identity anymore.

He shrugged in the dark.

They will come soon enough.

He hoped Beth and Meghan would hear him out before shooting him.

That's all I ask.

Chapter 50

———⟨∞∞⟩———

They were like shadows in the dark of the night.

Ghosts. Some of the most lethal people in the world.

They came to the Tripoli Paradise after parking their Range Rover several streets away.

Werner had found that Latif Wakil Misfud had rented a room there for the night.

'Is it a trap?' Meghan had wondered when their AI program had alerted them. 'Why would Zeb use that name?'

The seven of them had looked at one another. The hotel wasn't a fancy one. The only reason Werner had found out was because the manager had made a late entry into the reservation system.

'He wants us to find him,' Chloe offered.

'Why?' Beth asked, tightly. 'He probably thinks we're out to kill him.'

He's okay with that. It came to Meghan suddenly. She turned away from her friends to hide the whitening of her face. *He's tired of running. Escaping. He wants to finish his mission, but he knows the odds are against him.*

It made sense because, she, they, knew how Zeb thought.

How he lived. His code. She blinked back the onset of tears and composed her face.

'We need to check it out,' she told her friends, and that decision, at 11 pm, had led to them filtering through streets and past houses to arrive at Tripoli Paradise.

They were geared up. Earbuds, throat mics, handguns, body armor concealed beneath their Tees and jackets.

'Check out neighboring cars,' Meghan whispered.

She and Beth went down one street behind the hotel; Bear and Chloe took the one to its left, while Bwana, Roger and Bear took the one to the right.

They were searching for other shooters. *Other teams could have had the same idea we had; they too could have located the hotel.*

'Clear,' Beth whispered, after they had peered through every vehicle on their street.

'Clear,' Chloe echoed.

'No teams here,' Bwana replied after a while. Disappointed that he hadn't gotten the opportunity to put down any badasses.

They gathered at the front street and went down single file. Past the driveway, through the lobby, tiptoeing past the slumbering night clerk.

Meghan took the lead as they approached the hallway, which was a turn away from the reception desk. Vending machines for drinks and snacks. Dim lighting on the ceiling. A slightly opened door, which turned out to be the laundry room. Coin-operated washers and dryers, some of which rumbled with a load in them.

She counted doors, her nerves tight with anticipation; signaled for Bwana and Roger to go past her once she reached it.

Knock or call out?

Knock. Using his name wasn't prudent. Not at night, when there could be nosy neighbors in other rooms.

She raised her knuckles.

Zeb woke up instantly. He didn't know what had warned him. It wasn't the presence of danger. No, that came with a different kind of tingling in his body.

He looked at his screen and froze.

There, despite the low light outside, he could make out Meghan's profile as she was preparing to knock.

Beth to one side. Broker, Chloe and Bear with her. Bwana, tall, dark, and brooding on the other side of the door, Roger behind him.

Zeb looked at his Glock, which was on the floor.

No. I won't draw on them, no matter what.

No rage, no bitterness in him.

Just an empty feeling.

All those years of working together, sharing good times as well as bad, seeing the sisters cry, holding them, saving them, seeing Bwana grin, Broker, who was the oldest of them all … all those times together, and it came down to this.

Dying at their hands in the Tripoli Paradise in Libya.

I am coming. A few minutes, no more than that, he told his wife.

She didn't reply.

The knock sounded. Meghan's jaw firm, her face tense.

Zeb got up and went to the door.

Meghan's heart constricted when the door opened.

Zeb stood there, his hands standing loose by his sides.

Something like resignation on his face.

She reached beneath her jacket for the gun she had hidden.

Brought it out and shot him between the eyes.

Twice.

Chapter 51

Zeb stumbled back.

He wiped his face; his hand came away wet.

Meghan, grinning widely at him.

Water pistol? Not a bullet?

It didn't compute. His brain was working sluggishly.

The ball of energy by her side, Beth, flung herself at him.

'ZEB!' She crushed him tight.

He staggered back from the impact, his left hand going around her automatically.

She didn't shoot me.

He didn't realize he had said the words aloud. Meghan's smile faded. She came to him, too, her arms going around him.

'How could you even think that?' she asked, her voice muffled against his shoulder.

Chloe, tears down her cheeks, her fingers gripping Bear's arm. Bwana, Roger, Broker, all of them in his room. Anxious looks. Heads nodding at Meghan's words. Beth sniffling against him.

She's crying, Zeb thought. He felt as if he was in a dream.

Everything, everyone was moving slow. His mind was like sludge; it was taking forever to process anything.

'I … didn't … do … anything.' He found his voice, but the words came out cracked, raw.

'We know,' Meghan said, nodding, her face still against his chest.

He *felt* her reply before her words registered.

He shuddered.

His free hand came up to hold her as well.

The smell of their hair. He closed his eyes, breathed deep until it filled him. When he opened them, he felt the warmth from his friends. Bwana, his dark face split by a smile so wide it stretched from one end of the earth to another. Broker, grinning in that lopsided way he had. Chloe, her cheeks wet with tears, leaning against Bear, whose beard couldn't hide his delight. Roger, leaning against the wall in unconscious elegance, winking at him.

The world slowly tilted back to normal as something loosened in him, that tightness in his belly relaxed.

'You fool,' Beth shook her head and gave way to heaving sobs, and he held her tight, her sister as well. Zeb buried his face in their hair, between their faces, and held onto them.

Somewhere dawn broke, and somewhere else the sun set, but there, in his room, with his friends around him and the twins holding onto him, it felt like his hotel had finally lived up to its name.

Hours seemed to pass before Beth lifted her head up and dried her face, her lips twisting wryly. She used the flat of her palm to wipe the water from his forehead.

'We thought it would instantly make you feel at home.'

The sisters pranked him with the water gun a few times a year.

He nodded dumbly, aware that Meghan was looking at him. She touched his temple lightly where Amelia's stitches were healing slowly. She fingered his left shoulder, feeling the dressing underneath his Tee.

She took a long, trembling breath and composed herself.

'We never, ever doubted you,' she said, her eyes full.

'It was all an act that we had to go through.' Bwana pushed forward and enveloped him in a bone-crushing hug. Bear thumped him on his back so hard that he stumbled; Roger punched his shoulder, his teeth flashing; and Broker, his oldest friend, came to him and clasped his hands in a simple gesture and squeezed.

It looks like you'll have to wait longer than a few minutes, he told his wife.

Oh, honey, you still have a lot to learn about people. Meg, Beth, your friends, would never harm you. Her laugh spread warmth through him. He could see the tiny wrinkles at the corners of her lips, the way she cocked her head when she was amused.

He nodded unconsciously, and when he raised his head, Meghan's green eyes were on him. There was something in them, as if she knew who he'd been talking to.

'Say something,' Beth demanded, and that drew a wry smile out of him. Bear chuckled. His friends ranged themselves around the small room, Chloe occupying the single chair.

Zeb sat on the bed, flanked by the sisters.

'What happened?' he asked.

Chapter 52

Zeb watched the fake videos when Beth and Meghan had finished their narration, right from when Clare had taken down the systems to their confronting her with what the elder sister had discovered.

'No,' Chloe shook her head. 'We don't know who made and sent those. Werner's investigating everything, but that's a very wide remit, and the players will be careful.'

'It could be anyone,' Meghan resumed. She briefed him on who was present at the kill meetings and the information the president had received.

'How many kill teams are there, in Tripoli?'

'Many. You took out two CIA teams.'

'Two?' he frowned. 'I know of only one.'

'The one who hit you today, that was CIA too. That helped us find you.'

Beth took over, told him about their finding Amelia and Wahab, and how they had backtracked to the triangulation point.

'And then, Werner found you here. After we read your message. The CIA case officer filed a report a few hours back.

Werner spotted that, and we used that as a starting point to triangulate you.'

Zeb looked at Beth, squeezed her hand. She squeezed back.

'It's real,' Meghan told him softly. 'We *are* here with you. You aren't dreaming.'

Something else loosened inside. A relaxation of not just his muscles, but also the tightness in his chest. He sat quietly for long moments, his head lowered, and when he looked up, his friends were still there. Strong, reassuring, warm faces.

His team.

'We never ever doubted you,' Beth repeated. 'Not once. We would never draw down on you.'

He held out his hands blindly and crushed her tight and held her and closed his eyes, and when he opened them, his world was right again.

'Amelia and her—'

'Are getting out of town. They're taking your advice. Oh yeah, add Kattan's men to those hunting you. I bet some of them will be searching for that shooter, too.'

'Your turn,' Meghan turned to him.

He broke it down quickly for them, right from the attack in his first hotel, eight days ago, the meeting with Abu Bakhtar, his missile recoveries, the various shootouts, down to the one at the school.

A silence fell over them when he had finished.

'Only that X gave me a clue,' he said, nudging Beth with his shoulder. 'I knew y'all would come. I didn't think it would be like this.'

He winced when she punched him hard on his good shoulder, her eyes blazing.

'THAT'S. A. REMINDER. TO. NEVER. DOUBT. US.'

'Yes, ma'am,' he said meekly, which brought a grin to her face.

'Zeb,' Meghan said urgently. 'Surely, you suspect someone, you must have found something.'

'No,' he confessed. 'I've been trying to stay alive. And finish the mission.'

Her face fell. Bear swore. Roger paced the room slowly.

'We thought you would have made some progress.' Meghan couldn't keep the disappointment from her voice.

'Go through it again.'

She repeated it all, and then again when she had finished. Patiently, because she knew how he worked, but Beth growled, 'We've been through everything, Zeb. Over and over. There's no obvious player.'

'Who was Shaming Chia's handler?'

'Who?'

'The Chinese double agent,' Meghan told her sister impatiently. 'Who said—' She broke off, then her face lit up. 'He said someone Hsu was running gave him up. We assumed it was Zeb.'

'But Chia's disappeared. Probably killed,' Bear said, puzzled.

'Jeez, keep up, Bear,' Chloe said. 'It was Chia's handler who put that statement out.'

'No,' Meghan corrected her. 'He was repeating what the report said. Zeb was not named.'

'You questioned him?' Zeb asked the twins.

'No. We don't even know his name,' Beth replied. 'Clare's not investigating that angle, either. You think Chia was leaned on to implicate you?'

'No. I want to know who gave him up. How did Hsu know we were running him?'

'We never considered that,' Meghan replied slowly. 'The entire focus of that investigation was on you.'

'I know. We find who leaked Chia, we might get somewhere.'

'He could have slipped up, Zeb,' Bear warned. 'In his position, the pressure he was under, a mistake could have been made. We all have been there.'

'Yeah, but it's the—'

'The timing,' Meghan guessed. 'It's too coincidental.'

'Chloe and I will go,' Bear announced. 'We'll ask this handler.'

'Nicely,' the elder sister reminded him. 'We want him alive. You're thinking of something else?' she asked Zeb, reading his expression.

'Why now?'

Her forehead creased momentarily, then cleared when she caught on.

'You think there's some link to Libya? To your mission? To taking down Almasi?'

'If our enemies wanted to discredit me and the Agency, they could do it anytime. Those videos, the supporting narrative, they would be believed. Why wait till I was in Libya?'

'Who benefits, though?' Beth asked thoughtfully.

'That's where I am stuck,' Zeb admitted. 'Who benefits from letting Almasi operate?'

Chapter 53

'Any news on the missiles?' the speaker was dressed in a white dishdasha. The transparent glasses over his eyes, the neatly trimmed facial hair, gave him a professorial air.

There was nothing academic about his actions.

Nasir Fakhir Almasi, the terrorist leader, sipped his tea slowly in his heavily guarded building in Sirte and waited for an answer from Abu Bakhtar.

From the outside, the building looked like it would collapse any moment. It was three stories high, concrete, brick and mud, large holes where once had been windows. It was in a central neighborhood, surrounded by other dilapidated buildings. Narrow alleys separating them.

Snipers on rooftops, armed men on the ground. A pantry, a makeshift hospital, a bomb factory several buildings away. Hundreds of rifles, magazines, burner phones, SIM cards and electronic jamming equipment. Laptops, recording and broadcast equipment for the leader to make his pronouncements.

No stranger could enter the neighborhood without the terrorists knowing. Straying refugees or civilians who had returned to Sirte were either turned away, beaten up, or shot.

A drone strike could destroy the building, but the GNA and its Western allies were wary of innocent casualties.

Besides, the West was weary of war. UK, Germany, France, the US, none of them wanted another protracted engagement in the Middle East.

Almasi took full advantage of that inertia. He was protected by his people, hid his base amidst innocents. His people were digging tunnels beneath the buildings, escape routes for him should the need arise. Only a few of them were ready, but time was on his side. He was well on his way to returning the terrorist group to its former strength.

'No, sayyidi,' Abu Bakhtar replied. 'I have a way of contacting Misfud, but we met only three days ago. He will need some time to gather the Javelins.'

'Let's wait. We should not appear desperate. He might increase the price.'

'Yes, sayyidi.'

'What do you think of Saharol?'

'Sayyidi,' his deputy stroked his beard. 'That approach from him. Totally unexpected.'

'It's a big company.'

'Very big. Billions of dollars big.'

'Why would they want to meet us?'

'The messenger didn't say anything, sayyidi. In fact, he never said he was from Saharol. As you know, he reached out to some of our soldiers and said there was a big party who was interested in discussions. A private party who was into oil. Whose name is everywhere.'

'It's Saharol,' Almasi said definitively. 'I have a feeling about it.'

'But why? It could be a trap. These Americans are cunning.

They might be using the company as a cover.'

'Yes, I have thought of that. But, think of this as well. We know Saharol is growing fast. We know no oil company likes the attacks we have been making on NOC. What if they want to offer us protection money?'

Abu Bakhtar thought for a moment and then shook his head. 'Sayyidi, no Western government or company wants to negotiate with us. They all want us dead. I smell a trap. We should not talk with these people.'

'No,' Almasi ordered. 'Let's hear them out. But send someone junior. Someone expendable. And meet them well away from Sirte.'

'Yes, sayyidi.'

Hsu's killers were some of the best in the world. They were some of the smartest, too.

They were already in-country, in Tripoli, when the spymaster greenlighted them.

Dante Abrahms, the leader of the seven-person team, hadn't bothered to find out where Carter was. He didn't go through the various disguises and send his men to question various hotels.

He knew everything there was to know about the American. Hsu had sent him the complete file. Carter's mission, the missiles, their locations, Abrahms was well-informed. He too could have based his team at the Javelins' hiding places, but he didn't do that.

No, his approach was different, and he was confident it would deliver results.

Better than all those other teams hunting him.

The South African was huge. Six feet four and built like a

barrel. His size belied his movement. He was light on his feet and could explode into action like a panther.

His shaven head and perpetually cold eyes kept people at a distance. Even his team members, with whom he had worked closely when they all had been with the State Security Agency, SSA, weren't close to him.

Abrahms had quit the South African Intelligence Agency, had taken his best people and had gone freelance several years back.

They carried out assassinations in the African continent. They killed politicians in Italy. They threatened and terminated business magnates in the US. There weren't many continents they didn't work in.

Their income stream exploded upwards when Jian Hsu sought out Abrahms and, after a long courting period, appointed the South African team as his deniable execution squad.

They had landed in Tripoli the moment the Agency had shut down its systems. They had familiarized themselves with the city and had studied every detail on Carter's file.

And when Hsu told Abrahms to be ready, he decided to watch the airports.

The way he looked at it, Carter's friends would find and kill him before any other team.

Follow the Agency operatives, and they would find Carter.

It was simple.

And if his friends killed Carter, then great, because they would still get paid.

However, if they didn't, then Abrahms and his men would carry out the execution. And they would kill the Agency operatives as well, as a free bonus.

When Hsu gave the go, he and his men were following the Range Rover in several vehicles. A complicated maneuver that meant no single car was behind the Agency ride long enough to be made.

They watched the operatives circle Tripoli Paradise. 'Proceed on foot,' Abrahms ordered when the Range Rover was parked streets away.

His caution paid off when the Americans checked every vehicle surrounding the hotel. The South Africans watched through their NVGs, from a distance, lying beneath trucks or jammed between alleys, as the operatives did a clean sweep and only then proceeded towards the hotel.

'Carter must be in there,' Morne van Zyl rasped on their comms. 'We can go inside, take all of them.'

'No, we don't know the inside. We've no idea whether they're confronting him, staying in different rooms. We wait here.'

They waited.

Chapter 54

Zeb got up early in the morning. For the first time since he had been on the run, the world felt right.

They had talked late into the night, watched the videos over and over again, considered the question of who benefits, but had made no progress.

They called Clare on a burner phone; she started off with, 'You understand?'

Zeb knew she was referring to his being cut loose, reporting the video and the kill meeting.

'Yes, ma'am.' He did. She was the director of the Agency. She had to follow procedure.

'I couldn't warn you.'

That tone, that guilt and shame in her voice made him swallow and grip the phone tightly. She had approached him when he had been a mercenary. Had asked him to build the Agency along with her. She had stood by him, had never questioned his judgment or his methods. *She never told me how to go about a mission.*

'Ma'am,' Beth took the phone from his hands when he couldn't reply. She put it on speaker. 'Zeb's gone all emotional.

Pretty soon, he'll be turning on the water works.'

'I'm sure you were dry-eyed,' came the sarcastic reply.

'Very few of us were, ma'am.'

'Ma'am.' Zeb leaned closer to the phone. 'Who was Shaming Chia's handler?'

Silence at her end. 'Of course,' their boss said slowly after a while, making the connection that Zeb had. 'I should have thought of that.'

'Frank Ibarra. Career CIA. Worked there ever since he graduated from Princeton. Works in the SOG. Not a field agent. Chia was the most valuable asset he ran.'

'He's still with the agency?'

'Yeah. Lives in Virginia.' She rattled off an address that Beth took down.

'You intend to talk to him?'

'Yes, ma'am. I am guessing no one did.'

'No. I never thought of that angle.' Guilt in her voice again.

'Ma'am—' Zeb began.

'I know,' she said, her voice trembling faintly, 'back when you were the Agency's only operative, when we were just starting out, I never imagined it would come to this. That I would sit on a kill meeting to terminate you.'

'He's still alive, ma'am,' Meghan said forcefully. 'We are with him. The Agency's in business.'

'Zeb.' Clare chuckled, her voice stronger, firmer. 'I bet you missed the twins.'

'I did, ma'am. All of them.'

They discussed the conspiracy with her and, after it was clear Clare hadn't made much progress, they hung up.

'What about Avichai, Dieter and Alex?' Zeb asked his friends.

'None of them believe the videos,' Broker chuckled. 'They all had a few choice words for us when Clare called them. However, they've made it look like they have sent teams too. They keep reporting to the kill meetings that their agents are in the city, looking for you. All made up.'

'And Francois?' Francois Armand, the director of the DGSE, another close ally.

'He,' Bear snorted, 'flat-out refused to cooperate. He said if you were a traitor, then we might just as well curl up and wait for the world to end. He hasn't sent any shooters.'

Zeb blinked. Squeezed Beth's hand when she gripped his. *I'm okay. Now.*

'When I told Mark,' she snickered, 'he said it was good we were leaving town, or else he would have to arrest us for stupidity.'

Mark Feinberg, an NYPD detective. Beth's boyfriend.

'Hope Langley will give us something,' Chloe said. 'We'll go in the morning.'

'We'll run your photographs,' Meghan said, referring to the dead shooters' images on Zeb's phone, 'and see who they are. We might get something there.'

'We need to complete the mission. Then see what happens,' Zeb said. 'Those killers, they've all been sent by some outfit or the other. We might not get anything there.'

'That's where you're wrong,' she asserted. 'If I was the one setting you up, I would send some of my people too.'

He watched her, turning it over in his mind.

Beth was the impulsive one. She wore her heart on her sleeve. Meghan, though, she analyzed everything. Looked at a problem from numerous angles. The sisters, together, were a high-octane combination of smarts and emotional intelligence. They complemented each other, and their lateral thinking was one of the reasons the Agency had such a high success rate.

'You've got a point.'

'We always have,' Beth snorted.

They talked about past missions, joked, laughed easily. When they were talked out, the twins hugged Zeb and followed the other operatives out. They got rooms in the same hotel, and when Zeb closed the door, he found himself grinning.

Yeah, things were looking up.

He stretched, glanced at his watch. Five am. He changed into track pants and a jacket and went out. Took the stairs to get to the roof of the hotel.

Stopped in his tracks when he saw Beth and Meghan already there, going through their warmup routine.

'You took your time, slowpoke,' Beth snarked. 'Meg said you wouldn't come, all that crying you did in the night.'

He fist-bumped them and joined them in an intense session. Push-ups, sit-ups, free-flowing katas, slow, medium, fast, fast, fast, fast, till sweat was pouring off them and their tops stuck to them like a second skin.

They cooled down by watching the sun rise, gold and orange painting shadows on the buildings and awakening Tripoli.

'Those the ones I gave you last night?' Meghan pointed at his shoes.

'Yeah.'

She had brought out the pair, along with a jacket, and had tossed them at him. 'GPS trackers in them. We aren't going to lose sight of you again.'

'What's on for today?' she asked.

'Let's recover the rest of the missiles.'

They left the hotel at 10 am.

The plan was to drop Bear and Chloe at Mitiga International Airport, where they would take a commercial flight to DC.

The rest of them would stick with Zeb.

He was with the sisters, the rest of the operatives ahead, all of them walking to the Rover, which was parked a distance away.

He donned his shades and inserted the earbud and adjusted his throat mic. Gear that Beth had given him in the morning.

Meghan laughed at something her sister said and caught his shoulder as if to share the joke.

'Two men,' she said. 'Behind us. One of them leaning against a tan car, the other lighting a cigarette.'

'What about them?' Zeb asked, turning on the rear-view on his shades, rotating his head slightly to get the men in view.

'Car man raised his wrist to his mouth. Like speaking into a mic. Too casually. He glanced once at us before doing that. Cigarette dude hasn't looked at us.'

'So?'

'Well,' Beth drawled, 'You gotta admit, Zeb, most men look at us. Besides, this is Tripoli. Every man will look at a Western woman.'

'She's right,' Chloe joined in over their comms. 'And they're not alone. On our two, man tying his shoelace, in front of that barber shop.'

Zeb spotted Shoe Man on the other side of the street. The beast woke up. The first two men were two car lengths behind them.

Shooting distance. But their hands are empty.

Which didn't mean much, because their shirts were loose, free, and one of them was wearing a jacket.

Bear and Chloe split away at the front and stopped to peer into a cake shop. Bwana and Roger doubled over in laughter and playfully shoved Broker away.

All done casually, to spread them out.

Three possible hostiles. Any more?

'Car entering the street ahead. Approaching us.' Roger chuckled. 'No other vehicle. Can't see inside. Sun's on the windscreen.'

They've boxed us neatly, Zeb thought swiftly. He made a show of pulling out his phone and checking it. Which brought his gunhand closer to his shoulder-holstered Glock. *That car might be stuffed with gunmen; the two men have our rear, Shoe Man has our right side, no one required at our left, because it's a compound wall running down the street.*

He resumed walking. Beth to his left, Meghan to the right.

Faint laughter. Cigarette Man and Shoe Man had cracked a joke and were ambling down towards them.

Shoe Man had straightened and was talking loudly on a phone, half-turned towards Bear and Chloe, who were to his left, still looking through the window.

He and the men at the back were closing in on Zeb, the sisters and the couple. Ahead, the approaching car was narrowing the distance to Bwana, Roger and Broker.

Zeb gave nothing away. He switched his phone to his left hand and shook his head in disgust.

Sunlight winked off the approaching car. It caught his attention for a moment.

In that instant, two men scaled down from the compound wall to their left.

Chapter 55

A glint of metal. A muttered curse from behind. Gas fumes and the faint smell of baking in the air. Meghan's sharply drawn breath.

Everything registered on Zeb unconsciously even as he moved. He threw himself to the right, shouldering the elder sister towards the cracked pavement. Grabbed Beth by her hair and yanked hard.

She grunted and fell back just in time as the first bullets ripped over their heads, as the wall shooters landed and opened fire.

Zeb lost balance, fell on top of Meghan, rolled away.

A snapped glance to his left. Car Man and Smoker were crouching, their guns rising. To his right, Shop Man was turning to Bear and Chloe.

Zeb's Glock bucked. His first two rounds went wild but caused the wall men to duck and spread out. He kept rolling away from the sisters.

They want me. Draw their fire.

He was dimly aware of shooting ahead. Shoe Man spinning around. Dirt exploded in his face as a round smacked the street in front of him.

He came to a stop.

He would offer a target.

He raised his gun, classic rollover prone shooting stance. One of the wall men was darting to the left, his assault rifle chattering, spraying blindly, coughing up dirt, shattering windows.

Zeb anticipated his move and let rip with his Glock, a long burst that made the shooter fall to the ground.

Did I get him?

No time to check, because the second shooter was more methodical. He wasn't running. He had dropped to a knee. At that distance, he couldn't miss.

Zeb saw him too late, as the shooter trained, paused for a fraction of a second.

Here it comes, he thought. *Death.*

He triggered, knowing he had reacted too slowly, knew he had missed—but the shooter fell back, his body shuddering under the impact of several rounds.

Zeb saw Meghan slap in a new magazine from the corner of his eyes.

She got him. Maybe Beth shot him, too.

He turned. Just his arm and head moving, the rest of his body still.

The shooters at the rear were sprinting away, realizing the momentum had turned. He chopped one of them down. The second man fled down the street, darting between cars.

Zeb pressed his cheek as close to the ground as he could get. Spotted the man's feet beneath the chassis of a vehicle.

A bead of sweat dripped off him. His temple was throbbing. He sighted, fired once, saw the man stumble, fired again, and the shooter went down.

Time started speeding up to normal. Sound returned. Screaming. No more shots.

Meghan, now to his left, face cold, her gun trained on the second wall man, who lay on the pavement, his chest a bloody mess. Beth, a smudge of dirt on her cheek, her Glock on Cigarette Man, who was slumped, motionless.

Bear and Chloe, standing tall over Shoe Man, his face a bloodied mess.

'Finally,' a voice said.

Bwana, approaching them, his light voice belying the concern in his eyes as he checked them out swiftly, his shoulders relaxing when he saw they were unhurt. He hauled Beth up carefully, staying out of her line of fire.

'Finally, what?' Meghan asked,

'I shoot some badasses.' His teeth flashed.

Zeb went to the bodies by the wall, Bwana covering him. Both were dead.

He got a thumbs-up from Chloe. Their shooter was finished, too.

'Only one man in the car,' Roger came to them. 'Not much left of him.'

'Zeb?' Beth called out from down the street, where she and Meghan had gone to check out the shooters.

'Yeah?'

'This one's alive.'

Chapter 56

Abrahms was sitting in a café several streets away. He was watching the shootout go down on his tablet computer, discreetly positioned away from foot traffic.

Each of his men had small body cams that fed sight and sound to his screen. The South African sipped his coffee, his face expressionless as he watched his men being taken down expertly by the Agency operatives.

Carter was there, between the two sisters. He had been the first to react when Abrahms's men leapt over the wall.

The former SSA killer's heart sank when he saw the speed at which the American had acted.

I underestimated him, he thought grimly as he watched the Americans explode into action and kill his men.

His team wasn't supposed to engage. Wait for the right opportunity and only then attack—those had been Abrahms's instructions.

However, they had no choice.

The South African knew Carter and the sisters had made Wikus Marx and Morne van Zyl. He read it in the way the American adjusted his shades and that woman cocked her head.

They seemed to have comms too, to communicate with each other, because an instant later, that couple near the store glanced casually at de Bruyn, and those three men ahead, they stiffened.

Sure, none of them gave their tells away, but Abrahms knew. The South African had been in the game for so long that he had developed a sixth sense.

And that was when he had given the order to attack.

Pienaar and Lombard should have fired from the top of the wall itself instead of waiting till they landed. Ricus should have fired from the car the moment it drove into the street.

Those delays had given away their element of surprise. He gritted his teeth. *This is on me. I got overconfident. Complacent. How difficult could it be to take out eight Americans who were boxed? That's what I thought. I should have gone the long gun route. Sniper shot to Carter as he came out of the hotel.*

A part of him, the professional side, couldn't help admiring the speed at which Carter and his people had reacted. They had moved like a smooth, well-oiled machine. No wasted moments, every one of them focusing on targets without any commands that he could hear.

He stiffened when he heard one of the women shout. Her voice was faint, but clear. And when he made out her words, he knew he had a problem.

Wikus was still alive.

Bob Marin was flanked by his security team when he entered the Ministry of Finance office on Tariq Al Seka road. In the cool interior, he folded his shades and broke into a smile when Nashaat Munjid Kanaan approached him.

The Libyan was in a business suit, accompanied by several men, some of them in dishdashas, others in Western wear.

'Mr. Marin, it's a pleasure to meet you,' the deputy minister of finance greeted him in fluent, Oxford-accented English. 'You are alone?'

'Yes, minister.'

'Come.' The official patted him on the shoulder like a long-lost friend and led him to his offices.

They entered a boardroom and arranged themselves around a polished wood table, the Libyans on one side, Marin and the minister on another. A seating choice that the Saharol CEO made deliberately.

It was about optics and perception. Sitting next to the minister gave the impression they weren't adversaries. That they weren't there to thrash out one of the most important deals in Libya's history.

Okay, that might be an exaggeration, Marin thought as he politely sipped his tea and waited for the small talk to be over.

He looked pointedly at the flunkies Kanaan had brought to the meeting. Each had files and notepads in front of them. All of them would take notes, each would flick through pages of material to help their boss. It was how government hierarchy worked. The more important a minister, the more flunkies.

'They are all cleared for our discussions, Bob,' the Libyan said. 'None of what we talk about will leave this room. Will it?' he looked at his men with a steely glance, and they shook their heads.

They'll probably be killed if they leak any of the discussions, Marin thought. *The minister must have threatened them and then tapped their phones, had them followed, to ensure secrecy.*

'Let's proceed, in that case,' the official said. He pasted a fake smile. 'You have wasted your time, Bob. We aren't interested in any deal.'

The Saharol CEO didn't react.

He was expecting just that reaction.

It was merely the start of negotiations.

Chapter 57

'Anyone recognize him?' Zeb asked as he looked down at the survivor.

The killer had two rounds in his legs and one in his chest.

'Nope,' Beth replied. 'We haven't seen any of these shooters.'

The other operatives agreed. They had checked the killers, taken their photographs, and now stood around the one who was alive. Just about.

Zeb knew they didn't have much time. *Police will be here soon.* They could hear sirens in the distance. A few brave people were poking their heads out of windows.

I'll have to disappear.

He and his friends had worked out the story they would tell the police. They were State Department officials who were hunting Zeb Carter.

They had located him at the hotel, in his Misfud identity. They were proceeding to capture him when these gunmen had attacked them. They had defended themselves but, hearing the shooting, Carter had fled.

The Libyans won't believe their State Department story.

Not with the guns on them and their shooting. They'll think they are CIA or some other agency. Which was fine, because Clare would make sure the Agency operatives' story was backed up by the US Embassy.

He knelt over the fallen man. Two rounds in his legs, one in his chest. *One of my shots must have ricocheted off something and caught him high.*

'Who sent you?' Zeb asked him, first in Arabic, then in English, followed by several other languages.

The man remained unresponsive. His brown eyes were wide, distant, his face grimaced in agony, his breathing shallow, his hands clutching his chest.

I hope he survives, Zeb thought as he inspected the man's wound. The round in his upper body looked to have punctured his lungs. His breathing was harsh and loud. He ripped the man's shirt and wadded it around the wound to prevent more blood leakage. Searched him swiftly. Nothing, not even a wallet. He found a mic around the man's wrist and earbuds. Removed and inspected them. Good quality gear, but nothing exceptional. Those could be bought from any store that sold advanced comms equipment.

'No identification on any other body,' Broker told him. 'Similar equipment on all of them.'

'You need to leave.' Meghan caught his shoulder as the sirens grew closer. 'We'll handle this.'

She's right.

He got to his feet, took one last look and ran towards the hotel, his head bent down. He went to the parking lot and got into his van. Drove out slowly just as the first cruiser arrived at the scene.

Zeb drove a block away and found another parking lot.

Stopped his vehicle in an empty space and waited for his friends to make contact.

Who were those killers? Were they from some US outfit, or from whoever set me up?

Sunlight streamed through the windscreen and warmed him up.

An idea came to him. He turned it over in his mind. Yeah, it could work. Besides, what did he have to lose?

He brought out one of the burner phones Beth had given him. Scrolled through a list of numbers on it. They were all single-use numbers for their boss. She would cycle through phones at her end after every call.

'Zeb?' Clare answered immediately.

Eleven am in Tripoli was 5 am in DC. The director sounded alert, as if she had been up for a few hours.

'Ma'am, we were attacked by a team. A few moments ago. Nope,' he hurried when he heard her sharp intake. 'We're unharmed. Not even a scratch.'

He briefed her quickly on what had gone down. 'Beth or Meghan will run their pictures through Werner, but that isn't why I called you.'

His boss waited.

'We should try to take control of this. All along, we've been reacting to someone else's playbook. It's time we wrote our own scenes.'

'How?'

'You should report this shootout to the president. Add a few more details. That I was shot by the Agency operatives, but escaped.'

'How will that help?'

'I shouted that I was innocent. That I was set up and knew

who was behind it. I was coming after them.'

'You didn't say who it was?' Clare asked. He heard the smile in her voice and knew she had caught on.

'No, ma'am.'

'I'll make sure the president knows of this.'

'Bear and Chloe are coming to DC, ma'am. To interview Shaming Chia's handler.'

'I've been thinking about that since your last call. He didn't name you. He might not know anything.'

'I know, ma'am. But someone leaked Chia. He's disappeared. We can assume Hsu found out about him and had him arrested or killed.'

'Killed. We know how Hsu works.'

'Yes, ma'am. But how did he know about Chia?'

'But won't that mean Hsu's involved as well?'

'Not necessarily, ma'am. Whoever's behind this could well know the history I have with the MSS. They could have scripted the story and made those videos.'

'But Hsu—'

'Ma'am, why would he wait till now to get at me?'

'He got us as well. Your friends might have told you. Officially, the Agency is shutting down. Hunting you is the last mission. I am retiring. The president has let that be known.'

'Ma'am, discrediting us ... Hsu or Mostofi, let's not forget him too, they could do it any time.'

'It didn't have to wait till Libya, is what you mean?'

'Yes, ma'am.'

'The timing could be a coincidence.'

'Yes, ma'am.'

'But you are not convinced. That's why you want Bear and Chloe to question Frank Ibarra.'

'Yes, ma'am.'

'He was interviewed as per procedure, but no one doubted Chia's report. I read it myself. There wasn't much in it. That he'd been betrayed by someone on our side whom Hsu had turned.'

'Bear and Chloe, ma'am, they won't be subtle.'

'You mean they'll say they are from the Agency?'

'Yes, ma'am.'

'That's fine.' Another smile in her voice. 'I'll handle the heat.'

'How, ma'am?'

'I'll just say, since killing you will be my last order, I want to be satisfied it was the right decision. What can they do? I am already on my way out.'

Chapter 58

Washington DC

President Morgan looked over those assembled in the Cabinet Room. The Veep, Bryan Thiessen, all his secretaries, they were all present. Mike Hoosier, the DNI, was there too, at his request.

He started the meeting with the state of the economy, jobs, unemployment, interest rates, the forest fires in California, and then moved to international matters. Brexit and a new relationship with the United Kingdom. European Union, a trade war with China.

He went through every item on the agenda and then stretched during the coffee break.

He looked at Lester McClellan, secretary of defense, and Paul Vaughan, secretary of state.

'Preparations for your Libya visit?'

'We're going through those, sir,' McClellan answered. 'State's working with Prime Minister Sabbagh's office. We should get dates soon. From our side, we are ready to go.'

'Oil—'

'Oil, Kattan, defense, ISIL and the migration routes.' Vaughan flashed a smile. 'Those will be our key points.'

The president nodded as he studied the men. One, craggy-faced; the other, movie-star handsome. He wasn't close to them. He wasn't friends with any of his cabinet members. That was a significant departure from previous presidents, who often appointed people whom they knew well, had gone to college with, had worked with, or were in their network.

President Morgan had no interest in carrying on with the old boys' club. He hand-picked people who were suitable for the job. He cast a wide net during selection and was satisfied that his cabinet was staffed with the most capable people available.

He maintained warm, professional relationships with his secretaries, but none of them were his buddies. There was only one person in his entire team he was friends with, and that was Daniel Klouse. The National Security Advisor was present at the meeting too, but not at the table. He was in a chair, in a corner, observing keenly.

He and Clare. The only two people in DC that I trust.

'Where are we with ISIL?' he asked.

Mike Hoosier spoke up. 'Sir, we are in a holding mode. We have restricted our aerial bombing to let the Libyan military deal with Almasi. Unfortunately, Prime Minister Sabbagh is stretched thin. He has to deal with Kattan, too.'

The president waited for anyone else to chime in, but there was silence. The DNI and Catlyn Feder knew that Zeb's mission had been to take out the ISIL leader. *Before he was declared a traitor.*

He shut down that train of thought. Clare had given him specific instructions. He would follow them and report back on reaction. After that, it was down to her to progress.

'We have enough intel sir,' the CIA director spoke up, 'to mount an operation to take him out. Clandestine.'

'No. Let's stay back for now. There's been another development overnight that none of you are aware of.'

He pretended to study a confidential report in front of him. 'All of you know of that one of our black ops outfits is under investigation. Their agent leaked national secrets.' Heads nodded. 'Some operatives from another *agency* cornered him in Tripoli.' He watched them keenly as he emphasized the word.

While everyone in his cabinet would have heard of the kill order, few of his cabinet knew that outfit existed and even a smaller number were aware that it was the one he had referred to.

There was no reaction from the attendees.

'Shots were fired,' he continued, 'but he escaped unharmed. He said something about being set up. That he would be coming after whoever was responsible. Expected reaction from a traitor,' he said, shrugging dismissively. 'However, I don't want to muddy the waters in Tripoli. Let these agents find him. There are other agencies hunting him too. He won't last long.'

Some cabinet members murmured assent. Feder and Hoosier made no objection.

He carried on with his daily briefing and, when the meeting had finished, got Vaughan and McClellan to stay back.

It was unusual for both the secretaries to visit Libya at the same time. It was needed, they said, to demonstrate to Sabbagh that he was valued, that the US was with him. They had to be pragmatic, too. They had to be prepared that he might lose power.

'You'll be meeting Hazim Kattan as well?' the president asked.

'Yes, sir,' Vaughan replied. 'My department has made contact. They are setting it up.'

'How will Sabbagh react?'

'He won't be happy, sir. There isn't much he can do, however.'

'We will make him feel important, sir,' the defense secretary added. 'There are arms deals to close and we will make a public statement that we are fully with him.'

It was an open secret that both Vaughan and McClellan wanted to run for the presidency, though neither had publicly declared it.

Each would claim this visit to be a success because of him.

President Morgan suppressed a wry grin. He knew how the game was played. *I did the same.*

'I am worried,' he said. 'Both of you at the same time. That's a security risk.'

'DSS and other intelligence agencies have cleared our visit, sir,' Vaughan said. The Diplomatic Secret Service, a law enforcement and security arm of State, was responsible for the secretary of state's protection. 'It would be wrong to back out now.'

'You know the drill. They have final say on your schedule. You don't deviate from it.'

'Yes, sir,' both men chorused.

'What do you think?' the president asked Klouse once the men had left.

'I think, sir, one of your cabinet must be feeling nervous. If they were responsible for Zeb's circumstances.'

'How is he?'

'He's alive, sir, and with the other operatives.'

Clare and the National Security Advisor had updated the president on the shooting the previous day. It was during that briefing that the Agency head had passed on Zeb's suggestion. The president had been happy to play along. 'Anything to find out who's the real traitor,' he had said grimly.

The politician was worried, but he didn't show it as he conversed with his cabinet colleague. 'This Libya visit should go smoothly, shouldn't it?'

'Yeah. It's not as if DSS is doing this for the first time,' the other man chuckled. 'Everything's agreed with Sabbagh for the weapons deal?'

'Yes, all he needs to do is put pen to paper when we are there.'

'Great. I take it you'll announce you are running after that?'

'Funny,' the politician said, slyly, 'I was going to say that to you!'

He waited until he was in his vehicle and then fired a message to Spears.

Carter's threatened to come after me.

How do you know?

The politician sent him a terse reply and sat back, brooding.

I'll get our man there to find out what happened. Worth checking with our mutual friend. Didn't he tell you his people were supposed to take care of Carter?

The politician erased all messages and drew out another phone. This one was for communicating with Jian Hsu.

Our friend is still out there. I heard he's looking for us. Haven't your folks met him?

Chapter 59

───⊗⊗⊗───

Beijing

Jian Hsu looked at the politician's message. Didn't reply immediately.

Dante Abrahms had briefed him on what had gone down in Tripoli. Carter survived, and it looked like his friends had joined him. *They don't believe he betrayed them.*

It was the first time the South African had failed him. Hsu was disappointed but not angry. *Dante lost all his men.* That was a heavy price to pay.

Not all of them. One of them is alive.

He pondered that for a moment and then turned his attention back to Carter and his friends. They were more important.

The message they had sent back to the Agency, that the American was hunting whoever had set him up, was a smart move. *I would have done the same. Shake the trees and see what falls. See who makes a mistake.*

He looked out of his office at the city skyline. He shared his president's vision of making China the most powerful country in the world. Having some control over Libyan oil flow was a crucial piece in the jigsaw that would lead to that goal.

Carter. He seemed to have more than nine lives. Initially, Hsu had thought the man simply lucky. Was he, though? Or was he supremely competent?

The Chinese man shivered, even though the air-con wasn't turned to low. He rubbed the jade ring on his finger, an unconscious gesture to ward off bad luck, and then frowned impatiently.

Okay, so Carter was good. So what? What did this development mean to his plans? How should he proceed?

Hsu could leak the news to the American intelligence outfit. That Carter was now hooked up with his friends. That would certainly bring retribution on the Agency. Another kill meeting would be convened; this time, to issue termination orders on those operatives. Its director would face severe consequences.

Hsu smiled. There was justice in that.

But there was a risk. The Americans might wonder who was behind that intel. No other US outfit knew that the Agency operatives had gotten together. They might look again at the video evidence.

That by itself wouldn't lead anywhere. The MSS head had covered his tracks well. The men who had made those fake videos were dead. They were single, from distant provinces in the country, and there was no one who would miss them. Shaming Chia's last message to his CIA handler had been doctored to implicate Zeb. The Chinese double agent was dead, too.

We are in a good position. The Agency knows someone is behind all this, but they won't find out who.

Which brought Hsu back to the politician's message.

Should he tell him what really happened?

What if he panics?

The spymaster studied the problem, weighed his options and decided on his course of action.

Say nothing to the politician.

What about Spears and Marin? They had a good network in Libya. They would have heard of the shooting.

I'll tell them and instruct them not to let the politician know. Let him believe whatever's told to him officially. Getting the NOC deal is most critical. Nothing could come in the way of that, and worrying the politician would just complicate matters.

Our friend doesn't know where we are. We will surprise him. In any case, my people are due to meet him soon.

He sent the message and then sent an instruction to Dante Abrahms.

Follow Carter and his people. Take him out. Kill your survivor.

Chapter 60

Washington DC

Spears listened to the politician rant.

'When will someone kill Car—'

'No names,' he interrupted sharply. They were using burner phones and a secure channel, but still, protocols had to be observed. There couldn't be any lapses in security.

'Our man in the East,' the politician restrained himself, 'said his people will attend to the Tripoli man. Soon.'

'I agree with him. In any case, I think we need to look beyond this particular problem.'

'What do you mean?'

'Turn on your phone's camera.'

The politician appeared shortly on Spears's screen. The ShadowPoint executive took a sheet of paper, scribbled rapidly on it and held it up. He wasn't going to speak out loud what he had written.

Carter is posing as an arms dealer. That's how he intends to get to Almasi.

'Yeah, I am aware of that,' the politician replied impatiently.

He's got Javelins that he wants to sell to ISIL.

'Get to the point,' the politician growled.

What if Almasi knew where those missiles were? Without Carter's involvement?

'I am listening,' the politician said slowly.

You don't need to know anything more. I might have to talk to Hsu.

'Go ahead.' The politician's face brightened. 'Hope whatever you have in mind, works.'

'It will,' Spears replied and hung up.

The idea had come to him while he was listening to the politician's tirade.

It was brilliant, even if he said so himself.

Let Almasi know their location.

The terrorists would try to recover the missiles. *CIA teams and all those hunting Carter will be waiting for the traitor there. They should be, if they have any sense. Those locations are where Carter will head.*

Those teams would put down the terrorists, and that wouldn't be any loss. But that shootout would get back to Sabbagh, and that would make the Libyan government nervous. That the terrorists were actively seeking to arm themselves.

That will play into our hands. They will want the protection that ShadowPoint, through Saharol, can offer. They'll speed up the contract negotiations.

What if Almasi's people managed to get some Javelins?

Spears looked blindly out of a window, thinking furiously.

The terrorists could blow up anything, in that case. That would still make the case for the Saharol and NOC partnership. The politician's visit, that wouldn't be affected either. DSS would be on top of it once they knew ISIL had the missiles.

No, there was no downside to letting the terrorists have that information. But only one location. Not all of them. No point in giving Almasi more firepower.

We have to negotiate with him, too.

He turned his idea over in his mind again, looking for flaws. Found none.

Bob Marin could discreetly do the leaking. He had already made contact with the terrorists to request a meeting.

I am a genius. Randy Spears congratulated himself and went to open a sixteen-year-old Lagavulin.

Chapter 61

Tripoli

Bob Marin realized Nashaat Munjid Kanaan wasn't discussing anything of importance.

They were four hours into the negotiations and all that concerned the deputy finance minister was Saharol's contributions to various ministries. A few million to the Ministry of Economy and Industry. Another few to the Ministry of Education. A donation to this charity, a contribution to that institution which was dear to Sabbagh's heart.

When's he going to discuss NOC?

In fact, the proposed equity stake wasn't even in the draft contract that the minister had drawn up and given to him.

What was in front of him was nothing but bland text for *Enhanced Collaboration.*

He let his impatience show during a tea break.

'This isn't what I came for,' he hissed.

'Wait,' Kanaan smiled and patted him on the arm.

After another three hours of interminable discussions, the minister leaned back. 'I think we have something here, Mr.

Marin. I can present this to the cabinet and the Prime Minister. I am sure they will pass it.'

The Saharol man opened his mouth angrily to protest, but something in the Libyan's eyes warned him. He controlled himself.

Kanaan inspected the notes a flunky had made, corrected here and there, closed the file and handed it back. He nodded once and his team stood up. They collected their papers, thanked Marin and the minister, and trooped out.

'That was for show,' the Libyan official said when they were alone. 'This is what you wanted to negotiate?' He slid across a few sheets of paper.

Marin skimmed them swiftly and fist-pumped mentally. Yeah. This contract contained the meat of the discussions. Ten percent of NOC was what was being offered. That wouldn't do. He wanted more, but at least this was a start.

'This isn't enough,' he said bluntly. 'NOC cannot survive without Saharol's help. You have Kattan, ISIL, so many militia groups, all of them wanting a piece of your oil. We are the only company who can not only protect your assets but also market it worldwide.'

'We don't need your marketing help. Countries come to us to buy our oil.'

'All it takes is one sanction from the US government to stop that.'

'President Morgan would never do that,' Kanaan blustered. 'Libya is your ally in the fight against terrorism.'

'Ally?' Marin scoffed. 'Almasi is camped in Sirte. His people are attacking at will. Every day there's a suicide bomber. Some oil facility is destroyed. What fight are you talking about? Your government is incapable of taking him out. Don't you think President Morgan must be wondering what exactly your government is doing?'

'ISIL's not the only challenge we have,' the minister said defensively. 'Kattan—'

'And that's why'—Marin slapped his palm on the table for dramatic effect— 'you need us. Have you seen any Saharol facility attacked? No. That's because we know how to protect our assets. Are there any other foreign oil companies who have not been attacked? No. Very few of them are willing to invest in Libya for the long term, and those who are here aren't as security-conscious as we are.'

'The US will never impose sanctions on us. That would destabilize global oil prices. And why would your secretaries of state and defense plan to visit us, if you're planning that?'

Marin smiled silkily. 'I never said our government will impose tariffs or sanctions on Libya. What I meant was, there's a limit to what President Morgan will tolerate.'

'You don't speak for your government. You are a private corporation. Saharol isn't that powerful. You can't influence your president.'

'You think so?' the CEO said softly. 'Don't underestimate how much juice we have in the US government. Did you hear that senator's speech last week? Praising Prime Minister Sabbagh and his efforts to make Libya a peaceful, progressive country? Are you aware that same politician was bitterly opposed to your country? Have you noticed NOC's offices around the world are getting more enquiries in the last few months? Nothing has changed in your oil output or in the global supply. Other than our involvement with you.'

'Ten percent is enough,' Kanaan said.

Got him! Marin exulted internally. 'No, sir, it isn't. We're doing the heavy lifting here. We need an appropriate compensation in return.'

'Twelve percent.'

'Thirty.'

'Thirty?' the minister blanched. 'That will never get passed. That … no!' He made a move to snatch the contract back.

'Twenty-eight,' the CEO proposed.

'Twenty,' Kanaan countered.

'Let's meet in the middle. Let's go for twenty-five.'

'That's still too high. The prime minister, the cabinet, they won't—'

'We will give employment to all their adult children. In the US.'

The minister stared at him for a moment. 'We have other demands.'

'I expected those, sir. What are they?'

Kanaan looked around as if to confirm they were alone. 'If Kattan gains power,' he swallowed, 'the prime minister, all of us, will be in trouble.'

'I understand. I am sure our government will not let that happen. But in case that happens, Saharol will make sure you can escape to the US. Seek sanctuary there.'

'You can promise that?'

'Yes, sir. I told you. We are plugged into Washington DC. Tightly. But this offer isn't for all. We can't airlift the entire cabinet. It will be for you and your family, the prime minister's, and two more cabinet ministers. You can decide who they are.'

'We have other needs.'

He's talking about money. It always comes down to that.

'We'll take care of those, too, for yourself, the prime minister and the two ministers you suggest. We'll make payments into offshore bank accounts.'

'We have those.'

I bet you have. There's no politician in the Middle East who doesn't.

'We have more requirements,' Kanaan said and pulled out a list from his jacket.

Marin skimmed through the items swiftly. Admission to US universities for children. Purchases of second and third homes all over the world. None of those demands were unexpected. He, Spears, the politician and Hsu had anticipated them and had made budget provisions.

We'll use some of our slush funds as well as what MSS provides.

'We'll accommodate those,' he returned the list to the minister. 'I have a demand from our side.'

'What's that?'

'Your government will need to buy some arms from ours. An announcement will have to be made when the secretaries meet the prime minister.'

The politician had suggested proposing this. *I'm doing his job for him,* Marin snorted. *He'll make the grand announcement to the press, flanked by his cabinet colleague and Sabbagh. It will go down well Stateside. His media ratings will improve.*

The CEO didn't mind making the case, however. *It helps all of us.*

'Why should we buy arms from your country?' Kanaan asked, astonished, 'and why are *you* making this suggestion?'

'Sir, surely you don't think the secretaries are visiting Libya just to press flesh? They are demonstrating that your country is very much on our radar. In return, we want a show of faith. And, as to why, it's me who's proposing this.' He smiled enigmatically. 'That should give you a clue how plugged-in we are to DC.'

He waited while Kanaan browsed through the shopping list the politician had sent across.

'We are a poor country,' the minister protested. 'We can't afford these weapons.'

'You have cash reserves of several billions of dollars, sir. We are asking you to spend a fraction of that, for the security of Libya.'

'If we got all these weapons, why do we need Saharol?'

'The US government will not fly you out to our country in case Kattan topples you. They will not find the best universities for your children, sir. Those arms, they are just a small gesture of your commitment, sir.'

'I will have to run this past the cabinet.'

'I understand, sir. On the NOC ...'

'I will come back to you on that, too.'

'We need to seal this quickly, sir. My sources tell me ISIL is preparing for something big.'

Marin didn't know if that was true, but it was a safe bet that the terrorists were always looking to attack.

The minister nodded, his head bent, crossing something out on a list, and when the CEO saw what he was doing, he knew the contract would be signed.

Nashaat Munjid Kanaan, the deputy minister of finance, was making sure all his demands had been agreed to.

'We've got Sabbagh too,' he exclaimed into his phone, the

moment he was in the privacy of his vehicle.

Spears congratulated him, asked for details and listened to Marin's briefing.

'You think we can nail this by the time the secretaries visit?'

'When's that happening? I've heard talk on the TV channels but no date has been agreed, has it?'

'In about a week. Sooner, if you can wrap this up. Our friend wants to have a glory meeting with you as well. Congratulating Saharol on being the largest American company committed to Libya. Lots of photographs, media interviews, you know how those go.'

'The next negotiation will be the most difficult. And dangerous.'

'I am aware of that. Speaking of that one, you need to do one more thing.'

'What?'

'You need to let them know where one lot of missiles is.'

Chapter 62

—oooo—

'We need to recover the rest of the missiles,' Zeb told his friends when they rejoined him several hours later.

They had given their statements to the police, who had taken copies of their identification, had cross-checked those with the US embassy, and had finally let them go.

Luckily, there were no other eyewitnesses, and so their version of the story held. Just seven of them in the shootout, not eight.

The hotel manager backed them up. He told the police that Misfud had been a guest at the hotel, but his room was now empty. Yes, he was aware of the police circulars. No, he didn't make the connection to his guest.

He made no mention of the seven American operatives entering the hotel the previous night, nor that they had spent time in Misfud's room.

Money talked. Or rather, a lot of it, in greenbacks, bought silence.

In any case, Libyans had a healthy mistrust for the police and feared terrorists more. The manager was happy to take the bribe and keep his mouth shut.

The surviving shooter had been taken to the nearest hospital. The EMS crew said he couldn't talk; he might not even survive.

'You need to have protection for him,' Meghan had warned the police. 'We don't know who he is. Someone might want to kill him before he speaks.'

They had looked at her speculatively, assessed her friends, and then the most senior officer had ordered an around-the-clock watch at the hospital.

'Let's get Bear and Chloe to the airport, first,' Meghan replied.

Bwana took the wheel and drove them to Mitiga. All of them alert, eyes ceaselessly checking the mirrors and side windows.

'I briefed Clare,' Zeb broke the silence. 'Told her what had gone down. She's going to let the president know that I escaped. And that I am hunting whoever is responsible.'

He grinned when heads turned to him in surprise and explained his idea.

'It might work. Mystery Person might just make a mistake,' Beth said.

'Or, maybe not,' Meghan replied, doubtfully. 'It's not as if they have goofed up so far.'

'She's going to send Frank Ibarra's details to you.'

Beth fumbled for her phone, squinted at it and fist-pumped at a message.

'Yeah.'

'Werner's running facial recognition on those killers,' she said. 'So far, nothing, which could mean none of them are from any outfit back home. Or from a military contractor.'

'If we strike out, we'll send those to Mossad, MI6, BND and DGSE,' her sister added.

'What about the previous attackers?' Chloe stretched her legs in the cramped space. 'Any luck on them?'

'The CIA shooters,' Meghan replied, 'we identified those easily. The attack in the fruit market, those were Germans. Appointed by an outfit back home.' She mentioned a name. 'Werner hasn't had any luck with all the other shooters.'

'They must be in some DoD files,' Bear said, frowning, 'if they were US military. Most American mercenaries have served in our forces at some point.'

'They aren't,' the elder twin snapped. 'We checked. Which means—'

'Werner's looking into the various international outfits it's hooked into. Zeb, did they say anything? Speak in any language?'

'Nope.' He shook his head. 'Not that I was paying much attention. I was trying to escape.'

He held his hand up when the sisters mock-laughed at his lame joke and turned to Bear and Chloe as the Range Rover turned into the airport.

'Be careful,' he warned. 'Ibarra might have watchers.'

'Yeah, I'm hoping for that. I want to hit back.' Bear fist-bumped him, waited for Chloe to hug the others, and the two of them disappeared into the lounge.

'The missiles?' Meghan asked when they were out of sight.

'Yes,' Zeb said. 'Let's get to them.'

Dante Abrahms watched them from the safety of his stolen car. He had decided to stick with the larger group of Agency operatives when Carter had escaped.

They'll meet up, once the police leave.

He was right.

Carter's friends drove to the parking lot and, as the South African watched, seemed to be briefing him on the police interrogation.

That van. Something's in it. It's riding low.

Then it came to him.

The missiles.

Does Carter intend to drive those around with him?

Abrahms wished he had his McMillan Tac-338 sniper rifle with him. *I could take out Carter right now.*

But his weapons were back in his hotel room in central Tripoli, securely hidden under the floorboards. All he had was his Smith and Wesson M&P 2, tucked into his jacket pocket, and some gear in his go-bag.

No, he wouldn't act hastily. That was why his team had been wiped out. Abrahms was an old hand at such missions. He would follow where Carter and his team were holed up. He would find what they planned to do, and only when he had a clear opportunity, an exfil route, would he make the kill.

Got to attend to Wikus, too.

He had no qualms about killing his own man. There were several missions in his past when he had done just that.

Dante Abrahms was one of the most successful killers in the world because he was a survivor. He hadn't needed Hsu to tell him to eliminate his injured team member. He would have done it regardless.

A loud laugh got his attention. The black man slapping the side of the Range Rover at a joke from the younger sister.

It was as if the shootout hadn't happened, the way they were standing around, talking, joking.

Not for long, he promised himself.

He huddled down when Carter looked his way, casually.

The South African's car, a Ford, was one of many anonymous-looking vehicles in the city parking lot. It looked like office workers and shoppers drove into the place, left their vehicle for a few hours or even the whole day, and went about their business before returning. Like a million other parking lots around the world.

He was sure the American hadn't spotted him. The former SSA assassin could lower his chi, become one with his surroundings so that another hunter didn't detect his presence.

At the far end was a food stall where an enterprising middle-aged man was serving street food and drinks.

Abrahms's heart leapt in his chest when the operatives looked towards the stall. The younger woman said something and led them to it. Taillights flashed on the van and the Range Rover as they locked the vehicles. The older sister, Meghan, flicked her hair back and said something to Carter, who looked quizzically at her and smiled.

Wikus would love to play with those two. His team member had twisted desires and indulged in them whenever there was opportunity and safety.

There was a trail of dead bodies, raped and mutilated women, in the countries Marx operated in.

Abrahms didn't interfere. His team was free to live their life the way they wanted it, as long as they didn't jeopardize a mission. Neither did he pass moral judgment. Heck, he killed people for a living. Who was he to play God?

In any case, Marx didn't have long to live. Not if Abrahms had any say in it.

He waited till the operatives were out of view, shielded by

a pickup truck. He palmed the GPS transponder that he had removed from his gear and exited his car.

Approached Carter's van, his cap pulled low over his head. Whistled tunelessly, as he walked, head down, free hand fiddling with his phone. Just another parking lot user.

There was open space between two vehicles, which gave him a clear view of the food stand. Carter was there, ahead, with his people.

Abrahms sidled around a truck, used its body to shield himself, ducked as he ran behind a Toyota, smiled absently at a couple who were arguing about how much they had spent shopping, and reached the rear of Carter's van.

Thin, transparent gloves over his palms. His prints weren't in any system, but Abrahms wasn't taking any risk. He hadn't lived this long by being reckless.

He fingered the bottom of the vehicle, checked that no one was watching him, crouched down. It took less than a minute for him to fasten the transponder to the base of the vehicle.

He rose and ambled back to his car. Ducked around that truck—just in time, as he saw Carter hurrying back from the corner of his eyes.

Did he see me?

He wished he had brought his gun with him. He broke into a trot as he used the cover of other vehicles to race back to his car. Climbed into it and grabbed his M&P and leaned towards the dash to play with the radio.

No Carter in sight … there, he was opening his van. Was he driving away? No, he reached for something, slipped it into his pocket, closed the door, locked the van, and went back to the food stand.

Abrahms went to an app on his cell phone. Grunted in

satisfaction when he saw the steady green dot on it.

He had eyes on the van as long as the transponder wasn't removed.

Why did Carter do that? He doesn't know about me.

Zeb saw the man filter between the vehicles, heading away from his van. He didn't pay any attention to him. His radar was quiet.

He opened the cab and caught hold of the phone that he had forgotten.

Turned back towards his friends when Broker yelled at him.

Later, much later, he would regret not inspecting his van.

Chapter 63

Langley

Frank Ibarra polished his spectacles, finger-combed his thinning hair, and inspected himself in the hallway mirror.

Dark suit, white shirt, red and blue tie, polished shoes. Yeah, he looked no different than the millions of accountants and bankers who were heading out to work that day.

Not that he was in any of those professions. He was a spy. *Not anymore.* He shut the door behind him, stood for a moment on his porch and bathed in the sunlight that was streaming through the leafy trees. He checked that he had locked his house, clicked his Toyota Camry open and got inside the vehicle with a grunt.

His briefcase went onto his passenger seat, his jacket to the rear. A quick glance in the mirror. No one in the driveway.

He backed out, the view of his house filling his windscreen. Four beds, three baths. A big house for a single man. He had been married once, had kids, but life in the CIA was rough on families. His wife had demanded a divorce, to which he had agreed. He hadn't cheated on Barbara, no sir. Not once in his twenty-three years of marriage had he even glanced lustfully at another woman. Nope, that hadn't been the reason for their separation.

She was alone, bringing up Shannon and Jamie. *It was hard on her, on the kids, too. I was away a lot. Was often posted in different countries. She was right to leave me.* He shook his head as he joined Rocky Run Road and began his morning commute to Langley.

Gainesville to the CIA headquarters in Langley was a forty-minute drive. Past the school to join the 619 W, go down that road where the cinema and his favorite grill was. Join the 66 and head east, follow the crush of other commuters.

He had been angry and bitter at that time, but not now. Heck, his kids were grown up. Shannon was studying English literature in NYU, while Jamie was working at a law firm. Barbara had married again, to a dentist. Dude was okay, and he treated her and the kids well.

Nope, the separation had been tough, but it had worked out. He didn't mind the maintenance payments. He was alone, dated rarely. What would he spend his money on?

He braked suddenly when taillights flared ahead. His brief-case slid across the seat and crashed to the floor. It reminded him of Shaming Chia. How that had turned out!

Ibarra had cultivated the MSS officer when he was posted in the US Embassy in Beijing. Chia handled vital military intelligence, massaged information on new research and development into easy-to-read language for his superiors. As a result of his position, he had access to highly classified information on the People's Liberation Army, weapons systems, prototype designs, troop movements, planned maneuvers.

He was a prime target for turning.

He started courting the man over a shared love of Chinese opera. It was at one showing in the Liyuan Theater that he had *bumped* into Chia and had spilled his drink on the man's suit.

That beginning had led to long dinners, boozy nights, philosophical discussions on politics and government.

'I wish I could live in America,' Chia had said once; it was the move Ibarra had been waiting for.

He never revealed he was CIA. He said he was a low-level officer at the embassy. A translator who often accompanied the ambassador and other US visitors.

I don't think he believed me, Ibarra reflected as he drove past a stalled vehicle, sounding his horn in disgust. *But he never asked and I never volunteered.*

It took several months more to land Shaming Chia, to turn him. Evenings of quiet dinners, suggestive questions, discreet conversations. Ibarra's heart had nearly burst when the Chinese man had finally asked, 'What will it take for me to move to the US?'

'Information,' he had replied. 'Something that will be valuable to my people.'

'You're asking me to be a spy? Betray my own people?'

'Do you see the line of people outside the US embassy? Why would my country treat you any different from the millions of people applying for migration? What's special about you?'

'What you're asking me to do is dangerous. I have a wife, a small girl.'

'I am not asking you do to anything,' Ibarra shrugged. 'You asked, I told you. In your position, you come across a lot of intelligence that can be useful to my people. That's all you've got to trade. Forget all this. Let's have a few more Tsingtaos.'

A month later, Chia slid an envelope across to Ibarra as they were having dinner after a show.

'What's in it?'

'Plans for our new nuclear submarine.'

The CIA officer stopped chewing. He looked around swiftly. No one seemed to be paying attention.

'Are you out of your mind?' he hissed angrily. 'You're passing me that information just like that? Do you know what will happen if you get caught?'

'Do you know what my life is like?' the Chinese man whispered, back. 'I do nothing every day. Just type reports and say "yes sir" to my bosses. I go home late at night. I leave for the office early in the morning. I have not taken my wife out for dinner for months, because she is working too. We don't have a life of our own. Sun Huan is seven years old. She sees me for a few hours on Sunday. That's all. Is this any life for us? In America we will be free.'

'My country isn't the paradise you think it is,' Ibarra replied. He had grown fond of the Chinese officer and wanted to help him, but he still had to play hard to get.

'Our lives will be better there than what we have here.'

'Chia, you need to think about this carefully. You need to know the risks. Your family—'

'I have thought about it. I know what I am doing. Can you help me?'

'I can't,' Ibarra demurred. 'I will have to see who can.'

'NO! If this goes any further, I want to deal only with you.'

Got him! The CIA officer kept a straight face as he pushed back the envelope.

'I will see what I can do, but we cannot meet like this anymore. You shouldn't give information like this. We will have to make arrangements. Be security conscious.'

They went low-tech. Messaging protocols that used search engines and keywords. Social media platforms that hid intel in innocuous posts. Designs that had to be pieced together from family photographs.

Ibarra returned to the US, but not before committing to Chia's extraction once specific information dump milestones had been reached.

And then, that last message. That he had been betrayed. I still don't know what happened.

The CIA officer thumped the wheel in anger and frustration. He knew Chia was dead. Jian Hsu must have tortured him and his family before killing them.

He blinked rapidly to prevent tears escaping. He had run many agents, but Chia, he was different. He had become a friend.

In his anger, he didn't notice the car following him.

Chapter 64

Ibarra returned home at 10 pm. He could have arrived earlier, but what was the point?

There was no one to greet him, no warm dinner waiting for him.

He tossed his jacket onto a couch, slipped off his shoes and went to his bedroom. He washed away his tiredness in a long shower and went to the kitchen.

A beer and a microwaved pasta in front of the TV was his dinner. He watched a ball game until he felt himself dozing. Got up with a grunt, tossed the dirty dishes into the sink and threw himself on the bed.

The urge to pee woke him up in the night. He stumbled to the bathroom, relieved himself and washed his hands. Returned to the bedroom when a faint sound caught his attention.

He hadn't turned off the TV?

He cursed himself and traipsed downstairs. Yeah, the flickering in the lounge, that was the TV. Some movie rerun.

He entered the room and stopped suddenly.

'We were wondering if you'd notice.' A petite woman glanced at him. She flicked channels on the remote until she came to a Western and made herself comfortable.

'What ... who are you?' Ibarra mumbled. Alertness flooded him. He was trained in self-defense. He had guns hidden in various rooms in the house. Why there was a woman under that ... and then he saw the large man.

He was big. Bearded. Inscrutable face. Had his feet up on that sofa, beneath which was Ibarra's Glock.

'You need to leave.' Ibarra projected anger. 'Whoever you are, go now. Otherwise I'll call the police.'

The large man got up so swiftly and smoothly that it caught the case officer by surprise.

'The only people who might be called are the paramedics,' he said.

With that, he picked Ibarra up by the scruff of his shirt as if he weighed nothing and flung him against the wall.

The CIA case officer howled as he crashed, back-first, on concrete and slid on the floor.

'MY SHOULDER!' he yelled, grimacing in agony as he clutched at the joint.

Not all of it was an act. One part of his brain was assessing how far it was to the couch, which had the gun. The savage, for there was no other way to describe him, leaned down and yanked him upright, sending a fresh burst of pain through Ibarra. *I can run around him. Dive, get my gun and turn on them.*

'You can't,' the woman replied as if he had spoken aloud. Something glinted in her hand. His Glock. 'Put him down,' she told her companion.

Beard shoved him onto the couch, which slid back a few inches under the impact. He went to the kitchen and returned with an ice pack. Threw it at Ibarra, who caught it clumsily and applied it to his shoulder.

'Can't I beat him up some more?' The look on Beard's face sent a shiver through the CIA officer. These two, whoever they were, had broken through his security as if it was nothing. They were supremely confident in themselves.

They were as good as the some of the agents in SOG that he had come across. Maybe better. Because who would assault a CIA officer unless they knew they could get away with it?

'Do you know who I am?' he warned through gritted teeth. 'You'd better leave. I promise I won't describe you to the cops.'

'Will you look at him?' Beard sniggered. 'He's got a dislocated shoulder. I haven't decided whether to knife him or shoot him, and yet he's offering an escape route.'

The woman went to the dining table and dragged over two chairs. She sat in one, close to Ibarra; Beard spun the other around, back to front, and dropped into it. It creaked beneath his weight but didn't give.

'Who are you?' Ibarra's voice cracked. He had been trained to withstand torture. He had gone through assessments for mental and physical fitness, weapons expertise, various other courses that the agency conducted for its agents. *Not one of them's been useful so far. There are those panic buttons. One's next to that coffee table, behind Beard.*

It was mounted in the floor, beneath the carpet. It had to be stomped on in a particular manner for it to work. An alarm would go off in Langley, which would send the cavalry.

'Disconnected,' the woman sighed. 'Please don't take us for amateurs. There's no rescue coming.'

'What do you want?' Ibarra asked. *I turned Chia, right under the noses of the MSS in Beijing. If I could survive that, I can live through this.* He crossed his fingers mentally. There was a lot of hope in that thought. Beard had already demon-strated what he was capable of. The woman, she'd moved just once to get the chairs, but Ibarra wasn't going to underesti-mate her. *She's just as lethal.*

'Shaming Chia,' she replied.

He jerked up so fast that his shoulder sent fiery pain through him in protest. He bit his lip to cut off a moan and struggled to sit upright on the couch.

'Who?'

'Oh, come off it, Ibarra,' she replied in disgust. 'We know all about you and him. Or, do you want Bear to work you over some more?'

Bear. Ibarra squinted at the large man, who was looking at him with a bored expression. *He looks like it.*

'I don't know what you're talking about.'

The large man backhanded him without rising from his chair. A casual blow that had enough force in it to send Ibarra sprawling to the floor.

He groaned, his head ringing. He spat blood and propped himself up with one hand. Tried to get onto the couch, gave up when his vision turned blurry. He swallowed and blinked back his tears.

'Are you Chinese?' he whispered hoarsely.

'Do we look Chinese?'

'Who are you, then? Which agency? Are you from OIG?'

The Office of Inspector General was an independent over-sight body that held the CIA accountable.

'Why would we be from them? Have you been doing something you shouldn't?'

'Why do you want to know about Chia?' Ibarra bit his lip the moment the words escaped him. With that question and his previous ones, he had verified that he knew of the Chinese agent.

'Ibarra,' the woman said sharply. 'We can play games all night and morning. They won't be the kinds you'll enjoy. We *will* break you and get what we want. You can make it easier by cooperating.'

'That's what every torturer says.'

'Your choice.'

Beard—Ibarra refused to refer to him by his name—rose at some gesture from her and approached the couch.

'Wait!' Ibarra cried. 'What do you want to know?'

If there was a chance he would live through this and continue seeing Shannon and Jamie, he would take it, and the CIA be damned.

'Who knew of Shaming Chia?'

Chapter 65

Tripoli

'You want me to reach out to ISIS?' Abrahms growled in his phone. It was a secure call that required iris and voice identification. 'Tell them about some missiles?'

'Yes,' Hsu replied, from the comfort of his Beijing office. 'One of my people could have done that, but he's busy.'

He didn't explain that Marin had pushed back at Spears's instruction. The CEO said he could not afford to be seen in the underground network he had cultivated.

He had a point. Negotiations were delicately poised. Almasi had yet to be reached out to. The secretaries' visit was being planned, various dates were being considered between DC and Tripoli. The visit would happen after ISIL had come on board at the promise of money and illegal supply of arms. That could mean the visit was still a week or ten days away. It would take that long to get all the moving parts into place.

Hsu had cursed Spears initially when he heard of the man's idea to let ISIL know of the missile location. Then, he had come around to it. It would be a gesture of good faith. It could make the terrorists more amenable to the negotiation. It would certainly spur Kanaan to move faster, get the contract approved by other cabinet ministers and the prime minister.

With Marin excusing himself from the location leak, Abrahms would have to do the deed. The South African didn't know of Saharol's involvement or anything about the conspiracy. He didn't need to, to carry out Hsu's orders.

'What of Carter?' the South African asked. No emotion in his voice. No sullen anger. He was a pro. If the MSS chief wanted him to do something else, he would do it. After all, he was being paid handsomely for it.

'You said you're tracking him, aren't you? You can take him out, after this job. All you need to do is go to that bar. Act drunk. Say you saw someone unloading something that looked like missiles, in that location.'

'Why would they believe me?'

'That bar is an intel gathering place for the terrorists. They'll be interested in that information. And if they question you …' Hsu smiled. 'I'm sure you can take of yourself.'

'I want Carter,' Abrahms said coldly, unmoved by the praise.

'I want him, too. Dead. But you can get back to him once you do this. It's not as if he's leaving Tripoli soon.'

Abrahms hung up after agreeing. He checked Carter's location. In a hotel. *They'll recover the missiles in the night. What if they go after the ones in Hsu's location?*

He shrugged his shoulders. It wasn't his problem.

Two hours later, he was leaning drunkenly against the wooden counter in a bar in Al Dahra. It was a seedy establishment. Barred doors on the outside, entry needing a coded knock and a password. The security was necessary because Libya was a dry state, but underground bars flourished for those who knew of their existence and could gain entry.

Dim lighting inside. The thick smell of alcohol inside. Uneven floor. A few tables. A counter behind which the bartender stood. No display of drinks on the wall. No glasses. No refreshments of any kind. Patrons asked for what was available, the bartender told them, reached beneath the counter, poured it into dirty glasses and served.

It wasn't a fancy establishment, but needs had to be met and, judging by the few men in the place, their needs were being very well met. All of them were on their way to being drunk.

'Missiles,' Abrahms mumbled in Arabic as he cut to the chase. He swayed as if intoxicated. 'Who would put missiles in that place?'

'What did you say?' the bartender, a swarthy, bearded man, asked him sharply.

'Nothing.' The South African backed away. He gazed morosely into his glass and signaled for a refill. 'Why there?' he asked himself.

'What're you talking about?'

'Mind your business,' he slurred, as he slipped, grabbed hold of the counter and righted himself.

He downed his drink and motioned for another. That went down his throat, too. He idly drew circles on the wooden surface, conscious that the bartender had sidled closer, trying to overhear his mutterings.

'Were they missiles? I could be wrong. But what else would be in that box?'

He shook his head heavily and blinked owlishly. 'One last

one,' he told the bartender. After downing it, he shuffled his way outside.

He went to a rear alley, unzipped and peed against a wall.

Heard the rushing feet. Zipped up hastily and turned back. Three men, faces covered by dark shemaghs, running towards him.

'What—' he cried and then fell back when they landed on him and began punching him.

He groaned and cried out in agony. Twisted and turned his body to take the blows. They were amateurs and he could take them out easily, but that wasn't the point.

'WHAT WERE YOU SAYING INSIDE?' one of them raged.

'What? Where?' he mumbled.

'IN THE BAR! ABOUT MISSILES!'

'I didn't say anything.' He yelped when a blow caught him on the face. Another in the belly made him double over.

'YOU SAW MISSILES.'

'I DIDN'T SEE ANYTHING,' he whined.

'THEN WHY DID YOU SAY THAT?'

'Don't hit me,' he blubbered.

'TELL US WHAT YOU SAW.'

'A BOX.' He yelled as he shoved back his attackers, but they pounced back. One man sat on his legs, another held his hands, the third sat on his chest. 'I HAVE SEEN THEM BEFORE. THEY HOLD MISSILES.'

'WHERE DID YOU SEE THIS?'

'In an oil company's place,' he said sullenly. 'On Al Shat Road. It's the only one there.' He winced when Chest Man raised his hand to strike. 'I'm telling you,' he said angrily. 'One man was dragging it inside, from a van. He didn't see me. I was sleeping under some debris. He went inside, came out and drove away.'

'Did you see his face?'

'No.'

'Was he alone?'

'Yes.'

'Was anyone else in that building?'

'Stray dogs.' And then he cried out when the man hit him. 'All those buildings are empty. No one lives there anymore. No one goes there. There can be unexploded bombs.'

'Why do you go there, then?'

'Because I have nowhere else to go.'

'How do you know it was a missile case?'

'I DON'T KNOW,' he yelled. He tried to sit up and was shoved back. 'I WAS A MANUAL LABORER HELPING OUT IN THE ARMY. I USED TO CARRY SUCH CRATES FOR THEM. I THOUGHT IT LOOKED LIKE SUCH A BOX.'

'Who are you?'

'Ilyaas Noor,' he said sullenly. 'I work in restaurants, hotels, anywhere. I clean toilets, wash dishes, wipe floors. I am homeless. WHO ARE YOU?' he asked in sudden anger.

They started hitting him, but this time, Abrahms had had enough. He had passed on what Hsu had instructed him to. He heaved suddenly, catching his attackers off-balance. A sharp elbow in one man's face, a knee to another's back, and they fell away.

He could kill them, but that wasn't the objective. He kicked them savagely and fled down the alley, hearing their curses recede.

I hope they were who I think they were and the information gets back.

Chapter 66

Virginia

'I've been through this a million times,' Ibarra said wearily. 'I've been through our internal investigations. We covered this ground thoroughly at the Company. I was questioned, my records checked, my phone, email, heck, my whole life was taken apart. I was even shadowed by other officers. And it wasn't just me. Everyone in my department was similarly checked. Bottom line, no one from the CIA gave up Chia.'

They were still in his living room. His body was throbbing from the beating it had received from Beard. The ice pack had long since melted. Sitting around them were empty bottles of water they had all drunk as the interrogation had progressed.

'Catlyn Feder and Brad Slaughter,' he continued. 'Those were the only two who knew. Slaughter had to know because he was my boss, the deputy director of operations. All of us who run high-level assets report to him. The intel feed goes only to him. No one else. Chia was so senior and his information was so valuable that Feder got into the loop too.'

'No one else?' the woman asked.

'No. How many times do I have to repeat myself? I know what you're trying to do, to see if I'll slip up. Have I, in these hours?'

Ibarra couldn't read the glance the two exchanged, but it looked like he was right. *I'm telling the truth. Why would I lie to these two?*

'Can we get some coffee?' he asked. 'I'd like to feel human. Unless you want to start on my nails,' he held his hands up to Beard.

Not that the giant needed to resort to those torture tactics. His size and wallops had been enough to get the CIA officer to talk.

Why do I get the feeling they aren't the bad guys?

Frank Ibarra was an excellent reader of people. A skill honed in various countries that he had grown to rely on.

It was clear the two intruders weren't just pros; they had an intimate relationship as well. It was also obvious they weren't there to kill him.

Maybe they're so good that they've fooled me and will leave me with a bullet between my eyes, he thought morosely as the two rose and went to the kitchen.

'Coffee's in the third drawer beneath the counter,' he shouted at them. 'I take it black. No sugar.'

He glanced at the door. At his cell phone and car keys that were on the table. Could he make it out?

'You can't,' the woman said loudly.

He jerked his head up in surprise. No, she was out of sight. How did she know what he was thinking?

If they're that good that they can sense my thoughts, I'll be dead before I take two steps.

He sagged back in his couch and closed his eyes in despair.

Opened them when he smelled his drink.

'Thanks,' he told the woman and wondered why he was saying that to someone who had broken into his house, roughed him up and threatened to kill him.

'Chia's last message didn't have any names?' she asked.

'Can we move on to something else?'

He shrank when Beard moved threateningly. 'NO! I SAID NO.'

The two looked at each other as if they knew what had been in that communication.

'His messages, your reports, are encrypted?' the man growled. 'No one else sees them but you and Slaughter?'

'No. Not even Feder. That's how we work, especially when it's a prized asset like Chia.'

'No one else could have known of him? Water-cooler gossip, a casual word to another officer? A team debrief?'

'No. We're the CIA, for chrissakes.' He dragged a palm over his face. It came away wet with sweat. He wiped it on the couch. 'We've been running agents for decades. You think we don't know how to contain information, especially this critical?'

'The debriefs with Feder, it was just the three of you?'

'Yeah.'

'In her office?'

'Yes.'

'How were they set up?'

'Doug arranged that.

'Doug?'

'Doug Belden,' he explained, sensing the sharp interest in them. 'An officer who's the EA, executive assistant, for the director and deputy directors. Shared resource—'

He stopped and straightened suddenly. 'I need to make a call.'

'Why?' the woman said tautly.

'Belden,' Ibarra blanched. 'He's like furniture. He's been there for so long, no one pays much attention to him.'

'What about him?'

'He served coffees several times.'

'He knew,' Beard said softly.

'Yes,' Ibarra said soberly. 'And while he'd have been investigated, too, it wouldn't have been as rigorous as mine.'

'Just because he was—'

'He was furniture,' Ibarra replied savagely. 'What could be more perfect than that?'

Chapter 67

———⦿⦿⦿———

Tripoli

The fourth crate was on Al Kurnish Road, on the beachfront.

Zeb had hidden it in a dump yard where rundown cars, broken furniture, household waste were thrown. There was no city-operated recycling or cleanup operation. The garbage piled up and emanated a stench, but the officials didn't do anything about it. They had more pressing matters, like trying to keep peace in the city.

The approach to the yard was a long dirt track through destroyed buildings. A few cars on the main street, but no vehicles in the alley. No pedestrians, either. The abandoned buildings had an ominous look; that, along with the smell, put off even the curious.

Zeb was with his team, the faint breeze carrying the smell and taste of the Mediterranean Sea.

They were a hundred yards out, huddled in a natural dip in the ground. Fully geared out, dark clothing, HKs, Glocks, body armor, the full works.

The Range Rover and the van were well behind them,

parked out of sight of passing traffic.

NVGs showed no presence of anyone. But the twins weren't that trusting of the binoculars. They launched a drone, Beth operating it, Meghan watching its feed.

The device was a stealth type made of composite material, painted with radar-observant pigment, all kinds of tech gear to nullify infrared and laser detection. Whisper-quiet engines that couldn't be heard even from a few feet away. Night vision, LiDAR, thermal imaging—the drone was fully equipped for clandestine surveillance.

The missiles were there, buried inside the hulk of a car. The GPS transponders on them gave a clear signal. However, the twins weren't interested in the Javelins.

They were looking out for other kill teams.

One pass. Bwana scratched his neck, the rasp of his nails loud in the night.

Another pass. Zeb leaned over Meghan's shoulder. Dimly lit screen showing the ground's topography, bushes, dips and hollows, nothing that indicated shooters.

'We're good,' he said.

She snapped her head at him. 'You're seeing what I'm seeing?'

'Yeah,' he asked, puzzled. 'Thermal's not spotted anyone.'

'There are eight men out there. Two snipers in those buildings, covering the approach from their side. They're the watchers, the early warning men. Look at this shadow,' she stabbed the screen. 'It's unnatural. Those two lines, those are his legs. There.' She pointed to another one. 'That's another shooter. These men are wearing custom combat suits. They cloak their heat sigs; that's why thermal isn't picking up anything. However, we've got Werner hooked to the feed, and it's analyzing every shadow.'

'This man,' she gestured to a vertical shadow in the dilapidated house to their right. 'That's a gunman. If you watch long enough, he moves occasionally. There's another one in the opposite house.'

'They've seen us?'

'Nope. Nothing about them says so. We are hidden, we have cover, and we are not on the track. If they have the same NVGs as ours, they'll be ineffective against our suits.'

'They're waiting for you,' she added.

'Good thing you didn't treat it like a walk in the garden.' Roger's teeth flashed in the dark. 'How do we handle this?'

'We'll cover you.' Beth kept the drone in a hanging pattern and drew out her HK. 'The four of you,' she said, smirking, 'you should be enough.'

'No killing,' Zeb warned. 'They might be from friendly agencies.'

'Friends don't send out kill teams,' Broker retorted.

'You know what I mean. I'll take the one on the right. Bwana, you take the left. Broker, Roger, you take the six others, but you move only when we have cleared out the snipers.'

The operatives nodded. If the shooters turned out to be from US or allied agencies, they would be captured. If they were anyone else, they would be interrogated.

'Aren't you forgetting something?' Beth smirked.

'What?'

'You're going to show yourself to them? We intend to let them go, right? After capturing them. Won't they recognize you and see you're with us?'

She shook her head sadly as she tossed him a balaclava mask. 'You're getting old, Zeb. We've got to do the thinking for you, as well.'

'We've got to send a message,' Bwana said grimly. 'If they're from a US agency, they need to back off.'

'Won't that give it away that Zeb's with us?'

'Not with what I have in mind.'

'No killing,' Zeb warned him.

'You sure do take the fun out of this,' his friend said morosely and disappeared in the dark.

Zeb suppressed a grin, pulled on the mask and went the opposite way. He took a circular route to go behind the building where the hostile was located.

They picked their spots well. If we had proceeded, we would be out in the open.

He breathed shallowly, moving with the wind, using every available contour in the ground to camouflage his movement.

We could ask them to surrender. We know where they are, and we could easily take them out.

But that could lead to a firefight, which wasn't what he was after. Knowing who they were was vital.

'STOP!' Meghan ordered in his earpiece.

He froze. Ahead was the shape of the building. Something dark in his path.

'That's a girder. Must have fallen from the building. You'll have to go around it.'

'Got it,' he murmured. 'How's Bwana doing?'

'You let us worry about him,' she said impatiently.

Zeb went closer to the shadow. It was a beam, lying unevenly on the ground. He pushed it lightly with his fingers. It moved. *Isn't firm on the ground. Can't risk climbing over it.*

He did what Meghan had ordered him to and entered the building through a cavernous opening. Blocks of concrete on the ground. Crumbing pillars. Moving slowly, directed by the elder sister's commands.

He froze at a sound in the distance. It sounded like a cough. Pictured what little he knew of the layout. Just a vast open space, with pillars in between. It had once been a block of apartments but now was just a concrete and steel skeleton.

'He hasn't heard you. Hasn't looked back. He's still watching the track.'

Zeb became the air. He moved lightly on his feet, pillar to pillar, heading to where the shooter was.

There, that shadow, looking carefully out of a jagged hole in the side of the building.

As darkly dressed as the Agency operatives, his hands cradling some kind of weapon. Barely moving, just his head minutely shifting.

Twelve or fifteen paces separating them.

Don't want to shoot him. Don't want to give him time to react or alert his crew.

Which meant Zeb had to go closer.

It must have been grit, loose pebbles on the ground, that gave him away.

Because the sniper stiffened suddenly.

Chapter 68

He's sensed me. Will he turn or will he warn his team?

The sniper started turning. A move so smooth this could be a ballet. A half-swivel of his body, simultaneous drop down to a knee, his weapon coming up to cover the source of the sound.

Zeb was no longer there.

He was airborne, thrusting off his feet, hands reaching out, a brief moment of time when he defied gravity.

Then he crashed into the hostile, hands connecting, blindly searching for his face, seeking and finding the wired earpiece, ripping it out and flinging it away, gasping when a sharp elbow found his throat, the blow blunted as he turned his head away just in time, kicking out savagely, wrestling with the shooter for control of the rifle.

Zeb fell off the sniper when the man reared and twisted.

Braced himself on his hands, pivoted his body around, his legs flying out, straight and hard. They caught the hostile in his chest, slamming into him with the force of a truck.

Momentum did its job. It sent the shooter back. His head slammed into the wall with a sharp crack. His body collapsed.

What the—

Zeb drew out his Glock, trained it on the man and got to his feet cautiously. *At this range, he can't miss if he lets loose with his rifle.*

The sniper offered no resistance when he kicked the weapon away.

Zeb crouched cautiously, well away from the man's reach.

Was he? Yeah, he was unconscious. *That blow against the wall must have taken him out.*

He secured the man quickly with plastic ties, taped his mouth, made sure he could breathe freely, and then began searching him.

No identity of any kind. The rifle turned out to be a Heckler and Koch G28. *Our Army uses them. Many special forces units and black-ops outfits, as well.*

The weapon gave no clue to the man's identity.

I can't wait for him to revive and ask him. My voice might give me away. He looked out in the darkness towards where the twins were, hoping his friends had had better luck.

Bwana's approach was easier than Zeb's.

The building the sniper was hiding in had more pillars. Blocks of concrete lying on the ground. Ample cover for the Agency operative as he moved stealthily, guided by Beth's whispered directions.

That element of surprise was in vain, however, when he snuck a fast look and caught the shooter looking right at him in the midst of a yawn.

The man froze in shock. His eyes bugged out. Not for long, however. Training and experience took over. His rifle came up. His mouth opened to shout, but only a grunt escaped him when Bwana tackled him, casually swatting the rifle away as if it was made of straw.

A brief exchange of punches, but he was no match for the operative's power and momentum. A few seconds later, he was on the floor, Bwana's forearm crushing his windpipe, a knife pricking his skin just beneath his right eye.

'How about some introductions?' the Agency operative smiled.

The sniper tried to shake him off.

'I'll go first. I'm from the Agency. You've heard of it?'

The man heaved with his knees, choked out a gasp and flailed limply when Bwana applied more pressure on his neck.

'Help me, man. Let's have a conversation here. You speak English? Arabic?'

The man's face turned dark in the dim light. He sucked lungfuls of air harshly when Bwana eased the pressure on him. He opened his mouth to yell. It turned into an agonized moan when the forearm crushed his throat again. He scrabbled on the floor, thrashed, made unintelligible noises, eyes wide in terror.

'Promise you won't yell?'

He nodded rapidly.

'Which outfit are you from?' Bwana asked when the man had drawn air inside him. 'I can do this all night, but I would rather not. At some point I'll run out of patience and this blade will rip into your face. Let's not get that far, shall we?'

'CIA!' the sniper croaked. 'We're from the CIA.'

'You're hunting Carter?'

The man nodded jerkily.

'You figured he would come here because of the missiles?'

Another nod.

'Funny, we thought the same way. Don't even think of that,' he warned the sniper when the man looked at his earpiece, which had fallen away in the fight. 'Your friends aren't coming to help. Let's say they've met overwhelming force.'

He slammed a fist into the man's jaw, stripped him of his weapons and secured him.

'Spread this message,' Bwana said silkily as the man looked at him blearily. 'Zeb Carter is our problem. We'll deal with him. Back off. If we come across you again, you won't live.'

'We're the CIA!'

'Yeah, and look where that's gotten you.' He taped the man's mouth roughly and vanished in the dark.

'I should be in Hollywood,' he told himself once he was away.

'Yeah,' Beth agreed snarkily, reminding him that he'd spoken aloud. 'You're a blockbuster all by yourself.'

Zeb stayed back with the twins while the remaining operatives recovered the Javelins and lugged the crate to the van. They had captured the rest of the CIA team and had delivered a similar message to Bwana's.

'Any problems?' he asked when Broker dusted his hands and climbed into the Rover.

'Nope. Let's see who we come across at the next location.'

Chapter 69

Dante Abrahms was nowhere near Zeb Carter.

He could have tracked the American after delivering his message to the terrorists, but he had a more urgent matter to attend to.

He had to kill Wikus Marx.

He had made several phone calls, bribed ambulance drivers and had finally located his man.

Alkhalil Hospital on Az Zawiyah Street. That's where the emergency services had taken the survivor.

No, the driver confirmed, the shooter hadn't talked. 'They're operating on him,' he said, swilling water in his mouth. He spat and looked at Abrahms. 'You're a relative?'

'In a manner of speaking.'

'What went down there, man? What's he involved in?'

'I've no idea.' The South African peeled several dollar bills, stuffed them in the driver's hands and left him.

He lingered around the front of the hospital, watching, waiting. The usual traffic in front of such a building. A steady stream of ambulances. Distressed relatives and friends. Weary doctors and nurses emerging.

That man over there, he was in a doctor's coat. Same build as Abrahms.

The SSA man followed the medic as he turned a corner, stepped behind a parked ambulance and lit a cigarette.

Abrahms scanned the alley. Parked vehicles. Some foot traffic, but there was cover.

He made a split-second decision.

'Got a light?' he asked, his hand reaching into his pocket.

The doctor nodded as he blew out a stream of smoke. He groped in his pocket and came out with a lighter.

Abrahms punched him in the throat and smashed his face on the wall behind. He caught the doctor as he sagged and laid him on the ground. Stripped him of his coat, his phone, his stethoscope, and rolled him under the ambulance.

He walked briskly out of the alley and entered the hospital. Snatched a pad from a gurney nearby and headed to the reception desk.

'I'm just starting my shift,' he told the attendant. 'Where's that patient? The one who was in a shootout near the Tripoli Paradise?'

The harried woman barely looked at him. She was juggling a phone cradled between her shoulder and neck, her fingers flying on her keyboard. There was a crush of visitors and patients through which Abrahms had shouldered his way.

'Fourth floor,' she told him, 'Intensive Care, Room 403.'

Abrahms thanked her and strode away to the nearest elevator. He changed his mind when he saw the stairs nearby. Elevators were enclosed spaces. They had cameras. There were chances a doctor or nurse in them would make out that his face didn't go with the name plate on his coat.

He climbed quickly, riffling through the pad, looking busy.

No one stopped him. Patients and visitors made way for him. The power of a doctor's coat.

Room 403 was in the middle of a hallway of intensive-care rooms. A row of seats on which family and friends waited. Doctors and nurses hurrying in and out of rooms.

Two cops on duty. *Not really,* he corrected himself. The officers were leaning against a wall, arms crossed, bored. Standing well away from Wikus's room, looking at nothing in particular.

A young nurse walked past them, and the sway of her hips caught their attention.

Abrahms went past 403, head down, eyes flicking rapidly to the left. Caught everything in a glance. Glass door, blinds up. His friend on the bed, various tubes through him, hooked to machines. Alone.

He went to the end of the hallway, clicked his tongue impatiently and spun on his heel.

The officers were ahead, to his left, not paying him any attention.

Abrahms swept past them and inside Wikus's room.

Some kind of machine with dials and graphs against a wall. Its mirrored surface gave him a good view of what was behind him. The policemen hadn't moved a muscle. They hadn't even looked up when he entered the room.

Abrahms checked his pad, checked the various machines, nodded knowingly. He bent over Wikus and felt his breath.

Came to a decision.

He went to the window and lowered the blinds.

Crunch time. Would the officers enter the room?

They didn't. They were laughing when he looked through the door. Some joke … no, they were commenting on the nurses, judging by the looks on their faces.

He lowered the blinds over the door, too.

Waited a beat.

No one approached the room

Went to the bed swiftly and slashed Wikus's throat with the knife he was carrying.

Forgive me, my friend. I'll make sure your family is provided for.

Sheets? There they were, in a closet.

He rolled them out and draped them over Wikus's body, right up to his neck. Looked around one last time.

He was wearing skin-tight transparent gloves. No danger of leaving prints behind. Blood was seeping out of his friend but hadn't stained the sheets yet.

From the door … yeah, Wikus looked like he was sleeping. Job done.

He exited the room. Dare he risk this next step?

He dared.

'You,' he addressed the police officers, who straightened at his authority. 'Make sure no one enters that room. He needs to recover. I'll instruct the nurses too.'

'Yes, sayyidi,' they nodded, and Dante Abrahms left the hospital after taking care of one loose end.

Next step, Carter.

Chapter 70

Langley, Washington DC

'What happened to you?' Catlyn Feder asked Frank Ibarra when he entered her office.

A routine briefing meeting with her and Brad Slaughter on another agent he was running in the director's office.

She stared at him as the deputy director made an astonished sound.

'I was attacked,' Ibarra began and broke off when Doug Belden entered the room, carrying a tray of coffee and cups.

'Attacked?' Feder asked sharply. 'When?'

'At night. A couple. They were in my house, beat me up when I woke up to go to the bathroom.'

Cups rattled when Belden looked at him sharply.

'What did they want?' Slaughter winced as he studied the bruises on Ibarra's face.

'They said they were from the Agency.'

'The Agency?' he and Slaughter chorused in surprise.

'They were asking who knew about Shaming Chia.'

Belden muttered a curse as he spilled coffee on the table.

389

He apologized swiftly, cleaned up and picked the tray.

'Anything else, ma'am?'

'No, Doug,' Feder replied absently, 'thanks.'

Ibarra launched into the night's events loudly, before Belden had left the room.

The EA panicked. This wasn't what he had signed up for. He rushed to the bathroom, washed his face and stared in the mirror, waiting for his trembling to start.

It had started innocuously.

It still is innocuous, he told himself angrily. *He comes and goes in this office all the time. He knows the director, the deputy director, everyone. He's got security clearances. I wasn't leaking state secrets by telling him about Shaming Chia. I wasn't paid.*

That European vacation cruise that had been paid for, or the car rental agency that provided him a SUV for free that time, or the numerous other occasions when a fancy meal had no bill attached. *Those are not rewards,* he told himself piously. *That's him showing how grateful he is.*

Belden had been questioned during the security sweep after the Chinese agent's last message. The EA answered less than truthfully when he said he hadn't heard of Chia, but had been honest in saying, no, he hadn't leaked any classified intel to anyone.

He's not anyone. Heck, he was with the director the day I was questioned.

Why's the Agency interested in him, then? What are they after? Way I heard, they're shutting down.

He wiped his face and dried his hands.

'Ma'am.' He knocked on Feder's door and thrust his head in. 'I've gotta leave early. I can feel a migraine coming along. I've printed those reports for you and will leave them in your outbox.'

'Of course, Doug. Take care of yourself.'

Belden concentrated on keeping his voice steady. He discreetly wiped his forehead, picked up his bag and rushed out of the office, down to the parking lot.

He brought out his phone … No! Not here. There were cameras in the lot.

They can't hear you, doofus.

No, he couldn't take the risk. He jammed his phone back in his pocket and drove out of the parking lot.

Drove into a gas station a mile away. Turned off the engine and brought out his phone.

'It's raining today,' he blurted when a woman answered. 'I didn't bring my umbrella.'

That was code for *I need to speak to the boss in a hurry.*

The woman didn't respond.

She's checking my voice print.

A click.

A man came on.

'Doug,' Randy Spears asked. 'What's the problem?'

Bear gave a hundred bill to Chloe, who pocketed it triumphantly.

'Don't bet against me next time,' she grinned.

'If he's the leak, he won't make any calls from inside,' she'd told Bear when the two of them had mounted watch outside the agency's staff exit. 'He'll make some excuse and leave.'

Bear had challenged her.

She was proven right when, after Ibarra messaged them

with what had transpired, Belden's car nosed out through the security barrier.

They followed him at a distance, and when he flashed his indicator, they followed him. Chloe climbed out, filled up while Bear pressed his phone to his ear, turned his head cautiously and fired several photographs of Belden. The EA was hunched in his vehicle, his mouth working, as he spoke on his phone.

'He could've left the office for any number of reasons,' he said defensively.

'Ibarra said he left because of a headache. Does that look like a man in deep pain?'

Bear shook his head. Nope, judging by the way Belden was waving his hand and seemed to be shouting, he seemed to be angry rather than in agony.

'Werner didn't find anything on him. Mortgage, school-going kids, house, car, lifestyle very much within his means. No unexplained payments coming in. No signs that he's got any offshore accounts … we follow him?' he asked when the EA's headlights came on and his vehicle started rolling.

'Yeah.'

'We keep on him?'

'Yeah. If he's the one, there's only one way this will end.'

Someone will try to have him killed, Bear thought as he floored it and fell behind the EA.

And we'll be there, waiting for that hit team.

Catlyn Feder's hand reached for her phone several times, and on every occasion, she drew it back.

She knew she had to make that call but wasn't sure she was ready for it.

The news from Tripoli and Ibarra's disclosure had unsettled her.

Does Clare know?

Of course, she knows, she answered herself. *She's on top of everything.*

If she was, how did she not know Carter was a traitor?

And that, right there, was what was troubling her.

She had met the Agency director several times and, on every occasion, had come away feeling there was mutual respect between the two of them. As women, both had navigated the male-dominated intelligence world and achieved rarefied success.

We could have been friends. We could have had each other's backs. But they were often on opposite sides, rival agencies. *She's answerable to no one but the president. I have to report to Mike, whereas she goes in and out of the White House as if that's where she works. She probably does.* She jabbed her pen on paper.

You're just envious.

That made her sit back and recap the pen.

I probably am, she thought, smiling ruefully.

And what of her own doubts about Carter? She hadn't met him but had read his psych evals several times. None of those indicated he could have betrayed his country. Then, there were the Pentagon top brass. Generals, senior officers, who praised Carter.

They went quiet when they heard what he had done.

She firmed her shoulders. *It's not my job to prove his innocence. That horse has left. That kill order is taken. All I need to know is whether Clare knows what her operatives are up to.*

'Clare, it's me, Catlyn,' she said when the Agency head

answered her call.

'Let me guess,' came the reply. No 'hello, how are you'; straight to the point. 'You heard about Tripoli.'

'That your agents captured mine and told them to back off?' Feder said heatedly. 'Yeah. They're obstructing a kill order.'

'Obstructing? All they did was ask your people to back off. Carter is our problem. We'll take care of him.'

'By letting him escape?'

'Catlyn,' Clare said coldly, 'I'll forget you said that. I signed on to that kill order just as you did, just like we all did to many others. What you're insinuating—'

'Carter killed several of my officers.'

'I am aware of that.'

'Then, why did your people stop mine?'

'If the roles were reversed, would you put out your own fire or leave it to others?'

She's got a point. But Feder wasn't going to give in, not so easily.

'Are you aware,' she asked angrily, 'that a couple of your agents attacked one of my officers? Here, in the US, at his home!'

'Yes.'

'What's that about?' she yelled.

'You know I'm retiring?'

'I heard something like that,' she replied stiffly.

'And that the Agency's shutting down?'

'Yes.'

'Well, I want to be sure we made the right decision. That—'

'You want to revoke the kill order?'

'Did anyone find out how Chia's identity got out?'

Feder closed her eyes and massaged her forehead. This call … why did Clare have to be so logical? Why did she have to rouse her own doubts? Couldn't she just go away gracefully and let Carter be dealt with?

'No, and you know that. Our investigation didn't reveal anything. And your people beating up mine isn't gonna help, either.'

'Doesn't hurt to ask, Catlyn. In a different way.' Her voice softened. 'We're on the same side. I don't want it on my conscience that Zeb was killed for no reason. Do you?'

'No, but neither can I forget Carter killed my people.'

'Zeb Carter is the deadliest operative I know. You know his record. You think he would be taken down just like that?'

'Heck, Clare, what do you want?'

'Me? Nothing. You're the one who called.'

'What do you want me to do about this … message your people delivered?'

'Back off.'

'You know I can't do that! That's not how a kill order works.'

'Catlyn, I'm sure I don't need to tell you how to look like you're progressing with an order while doing nothing about it.'

Clare smiled when Feder swore and slammed the phone down. She leaned back in her swivel chair and half-spun.

She'll do it. She'll tell her teams to discreetly hold off. That message will go to other outfits, too. That'll give my people more breathing room.

What of Feder herself, though?

Clare spun a paperweight on her table and watched it reflect light.

She's clean. I'll stake my career on that. But what about her people?

Her team would find out. And then there would be a reckoning.

Chapter 71

———— ഇ ————

Randy Spears hung up after reassuring Doug Belden.

He had suspected such a day might come but hadn't thought it would come this early.

I can go to the CIA, ask Feder if she knows what's going on.

He had the security clearances. ShadowPoint did a lot of work for the company, and he was always in and out of Langley.

He discarded the thought immediately. *No. She might wonder why I'm asking so soon after Ibarra's attack.*

He could, of course, circulate a rumor that Clare was acting beyond her remit.

But we're nearing the end, now. Marin's just got to meet Almasi, agree with him, get Kanaan to move the contract quickly through the government, and we're home.

No. Doug Belden was a weak link and he had to be taken care off. Spears had anticipated and planned for this. It wasn't a course of action that he wanted to take, but he had no choice.

He opened his desk drawer and selected a phone. Went through the thumbprint and voice recognition security setup when the other person answered.

'It's me,' he said. 'You and Chad are activated. Target's Doug Belden. Make it look like an accident. He's got health issues. I'm sure you can make it look like he died of a stroke or something like that. I'm sending you the package through the usual.'

'Got it,' Rick Beavis answered.

Rick and Chad are good. Mercenaries. Two of my best men. They were like his personal hitmen, his cleanup team when he wanted any mopping up to be done stateside. Someone had to be killed so that it looked like an accident, they were his men. A politician had to be threatened, a senator blackmailed, Beavis and Travers got the job done. Without fail.

He created an electronic, encrypted file of Belden's photographs, residence address and car plates and uploaded the package to an online fishing site. His team would download it from decrypt and get to work.

He rarely sanctioned hits this close to home, but this one time he had no other option. He knew who the Agency's operatives were, the ones who'd assaulted Ibarra. Bear and Chloe. As dangerous as Carter.

I could have them followed, see where they are, take them out. Locating them wouldn't be difficult, not with the resources he had.

No. Going after the Agency was too risky.

Drop it, he told himself. Belden would be taken care off. Focus on success.

Chapter 72

Tripoli

Zeb drove the van inside the yard that fronted the strip mall–like row of shops in Al Hany, on the outskirts of the city.

Hardware stores, paint shops, hand tools, metal working outfits, beyond the Sharia al Jalaa road. Some of them empty, because times were tough and not everyone could afford the rents.

Zeb drove to the one in the middle, which was shuttered and locked. Reversed and parked a couple of feet from the concrete walkway that ran down the length of the retail area.

'Can't see any guns,' Beth chirped in his ear.

'Yeah, I can't sense anything either,' he responded.

He had decided to retrieve the next set of Javelins in broad daylight. They'd had enough action the previous night.

He grinned suddenly, remembering the way Bwana had described delivering his *message.*

Clare said Feder would respect it. But will her teams do so? I've killed some of their friends. That's hard to forget.

He waited in the van, taking in everything. A young boy

running down the walkway, serving tea and coffee. Men in vests unloading a metal grill from another vehicle. An old man snoozing on a chair, swatting flies away occasionally.

He shrugged. CIA, other agencies and black-ops outfits— he and his team would deal with whoever turned up.

Chloe and Bear are on Belden. They'll watch him. The couple had briefed them on the Ibarra development, and then their boss had updated them on her call with Feder.

Something has to give. Someone has to crack. We're shaking the trees hard enough.

But his mission hadn't gone away, which was why he was in the yard.

His friends were somewhere behind him. Each one of them occupying vantage points, watching, having his back.

He adjusted a ghutrah around his neck so that it half-covered his face. It was dusty and windy, and several men were similarly attired, so his appearance wouldn't draw notice.

The boy spotted him through his windshield and lifted his kettle up, mouthing, 'Shai?' Tea?

Zeb shook his head and climbed out when the server scampered away.

He slammed his door shut and stretched and yawned, taking the opportunity to check his mirrors. No one creeping up on his six.

'Quit dawdling,' Beth ordered.

'You missed ordering me around, didn't you?'

'You betcha,' she chortled.

Zeb got on the walkway and strode to the shutter. Bent down, unlocked it and rolled it up, just enough for him to slide sideways inside. He rolled it down after him and hit the lights.

The air was musty and thick. Smelled stale. Cobwebs in the

ceiling and on the walls. Thick layer of dust underneath. From outside, voices and sounds from the other establishments.

Thick iron sheets against the wall. Heavy-duty drill in one corner. Metal working table on which were clamps, vices and various tools. Power cords dangling from the roof, at the end of which were lights. A lathe.

Zeb had bought the shop cheap and shuttered it up immediately. He moved various pieces of works-in-progress and went to the back. To the table, beneath which were several cases of tools. Shoved them to the side and there, snug against the wall, was the missile crate.

He pulled it forward, grunting from the weight, and once it was clear from its hiding place popped it open. Four Javelins inside, capable of death and destruction.

'They're here,' he called out.

'You need any help with loading?' Bwana asked.

'Nope.'

Half an hour later of pushing, shoving and swearing, the crate, Faraday-caged, had joined the four others in the van. Zeb wiped his brow and patted his hands dry on his trousers.

'Sayyidi?' the *shai* boy came running up.

'Alright,' he relented, 'I'll have one.'

He lifted the tea glass in a silent toast to his friends, who he knew were watching, and sipped gratefully. The hot beverage had just the right amount of sweet and spice in it. It refreshed him. He tipped the server generously and watched him skip away.

'Move your ass, Zeb,' Beth said impatiently. 'We've got to retrieve the last one.'

'Not now,' he shook his head.

'What? Why not?' a chorus of protests in his earpieces.

He got into the van without replying and started it. Rolled

it out when Meghan spoke.

'You want to go at night,' she said. 'You want to see who else attacks us.'

'Yeah. We need to flush out the *friendlies* as well as the hostiles.'

'They're all hostile.'

'You know what I mean.'

Langley, Washington DC

Beavis and Travers shared an apartment in Foggy Bottom. Both had been in Delta, where they had come across Spears. They had served in Afghanistan, where they had developed into two of the best killers the US military ever had.

However, the men had a weakness for women. Young women. It was in a dusty village several clicks from Bagram that they had been caught with their pants down. Literally. Raping a girl.

Action had been swift.

A dishonorable discharge, a prompt flight back to the States and civilian life. Spears's intervention had saved them from a court martial and time in Leavenworth.

The ShadowPoint CEO had come calling once he had established his firm and appointed the two men. Off the books, paid offshore, paid generously, which had enabled them to live close to the heart of the city.

Travers shaved while Beavis read through the package. 'He's a spook,' he called out. 'In Langley.'

'We've never killed one of those.'

'We shouldn't?'

'You know that's not what I meant.' Travis washed his face, toweled it dry, joined Beavis and read over his shoulder. 'Huh! He's not a spook,' he said in disgust. 'He's a secretary. Why does Spears want him dead?'

'Ours is not to ask—'

'Yeah, yeah. Got his home address?'

'It's right there. In Herndon. Half an hour from here.'

'Let's get moving.'

Doug Belden kissed his wife, Martine, and Louise, his daughter, and went out to his car.

He hadn't slept well. Had woken up several times in the night and finally gone to the spare bedroom, where he had tossed and turned fitfully.

Ibarra's comments, his call with Spears, ate at him.

He knew what the consequences would be if it was found he'd leaked confidential information.

Yeah, leaked, he finally admitted to himself in the dark of the night.

He would go to prison. His family destroyed. He would see them rarely. *Martine might divorce me,* he shuddered. His wife was a strong-willed woman who had no time for traitors and liars. She would leave him, taking Louise with her. He was sure of that.

Then, what am I left with?

He had let none of that show on his face in the morning. He joined his family for breakfast. Laughed and joked with them and then left for Langley.

He was ten minutes into his drive when he decided he needed time off. He had to work through this. He called his office and left a message that he wasn't feeling well.

Joined the Leesburg Pike and headed to Tysons.

'He hasn't come to work.' Travers hung up.

Beavis was driving them to Langley in his Subaru. Both of them armed with throwaway guns. They hadn't decided how to dispose of Belden. They would figure that out when they got to him.

During the ride, Travers had gotten the idea of calling ahead and finding out if the EA had arrived at Langley.

Beavis swerved into an overlook and parked behind an RV. A family had put out a picnic table and were snacking at it. Parents, two kids, a boy and a girl, who, from the looks of it, were arguing.

'Randy,' Travers called their boss. 'Belden didn't go to work. Can you find out where he's at?'

They waited. Knew that Spears could locate modern cars fitted with LoJack. The men consumed their paper-wrapped burgers and swilled a bottle of water. Made idle talk as they looked out of the windows.

It was sunny. The George Washington Memorial Parkway was a scenic drive along the Potomac. A great day to be alive.

Or to kill someone.

Chapter 73

Tripoli

'Misfud's taking too long,' Almasi told Abu Bakhtar.

'Gathering the missiles in one place takes time, sayyidi.'

The terrorist leader turned on the TV, muted it and watched a news report on the imminent visit of the US secretary of state and secretary of defense.

'What about that location?'

'The one that drunk said in that bar?'

'Yes.'

'He's a drunk, sayyidi,' Abu Bakhtar scoffed. 'We should not rely on such information.'

'But what if he's right?' The leader's glasses glinted in the light as he turned towards his second in command.

'Sayyidi—' the deputy waved his hands helplessly. 'If we acted on every such—'

'Send someone. Tonight.

'But—'

'Someone junior. Someone who is expendable.'

'You think this might be a trap?'

'I am not thinking anything other than there *might* be some missiles out there. If Misfud is taking his time, this is worth exploring.'

'I can send Firas Siddiq. He has four men with him. He joined us in Syria. He doesn't know much, even if he's captured. He's brave. He will follow orders. I've heard he's desperate to prove himself.'

'Do that. And call Misfud, also. Tell him we need these missiles urgently.'

Abu Bakhtar licked his lips nervously as the TV host droned on about the US dignitaries' visit. 'Sayyidi, are we going to … use those missiles on them?' He jerked his head towards the screen.

'What do you think?'

'It would be a great win for us. If we got the missiles in time and were able to get more intel on the meetings.'

'You don't sound very enthusiastic, Abu Bakhtar.'

'Sayyidi,' the deputy whispered, 'the Americans will wipe us out if we do that. They haven't bothered attacking us here because they don't see us as much of a threat. Not as large as before. But if we attack those officials—'

'Are you scared of dying?' Almasi's eyes were black pinpoints of light, nothing decipherable in them as he came up close to his deputy.

'Sayyidi, I would have run away like a coward, if I was. I am thinking of the long term—'

'You think I am not?'

Abu Bakhtar started sweating. The ISIL leader's fits of rage were well known. What he did during those bursts of anger to those he wanted to punish scared even the most hardened of them. Almasi had no favorites. He showed no liking for anyone. His deputy was in that role because he was the most capable, not because the two of them had history.

'Every step you take is well-thought, sayyidi,' Abu Bakhtar stammered.

'Relax.' The leader gave a small smile and patted him on the shoulder. 'We'll use the Javelins on the Libyan government and on NOC. To capture oilfields and territory. But it doesn't hurt for the outside world to think we might attack the Americans.'

'Sayyidi, you're several heads ahead of us in your thinking.' Abu Bakhtar bobbed his head in relief.

'Enough talking, bring Siddiq in.'

Firas Siddiq wasn't the smartest man. He knew that. He knew the other ISIL killers knew it. So, when he was led into a room and told about his mission, he was ecstatic.

He had seen Abu Bakhtar before, but only from a distance. Siddiq knew what a privilege it was to see him up close. And that other man with his back to them ... his knees almost gave out. That was the leader, Nasir Fakhir Almasi!

His heart thumping with excitement, he tried to control his trembling.

'You know what you have to do?'

'Yes, yes, sayyidi,' he cried. 'Go to that place on Al Shat, recover a box if it's there.'

'And if enemies are there?'

'Come back immediately.'

'Don't start shooting. Fall back in the night and leave immediately.'

'Yes, sayyidi.'

'If you succeed, you will be rewarded. If you fail ...'

'I won't fail, sayyidi,' Siddiq said resolutely.

He was turned and guided out of the room. As he was leaving, he heard Abu Bakhtar say something to Almasi. He caught one name and his heart leaped.

Saharol? They were providing the missiles?

Firas Siddiq wasn't the brightest bulb in the room. Hence, when he heard *Saharol* he thought, *they are giving us the missiles?*

He didn't stop to think that perhaps he had missed out on the rest of the conversation. If he had, events might have turned differently.

Chapter 74

⸺⚬⚭⚬⸺

Langley, Washington DC

Doug Belden paused to mop his face and pocket the cash he had withdrawn from an ATM.

Fletcher Street, Tysons. He was in the parking lot of a bank, heading back to his car. Some retail therapy was in order, hence the load of bills filling his wallet. Shoe shopping, followed by a medium-rare steak. Never failed to help him with his worries.

'Sir, you dropped something.'

Belden turned around to see a man approaching him, holding a wallet. He patted his back pocket. The heavy bulge was there.

'Not mine—'

He didn't get any further, because the man was on top of him, shoving him against his car.

'What—' Belden began, and then a rough palm clamped on his mouth. Another man appeared. Dug into his pocket and unlocked his car.

They were on him so swiftly that it took several moments

for him to work out that he was being attacked, in broad daylight, less than an hour away from Langley or his home.

Spears! He must have sent them.

Comprehension came too late. By then, he was jammed against the car by the two men, who smothered him and rendered his resistance, his kicks and punches, ineffective.

First Man applied pressure, so much force that he whimpered and bit the hand over his mouth, but it didn't move. Belden was pushed unwillingly inside his vehicle and settled awkwardly on his seat.

His eyes wide with panic, he tried to headbutt the man, tried to sound the horn with his chest, but rough hands pulled him back. A forearm jammed against his throat and started squeezing.

He struggled to breathe. He started hyperventilating. His legs kicked ineffectively.

Two pairs of eyes looked down at him, First Man and Second, both impassive.

I'm going to die. The thought clamored in his mind, trying to force his body to escape, get his mouth to signal for help.

His vision started to fade. His grunts grew weaker.

'Please …' he tried to say, against the hand over his mouth. With the last of his strength, he tried to shake himself free from the three men.

Three? There had only been two. Whose was that third head that came from behind?

First Man disappeared, as if he'd been sucked away by a giant vacuum. Second Man turned away, but by then Belden had fallen forward, on the wheel from the sudden loss of pressure, gasping and wheezing as his body drew much-needed air inside.

Bear and Chloe were a few moments late. They had been following Belden ever since he left his home. They had tailed him as he changed his mind and headed to Tysons.

A red light had held them up, and by the time they had turned in to the bank's parking lot, the two men were on top of Belden.

From a distance, it looked like the men were leaning over the EA's vehicle, talking to him. One of them leaning against the side, blocking a frontal view, the other covering side vision.

Knock him out quickly. Make it look like he's fainted. Drive him away, where he can be killed.

Bear and Chloe had worked so long together, having been in a relationship for a significant part of that time, that they both knew the other had arrived at the same conclusion.

Bear lunged out of the moving vehicle.

He gave no warning, which might draw weapons.

One man started turning even as he neared.

That didn't matter. Momentum and body size worked in his favor as he grabbed the nearest thug, wrenched him back from Belden easily and smashed his face on the hood.

The second man's hand streaked to his belt. He drew. Something dull and black appeared in his hand.

And then he was falling, cursing and swearing, as Chloe charged into him, punched him in the throat and wrestled the gun away.

Beavis and Travers were no dummies. The former reared back from the vehicle and elbow-punched Bear. The latter grabbed Chloe by her hair and attempted to shoot her.

Momentum and body size.

Bear used his large frame to give Beavis no room. He

absorbed the man's blows. Kept inching closer and closer until the shooter was bent over the hood, flailing, and with a contemptuous punch, knocked him out.

Chloe was smaller than Travis. But faster and no less strong.

She ignored the hair yank. Grabbed his wrist, forced the gun down, jammed her finger over his, and emptied the gun rapidly into concrete.

Someone screamed. A man yelled. She didn't look up. She hooked her leg behind, curled it around the attacker's leg. A twist and a heave, and Travis went tumbling over her shoulder.

She didn't let go of his arm. Instead, twisted it viciously and dislocated his shoulder. Staggered back when the attacker flailed wildly and caught her belly with a kick. And then he was on top of her, eyes grim, teeth gritted, as he headbutted her against Belden's vehicle and with his free hand drew a blade, which she trapped between both hands. She twisted her body away just in time for the knife to skitter against the car's roof, but the attacker groaned, forced his injured arm up and elbowed her in the neck, and when she gasped in agony, took a step back, which enabled him to free his knife arm and come at her wickedly. She was anticipating that. A block and a chop to turn the knife away. A vise-like clamp on the wrist. A pivot so that her back was against his chest, her hands guiding his blade.

She brought it down towards herself, still pivoting, still twisting, a few inches of space between her left shoulder and his.

That was the clearance she wanted.

The blade sank deep inside his chest. He yelled and attempted to free himself, but she thrust back, her feet holding on concrete, wedging his body between hers and the car. Despite his furious attempts, despite his body heaves and bites and kicks, she held him there until he faded.

'That's a new move,' Bear said, helping her upright. Swiftly noted the bleeding from her nose. Didn't make any more comments.

There was a gaggle of onlookers. Several people on their phones. They had to get away.

He hauled the man he had taken down and dragged him to their vehicle. Dumped him in the rear seat. Cursed when he checked the man and felt no pulse. Climbed behind the wheel and took off.

In the mirror, he saw Chloe follow, after she had shoved her attacker in the back and pushed Belden away to the passenger side.

They drove out swiftly, heads down.

'We need phones to be jammed,' he called Clare the moment he joined the street. 'A few people saw us, must have recorded us. They might have called the cops.'

'Give me a few minutes,' she replied. 'Head to our safe house.'

The safe house was in Reston. A cottage on Pony Lane, in the woods, secluded, secure.

'We'll be there in twenty.'

He hung up and dialed Chloe.

'We wanted one of them alive,' she said as soon as the call connected. 'You broke his neck, didn't you?'

'I can't help it if I am big and strong,' he said defensively.

'Bear,' she sighed, but there was a smile in her voice.

'How's Belden?'

'In shock. Frozen in his seat.'

'Probably thinking we're going to kill him, too.'
'Probably. We're going to the safe house?'
'Yeah.'
'He'll talk there.'

Chapter 75

—⊙≈⊙—

The temporary outage of the phone network was the easier job. All Clare had to do was make a few calls to select CEOs, invoke national security, and offer to patch them to the president if they wished more reassurance.

The executives fell in line.

But that won't help with the recordings any onlookers might have made. Who might post them on social media, later.

Besides, there was the matter of Belden. Whoever had sent his killers would be waiting for an update.

'Tony,' she said when a man answered her next call. 'I need a story to be published.'

The editor of DC's most prominent newspaper knew her as the director of strategy at the White House. There was no protocol she followed in such calls. Sometimes she called in favors, other times, she used the power of her office.

'It needs to go out immediately.' She briefed him on the story. 'Right now. On your online edition, followed by a detailed writeup in the print version.'

'Of course, it's true,' she replied.

True to the version I want out there.

She made more calls to other editors, got all of them onboard.

The next number she dialed was that of Fairfax County Chief of Police Brian Scheener.

'Brian,' she introduced herself, 'this is Clare, director of strategy at the White House. You can crosscheck my credentials at the following numbers,' she recited a string of them and waited for him to note them down. 'That incident in Tysons,' she continued, 'it should be recorded in a certain way. Yeah, I know what I'm asking. There's a national security reason for that, Brian,' she said softly, when the chief protested. 'I am not asking here.' A few more threats, softened by the promise of favors, and Scheener succumbed.

She made one last call.

'Beth,' she asked, glancing at her watch. Ten pm in Tripoli. 'Are you awake?'

'Yes, ma'am.'

'Meg's there.'

'Yeah,' the older twin joined in.

'I want Werner's bots to be activated. Spread a story on social media.'

They had learned from their enemies—Russian, Chinese, Iranian agencies—who used bots to spread fake news. Taking that cue, the twins had programmed their AI to manufacture its bots. To be used tactically during missions.

'Ma'am,' both twins began when she had finished. 'What—'

'Not now. Let me get this under control and then I'll get back. Yeah, Bear and Chloe are fine. Belden too.'

All in a day's work, she thought as she brought up Chloe's number.

'Question him,' she told her operative.

Chapter 76

Tripoli

'Belden's with Chloe and Bear,' Beth announced when she hung up. 'Two men attacked him. Both dead.'

'He talking?' Zeb asked

'Not yet. They're in the safe house.'

He nodded absently, aware of the time.

Another half hour, then we'll roll.

A video on Meghan's screen caught his attention.

'What's that?'

'You remember the shooter who survived?'

'Tripoli Paradise attack,' Beth reminded him.

'Yeah, him.' His brow cleared. 'We need to question him. Is he conscious?'

'He's dead,' Meghan said bluntly. 'Yesterday night. Killed.'

Zeb rocked back on his heels. The other operatives gathered around him. All of them stunned at the news.

'The hospital updated its records recently,' Beth said. 'And the police filed their report minutes ago. Werner's tapped into both systems.'

'Killed?' Zeb asked tightly. 'By whom?'

'This is who the police suspect,' Meghan turned her screen towards them. Played the CCTV video from the hospital.

A doctor approaching the shooter's room. Emerging after a while, saying something to the cops on duty and leaving.

Zeb squinted as he took in the man. Big. As large as Bwana and Bear. Equally muscled, going by the shape of his body beneath the white coat. Smooth, liquid movement. But it was the grey eyes and shaven head that caught his attention.

He reached over Meghan and replayed the clip.

Do I know him? Have I seen him before?

'Stranger to me,' he said, finally. Checked his friends' faces, got similar reactions from them. 'Have you—'

'Werner's checking,' Beth forestalled him. 'He's not in any database. We've sent the clip to Mossad, MI6, our allies. They'll get back.'

'What did he tell those policemen?' Roger drawled. 'It didn't look like they questioned who he was.'

'They didn't.' Meghan lips curled in disgust. 'That white coat was all it took for them to believe him. Some cops! All he told them was to let no one enter the room.'

'That would buy him time to get away,' Bwana said morosely. 'I'm guessing no other camera captured him.'

'He got away clean. He's in the wind.'

Zeb played the clip for the third time.

The killer moved confidently. No fear.

'He knows he's not in any database,' he said.

'And he's still out there. He could be coming after you,' Broker said ominously.

Dante Abrahms would have smiled grimly if he had heard

their conversation.

He was in his ride, slumped low, keeping a watch on the van that was in the parking lot of the hotel where the Agency operatives were.

He had followed them cautiously throughout the day. No opportunity had presented itself to take Carter out. He was either in a public place, with no escape route for Abrahms, or well-protected.

He had watched Carter retrieve the crate, which he assumed contained Javelins.

Will he recover the other case too?

He got his answer as the operatives exited their hotel. Carter and two men, Bwana and Roger, as he recalled from their files, got into the van. The sisters and the eldest operative got into their SUV.

The two vehicles took off.

Poor tradecraft. They should have checked their vehicles. They would have spotted my GPS tracker.

He followed them.

Bob Marin checked his phone and email for the thousandth time.

No response from Nashaat Munjid Kanaan, the deputy finance minister.

He thought for a moment and then fired off a text.

Is our file progressing?

As if on cue, his phone rang. The other one, which required the thumb and voice verification.

'Any progress?' Randy Spears asked.

'No. I just nudged Kanaan.'

'Why're they taking so long? We've given them everything

they asked for.'

'Usual government bureaucracy. I'll wait till tomorrow and then call him. How's our DC friend holding up?'

'He's getting antsy. He's calling me every day for status updates. He wants this Libya visit to be over and done with. But until Kanaan responds, there's nothing to progress on. And we've still not heard from Almasi's people?'

'Nope. I'll send a reminder there too, through the underground network.'

'They should have got one crate's location.'

'They might suspect it's a trap.'

'They might. But they're in the market for missiles. That's why Carter's there. I am sure they'll make an attempt for those Javelins. If they succeed, that's great news for us. What of Carter?'

'You should be telling me,' Marin said irritatedly, 'I've got enough on my plate.'

'Hsu's man, the one who survived, is still hunting him. My CIA contacts say they too are still hunting Carter. An interesting development. The Agency operatives in Tripoli captured a Company team. Delivered a message that they would kill Carter. He was their mess; they would tidy up.'

'They've backed off?'

'Hell no. The Agency can send whatever message it wants to. No one's listening.'

'Is there a chance Carter's friends are colluding with him?'

'No. I'm listening to the bugs in Clare's office. Her people will kill Carter if they get him.'

'What about our Beijing friend?'

'No panic from his side. He knows what we're planning requires time. Delays can occur.'

'I'll light a fire here.'

Chapter 77

———∞∞∞———

Reston, Washington DC

Doug Belden watched the woman move around in the house. The bearded man was somewhere outside.

He was sure they had mentioned their names, but he didn't remember.

He had frozen when they saved him. He shuddered when he recalled his attackers. Unconsciously, his hand went to his neck, gingerly. It felt tender, swollen.

He had been sure he was going to die, and then these two had turned up. He hadn't moved, he had been so scared. He had sat stiff, rigid, while outside the car, the fight had escalated. Grunts, blows, shouts, till it had ended and the woman had pushed him unceremoniously to the other side.

Panicked, he wondered if she was about to kill him herself.

He had seen her lips moving, felt her speaking, but no words registered, his shock was so complete.

Then she had taken the wheel and began driving, following her companion.

He had followed her obediently into the house. On some

level, he knew his brain had switched off and his body was reacting to automatic commands.

The numbness had gripped him so totally that he stared blankly at them when they asked him questions.

They gave up, finally, left him alone. And there he sat till the world returned.

The man entered the house, flicked the woman's ponytail. A gesture of familiarity that sent a shudder through him.

Reality beckoned.

'I need to call my wife,' he whispered.

They whirled around so fast that he shrank.

'Sure,' the woman said, after observing him. She slid a phone across the table.

He fumbled with it. Dropped it. Picked it up again and started dialing.

Wait. He stopped. Was this a trap? Would they trace where Martine and Louise were and kill them?

'Doug Belden?' the woman spoke, something in her voice getting his attention. 'If we wanted to kill you, you think we would have brought you here? You think we don't know where your family is? They're safe, by the way. They know you'll be late.'

'What … how?'

'You don't need to know that.'

'Who are you?'

'Chloe,' she pointed at herself. 'Bear,' she nodded at her partner. 'We're from the Agency.'

'Agency? No!'

He leapt out of his chair and dashed towards the door. Faltered when they made no move.

'You go out there, you'll be killed. Whoever sent those men will send some more.'

'Carter's—'

'Yeah, we know all about him,' the man began, and clammed up when the woman shot him a look.

'Doug,' she commanded. 'Come back.'

He returned unwillingly.

'Sit down.'

He sat.

She brought out a gun and placed it in front of him.

'Shoot us. Escape.'

He stared at the weapon and then at her.

'I'm just an EA. I am not an officer. I don't use guns,' he said nervously. 'I don't know anything.'

They didn't move. He didn't move. And then the large man approached, but this time, Belden didn't feel threatened.

'Why would anyone want to kill you, then, if you were just an EA?'

Randy Spears! The name was on the tip of Belden's tongue, but he held himself back.

'What are you going to do with me?' he said, summoning his courage.

'We saved your life, you dumbass,' the man growled.

'BEAR!' The woman said sharply, stopping him.

Her voice softened when she looked at Belden. 'He's right. We saved you. That should give you a clue. We aren't the bad people here.'

'But Carter—'

'Let's not discuss him. It's complicated. The more important question is, who wants you dead? And why?'

'I'm just an EA,' he repeated.

'An EA who heard too much? And talked to the wrong people?'

They know!

He stared at his trembling hands, wondering how he was going to get out of this.

'Doug?'

He met her eyes.

'We can help you. We can keep you safe. Your family as well. But you need to give us something.'

Doug Belden, executive assistant to the director and deputy director of the CIA, heard the earnestness in her voice. Saw Bear's clenched fists.

They can beat it out of me.

But they didn't.

'It was Spears,' he whispered. 'I am sure of it. Randy Spears.'

Chapter 78

———⊗⊗⊗———

Randy Spears wasn't worried when Beavis and Travers didn't get back to him immediately.

The two were known to take their time. They executed every job methodically, cleaned up, and only then updated him.

He reached home. Turned on the TV to the local station. Tossed his car keys and phones onto the coffee table. Poured himself a shot of alcohol and lowered himself onto a couch.

Took a sip. Savored it. Spat it out when he heard the reporters mentioning a shootout in Tysons.

He jerked his head up, grabbed the remote and turned on the volume. A shot of a bank's parking lot. Nothing there other than some vehicles and inquisitive people in the background.

She said the place had been the scene of a three-way shootout earlier, all men, all dead. The police were in the process of identifying them.

Tysons? No, that can't be them, Spears reassured himself. *There's no reason for them to have gone there.*

He snatched his phone and called Beavis. No answer. He tried Travers. Same result.

Dread pooled in him. He went online. Social media confirmed what the TV host was saying. A clip of two men against a car, a third barely visible through the windshield. Their faces couldn't be made out. The bank's security cameras weren't at the right angle. The vehicle's plates were just out of focus.

His fear grew when he noticed the build of the two men. *And that vehicle, that make's the same as Belden's.*

He called Langley. Assumed the name of a case officer and said he had to book an appointment with the director. The answering officer said the EA hadn't come to the office that day.

Spears tried Belden's residence. Same cover. It was normal for the CIA employee to receive late calls.

His wife answered, said the EA had left a message that he would be late.

They're all dead. Which means no loose ends.

But it nagged at him. Beavis and Travers were pros. A glorified secretary shouldn't have taken them out.

He looked up a number and dialed Fairfax County Police. Assumed the same case officer's name, an identity he knew would hold good.

'Chief,' he greeted Brian Scheener when he came on line, 'any more updates for us? We're all in shock here.' He decided to fire a shot in the dark, see if it landed. 'Doug Belden's been with us for a long time.'

'How many times will you people call?' Scheener said wearily. 'I can't magically turn up more information. Investigations take time. I've already told everything we know. To your director. Two men attacked your man, Belden, at that bank. From what we can work out, he had withdrawn cash, was returning to his vehicle, when these men set upon him.

Belden had a gun. He fired at them, but at least one of them fired back. All three died at the parking lot. Looks like a robbery gone wrong.'

'There's a video on social media—'

'Yeah, we're aware of that. We've urged people to not spread anything on the internet. This is an ongoing case. But you know how folks are. They have these phones, they think they can become the next internet star,' Scheener said bitterly.

'That clip,' Spears brought him back to his point, 'doesn't show any guns.'

'It was someone recording on a crappy phone from some distance away,' the police chief said angrily. 'Heck, it doesn't even have their faces. What do you expect? My officers have interviewed everyone at the scene. They worked out Belden's movements right from the time he left home. They've checked the bank's CCTV. I am confident what I told you is what went down. Now, if you'll excuse me, I've got a police department to run.'

'One more question, Chief, and then I'll get out of your way. Belden's identity not revealed—'

'WHY DON'T YOU ASK YOUR DIRECTOR?' Scheener lost his patience. He controlled himself. 'She wanted to tell the family herself. Besides, it would buy us more time to complete the investigation.'

'No clue about those attackers?'

'No,' and he ended the call.

Spears rubbed his brows, his mind whirling.

Belden's dead. He didn't talk to anyone. That's the upside. The downside was that his two best men in DC were dead, too. It still astonished him that they had gone down at the hands of the EA. But missions turned south. Often. All it took was one element of unpredictability, one piece of bad luck.

Beavis and Travis must have accosted him at the vehicle. Belden overreacted, went for his gun.

Yeah, that was how it must have gone down. His men had carried out similar kills before. They were ice-cold professionals. *Belden didn't know my men. He must have been jumpy, however. On a hair-trigger. No other reason why he drew.*

Job's done. Not the way I wanted, but Belden won't be a threat anymore.

There was nothing to link Beavis and Travers to him. The calls they had exchanged were from burner phones. None of them were recorded. That's assuming the cops could crack through the phones' security.

Their identities would come out eventually. Former military. Freelancing at various gigs. Private security. Bouncers. Anything where they could use their skills.

Vets down on hard times. Saw Belden with cash. Decided to make some easy money. Shootout. All dead.

That would be the conclusion the cops would arrive at.

Spears drained his glass and started relaxing. Sure, Beavis and Travers dying wasn't part of his plans. But they were expendable. And replaceable.

He folded his arms over his belly, stretched out and closed his eyes. Things were poised well despite this development.

His phone buzzed.

Hsu.

Everything under control?

Yeah, Spears replied and sent an abridged version of the events.

No loss, came the cold reply, which made the CEO grin. *We found the right partner in him. He's just like us.*

'I'm hearing rumors,' the politician said when he called a moment later. 'Belden—'

'You heard right. And he's not a problem.'

'Sure?'

'Yes. I checked with the cops. He died without speaking.'

'How—'

'I don't know. It doesn't matter. He was a loose end. What about things at your end?'

'All good. We're waiting for a confirmed date from Sabbagh's people. But we know why that's delayed, don't we?' His voice lowered. 'Any news from Marin?'

'I spoke to him. He'll chase Kanaan on the contract. And will get a meeting with that other party … you know, to the east of Tripoli.'

'Yeah. We're close, Randy, this close. Let's not botch it.'

'We won't.'

'What about Carter?'

'Stop worrying about him. He's as good as dead.'

The politician was still working. He had made the call to Spears and then joined the other secretary at the White House. They had discussed various matters with the president.

'No news from Prime Minister Sabbagh?'

'No, sir,' he answered.

In any case, I won't greenlight any date until Marin ties up everything.

They discussed defense and foreign affairs— Hong Kong, China, Saudi Arabia—and when they had finished, it was quite late.

President Morgan shook hands with them and walked them out.

'That went well,' the politician said.

'Yeah,' his cabinet colleague replied. 'I'll be glad when we get to Tripoli. A show of support is necessary.'

The politician *hmmed* in assent.

They turned a corridor and nearly bumped into a woman who was heading the opposite direction, going to the Oval Office.

'Clare?' the politician asked, astonished. 'I thought you'd left office.'

'I'm still here,' she replied coolly. 'Tidying up. I'm sure the president will announce when I've stepped down.'

'Carter's still out there, isn't he?'

'Last I heard, yes.'

'You can't imagine the damage he's done. Foreign affairs—'

'I am well aware of that. But I am sure he won't be around for long. And he wasn't the first traitor this country has had, and he won't be the last.'

The politician's eyes dropped beneath her steady gaze. He cursed himself for engaging with her in the first place.

His back prickled as he swept past her. He knew she was watching him, didn't dare to look back.

Clare watched Paul Vaughan and Lester McClellan depart.

There was something about the way the secretary of state had mentioned Zeb.

Am I overreacting? The entire cabinet knows his identity.

Her discreet investigation into the cabinet, the kill committee members, had turned up a blank. *Nothing new there. I wasn't expecting anything incriminating.*

She headed to the president, straightened her shoulders.

Belden's confession, however. I wasn't expecting that!

Was Randy Spears behind the conspiracy? He had the intelligence connections and the clearances and, in Shadow-Point, had the resources to pull it off.

But what's in it for him?

She didn't know. She hadn't informed Zeb yet and had asked Bear and Chloe to hold back for the night.

Don't want to distract Zeb and his team. Not tonight.

Chapter 79

Tripoli

Zeb drove down Al Shat Road, heading to the abandoned refinery where he had hidden the last case. Bwana and Roger filling the seats beside him. The Texan whistled tunelessly, his lips cracking into a grin when his friend stuffed his fingers in his ears.

Headlights in their mirror. Meghan driving the second vehicle.

'This place is empty?' Bwana asked, amazed, as the buildings came into view. Storage tanks. Pipes and cranes and tubing all over the place. Smoke stacks. Loading bays and offices.

'Yeah. ISIL attacked it; the Libyan Army tried to defend it. Lost. The terrorists killed several NOC employees and booby-trapped the place.'

'Booby-trapped?'

'Relax,' Zeb said, smiling. 'I have disarmed them, but no one knows that.'

He slowed and exited the road. Took a dirt track that seemed to head to the beach. It didn't. It ended up in a natural cul-de-sac, bounded by rocks.

'Discovered this a while back.' He jumped out of the van and locked it when his friends joined him. 'It's invisible from the road. No traffic comes here.'

The Range Rover joined them, Meghan parking sideways, behind it. Tactical move to block its exit in the event someone broke into it and attempted to drive away. Bwana, Roger and Broker unloaded gear from it and hoisted it on their shoulders.

Meghan surveyed their surroundings when she got out.

'Good?' Zeb asked her.

She flashed a thumbs-up. 'Even if someone breaks into the van, there's no way they can make off with the missiles.' She pointed to the rocky ground around them. 'That will make their escape impossible with that heavy load.'

Beth joined them and looked in the direction of the refinery. 'Half a mile away?'

'Yeah,' Zeb replied and led the way at a fast pace.

They launched two drones when they were three hundred yards away. Spread out, each barely within sight of the other, radio comms active.

'No human,' Beth announced softly. 'A few dogs, but not where we're going.'

'That's a big refinery,' Roger said doubtfully. 'An entire army could be hidden there.'

'They aren't showing on our screens,' she replied, testily. 'Shall I go into their coverage, their range?'

'Nope.' The Texan backed off gracefully. 'It's just that Bwana was hoping for a fight.'

'Yeah, it's been a long—' his friend began.

'Save it. We know,' Meghan cut him off.

Zeb tuned them out. He circled a large crude storage tank,

which took him several minutes. Another one nearby, sitting fat and round and squat. Its concrete dull and blackened.

'I thought they would be metal,' Bwana complained. 'I rapped one of them and now my knuckles hurt.'

'Bwana,' Beth sighed. What else was there to say?

A tower pierced the sky. For distillation, Zeb remembered from his study of the refinery. Smaller towers in the distance, smokestacks and coolers, for the crude oil heater, for gas treatment units, the catalytic cracker.

It was the admin buildings that he was after, which were some distance from the security barrier. The operational part of the refinery sprawled behind it. Concrete access joining the offices to Al Shat Road, which was a mile away.

We came in from the side. Through the rocky outskirts and not from the front. To flush out any hostiles.

Of whom there was no sign.

The smell of sulphur and oil was still strong in the air, even though the refinery had been unoperational for several months.

The offices came into view. A low-slung stretch of buildings, shaped like a U. Driveway. What had once been a fountain, but now a dry concrete bed. Crumbling pillars. Shattered windows, dark interiors.

'Still nothing?'

'Yeah,' Beth confirmed.

Zeb went down the left leg of the U. A concrete path running alongside. Curving, more buildings, and then a large open yard, at the end of which was a shed-like building. Storage for office and non-refinery essentials. Trucks would come through the security gate, detour around the offices and head directly to the yard. When the refinery was operational.

Zeb waited. Listened. Watched. Light wind from the sea sweeping through the deserted establishment. Somewhere, a window rattled.

He would have to cross the yard to get inside the storage. That was where the last bunch of Javelins were. GPS said they were there. Who else is inside?

'No one,' Meghan said. 'We got the drones to circle the entire refinery. No one here other than us.'

'I'm going in.'

'We'll cover you,' Broker replied.

The yard was uneven in places where weather and lack of maintenance had withered the cement away. Pot holes had appeared.

Zeb picked his way carefully, alert. The few minutes it took to cross the wide space felt like hours.

His face was bathed in sweat when he climbed onto the concrete walkway and disappeared inside the darkness. Dank air. Shapes he could feel but not see. *Empty boxes and crates. There's nothing of value left. The refinery was looted bare after its bombing.*

He felt his way in the dark, reluctant to use his torch. His radar was quiet, the beast too, but he was uneasy.

The rear wall had a stack of boxes. He leapt high and yanked the top-most one and jumped out of the way.

The loud crash would have woken the dead.

'You okay?' Meghan, worried.

'Yeah.'

He shoved debris out of the way. Sent up a silent prayer of thanks when he felt the hard surface of the Javelins.

'They're here,' he announced.

'So's company.'

Chapter 80

Firas Siddiq had recruited additional men. Four more fighters, taking his strength to nine.

He had outlined the mission to them and made a motivating speech.

'We'll be heroes if we come back with those missiles. We'll be heroes even if we die there.'

He looked meaningfully at each of them and raised his AK47. 'We cannot be captured alive,' he said, just in case anyone hadn't understood him. 'Are you ready to be heroes?'

'Yes, sayyidi,' they shouted.

'Are you ready to be martyrs?'

'Yes, sayyidi.'

He inspected them again. All of them in dark clothing. Loose shirts and trousers. AKs and several magazines with each of them. Some of them had knives and handguns as well.

'Cover your faces,' he ordered as he wrapped a bandana around his nose and mouth.

He led them in two vehicles. Three with him, the others in the second vehicle. Adrenaline and determination surging through all of them.

It should be easy. Saharol will make sure there will be no one else there.

He didn't know that, but that was a reasonable assumption to make, given that the oil company was gifting them the missiles.

He was cautious, however. The military, police, the Americans, just about everyone in Libya and the world was hunting them.

It wouldn't do to be captured, and so, he halted his entourage a good distance away and proceeded on foot. He imagined he was leading a ferocious army as he broke into a jog, his men at his side and behind. 'Lead from the front' was his motto.

Wariness kicked in when they entered the site. They spread out at his hand signal. He still was in the front as he went around the offices and stopped at the edge of the yard.

Everything was dark. Everything was still. Waves crashing in the distance. Blinking lights high above. He tensed, then relaxed when he saw it was an airliner.

'Go,' he commanded when he was sure the night was theirs.

He charged forward, his heart thumping, his men taking his lead.

And then the night turned into day.

Chapter 81

---∞∞∞---

The blaze from the headlamps pinned Siddiq and his men.

'Scatter!' he cried, 'keep going.'

'STOP!' Someone shouted. A burst of shots landed at their feet.

'ATTACK!' Siddiq ordered. It didn't matter that he couldn't see anyone behind the glare of the lights. Offense was the only way forward.

He cut loose at the nearest light, figuring that the darkness would be their friend. Some of his men took his cue, more followed, and the night filled with the chatter of AKs.

Zeb watched in dumb amazement at the reckless charge. The intruders hadn't heeded his command.

That man in the center, he seemed to be the leader. He shouted something and fired. His men followed.

'They're going after the lights,' Roger said.

'Let them,' he replied. They hadn't had enough time to mount the lamps. Their dying out was a calculated risk.

'Zeb,' Beth said uneasily, 'these don't look like CIA or any home outfit. No professional would keep going like this.'

He didn't answer. The same thought had struck him.

One light died. Another, and when the last one flickered out, he moved. 'Take them down. Alive.'

Nine of them against six of them. His team was scattered; they were bunched together. His friends were some of the deadliest operatives in the world. These intruders … they were bold and reckless for sure.

But we are concealed. Whereas the attackers were in the open.

He crouched inside the storage building as his friends opened fire from the sides. He didn't shoot. He didn't want to give away his position.

Rounds flew over the attackers' heads. That slowed their charge. They looked uncertainly at their leader.

They're still blinded by the light. We've got a few seconds of advantage.

'STOP! SURRENDER! YOU'RE SURROUNDED,' Broker shouted. He repeated it in Arabic.

'ATTACK,' the leader screamed.

Zeb froze when he heard the command and the corresponding yells.

They're Libyans?

The intruders split up. Several of them fired blindly in the dark and went sideways, seeking out where the incoming rounds had come.

The leader fired at the storage room. He and two men resumed their run.

'Zeb,' said Meghan, 'You can handle them?'

'Yeah.'

A startled exclamation from her over their comms. The sound of a blow. A flurry of shots.

'Meg?' Beth asked cautiously.

The darkness made it difficult to make out shapes. They didn't want to risk using their NVGs.

'I'm fine,' her sister gasped. 'This dude … he shot himself when I disarmed him. A gun hidden in his clothing.'

More shots sounded.

'Mine, too,' Roger panted. 'Zeb, these men won't surrender. They won't be taken alive.'

Suicide mission? No, that can't be right. They've come for the missiles.

It came to him just as the leader mounted the walkway.

They are terrorists. Who else would kill themselves?

How did they know this place?

Answers would have to wait.

The three men were entering the storage building.

Chapter 82

Zeb swung.

The plank he was holding slammed into the middle of the three men.

They doubled up. Cried out in agony. Two of them lost their AKs.

Not the leader, who swung his rifle and fired a loose round. Sprayed the inside of the building.

The man to his left, nearest to Zeb, clawed at his waist. Brought out a gun.

Zeb shot him.

'OUR LEFT. ZAKIR!' The leader shouted at his remaining man. He rolled on the ground. Kept shooting, bringing the AK towards Zeb. His man groaned, clutched at his belly and scrabbled on the ground, searching for his fallen rifle.

Zeb shot him, too.

He felt the blur of movement. Couldn't react in time as the leader lunged at him, a roar escaping him.

Something hit him in the chest, a hammer blow.

He was shot.

No. It was the attacker's rifle. He was wielding it like a

club. It looked like his AK had run dry.

Another swing caught Zeb on his left shoulder, right on his wound. He fell to the ground, a groan escaping him.

The leader fell on top of him, eyes fierce, teeth flashing, something in his hand … a handgun!

Zeb threw him off just as the round entered the ground next to his head. The sound of the shot set his ears ringing.

He rolled to his side. Met the man's fist, took the blow on his chest. Headbutted him, grabbed at his gun arm, wrested loose the weapon, which slid away from both of them. His other hand went around the man's throat and pounded his head on the floor.

'Who are you?' he raged in Arabic.

The man spat at him. Bared his teeth and reared forward to bite him.

Zeb threw him off to a side, a heave that sent the man rolling towards his companions' AKs.

'TRAITOR!' he screamed. 'YOU BETRAYED US!'

Zeb paused for a fraction.

Those words didn't make sense.

His freezing was a mistake.

The leader dived for the nearest AK. Caught hold of it. Started bringing it around just as Zeb dived at him, grabbed him by the waist and brought him down.

He chopped at the man's hand with the side of his palm. The rifle slipped in the man's hand. A punch to the man's neck. He gasped, choked, tears streamed down his face, but he didn't let go of the rifle. With what looked like superhuman strength, he brought the gun up.

Zeb had had enough. He caught hold of the AK's barrel and smashed it on the ground, trapping the man's fingers between hard floor and weapon.

The man screamed. He let go of the rifle, writhing in pain, but his fighting instincts didn't die. His left hand flew to his belt and drew out yet another handgun.

Zeb shoved his hand away just as he shot wide. The two men grappled in near-silence, broken only by harsh breathing and grunts. Zeb tried to keep the leader's hands pinned down, while he tried to break free.

'You're ISIL?' Zeb asked with gritted teeth.

The man prepared to spit, but howled in pain when Zeb headbutted him again and split his nose.

'FILTHY PIG,' he screamed. 'FIRST YOU BETRAY US, THEN YOU—'

'WE ARE NOT SAHAROL. WHAT MAKES YOU THINK THAT?' Zeb yelled over his shout.

The man stopped resisting. His eyes widened. He twisted his head to look at his fallen men.

'You're American,' he whispered. Before Zeb could react, he brought his gun to his own temple and blew his brains out.

Chapter 83

———— ⊷⊶ ————

Zeb staggered to his feet, winced as his shoulder throbbed, and felt his face. *Nothing bleeding.*

His head was still throbbing from the close-range shots and his body was a mass of pain. *I've been here before. I'll recover.*

Footsteps behind him.

He turned to see Beth and Meghan racing, skidding to a stop, the other operatives following.

'I couldn't stop him,' he said.

'All of them killed themselves,' Bwana said bitterly. 'The moment they saw they would be captured, they trained their guns on themselves.'

Zeb nodded. He felt hollow. *All this, the stakeout, the ambush, and we got nothing.*

Wait! That's not right.

'Why did they think we were Saharol?' he said slowly. It didn't make sense. Why would that oil company be connected with the Javelins? 'And, how did these terrorists know of this location?'

'You're sure they're ISIL?'

'He,' Zeb looked at the leader, 'died before I could question him more. He didn't deny it when I questioned him. Called me a filthy pig.' His lips quirked when Beth snorted in amusement. 'Yeah, I think we can safely assume they are terrorists. Searched them?'

'Nothing on their bodies,' Meghan said disgustedly. 'Just spare magazines. No phones.'

Zeb patted down the leader, shook his head when he had finished. 'He isn't carrying a phone, either.'

'A suicide attack then?' Roger mused. 'That makes no sense. They weren't expecting us. They were looking to retrieve the Javelins.'

It came to Zeb in a flash.

'They know Almasi's location.'

They gathered their weapons; Bwana and Roger grabbed the case. Zeb took one last look at the refinery as he led his team back to their vehicles.

The terrorists didn't know of the other missile locations. Only this one.

He swore beneath his breath, frustrated that he was missing some piece that would help him see the picture.

Meghan caught up with him.

'You were expecting this? That's why you decided on tonight?'

'Not *this!*' he said, laughing humorlessly. 'I was thinking whoever was hunting me would stake out this lot. They would know the other Javelins were moved. It followed that I would come here. Best opportunity for them to nail me.'

'What does it mean?' She bobbed her head backwards at the establishment.

'Hell if I know!'

'Time to ask Saharol?'

'That some terrorist took their name? They would laugh us out of their fancy offices. They're a billion-dollar business. Heavily invested in Libya. Businesses like peace. They don't like disruption. Why would they want ISIL to have these missiles and destabilize the whole region?'

He kicked the van's tire in frustration when they reached it and reluctantly broke into a grin when she chuckled.

Bwana and Roger loaded the crate silently. Climbed into the passenger seat. Zeb turned on the van and was preparing to back out when Beth came running, slammed a palm against the window.

'We've got to take this.' She held her phone up.

She, Meghan and Broker climbed into the rear before Zeb could ask any questions.

She turned the speaker on.

'Zeb?' Clare came on, alert.

'Yeah, we're all here.'

'Beth told me what went down. Y'all are okay?'

Trust her to lead with that. It shows why she's a leader.

'Yes, ma'am. A few scratches. Nothing serious.'

'Chloe and Bear are on the call too.'

His brows furrowed as he greeted them automatically. *Belden. I forgot all about him.*

'What do you have?' He raised his head when he felt Beth and Meghan's intensity.

It must be big.

It was.

'Randy Spears. Belden told him about Chia. Spears sent killers after him.'

Chapter 84

———∞∞∞———

The expression on his friend's faces reflected the shock Zeb felt.

Spears?

Zeb knew of ShadowPoint and its CEO. They all did. *Heck, they are as good as an official government outfit, they do that much work for various agencies.*

'Zeb?' Clare spoke sharply.

'I'm here, ma'am. I heard. I'm digesting this. Chloe, Bear, what else did Belden say?'

His friends narrated the EA's confession, which wasn't much. That Spears had befriended him a while ago, had made him feel important, had paid for a few luxuries, vacations, concert tickets, meals. Frequently took him out for a drink, and it was at one of those outings that Belden had blurted Chia's name. He hadn't mentioned it to anyone because it hadn't felt important and guilt had set in only when the Chinese agent had disappeared. By then, it was too late.

'Spears set up a protocol for him. To get direct access, Belden had to call a certain number, speak a code.'

'Why?'

'Bear and I discussed this. We think it was to make Belden feel important. He would volunteer more information if he knew he was special.'

'Did he?'

'Not according to him.'

'You believe that?' Bwana asked sharply.

'Yeah. He's scared. He knows he's in so deep that telling the truth is the only way out. I don't think he's a traitor. Not in that sense.'

'You briefed them?' Zeb asked the sisters.

They nodded.

'Have you gone against Spears at any time?' Clare asked him.

'No, ma'am.'

'Does any of this mean anything to you? Spears, Saharol, ISIL?'

The van was warm from their body heat. Secure. Containing the most lethal people in Libya. To one side was the Mediterranean Sea, separating Europe and North Africa. Around or near which several of the world's hotspots were located.

'ShadowPoint can pull this off, ma'am. It—'

'Yes, but why? And what's the oil company connection? Why would any American outfit, government or private, associate itself with terrorists?'

'Maybe there's no link, ma'am.' His words sounded weak, even to himself.

His hair rose when Meghan looked up from the screen she was working on.

'There's a connection between Spears and Saharol. Bob Marin, the oil company's CEO, is ex-ShadowPoint.'

Zeb drove almost in automatic mode, thinking about the call, the revelations, the attack.

Even if there was something going on between Saharol and ISIL—. He stopped himself.

A billion-dollar US firm colluding with the world's most wanted terrorists? How was that even possible?

What if that's precisely the reaction they're counting on if someone investigates them?

The twins had already put Werner to work, but he was sure, smart as their AI was, there would be nothing to be found.

Spears and Marin are too smart to leave a trail.

Another question presented itself.

Why frame me?

And that led to the question he had posed to his friends.

Why now? Why, while I'm in Libya?

'Zeb, Spears would know your mission, wouldn't he?' Beth. He was sure she was biting her lip as she worked on her screen.

'Yeah, if he's the one who hacked into us, he knows everything.'

'Let's assume he did. We never identified the shooters at your first hotel or in the second or third attempt. They could be sent by him.'

'But why—' Bwana began.

'We'll have to ask him that,' she said, drowning him out. 'And Marin, as well.'

Silence. The slap of tires on road. A stray vehicle passing them, headlights throwing his friends in sharp relief when he looked sideways. Lost in thought.

Those Tripoli Paradise shooters, that hospital killer ... those are Spears' men?

He swore when he realized he was flooring the gas unconsciously. Some layers had been peeled back, but the conspiracy was still shrouded in darkness.

Bob Marin, he decided—the CEO had to be questioned, and to hell with the niceties.

How urgent is that? I'm still alive, so if taking me out was Spears' goal, he has failed. Besides, Almasi knows by now his people have failed. If I were him, I would make contact with Misfud and speed up the purchase.

'Nothing has changed,' he announced, and when his comms squawked in surprise, he clarified, 'until Misfud makes his sale.'

Chapter 85

─────◦◦◦◦◦─────

One of the calls came in the morning as he was checking on the van.

It was where it should have been, in the parking lot of the mid-priced Tripoli hotel they were staying in. As oil company executives.

His phone rang as he was heading back to the room. He looked at the number, identified it as the Fashloum storekeeper, the conduit to Abu Bakhtar.

'Yes,' he replied.

'Our friends are unhappy that you are taking this long. They—'

'Tonight,' he cut in. 'Do you know that open space on Omar Almukhtar Road, after the Municipal Beach?'

That's where Almasi executed a French journalist. Posted it on the internet. Abu Bakhtar will know where.

'I don't.'

'Our friends will,' Zeb replied.

'How come you're ready so quickly?' the Libyan asked suspiciously.

'I had everything in place a couple of days back,' he lied.

'I was scouting for a good location and found this one only yesterday. You called me in time.'

'I am sure they'll not like the delay.'

'Are you going to pass the information, or not?' Zeb snarled.

The storekeeper hung up.

That location ... it's like where we parked the van at the refinery. Entry or exit through just one way. Isolated. Easy to set an ambush or a trap.

He went to the twins' room, confident that there was where he would find the rest of his team.

He was right.

Everyone converges around them.

He explained his plan and couldn't help laughing at their expressions.

'That's it?' Broker asked, astounded. 'You'll take a case, fire a missile, and then agree on a date for a sale?'

'And a price. I'm sure they'll negotiate.'

'THEY'LL KILL YOU!' Beth said heatedly. 'And take your Javelins.'

'Not if y'all are there to dissuade them. You'll be out there. Sniping positions. Booby-trap the exit. Maybe shoot one terrorist, to show that I have backup.'

'It might work,' she said, grudgingly. 'What makes you think Abu Bakhtar will turn up? They'll know their raid failed. Will they suspect anything?'

'No. My credentials are rock-solid. And they will show if they are desperate for weapons. Which, I think, they are. The missiles will help them get back some power.'

Meghan, who had been watching him, snapped her fingers. 'You want them to take your missiles today.'

'Yeah,' he grinned.

'And then you'll blow them up.'

'Correct.'

'Surely, they'll store the weapons well away from Almasi. There's no guarantee you'll take him down.'

'The missiles are to reduce their Sirte hideout to rubble. We've always known that they're in that city, but where precisely is something we haven't found. As for Almasi'—he headed to a bottle of water, drank from it and held it to them—'this will help.'

Chapter 86

—⟨∞⟩—

'Can we trust him?' Almasi asked Abu Bakhtar when his deputy relayed the storekeeper's message.

'Sayyidi, we have checked out Misfud so thoroughly that we know every wart on his body. We know his customers, his business in Syria, his entire life story. Everything checks out. Yes, we can trust him. All he wants is to make money. By selling arms.'

'What happened yesterday?'

'As you know, Siddiq and his men never returned. Our people report a gunfight at the refinery. Nine people dead. Our men. I think the killers were Americans. We don't know for sure, though. I had asked Siddiq and his men to leave their phones behind so that there was no way anyone could track them.'

'You were expecting a trap?'

'Sayyidi, why would anyone leave missiles like that in such a location?'

'You think the Americans—'

'I am not sure they were Americans, sayyidi. They could be anyone. Libyan Army. I have a feeling that rumor was spread deliberately to see who turns up. Lucky for us, Siddiq and his men didn't talk before dying.'

'You're sure of that?'

'Sayyidi, don't you think we would have been bombed by now if our enemies knew of our location? A drone strike.'

The light flashed off Almasi's glasses as stared into space. He patted his deputy. 'You're a wise man, Abu Bakhtar. A good leader. You think of all angles.'

His second-in-command flushed and looked down, embarrassed.

'Go, meet Misfud. Get his Javelins. Buy them. Or, kill him and get them.'

'Yes, sayyidi. Saharol has made another approach. They want to meet. This time, I'm sure it's the oil company. They left a business card.'

'What do they say?'

'They want to make an offer. One that will benefit us and Libya.'

'Who cares about this country?'

'Their operation is based here, sayyidi.'

'What do you think?'

'I think it's worth hearing them out.'

'We can always capture their executives, kill them and broadcast it.'

'That's what I was thinking, sayyidi.'

'Go, get the missiles.' Almasi patted Abu Bakhtar on the shoulder. 'Then, we'll meet the oil company.'

Bob Marin couldn't suppress his *gotcha* when word got to him that the terrorists were ready to meet.

Apple has been bitten, he messaged Randy Spears.

Congratulations! When?

They'll let us know.

Good work. Set it up asap. Any progress with Kanaan?

Working on it. You heard about the refinery shootout?

Yeah. Terrorists killed. Agencies here think they were trying to retrieve the missiles.

Any blowback to us?

No one suspects we were involved.

Who killed them?

No agency is owning up. I think it's the CIA. But they're playing cagey.

Could the killers be Carter's friends?

No. They're out there in Tripoli. Still hunting him. Forget about him. Someone will get him eventually.

Yes, Marin nodded. The solitary Agency operative wasn't his problem. His job was to get the contracts with all the Libyan players.

The second call came when Zeb and his team were driving to the meeting point on Omar Almukhtar Road.

'It's Avichai Levin,' said Beth, excited, in his earpiece. 'Conferencing all of us.'

'Zeb?' The Israeli came on after a moment. 'You're proof.'

'Proof of what?'

'That your agencies are incompetent,' the Mossad chief said, chuckling. 'So many of them hunting you and here you are, alive. Now, if it had been one of my teams …'

Levin took every opportunity to prove that Mossad was better than any US outfit. *And he's probably right about that,* Zeb thought, his lips curved in a reluctant smile. He and the Israeli had history, a bond that transcended any inter-agency rivalry. If Zeb asked for help, the Mossad director would come running. In person.

'How are you, my friend?'

'Bruised. Sore, but as you guessed, alive.'

'I told Clare—'

'We'll talk about all that over a drink one day, Avichai. You called?'

'Danie Vlok reached out to me.'

Zeb slowed the van involuntarily. Vlok was the head of SSA, the South African State Security Agency. He had met him a few times but didn't know him well.

'Yeah? What about?'

'Beth and Meg sent out a photograph—'

'The hospital killer,' the younger sister chimed in.

'He isn't in our system,' Levin continued. 'But Vlok knows him. He's South African. Dante Abrahms. I'll send the twins his dossier. It isn't much. He's a killer. No other word for it. He was the best the SSA had before its restructuring.'

Zeb nodded unconsciously. He knew the history of the South African agency. It had a notorious past, having run kill teams that took out political opponents, at a different time in the country's history.

'He and seven others quit when the outfit was restructured. He dropped out of sight, but there were rumors that he became an independent operator. Contract killer. Vlok kept tabs on him and, when he got that photograph, contacted me.'

'Why not us?'

'Because he heard about you and the Agency. Wasn't sure if this was an official request from an outfit that was shutting down.'

'Got it.'

'This is where it gets interesting.' Levin paused for effect. 'Vlok heard that Abrahms is working for Jian Hsu.'

Zeb lost control of the van momentarily. It swerved and nearly ran off the road. He fought for control, steadied it, acknowledged the Range Rover's headlight flash from behind with a hand wave.

'You heard me?'

'Yeah,' he replied, aware that his voice sounded distant.

'It was Hsu all along.'

'Looks like it,' he replied thinly.

Him and Spears.

The two together made a formidable combination. ShadowPoint's worldwide reach and resources, MSS's capabilities and the unlimited budget they seemed to have.

The shape of the conspiracy became clearer. But its heart was still a mystery. The *why* and *why now* were still unanswered.

'Later, Avichai,' Zeb told his friend as the Municipal Beach flashed past.

It was time to focus on Abu Bakhtar.

'Don't forget Abrahms. He's hunting you.'

Meghan, out of the corner of her eye, saw Beth typing furiously when Levin hung up.

'What's up?' she asked, surprised that she could speak normally. Her head was still reeling from the Mossad director's revelation.

'Getting Werner to see who else connects Spears, Hsu, Marin and Saharol. And to see what news items link the four.'

'Makes sense. What do we know of Saharol?'

'Private company. Some investment bank came up with

the idea of an oil company focused on Libya. It got together other firms and raised private equity. Marin got appointed.'

'Any Chinese connection?'

'Not traceable, but I wouldn't be surprised if some investors were Chinese. They've put money everywhere.'

Is Saharol an MSS front? Meghan worried her lip as she drove. It was possible, but unlikely, she decided. Intelligence agencies did not own companies that large and high-profile. There was too much scrutiny about such firms. It was a risk they couldn't afford.

Hsu and Spears ... the stakes just got bigger, she thought grimly.

Abrahms had followed Carter the previous night. He had shadowed them on foot, but when he saw the women launch the drones, he had dropped back. There was no point giving himself away.

Time's on my side, he reflected as he tracked the American's van on his screen. It looked like Carter was heading to the west of the city. The South African didn't know the area well. He had no intention of carrying out a kill in alien surroundings.

He'll return and will be alone at some point. I'll take him out then.

Chapter 87

⸺❧⸺

Abu Bakhtar arrived at dusk, when there was still light.

Three vehicles bristling with his men, all of them bearing weapons that they brandished openly once they were outside the city limits.

One vehicle parked on the road and cut off access to the clearing where the meeting was to take place.

Another vehicle stopped midway and unloaded its killers, who surrounded the venue.

The third kept coming and stopped a few yards from Zeb. Armed men got out. Gave him the badass look and checked out the surroundings. There wasn't much to see. Rocks, a distant line of trees, and the sea facing them. The dirt track the sole means of access. Any approaching vehicle could be seen for miles, and if it turned hostile, there were numerous nooks, crannies and hollows for the terrorists to melt into.

Two men approached Zeb and searched him. They took his phone, his weapons, and headed to the two cases on the ground.

'Don't touch them,' Zeb warned.

They stopped. Looked hesitantly at him, shrugged. One of

them made a hand signal to the vehicle.

A robed man, face covered, got out. He came to the clearing and unwrapped his face.

Abu Bakhtar.

'You know this place.'

'The whole world knows it,' Zeb replied dryly. 'You made it famous.'

The terrorist's eyes flicked to the case on the sand. 'Those are the missiles?'

'Four of them. Shall we not do the thing about your killing me and making off with them?' He raised his hand and snapped his fingers in the air.

Abu Bakhtar jumped in surprise when a round landed in the sand in front of him. His men reacted instantly. Covered Zeb with their weapons. Angry shouts.

'It's a trap, sayyidi!' someone yelled. His bodyguards rushed forward to surround him protectively.

'It's not a trap. It's a precaution. A warning that I am not alone. We are here to complete a business transaction. Don't try to hijack the missiles.'

Abu Bakhtar searched the horizon for the concealed shooter. Didn't see anyone. He was impassive when he turned to Zeb.

'How many do you have out there?'

'Enough to kill you if you make a wrong move.'

They could have staked this place out before us, but they didn't. They can't risk being in the open that long. Someone might spot them.

The disadvantages of being the wanted men had played into Zeb's hands. That, and their desperation for missiles. *There's no other reason Abu Bakhtar would have left his hiding place.*

'Shall we do business?' he asked, mopping the sweat from his face. He jerked a shoulder toward several bottles of water in the sand. 'I can't offer you hospitality. If this had been a different business, I would have an air-conditioned office, assistants to bring tea and snacks. Water is all I have.'

He bent down, uncapped one, dragged deep and tossed it in the sand. He offered another to Abu Bakhtar, who, too, was perspiring in the evening. The sea breeze was doing nothing to dispel the humidity and the waves of heat radiating from the sand.

The terrorist hesitated. Looked at one of his guards, who took the bottle, broke its seal and drank and then passed it to his boss.

'It's not poisoned,' Zeb said, laughing sardonically. 'If I wanted you dead, don't you think my shooter would have fired into it?'

Abu Bakhtar didn't react. He drank and wiped his lips.

'Show us,' he ordered.

Zeb opened the case. The terrorists stepped closer and soft murmurs spread through them at its contents.

He lifted one missile, mounted it into the tube assembly. Reached into the smaller case and extracted the CLU, Command Launch Unit. He instructed the terrorists on each piece of the missile, gave them operating instructions as he attached the tube to the CLU, sat on the ground and rested the missile on his shoulders. The entire unit weighed just over forty-nine pounds and vaguely resembled a pair of weights on either side of a tube.

When the terrorists came closer to him, he demonstrated the various views: the DFOV, Day Field of View, WFOV, Wide Field of View, NFOV, Narrow Field of View, and SFOV,

Seeker Field of View.

The WFOV on the CLU was for thermal representation of the area the target was in. NFOV, which was on the launch unit too, was for identifying the actual target, and once that was done, the gunner would pass the electronic message to the missile-mounted SFOV. The missile tracking of the target made Javelins a fire-and-forget weapon and enabled the gunners to move immediately after firing.

There was no target to home in on, so Zeb pointed the missile at the sea, looked at Abu Bakhtar, who nodded assent, and fired.

Some of the terrorists jumped back at the back blast, others clapped when the Javelin raced into the sky with a dull whump. With an effective range of a mile and a half, the missile disappeared into the night.

'Boom,' Zeb said softly. 'If you were targeting something, a building or a tank, it would be destroyed.'

'Impressive,' Abu Bakhtar said after a pause. 'How do I know the other missiles are not decoys, rigged to explode?'

Zeb pointed to one of his bodyguards. 'You, come and fire the next missile.'

The terrorist looked at his leader, who nodded. He came forward eagerly and started reaching out for the missile Zeb picked.

'Not that one,' Abu Bakhtar said. 'Humaid, you take any one of the other two.'

'You don't trust me?' Zeb asked.

'No,' the leader said coldly.

Humaid reached into the case and nearly dropped the Javelin, surprised at his weight. Zeb steadied him. Showed him how to complete the assembly. Taught him a basic sitting posture for shooting and then stepped back.

A second Javelin flew into the sky minutes later and landed into the sea a short distance away.

'You shot too high,' Zeb told the man. 'With practice it will become easy.'

'You wanted twenty, didn't you?' he addressed the leader. 'I can get them to you tomorrow.'

'We are taking these with us today,' Abu Bakhtar said firmly.

'That wasn't what we agreed on. Your boss—'

'Those were your conditions. I never agreed to them.'

'You did.'

'I am the buyer. I decide the terms.'

Zeb was going to relent. That was the plan. But he had to make a show of protesting. Latif Wakil Misfud was no push-over. That reputation had to be lived up to.

He and Abu Bakhtar argued for a long while until he finally threw his hands up in the air in resignation. 'Do what you want. But I want to be paid right now for these four.'

'Two,' Abu Bakhtar's teeth shone in the night. 'The first two missiles were for you to demonstrate they worked. They are to your account.'

'No—'

'Enough talking,' the terrorist leader snapped. 'Humaid, go get the money.'

His flunky ran back to the vehicle and returned with two heavy satchels that he tossed at Zeb's feet.

'That's the price we agreed. For two missiles. I am not even negotiating on that,' Abu Bakhtar sneered.

'Why would you? You got four for the price of two,' Zeb retorted. He opened one bag and checked its contents.

Bundles of greenbacks in used notes. The other one had similar contents. 'These are genuine?'

'Take them to a bank and see for yourself,' the leader said arrogantly, fully aware that Zeb would do no such thing.

'Don't underestimate me, Abu Bakhtar,' Zeb said softly, menace in his tone. 'If you wrong me, I, not the Americans, will finish you.'

The leader's men stiffened. They lined up their weapons at the arms dealer. A tense silence was broken when Abu Bakhtar waved his hand dismissively. 'Load those into our vehicle,' he ordered his men, who scrambled to carry the two cases.

'Tomorrow,' Zeb reminded him. 'I'll tell you where to come.'

'Not tomorrow. I'll tell you when,' Abu Bakhtar replied.

Zeb watched the vehicles reverse and fade into the night.

'Tomorrow?' Meghan asked him in his earpiece.

'Yeah.'

That was when Almasi would die.

Chapter 88

Werner linked the politician to Spears and Marin easily. It didn't break into a sweat. Heck, it didn't even use a fraction of its prodigious computing power. The evidence was there, right in the open.

The military records of the politician and Spears, the DC man mentioning Saharol in several occasions, his photographs with Marin. There was no disputing that the three men had a connection.

Had they met?

No, Werner could find no proof of that. However, there were several occasions when the three of them had the opportunity. Bob Marin was a frequent visitor to DC and there were at least six occasions when they were within two blocks of each other. It wouldn't have been impossible for them to meet away from cameras.

What of Hsu?

The politician had been to Beijing several times, had been honored with state dinners each time. Werner searched for invitee lists and photographs, but found only what the government had put out. He had been to the Chinese Embassy in DC several times as well, and there was at least one occasion when Hsu had been in the US on an official visit. The men could have met.

But Werner had no proof.

It was similar with Spears.

The ShadowPoint CEO had visited China several times with a view to establishing operations there. But nothing on a meeting with Hsu.

Werner played *Go* with itself as it thought.

How about Saharol and its origins?

VC firms and investment banks funded companies. They didn't fund them, did they?

Excited, Werner stopped its game and pursued that thought. A quick scan of the company's bank accounts—yeah, the AI had hacked into them— revealed nothing.

What of offshore banking locations? Switzerland, the Caribbean, Jersey, many others, where it was possible for the scrupulous as well as the unscrupulous to open and operate bank accounts, no questions asked.

Werner snapped its fingers and commanded its prodigious chips to hack into those establishments that offered such services. Simultaneously, it attacked the public and private airports to get to their security camera feeds.

In one bank in the Bahamas, it hit jackpot. Not once, but twice.

Meghan was driving back from the Abu Bakhtar meeting, Zeb's van visible in the distance ahead, when she felt Beth freeze.

She snatched a glance, saw her sister had gone white.

'What?' she whispered.

Beth turned the screen towards her.

Meghan risked a longer glance … and nearly drove off the road.

She swallowed. Looked in the rear mirror. Broker was snoozing in the backseat, oblivious to the goings-on at the front.

'Why?' she asked.

'That, we don't know,' Beth replied. 'We should let Zeb know.'

Meghan considered it. The next day would be big. They would have to be at the top of their game.

Hsu's involvement had rattled all of them.

Can Zeb afford any distraction?

'No,' she told her sister. 'Let's hold off until Zeb deals with Almasi.'

Chapter 89

⸺⸺

'Sayyidi, we got them,' Abu Bakhtar exulted.

His men laid the cases on the floor and stepped back as Almasi approached.

The terrorist leader was in white robes and held sheets of paper in one hand. A speech that he would give to his followers the next day, exhorting them to attack Westerners, Libyan establishments and fight for the cause.

He bent over the Javelins and ran his fingers over a polished surface. His eyes were glowing when he straightened.

'Well done, Abu Bakhtar. I knew you could pull it off. What about the others?'

'We'll get them, sayyidi. We just need to tell him when.'

'Did he give any problems?'

'No, sayyidi. But I came close to killing him.' There was no need to tell the leader that Misfud had pinned them down with snipers. Minor details that the ISIL chief didn't need to concern himself with.

'Make plans to get the remaining,' Almasi said. 'And make a list of Libyan government targets. Start with NOC's facilities. Now, we'll win this war.'

The ingestible GPS tracker in the water that Abu Bakhtar had consumed started operating half an hour after he left with the missiles.

By the time Zeb and his team reached their hotel, the twins had located him.

'Still on the way to Sirte,' Beth told him when he checked her screen.

He went to his room and removed his Misfud disguise. *Will I need it again?*

He gave that thought while he showered.

Yeah, he would. He would go as the arms dealer to Sirte. Not the padding around his waist, though. That would slow him down. Just the facial alterations.

When he joined the twins, everyone else was there. Meghan was wrapping up a call with Clare.

'Nothing new at her end. She met the secretary of state and secretary of defense at the White House. Unplanned encounter. Paul Vaughan asked her about her departure.'

'They're coming to Libya, aren't they?' Roger stretched his legs and admired his handmade boots.

'Yeah.'

There's something she's holding back. Zeb waited, let the silence build, but Meghan didn't crack. *She'll tell when she's ready. Probably chasing down a hunch.*

'Chloe and Bear?' he asked.

'In the safe house. They have brought Belden's family, too. They've put out a message that she's gone to be with her family in Iowa.'

'Where's Abu Bakhtar?'

'In Sirte.'

He pulled up a chair, sat with his chest to its back and watched as she enlarged the map application on her screen. The green dot, for the ISIL deputy, was steady. Two more dots a distance away.

'That's his building. Those others, the missiles, are probably stored along with their weapons cache. Another building.'

She zoomed in on the imagery provided by the network of military recon KH-11 satellites. Rooftops of desolated buildings. Empty streets and lanes.

And those green dots, right in the center.

'Let's plan,' he said.

Chapter 90

They continued their planning the next day. Six of them crammed into Meghan's room; she sat next to her sister, screens in front of both.

Roger lounging in a chair, Broker on the bed next to the twins, Bwana peering out of the window, Zeb in a chair facing the sisters.

Satellite images of Sirte on their screens. Tall buildings in the center, which was where the terrorists were. Smaller construction and independent houses on the outskirts. Very few buildings were intact. Most of them had gaping holes, crumbling rooftops, and dangerously leaning walls. Narrow alleys and lanes, no signs of vehicular traffic.

Almasi's building was six stories high. the weapons store was smaller, three stories.

'How do you know?' Bwana straightened and shook his head, puzzled.

'Average heights of buildings in Tripoli, and in Sirte in particular, known details of floor sizes, comparison images …' Beth began impatiently, as she worked on her screen. 'Tech and algorithm stuff. You wouldn't understand.'

'Abu Bakhtar sleeps on the third floor,' Meghan jumped in before he could retort. 'Chances are Almasi is on the same floor.'

'No,' Zeb shook his head. 'He will be higher.'

'Power play,' he explained, when they looked at him intrigued. 'Leader of the group. He'll have a floor to himself. There will be no one important above him. Guards, probably, but no ISIL officer. What else do we know?'

'Snipers,' Meghan resumed, 'on rooftops on surrounding buildings.' She pointed at the screen and then dragged her nail to ground level. 'And more shooters at street level.'

'We won't be able to get past all that,' Roger said, shaking his head. 'It's best we blow up the missiles.'

'No,' Zeb declared. 'We need to get a confirmed kill. There's no guarantee a missile explosion will take out Almasi.'

'Can you see those foot soldiers?' the Texan said angrily. 'How will you get past them? The only people in that town are the terrorists. They'll identify us as strangers in a moment. They'll have radio comms as well. Some kind of password system.'

'We'll ask some of them, nicely.'

Bwana smiled. He liked that strategy. His grin faded at Zeb's next words.

'We'll take to the roofs.'

They left at 8 pm in the van and the Range Rover. Zeb with Broker, the sisters with Bwana and Roger.

Down the Al Shat Road, past the oil refinery, which had a TV truck outside, joining the coastal highway.

They stopped once at the edge of the Misrata district. The dark of the night was intense; traffic was sparse and became virtually nonexistent once they entered Sirte district and curved towards the coast. They drove parallel to the sea, and after a while, turned off their lights.

The moon provided them company. It illuminated their way and guided them to the town where evil lurked.

They parked their vehicles deep in a bombed-out house on the outskirts of Sirte and proceeded on foot.

All of them in loose robes, which had strategic slits through which they could quick-draw their weapons. HKs for all of them except Zeb, who carried a M107, the Barrett Light Fifty. It was in its case, over his back, with custom-made slings.

His go-bag had coils of explosives, detonators, nylon-coated ropes, a compressed air gun and several grapple hooks. They weren't of the kind Hollywood depicted. His did have claws, but also a special adhesive that the NSA had designed. It was quick-acting, stuck to any surface, and, along with the hooks, could fasten to concrete.

'You're sure that works?' Beth quirked an eyebrow at him as they jogged at a ground-eating pace.

'Works in training,' he replied. 'First outing in the field.'

'Zeb.' She sighed. 'I'm not sure of your plan.'

'There's no other way. Nothing that will give us a confirmed kill.'

He went through their plan in his mind as they ran. *That's not what it is. We've got a rough idea on execution. Everything will depend on the security and rooftop access.*

They came across the first perimeter in half an hour. A sentry was smoking a cigarette, leaning against a wall, chuckling to himself as he watched a video on his phone.

He jumped up when Bwana loomed over him. Made a desperate attempt to claw at his gun, went still when the operative's knife nicked his throat.

'How many people on the ground? What security setup do you have?'

The terrorist's eyes bulged at the dark man's fluent Arabic. He drew breath to scream a warning, choked off when Bwana drew blood.

'You can die here. Or, tell me what I want and live through the night.'

The sentry decided valor wasn't the right choice.

He spilled everything he knew and then slumped to the floor when the operative applied a cotton swab to his nose.

Its contents rendered adults unconscious. When they came to, they were invariably disoriented and confused. Special forces operatives had used it for a long time and found that the victims invariably didn't disclose they had been assaulted. No sentry liked to admit they had been overpowered easily.

'Three layers of guards,' Bwana explained when he rejoined them.

He tapped at the map on Meghan's screen. 'First layer is half a mile from Almasi's building. A loose circle of men in radio contact with each other. They patrol their section of the perimeter, which is about a couple of blocks. Central command is on the first floor in Almasi's building.'

'What about the snipers?' Zeb asked.

'Hold on, I haven't finished. Each perimeter has a unique password. Any stranger who doesn't know the password is turned away.'

'What if an outer guard wants to go inside?' Broker asked.

'Will you let me finish?' Bwana growled. 'Each layer knows the password to the next one, but not beyond. These men live in their zones and rarely need to get to the central area. If they do, they are blindfolded and escorted inside. Only those in the inner perimeter get access to Almasi's building.'

'The snipers'—he looked at Zeb— 'have the same setup. In their case, however, there's no need for any to move inside.'

'Do they have call signs?'

'No. They use their first names. Here's the thing.' He took the screen from Meghan and zoomed in to show Almasi's building. 'Two snipers on these two buildings.' He pointed to a couple, to the left and right of the target structure's entrance. 'They can see inside Almasi's room. That's by design, so that they can take out any hostile who enters.'

Zeb studied the layout, calculated distances. 'Three hundred yards from that roof on the right?'

'Yeah,' Beth confirmed after a moment. 'Downwards. You've taken those shots before. There's barely any wind. No cloud cover.'

'Yeah.'

The shot would be easy. It was getting to position that was the challenge.

'What's the password for this zone and the next one?'

'Jasmine and Kalashnikov,' Bwana replied.

'What about women and children?'

'That building,' he pointed to one in the outside perimeter, well away from Almasi's or the weapons store.

'They don't live together?'

'No.'

A weight lifted off Zeb's mind. Killing innocents wasn't his objective, and now it looked like there would be no such casualties.

We can do this.

'Let's go,' he said.

Chapter 91

———⊂⊃⊂⊃⊂⊃———

Abu Bakhtar was with Almasi, both of them having a very late dinner.

Neither slept much at night. It was during the day that they rested. It was a schedule that worked for them, given that they carried out their attacks in the dark.

'The NOC refinery in Al-Hany,' the deputy briefed his leader. 'We're getting plans for it. That will be our next target. It's the fourth largest complex the oil company has. The second target will be Libyan Islamic Bank. A lot of government accounts are there.'

'Both neighborhoods are well-populated?'

'Yes, sayyidi. We'll get lots of victims. A lot of coverage.'

'Good. The world should not forget that we exist. What about Misfud?'

'I'll make contact with him tomorrow. I have also sent a message to Saharol, asking who will be at the meeting.'

Almasi nodded approvingly and they ate in silence, unaware the night was not theirs alone.

Zeb scaled the first accessible building he came across, just inside the first perimeter.

The layout was in his mind. Almasi's building, to the northwest of where he was. A narrow alley running in front of it. The two sniper buildings on the other side. The weapons store was a short distance away, but it didn't matter for now.

He climbed up the sloping roof and got to the roof of the house. Went to its edge and peered down the alley. No sentry. Seven feet separating it from the next roof. *Jump's not possible. But that ledge over there, I can use that to step.*

The ledge was nothing but a block of concrete, a section of the roof that had split and was overhanging the street.

He tested it with a foot. No give. He climbed onto it. Yeah, it was solid. Four feet separating him and the next roof.

'You're good to fly,' Beth's amused voice in his earpiece.

They had separated once they had gone deeper inside the outside perimeter. Bwana, Roger and Broker would circle the target building and approach the lane at its front from each side. They would take positions there.

The twins had split, too. They sought out two houses and from there launched the drones. The birds had been kitted out with longer-life batteries that would keep them in the air for six hours. Two craft, not just for redundancy purposes, but also one for keeping an eye on Almasi and the other to overlook the terrorist base and guide Zeb to the ground operatives.

'You'll come across the first sniper if you proceed in a straight line. Four roofs away.'

Zeb took a running jump, landed easily and crouched down immediately.

'I said you're good.'

He got up sheepishly and headed to the end of the roof.

The next building was taller. Four floors. Impossible to jump across.

He reached into his go-bag and removed the grapple gun. Mounted the hook in it and attached one end of a rope to it. Applied the adhesive liberally to the hook. Took aim at a part of the parapet on the other roof and triggered.

The hook flew with a whistling sound and landed on the roof. He yanked at it until it stuck in the parapet and its claws extended at the impact. He looked around, found a large block of concrete and secured the other end of the rope to it.

Gave a hard tug to it. It held.

'Pray for me,' he spoke.

'Go on, don't be a wuss,' the younger sister chided.

Zeb donned thin gloves, went to the edge, leaned down, grabbed at the nylon and let his body swing off the roof.

His stomach clenched when the rope sagged. It stayed in position, however.

He stilled his body and looked down into the dark alley. No backup. He was a sitting target for any hostile. There didn't seem to be any.

He hand-walked along the rope, the going slower than he preferred, the weight of the rifle and his go-bag slowing him down. Sweat was streaming down his face by the time he reached the parapet, put a hand over it and pulled himself over. He lay on the roof, sucking huge lungfuls of air, and then got to his feet.

'Go to the roof to your left,' Beth commanded. 'There's a jump space, and then you can come to the sniper from behind.'

'What about Almasi?'

'Eyes on him,' Meghan answered. 'You were right. He's on the fourth floor. A room with a bed, closet for clothing. AK in a corner. Computer on a table, a couple of chairs.'

'What's he doing?' he asked as he went to where Beth had suggested, where there was a jump space formed from two jutting beams. He crossed to the roof and headed to the west, to the sniper who was on the next roof. *Have to question him.*

'Having dinner with Abu Bakhtar.'

'You can see this clearly?'

'None of these buildings have glassed windows. Just holes in the wall.'

He stopped at that. Pondered about it, and then it came to him. 'To prevent flying glass or debris in case they are attacked.'

'Yeah, and also, they can jump out if needed.'

'That will be a long fall.'

'That's the risk they might take. Better than being attacked and captured.'

Zeb crouched low and ran across the top of the building. Skirted piles of bricks. Looks like someone tried to repair it but gave up. Slowed when he came to the end of the roof and peered through the night.

He saw nothing but more roofs and the pale sides of residences. A shadow moved. Something whispered in the air. His footwear scraped on concrete.

'He isn't facing you,' Beth whispered as he squinted. 'You have a three-foot leap to get to that roof. You can make it?'

'I don't have a choice. Tell me when he takes his next drag.'

He hurried several steps back. Checked his bearing and where the neighboring building was.

I'll have to jump, land, take three or four steps to get to him.

'He's raising his smoke.'

Zeb broke into a sprint.

'In his mouth, now.'

He flew in the air.

'Head back. I think his eyes are shut. Can't be sure.'

He landed hard. *Too much noise.*

'He's turning around,' her voice rose.

One lunge.

His vision will have to adjust, too. His mind will have to catch up.

The terrorist reacted faster than Zeb expected. He dropped his smoke. An exclamation left him. He reached for the AK around his chest.

And then Zeb was on him, bodyslamming, bringing him down on the hard surface, his left fist smashing into the man's jaw, turning another shout into a grunt, and his blade came out and dug just beneath the man's right eye.

'Password to the next level?' he hissed.

The shooter squirmed. Went still when Zeb drew blood.

'I'll cut your eyes,' he warned. 'Nod if you understand.'

The man nodded rapidly; his eyes wide with fright.

'Password?'

'Khayyam.'

'Khayyam?' Zeb pricked him deeper.

'Yes,' the man babbled in fear.

'Not Kalashnikov?'

'That's for the second circle. This is the third.'

'What happened to the sniper there?'

'Asif, he wasn't feeling well. He went down.'

'Passwords for the next level?'

'No more. This is the final one.'

'What about for the ground?'

'Same passwords.'

'Where are the other snipers?' Zeb asked, even though he knew from Beth's briefing.

'Awad's the next one. Two roofs away. Shamon is four roofs away.'

'How high are those buildings?'

'Six stories.'

'How often do you check in?'

'Hourly.'

'When's the next one?'

'I just finished. Another hour.'

'What do you say?'

'Nothing, just my name.'

'Who asks?'

'I don't know. It's someone in central command.'

Zeb jammed his palm over the man's mouth and slashed his neck. Held him down until he went still.

'Three and four roofs away,' he spoke into his comms.

'I know,' Beth replied. 'Get moving. You'll have to do the rope thing again, and then you'll be on the line of buildings on this side of the lane.'

Zeb got moving.

Chapter 92

———— ∞∞∞ ————

Abu Bakhtar and Nasir Fakhir Almasi finished their dinner. Their plates were taken away by an attendant. The terrorist head went to the computer and fiddled with it until a news channel came on. He went back to his chair and the two men watched in silence.

It was how they spent the evenings when no attacks or raids were being carried out. Dinner. Watch world and local TV. Get ideas for their next attacks and recruiting more to their fold.

'Americans,' the ISIL chief said in disgust when the report turned to US politics. 'We need to be stronger, Abu Bakhtar. We need to have more soldiers. Then, we can carry out a big attack on the shaitan.'

'Yes, sayyidi,' the deputy agreed.

Zeb's climb through the air to the sixth-floor building was easier than he thought. The angle wasn't too steep. *Maybe I've gotten used to this.* He hauled himself over the ledge and caught his breath. Rolled over and got to his feet. One more roof to cross, and then he would be with the first sniper to the

491

left of Almasi's building.

That terrorist was yawning when Zeb came out of the gloom, and before his mind could comprehend what his eyes saw, he was knocked out cold.

Zeb trussed him up and sealed his mouth with tape.

'Good work. Don't be overconfident,' Beth warned him.

'Where are Bwana, Rog and Broker?'

'We're here,' the dark man replied in fake-disgust. 'Waiting for you to do something instead of strolling in the park.'

Zeb couldn't help grinning as he pondered the next building. Getting there called for a little parkour. He used the side of a water tank to lever himself off into the night and land on the roof. He fell awkwardly. Shot his hands out to stop the Barrett's case from thumping. Waited, chest pounding. Checked his ankle.

No sprain. Wiped his lips on his sleeve and got to his feet.

'Shamon's alert,' Beth told him. 'He's pacing down the roof line. Checking the lane once in a while.'

'Where's his rifle?

'Slung across his chest. Hands free. You've got a little luck. There's a water tank there.'

Zeb saw it now. It was dark and looming, cut his view from the front of the roof, where the sniper was.

'You can't use the grapple gun. He'll hear you. You'll have to leap. Distance is just about right. Four feet. But you will make noise when you land.'

Zeb checked the space between the buildings. The jump was doable if he had a good enough runup.

The landing noise?

Perhaps he could use it to his advantage.

Shamon took great pride in his vigil. He could see down and across the lane, right into their leader's window. There he was, with the deputy.

He patted his AK reassuringly. He took his duties seriously. Not like the others. He knew some of the snipers slept in the night … why, some of the ground sentries even went to visit their women!

Not him. Abu Bakhtar had him in that position not just because he was always awake, but also because he was the best shot.

What was that?

He whirled round when something clattered behind the water tank.

'Who's that?' he shouted.

'Shamon,' a voice called weakly. 'Help me.'

He didn't recognize that voice, but there were many new men in the group that he didn't know. Was it Awad, the nearest sniper? It could be. He hadn't spoken to the man much.

'Help me, Shamon,' the voice called out urgently, getting weaker.

The sniper left his post. He hurried to the tank, down its right side. If the injured man knew his name, he had to be one of them. Who else would dare enter the ISIL stronghold, and on the roof, too?

Huh? There was no one there. What was that? A bag?

'Awad? Where are you?' he called out, bending down.

Something struck him on the side of his head. He fell face-down. Another blow hit him so hard that he saw stars.

Something gripped his throat and turned him over. A man, not Awad. A stranger. His eyes fierce and dark in the night.

And then the questioning began.

Chapter 93

Shamon had confirmed what Awad had. Zeb knocked him out and secured him. Went to the side of the building and looked down at the light coming out of the fourth-floor window.

He unpacked the Barrett. Aluminum receiver, bipod, rear handgrip, recoil operated frame, chrome-lined barrel, muzzle brake and suppressor; he assembled the weapon swiftly and mounted the BORs, Barrett Optical Ranging Scope, on top.

The weapon was originally designed for anti-materiel purposes but was widely used for anti-personnel sniping, too. Its fifty-cal round delivered tremendous kinetic power that ensured that, if a target was hit, it stayed down. And was destroyed.

Zeb slapped in a ten-round magazine and lay prone in a classic shooting position. Brought his eye to the scope and made adjustments.

Almasi was as clear as day in his sights, as was his deputy.

Take your time.

He cycled down his breathing and summoned the grey fog that helped him for intense concentration.

He adjusted his shoulders. Planted his legs firmly and

curled his finger over the trigger, which when pulled would send death at close to two thousand feet a second.

Inhale.

Exhale.

Inhale.

His finger curled over the trigger.

Inhale.

Exhale.

His finger started depressing.

Almasi got up suddenly. Abu Bakhtar followed.

Zeb didn't move. He kept watching as the two men talked. He could take a shot, but kill probability was low.

The ISIL leader walked off abruptly. He went to the closet and brought out a coat. Shrugged into it and disappeared from view.

What happened?

'Sitrep,' he asked tightly.

'Everything normal,' Roger drawled.

'Same here,' Bwana and Broker chorused.

'He's heading down,' Beth said. Worry in her voice. 'I can see thermals. Abu Bakhtar is with him. Did something spook him? Did they get a call?'

'Negative,' Zeb said, 'I was watching them.'

He crawled to the edge of the roof and looked down. There would be sentries at the end of the lane. No one in front of the building.

'Still going down?'

'Confirmed,' Meghan replied. 'Now on the third floor.'

He whirled to the Barrett. Attached explosives to it. A remote-operated detonator that he could trigger with his phone.

Checked that his Glock was in its holster and his blade was in its sheath.

'I'm going down.'

Chapter 94

———— ∞∞∞ ————

Zeb ignored the protests in his earpiece. Returned to the front again. Nothing there by which he could get to ground level.

'Second floor,' Meghan intoned.

He could use the stairs. *What condition will they be in?* No, he couldn't waste time finding that out.

He went to the left. Just the side wall—wait, wasn't that a drain pipe there that went down to the narrow alley? It was several feet below the top. There was a window to its side.

Similar to how I escaped the first time.

He didn't stop to think. Straightened, faced the roof and dropped.

'ZEB! WHAT THE—' Beth screamed.

The fall felt like barely a second before his outstretched arms caught the rough concrete of the hole which was the window. His body slammed against the wall.

'First floor, entering the alley,' Meghan updated. Zeb kicked out with his right leg even as his grip slipped. An inelegant, sideways heave that sent him crashing into the drainpipe, which held, thankfully. He wrapped his legs around it. Sent another prayer of thanks for his foresight in wearing gloves and slid all the way down to the ground.

One second to orient himself from the descent. Check the small alley between the two houses. No hostile.

'They're going down the lane. Your left once you enter it.'

He crouched behind the shelter of the house and peered. Two figures were illuminated from the lighting within neighboring buildings. Abu Bakhtar, the taller of the two, on the left.

He looked right. No gunmen in sight.

Don't they have guards? It might be a power thing. The ISIL head and his deputy should have the freedom to go where they want without security. Besides, there are sentries at the ends, and snipers on top.

He stepped out. The grey fog returned. The beast woke up and filled him smoothly, silently.

His hand went to his Glock, fell back. No guns. The shots would alert every terrorist. He would have to use his knife. He drew it out and held it down his thigh.

One man against two deadly killers. In hostile terrain.

He picked up his pace. Got closer to them. Thought he heard one of them laugh. His comms was silent. His friends knew he couldn't be distracted.

He lowered his chi. Ghosted silently, head down, sensing them ahead.

But not quietly enough. Or it must have been a sixth sense that alerted Abu Bakhtar, because he turned back. Did a double take when he saw the man behind them.

'Misfud?' he asked in astonishment when light fell on Zeb.

That animal instinct must have warned him of danger. That the arms dealer's appearance wasn't normal. Because his hands flew to his AK.

Move!

Zeb pounced forward. Crossed the short distance between them in two swift strides. Was aware of Almasi turning as well. Saw his profile. Got confirmation that it was the ISIL leader.

And then he was on top of Abu Bakhtar, sending him stumbling back, his left hand clasping the terrorist's wrist, preventing him from triggering. He saw the deputy's mouth open. Knew a warning shout was coming. Thrust the knife in his throat. Not a clean cut. Felt Almasi move beside them. *Finish this fast.* He couldn't afford to get into a fight. Abu Bakhtar gasped hoarsely, his eyes wide, summoning his strength to struggle.

Jab, Jab, Jab. Zeb knifed him rapidly, all in just a few seconds, so fast that when he snatched a glance to his right, Almasi wore a shocked expression.

He recovered rapidly, however. Sprang back to give himself room, his hand grappling with something at his waist, coming up with a handgun, leveling it.

The beast acted. It powered Zeb's reflexes. He grabbed Abu Bakhtar by the shoulder, whirled him around and flung him towards the ISIL leader, who fired just as his deputy landed on him, his body twitching and jerking from the impact of the rounds.

Time seemed to freeze as Almasi looked in horror at what he had done. He cried with rage. He shoved Abu Bakhtar's body away, his eyes murderous as he brought his gun up.

Zeb slashed it away with his free hand, sending it skittering in the darkness, and plunged his blade in Almasi's chest. He was dimly aware of shouts down the lane, more windows being lighted. Almasi's shots had been muffled by his deputy's body, but they were loud enough to be heard in the night and had alerted the terrorists.

'GET GOING,' Beth yelled at him.

His knife jammed into Almasi's ribs; the man was punching and kicking and attacking with all the strength in his body.

Movement down the lane as hostiles spilled out.

Silence was no longer an option.

Zeb took a blow to his head, drew back, stumbled against Abu Bakhtar's body, lost his balance and fell.

Almasi roared in triumph. He made a fearsome sight with the knife sticking out of his chest, his face bloodied and feral.

He jumped on the fallen man, drew out the blade with a cry and brought it down on Zeb, who deflected it just in time, but the ferocity of the terrorist's attack was such that he recovered and slashed again, and this time, Zeb took the knife in his chest. It stuck in his plate armor, and the hard barrier confused Almasi for a moment, which provided the opening Zeb wanted. He lunged forward, snarling, teeth bared. The ISIL leader sensed his intent and drew back, giving more space for Zeb's hand to draw out his Glock and point it at Almasi's forehead—and blow his lights out.

Zeb followed through by firing a wild burst at the hostiles who were approaching rapidly. They scattered, giving him time to fire a killing shot in Abu Bakhtar's head, just in case he had survived the knife attacks and the rounds from his leader.

'TOWARDS US!' Bwana commanded.

Zeb took off, fumbling in his pocket for his cell phone, finding it and triggering the Barrett.

The explosion drew yells of alarm from the pursuers, who dived back into the buildings, suspecting an aerial ambush.

Zeb ran, zigging and zagging, firing at a shadow in front

that emerged from a building to his left. It disappeared.

The noise grew behind him when the shooters realized there was no ambush. He looked back. Fifteen, maybe twenty men, joining the hunt, yelling and baying. Sweat and blood—from a cut in his forehead that he hadn't been aware of—blinded him. He ran, his forearm against his face, but it was ineffective.

'Keep coming,' Bwana said calmly.

Two figures ahead, one on each side of the lane. One crouching, the other standing. He brought his Glock up.

'That's us,' Roger drawled, and then the night lit up as they opened fire. When he looked back, the terrorists were caught between the two operatives at the front and Broker, who had opened from the rear.

Something smashed into Zeb's back with the force of a log. He went down. Realized his armor had stopped a round. *Get up.* Beth was shouting in his earpiece, Meghan too. But his limbs refused to cooperate. His head was swimming, and then the darkness faded as the beast took over. But before he could rise, he was pulled up effortlessly and found himself looking up at Bwana's wide smile. 'Cavalry to the rescue,' his friend said, chuckling. He turned Zeb round and inspected his back quickly.

They were in ISIL territory, with deadly killers hunting them, and yet his friend found it in him to laugh.

'Thank you,' Zeb said, overcome with emotion.

Bwana read his face and gripped his shoulder. 'Anything for you. *Anything.*' He inspected Zeb's back, 'Low-caliber round,' he said. 'You're good.'

They sprinted to safety at the end of the lane, Roger and Broker pinning back the swarming terrorists. Just as they exited, the ground shuddered and trembled as an explosion rocked the buildings.

Meg's set off the missiles.

Zeb ran in the night, twisting and turning in lanes and alleys as they headed back to their vehicles, his friends ranging alongside him. Beth and Meghan joined last as they continued to fly the drones, taking video of the destruction and directing the craft to the rendezvous.

The cool air dried his sweat, renewed him.

Beth punched him when he stopped at the van. A furious blow on his shoulder that sent him staggering.

'DON'T. EVER. DO. THAT. AGAIN,' she fumed.

'Do what?' he asked as his friends laughed.

'That drainpipe thing.'

'Oh, that. I'm an old hand at it.'

They fist-bumped, climbed into the vehicles and set out immediately. Once they hit the coastal road, Broker broke their silence.

'ISIL'S finished.'

Zeb didn't answer, as murmurs of agreement filtered through his earpiece.

Is it?

It's driven by ideology and that isn't easily destroyed. It will take time, new generations, to overcome such thinking.

But, for sure, it's a setback for them. A big one.

My mission's done.

He relaxed and drove on in the night.

Chapter 95

Meghan told him when they stopped for a rest break just before entering Misrata District. At the same spot they had halted when going towards Sirte. To their right was the sea. To their left, a few hundred yards away, the highway ribboned away, no traffic on it.

She came to him with her screen, and something in her posture made him put his coffee flask down.

'Beth and I found this when we were driving up.'

'What?'

She showed him her screen instead of replying.

A brief bio of Secretary of State Paul Vaughan.

'I know about him,' Zeb began. Drew his breath sharply when she pointed to a few highlighted sentences.

Served with Randy Spears. Same Special Forces team as him. Bob Marin is SF, too.

He kept re-reading the bio, stunned to silence, and stopped her from the swiping the screen.

'It could be coincidence,' his voice cracked.

'It isn't,' she replied and brought up an image of a picturesque street. There, at the edge of the frame, two men: Vaughan and Spears. It wasn't the greatest photograph, but their faces were clear enough.

'Bahamas,' she said. 'To the left of them, not in the frame, is a bank that relies on discretion of service. Werner hacked into it. That bank records only numbers, no names. However, it cracked into several law firms there that specialize in offering offshore legal services. In one, it hit pay dirt. It found that account number linked to four individuals. That bank account is Saharol's. Vaughan, Spears and Marin are the signatories.' She flipped through more images, rapidly, knowing that he wasn't paying attention to them.

'Who's the fourth?'

She silently brought up the last photograph. It was an airport terminal, one that he recognized immediately. Lynden Pindling International Airport, in Nassau. One man, his profile to the camera, unrecognizable by the large pair of shades and low hat over his head.

'That's Vaughan. Werner ran all kinds of checks on that image and confirms his identity. And that person'—she tapped the screen at a second man who was angled away from the camera— 'is Jian Hsu. He's the fourth name associated with that account. They formed Saharol.'

Zeb sagged against the van as Roger took the screen from her and flicked through the images, the other operatives bursting out in surprise and anger.

The Earth continued its orbit, waves crashed on the beach not far from them, but Zeb didn't hear them, nor did he feel anything.

I knew there would be powerful people behind this. Didn't expect our own secretary of state.

Sound, sight and awareness returned to him after a while.

With it, an icy rage that made his hands shake. He jammed them in his pockets, but not before the older twin had noticed.

'What I don't get is why,' she said, without commenting on his reaction. All of them were aware of his shakes.

Zeb controlled his anger, shoved it deep down inside him. *Now isn't the time for it.* He didn't ask the twins if they were sure of the identities and of the information Werner had gathered.

'They didn't want me to kill Almasi,' he stated.

'Yeah, but why?' Beth cried.

'Do you have Vaughan's schedule?'

'No,' Meghan replied. 'His dates aren't confirmed yet. But some of the meetings he'll have are obvious and covered by the media. One's with the Libyan prime minister and various cabinet members. Another's with Hazim Kattan. Yet another,' her voice slowed, 'is a reception for US companies in Libya. Bob Marin is expected to be praised by Vaughan.'

'What if ShadowPoint offered security services to the Libyan government?' Broker voiced. 'They are a highly experienced, capable security force. They could either work with the Libyan military or take over from them.'

'And Sabbagh and his cabinet would take them on. They would need someone with that specialist expertise because, as long as Almasi was around, he was a threat,' Beth caught on excitedly, 'and their own military is corrupt.'

'That could be why Saharol, whose security partner is ShadowPoint, leaked the location of the missiles to the terrorists. To make them a more potent threat.'

Zeb rubbed his jaw. It made sense; however, he remained unconvinced. 'Why would ShadowPoint need Vaughan for that? They could work with Saharol alone in securing such a deal. And Hsu? Where does he fit in? He's not involved because of a security contract. His ambitions are bigger.'

'Zeb,' Meghan frowned, 'What if Saharol wanted to play a bigger role in Libya's oil operations? Right now, all foreign companies have only bit parts to play.'

He straightened instantly, a light bulb moment. *That must be it!* 'That's …' he trailed, thinking furiously, 'more like it. Saharol must be angling for an oil field. Because of its association with ShadowPoint, it can pretty much guarantee uninterrupted oil operations. Those have been disrupted because of Kattan and Almasi's attacks. Billions will be involved in such a deal. That explains Jian Hsu's involvement as well. It will give China a hold over Libyan oil, make it a much bigger and stronger player in North Africa than it currently is.'

'Vaughan, Spears and Marin will be billionaires overnight,' Roger said grimly. 'It will be easy for the secretary to hide his involvement. His offshore account, the incorporation documents, none of them are accessible to US authorities. Not by legal means. Even if someone comes across that travel blog and identifies him, he'll laugh it off and say he *was* in the country. Vacationing. Heck, Zeb,' he slapped his thigh angrily, 'this Saharol deal, it need not even be kept secret. If it's in the open, he'll take credit for facilitating it. A secretary of state helping US business? That's pretty much his job description.'

'And it will help that presidential run he's said to be interested in,' Bwana added. 'Greed, ambition, in his, Marin and Spears's case. And power and control for Hsu.'

'They had to maintain status quo in Libya. Almasi had to remain a threat, otherwise there's no need for a deal with Saharol,' Beth exclaimed. 'Spears must have heard of the Agency's mission through his security connections. Hsu knows what a threat Zeb is. He and Spears got those videos out, he took out Shaming Chia and they turned Zeb into a traitor, expecting that some team would kill him.'

Zeb climbed into the van without a further word.

'Where next?' Meghan took his cue and headed to the Range Rover.

'Bob Marin,' he said grimly. 'Let's ask him some questions.'

Chapter 96

⸺⸺∞⸺⸺

Zeb had driven a mile when he slowed suddenly.

'What's up?' Broker asked him.

'Beth?' Zeb spoke into his comms. 'Anything on the news or social media about Sirte?'

'Some chatter on the internet about an explosion. Nothing more than that. ISIL will not reveal anything. That's not how they operate.'

'You've told Clare?'

'Not yet.'

'Let's patch her in.'

'Almasi and Abu Bakhtar are down and out,' Zeb told her when she came on.

'You pulled it off,' she said wonderingly, 'despite all that was happening.'

'We did, ma'am.'

'You know, Zeb, no one would have minded, least of all me, if you had focused on clearing yourself. Almasi wasn't going anywhere.

'That's not who you are, right?' she said softly when he didn't reply.

'We lost four missiles, ma'am. Two to demonstrate they worked. Two, well, there's something on social media about an explosion in Sirte. That was us.'

'I'll record that in your file,' she said, a smile in her voice, 'that you are wasteful with government equipment.'

She turned serious when all of them stayed silent.

'There's more, isn't there?'

'Yes, ma'am,' Beth took over. 'You'd better fasten your seat belt. Paul Vaughan is involved. Our secretary of state.'

They sped through miles of highway and remote country-side as she briefed Clare on the Bahamas and their suspicion.

Something clattered. *Her reading glasses.* He pictured her putting them down and rubbing the bridge of her nose.

'Send those photographs to me. That bank account, every-thing.' Clare's voice was tungsten steel.

'Should be with you in a few.'

'I'll go to the presi—'

'Ma'am,' Zeb interrupted. 'We don't know everything. Which is why we're going to question Marin.'

'I can't sit on this, Zeb.'

'I'm not asking you to. Share this with who you have to. However, Vaughan, Spears or Hsu shouldn't suspect anything.'

'I'll take care of that. Hsu …'

'We'll deal with him when the time comes. I need a couple of favors. The president needs to delay the secretary's visit. Whatever plausible excuse he can make.'

'Done. The second one?'

'Sirte. We need to have some story out there. Maybe fight-ing between two militia groups that resulted in the explosion.'

'I know a few people who'll be happy to cooperate.'

'Beth, I think we need Werner's bots to spread this story

as well. Let's take the initiative before the real one leaks.'

'On it.'

'Zeb, we're forgetting something,' Meghan said quietly. 'Dante Abrahms. He's still out there.'

'Not much we can do about him until he shows himself.'

'That's just it. He might take a sniper shot.'

'He won't. If he's the kind of person I think he is, he'll want to make this personal. We wiped out his team. He had to kill his own man before us. They had been with him for years. That loyalty deserves revenge. Delivered face to face.'

'I hope you are right.'

Zeb was right.

Abrahms had followed them out of the city and had halted when they entered Misrata district. He guessed where they were going. An attack on ISIL. He could have warned Hsu, but what Carter did wasn't his mission. Killing him was.

The highway was remote, very little traffic on both sides. It was ideal for taking out Carter.

But what of his friends? He couldn't take them on as well.

Their vehicles weren't close to each other. There was a good fifteen-minute gap between them. Could he make use of that? He drove on, and when he found an opening, got onto the highway running the other way. Back to Tripoli.

Found a few spots, discarded them, until he got to the steep slope.

He stopped his vehicle and got out. There would be several minutes when one vehicle would be out of sight of the other. He could hide a getaway vehicle in the woods over there. By the time he finished Carter, he would be gone, long before his friends could track back.

They would hunt him, but where would they find him? Sure, they would suspect that he had escaped in another vehicle, but what if he ditched that too and got into another?

He checked the GPS on Carter's van. It was still heading to the east.

Abrahms made his decision.

Carter would die on his return.

Chapter 97

---∞∞∞---

Later, Zeb would blame himself.

He was distracted, thinking of Vaughan, Spears and Hsu. Wondering what motivated people like the secretary of state and Spears, who were already wealthy. He understood Hsu. The MSS head wasn't driven by wealth. For him, it was always about China and its preeminence in the world.

It was that lapse of concentration that cost him. The thinking and the idle conversation he was having with Broker.

He was aware of the lights in his mirror. The Range Rover, ahead, had disappeared from view, going down a slope. He was on the right lane, sticking to the speed limit even though there were no police around.

The other vehicle came onwards in the outer lane, started overtaking. He didn't pay it any attention.

It swerved into his van, rammed it hard and started driving it into the metal divider.

All in a split-second, before he could react.

Broker's 'Watch out!' lost in the thump of impact, tearing of metal, shattering of glass and squeal of tires.

He grabbed the wheel, but the van didn't respond. Jammed

the brakes hard as his ride smashed into the divider, their bodies rocking and buffeting with the crash. Metal crumpled. The front of the van collapsed. Their leg space cramped up as the floorboards buckled.

His engine spluttered, coughed and died. Steam escaped from the front. Dark smoke from rubber joined it.

And when a figure loomed outside his window, Zeb knew the crash wasn't an accident.

Dante Abrahms, a gun pointed straight at him.

He threw himself back in his seat, his fingers operating the recline lever. The shot missed by mere inches. It sped past him and then he heard Broker grunt, saw him jerk forward.

He's hit!

The beast roared in fury.

He clawed at his Glock even as Abrahms looked on contemptuously. His lips moved, but Zeb didn't hear.

Where's my gun?

'Not serious.' Broker's words were barely audible above the white noise in him. 'Scrape. Get him.'

His holster had slid to the side during the crash and was jammed between his back and the seat. He clawed at it. Released his seatbelt. Knew he was slow. Saw Abrahms get to the front. Raise his gun again.

His Glock came free.

Broker grabbed him and pulled him sideways as the South African fired. The round tore through the windscreen and punched into upholstery.

Zeb was at an awkward angle. Leaning on Broker, who was breathing loudly, harshly. He shot despite the angle; knew he had missed.

Anything to buy time.

Dante Abrahms didn't react. He didn't duck. He was stone-faced as he lined up his gun again, this time on Broker.

'*NO!*' Zeb shouted, knowing he didn't have enough time to aim, to stop his friend from being killed, and all because he hadn't been alert, hadn't been paying attention to the highway.

Meghan was alert. Beth was laughing at something Roger had said, but it didn't register on her. She was uneasy. She recollected Abrahms's file. *He's lethal. We need to look out for him.*

She checked her screen. Jammed her brakes hard when what she saw registered.

'ZEB! BROKER,' she yelled as the Range Rover slowed and yawed. 'They've stopped—'

Roger and Bwana reacted even before she had finished. They flung open their doors and dived out. The Texan landed on his shoulder, held his body loose and rolled twice to absorb the impact. Got to his feet in one smooth, fluid move, nodded to Bwana, who was up too and raced up the slope.

They burst into a full-tilt sprint when they heard the shots, their Glocks coming to their hands as if spring-loaded.

Roger didn't slow when he topped the rise and saw the van smashed into the barrier. The other vehicle hard against it. Cracked windshield. Fumes and smoke. Shards of glass on the road. One shooter in the glare of the headlights.

He didn't have to tell Bwana to go right, he would take the left. They were parts of the same whole.

He snapped the first shot. It went wide. He fired again, just as Bwana triggered, the double roar filling the night.

The shooter dropped to his knee and whirled to his side, triggering back rapidly. He jerked and shook and fell to the ground when Zeb opened up from inside the van.

'It's just a scratch,' Broker growled. He tried to push Meghan away and got a sharp rap.

Abrahms's round had grazed the front of his shoulder and scraped the front of his armor before flying out of the window.

'These would have stopped him in any case,' he said, tapping the ceramic plates across his chest.

'He was going for head shots, doofus,' Meghan snarled and deliberately tightened his dressing, making him wince.

She and Beth had joined moments later, by which time Abrahms had been killed.

'He's got a getaway ride there,' Bwana said, nodding towards the woods. 'A car. Looks like he had it planned.'

He would have succeeded, too, if Rog and Bwana hadn't acted so fast. If I hadn't noticed their GPS had stopped.

Meghan swallowed.

'How did he find us here?'

'This is how.' Roger came from behind the van holding a GPS transponder. 'He must have attached it at some point. We never checked our vehicles for surveillance or trackers.'

She noticed Zeb looking on from where he stood, by the side of the highway. He hadn't spoken since Abrahms's takedown.

That look when he saw Broker's shoulder. He'll never forgive himself for it.

'For chrissakes,' the elder operative said irritatedly, 'it's nothing. We get shot sometimes—'

Zeb turned his back on them.

She watched him for a long while as Roger and Bwana checked the Range Rover, declared it clean, and helped Broker to it.

Zeb became like this when any of them were injured. That coiled thing inside him, he called it the beast, unleashed itself and turned him into the deadliest person she had ever known.

She shivered.

I wouldn't want to be in Marin, Vaughan and Spears's shoes.

Or Jian Hsu's.

Chapter 98

Washington DC

Clare's first meeting was with Catlyn Feder.

'This is where the famed Agency is based?'

'You mean, *notorious*?'

'No. You did great work … Carter and your resignation does not diminish that at all.'

She glanced at the bare walls and the spartan-looking desk, on which there were no adornments. A screen. A notepad, a paperweight.

'You don't go in for decoration?'

'My personal and professional life are separate.'

'You said we had to meet.'

'Yeah. Belden is alive,' Clare said baldly.

'WHAT!' Feder clearly looked shaken. 'He died. The cops—'

'Said what I asked them to say.'

'What…? How…?' she trailed off, helplessly. Gathered herself and asked, 'How do you know? Where is he?'

'He's in a safe house, along with his family. He *was*

attacked. That much is true.'

Feder opened her mouth. Closed it. Opened it again as twin spots of color appeared on her cheeks. 'Clare, I am the director of the CIA,' she said, angrily. 'Doug Belden is my EA. Why don't I know any of this?'

'Because your assistant was the one who leaked Shaming Chia's identity.'

Clare took pity on Feder, who turned pale. 'He overheard a discussion you were having with Ibarra and Slaughter.'

'We questioned him, too.'

'Not seriously.'

'Who did he sell it to?

'He didn't do that. He confided in someone who he thought was trusted by you. In fact, was security cleared. He didn't think he was violating any confidentiality.'

'Belden's been around at the CIA for a long time,' she said heatedly. 'He should know well enough.'

'Not when the person he told is Randy Spears.'

Feder didn't react. Her head bowed. Her shoulder drooped. She stayed in that position until a laugh from an outside office roused her.

'You've checked ... of course you have,' she said dully, 'you wouldn't be saying all this if you hadn't.'

'Yes.'

'Everything,' the CIA head said monotonously, 'was fake, then. Carter *was* set up.'

'Yes.'

'By Spears? No, don't tell me. I don't need to know.'

'Why not?' Clare asked in surprise as Feder prepared to rise.

'I'll resign. There will have to be an investigation—'

'Sit down. You're going nowhere and doing nothing of that sort.'

'But—'

'Catlyn, sit down.'

The CIA director obeyed.

'You did nothing wrong. You got evidence and acted on it. I would have done the same if I had gotten something on your officers.'

'You went along with the kill order. That was a ruse?'

'Yes. I knew Zeb was implicated, but I didn't know whom to trust. I hoped he would survive until I or he got to the bottom of this.'

'Why're you stopping me from resigning?'

'Because you did nothing wrong. You aren't aware of this, but I offered to resign, too. The president laughed.'

'He knows about Carter?'

'He didn't believe it.'

'I don't know—'

'Catlyn Feder, you are one of the most intelligent women I know. Your smarts and your integrity are what make you the most qualified for that role. Besides, there aren't many of us. You, Lizzie at Homeland, me … we all need to stay together. Keep the men in line.'

The CIA director smiled wanly. 'You and I haven't gotten along very well.'

'We'll have professional differences. That does not mean we cannot work together.'

Feder squared her shoulders. 'Tell me everything. Spears is behind everything?'

'Not just him. Paul Vaughan, Jian Hsu and Bob Marin are involved too.'

'Any more bombshells?' the CIA director asked faintly when she had gotten her breath back.

'One more. Nasir Fakhir Almasi and Abu Bakhtar are both dead.'

It took an hour of telling and retelling, showing the evidence, walking through the timeline and sequencing of events for Feder to get up to speed.

'What do you want from me?' she asked. 'You invited me to your office for a reason.'

Clare raised her hand and extended her finger. 'Treat Spears no differently.' Another finger shot out. 'Your kill teams in Tripoli. Change their orders to *apprehend*, but do that discreetly. You can recall them when we wrap this up.'

'What about the other agency teams?'

'I know someone who can pass that message.' *Daniel, he can do that.* 'Thirdly, spread the information that it was militia groups warring between themselves that caused the Sirte explosion. No reference to Almasi.'

'I can do that. I will still need to brief the president and Mike.'

'Don't do anything until this is over.'

'What about Belden?'

'My people are protecting him.'

Feder assessed her and nodded slowly. 'I can see why the president has such high regard for you.'

Clare dismissed the compliment and walked her visitor out of the office, who lingered at the doorway.

'Too bland,' she said. 'You need to lighten it up.'

'I would,' the Agency head said with a laugh, 'if it was mine. This is a room I hired for our meeting.

'Remember, my office is bugged,' she explained when Feder's brows came together in astonishment. 'We could hardly meet there.'

'Sir,' Clare greeted President Morgan in the Oval Office that afternoon. 'You want the good news or the bad news first?'

She nodded to Daniel Klouse, who had arrived earlier at her request.

'The bad news, Clare.'

She spread the two Bahamas photographs on the Resolute Desk and let the men take them in.

'I don't understand,' the president said after a while. 'What am I seeing? That's Paul. Him I recognize.'

'Sir, that second man,' Klouse said softly, shock in his voice apparent, 'is Randy Spears. He's CEO of ShadowPoint.'

'Yeah, I've heard of them. So what? And this other photograph?'

'Sir, that person there, with the side profile, that's the secretary of state. And the one whose face we can barely see, that's Jian Hsu, head of China's Ministry of State Security.'

A stunned silence fell in the room. The president turned off the TV, crossed his arms on his chest and put on his game face.

'Tell us everything. How bad is it?'

'Very,' she said and began.

Briefing the most powerful person in the world and the national security advisor took less time because they didn't need to know everything.

The president went behind his desk when she had finished. He reached down and brought out a bottle of Uncle Nearest 1856 whiskey and three glasses.

'Purely for medicinal purposes,' he explained as he poured and served them, 'and for moments of shock such as these.'

Clare stayed quiet as they sipped. *He's working it out. Assessing the damage, political as well as personal.*

'This cannot be made public,' he said gravely. 'Ever. We cannot have that spectacle, that of a cabinet secretary colluding with other countries.'

'Yes, sir.'

'How bad is the damage to our intelligence agencies?'

'Containable, sir. My outfit was hit hardest. But my team is also the smallest; we rarely run double agents. We'll recover from this, sir. The CIA, too.'

'You've spoken to Catlyn.' A statement, not a question.

'Yes, sir.'

'What do you think?' he looked at Klouse.

'The Agency is good at this, sir. Let Clare handle it.'

His face lightened momentarily. 'Clare, whose resignation I have accepted and whose outfit is to be disbanded, will you handle it?'

'Yes, sir.'

'What of Zeb?'

'He's good, sir. My team is together. They're the ones who found all this.'

He nodded absently, looked at the photographs and for a moment, anger flashed in his eyes. 'I trusted him,' he said bitterly.

He collected the images and handed them to her. 'You *will* clean this up.'

'I will, sir.'

'You had good news as well?'

'The best you have heard in a few days, sir.' She spread

more photographs taken by the drones over Sirte.

'That's Almasi'—she pointed to one body and then to the other— 'and that's Abu Bakhtar. Zeb Carter completed his mission yesterday.'

President Morgan didn't whoop or holler when he finished studying the photographs. He clasped her hand and shook it hard. Thumped Klouse on the shoulder, poured them another round and raised his glass in a toast.

'That *is* the best news I have heard in a while.'

'Clare,' he accompanied her to the door. 'Jian Hsu. I hope he's included as well in your cleanup.'

'I'm sure Zeb's already making plans for him, sir.'

Chapter 99

Tripoli

They were ghosts in the night as they arrived in Gergaresh, where the politicians and the wealthy lived in their fancy villas, inside walled compounds, protected by private security teams. Many of them had Tripoli's police cruisers patrol their streets, such was their power and influence. Even the militia groups left those residences alone.

Zeb had no such reservations. He parked their vehicle several streets away and filtered through the shadows, Broker tagging with him.

The elder operative had furiously argued when asked to stay back. 'IT'S. JUST. A. FRICKING. GRAZE,' he had yelled until Zeb had worked out a compromise. He would stay back with Beth on the drones, while Meghan joined the inside team.

The Range Rover's occupants proceeded down on the other side of the leafy lane. The sisters holding their dim-lit screens, guiding the craft high above them.

Zeb stopped when the gated entrance to Bob Marin's home

came into view. The Saharol CEO wanted privacy, and he got it.

He's chosen it well. Middle of the street. Any vehicle stopping near it will be noticed. There were two other villas on the same side, but they were spread out. The nearest residence on the opposite side was set back. No house had direct sight of the other.

'Here we go,' Beth murmured, just as two vehicles turned into the street, coming up from behind them. Loud music and raucous yelling from them as they drove side by side.

One of them swerved when it neared the Marin gate. The second vehicle overcompensated, crashed into the first and sent it careening into the compound wall.

Both drivers got out, cursing. They swore at each other, blaming the other. The crash and their furious argument brought the guards out. They hustled angrily towards the fracas. *Didn't those fools know whose house they had crashed into?* They separated the quarreling men. And stood frozen when Bwana and Roger appeared out of the night and jammed their Glocks into their mouths.

'Got the gate keycode,' the Texan announced.

'Send the birds.' Zeb raced to catch up as Roger and Bwana were opening the gates. Meghan joined him a moment later.

The drones shot over the tree line, went over Marin's compound and fried its security system with an intense EMP burst. Simultaneously, Werner tripped a switch in the city's power supply and turned the street dark. The villa had a backup generator, however its electronics had been toasted by the electromagnetic wave. Several of the AI's bots dialed the Tripoli police number, reported militia attacks in various part of the city, and hung up before the call center could verify.

Those calls will keep the police busy.

Zeb separated from his friends, who split and went separate ways through the villa's gardens. *They'll take care of the remaining guards. Meg, Bwana and Rog will be more than enough for them.* He frowned immediately. 'Bwana, no killing,' he said in his mic. He couldn't help grinning when the reply came.

'Spoilsport.'

Bob Marin was seated at his dining table when the lights went out. Battery-powered ones, independent of the generator, came on instantly. He gave no thought to it. Tripoli wasn't known for reliable power supply.

He was cutting into his steak when his security manager, Raoul Daschel, hurried in. 'Some problem with the cameras. They're all down. Phones are dead, too. I've lost contact with our men.'

Marin chewed his meat and glanced at his cell phone. No signal. He had checked in with Spears earlier, had told him that Kanaan was moving the file through the cabinet. Almasi hadn't responded yet. Matters were progressing, a tad slower than they wanted, but hey, this was Libya. Time had its own pace.

'Anything I should be worried about?' he asked Daschel.

'No, sir. I'll investigate and loop you in.'

The Saharol CEO resumed his dinner when his manager left. He was cutting another slice when a faint exclamation came to him.

'Daschel?' he called.

'He won't be joining us.' A man entered the room.

Bob Marin, special forces veteran, combat-hardened, recognized Carter in a flash and acted.

Zeb wasn't expecting the speed at which Marin reacted. Nor the *how*.

The CEO upturned the dining table. Its top, which seemed to be hinged to its legs, swiveled and presented a vertical surface, giving him cover. Crockery and cutlery crashed to the floor, their sounds drowned by gunshots, as Marin fired blindly.

Zeb threw himself to the floor. Slithered back rapidly, seeking cover behind a couch. *Should've drawn on him without any warning.* He cursed himself as rounds whizzed above him and windows shattered.

He's firing blind. He snatched a glance and saw Marin's gun hand over the edge of the table. Fired at it rapidly. The hand disappeared.

He continued firing, keeping the Saharol man pinned behind the table. *It's steel-lined. He probably had a gun taped beneath it.*

His own position was perilous. Marin had cover and could wait until he was empty. There wasn't much cover in the dining room, just the couch, whose upholstery was already wrecked. A few decorative tables and chairs. Lightweight, when he felt them. To the left of the table was a side wall. To the right was the hallway through which he had arrived.

That'll be his escape route.

Zeb fast-changed and kept shooting, not allowing Marin to show his gun hand, searching the top and sides of the table with his shots.

'YOU'RE TRAPPED. YOU CAN'T ESCAPE,' Marin shouted. 'MY MEN ARE COMING.'

Zeb's gaze fell on glass vases on a side table. Several of them, stuffed with flowers.

He picked up one and hurled it at the wall behind Marin. It splintered into pieces. Threw another one. A third followed. A yelp from behind the table. He flung the last vase with all his strength.

He got the result he wanted.

Bob Marin shot out from behind the table, firing wildly, and hurtled towards the hallway.

Zeb grabbed at a chair. Threw it at the fleeing man. He flung another. Shot out from behind the couch. Saw that his second missile had brought down Marin, who was turning around desperately, searching for the gun he had lost.

Zeb landed short, slid on the smooth floor just as Marin found his gun and started bringing it up.

Marin howled in agony and his gun went clattering when Zeb plunged his knife through his shoe. He wasn't done, however.

His free leg came up in a vicious kick. Zeb twisted to avoid it, which gave Marin time and space to rear up and remove the knife from his foot in a short, savage motion. Zeb threw himself forward, caught his knife wrist, used his body momentum and the upward arc of Marin's hand to keep the blade moving up and around and buried it deep in his right shoulder.

Marin's scream turned into a choking groan when Zeb landed his knee on the man's gut and thrust hard.

'I'm tired of people shooting at me,' he grated, while twisting the knife. 'I want answers.'

Bob Marin's breaking point came when Zeb punctured his body several more times and made to jam the knife in his groin. That, along with the promise of an easy jail term, got the CEO to spill.

Zeb tapped his mic once to get Beth and Broker to record once Marin began talking. He listened silently, stunned by the scope of Paul Vaughan's ambition and greed.

'It was his idea,' Marin panted. 'He got Spears on board. They made me CEO.'

He detailed Hsu's involvement, the deal, the meetings with Kattan, the deputy prime minister and the reach out to ISIL.

They thought of everything, Zeb thought bleakly. He and his friends had come close to identifying the conspiracy. *We underestimated the scale, however. Saharol a shareholder in NOC.* That was a game-changer, one they hadn't even considered. *For that big a prize, no wonder they pulled out all stops to kill me.* Jian Hsu's involvement made perfect sense.

Marin's voice cracked as he finished narrating. He lay on his back, bleeding from multiple wounds, shiny-faced with sweat, eyes half-closed in agony.

'I'll be your star witness,' he whispered. 'Closed trial, open trial, you name it, I'll do it. Give me leniency in return.'

Zeb studied him.

He was the man on the ground. Nothing would have happened without him. He got Abrahms to leak the missile position.

The cold rage returned.

And he was going to negotiate with ISIL.

'Sure, I'll be lenient,' he told Bob Marin. 'I'll kill you quickly.'

And shot him.

Chapter 100

———⚬⚬⚬———

Beth and Meghan hacked Marin's phone and found a series of messages and calls to Spears. Nothing incriminating in them; however, they weren't looking for more proof.

They were looking for his schedule, the frequency of his communications with his conspirators. It turned out the ShadowPoint CEO was the only one he talked to.

'Makes sense,' Zeb said when the sisters outlined it to him. 'Spears, he's probably the one who keeps Hsu and Vaughan in the loop. Can you do it?'

'Ask something more challenging,' Beth snickered.

It was to keep up the pretense that Bob Marin—lying dead on the floor, his brains blown out—was alive and well.

Werner studied the CEO's emails, learned how he wrote them, how he addressed his staff. It sent out a message to his reports saying he would be working from home for a few days and wasn't to be disturbed.

It learned Marin's speech patterns, the words he used, his pauses, and created several brief clips that it would play back if anyone called his phone. Like, *Hey, John, I'm with someone now. Shall I call you back?*

Those clips wouldn't withstand a lengthy conversation with someone who knew Marin well, but they would buy time.

Until we get to Spears.

Zeb watched as Meghan sent a terse message to the ShadowPoint CEO from Marin's phone.

Almasi responded. Will be meeting his people. Going dark for a couple of days.

They left the villa the way they had arrived. Stealthily, leaving behind one dead man and several bound security guards.

Bwana and Roger met a bunch of Delta operatives the next day in a city parking lot. The Agency men identified themselves, checked the credentials of the officers, made a call to Clare, who verified them, and led them to the van.

'Twenty-one Javelins,' Bwana said, pointing to the cases. 'Take them away.'

'You've been driving these around?' A short, bristly-haired officer chewed gum as he opened a crate and inspected its contents.

'Something like that.'

He snapped his fingers and looked up quickly. 'Say, are you the ones who're hunting this dude Carter? We heard something—'

'You see twenty-one missiles?'

'Yeah.'

'We're done, here.'

Chapter 101

Washington DC

Randy Spears was uneasy.

He was on his seventeenth-floor office on Pennsylvania Avenue, a short distance away from the White House. Shadow-Point owned the building outright but occupied only two floors. The remaining were rented out to other businesses. Mirrored glass, anti-surveillance tech, biometric entry, gait analysis— his two floors had every bit of high-tech gear expected in one of the world's most prominent military contractors.

The building had a basement parking lot, but Spears didn't use that one. Nope, he didn't mix with commoners. He had a private lot, just for his vehicle, which opened discreetly on Twelfth Street.

'Hold my calls,' he told his EA and rocked back on his two-thousand-dollar, air-cushioned leather chair.

He couldn't put his finger on what troubled him, but the feeling persisted.

He recalled that day in Iraq when he was leading his team

of operatives. Their target was a building in Baghdad that was supposed to be abandoned. Intel had suggested it was where a wanted terrorist was based. The street was silent, hot, dusty. Nothing moved on it. Spears was crouched behind a bombed-out car, eyes on the building's entrance. Thermal imaging had confirmed the presence of one person; his snipers on nearby rooftops and buildings had sighted the hostile. He was alone, unarmed, as he slept.

It looked like a straightforward smash-and-grab operation. There wasn't anything to smash, either. There were no doors in the building.

Still, Spears hesitated. Something held him back from giving the *go.* A chunk of concrete moved as he watched, rippling in the hot wind. He gawped in astonishment. Concrete blown by breeze? He raised his binos and looked closer, letting his peripheral vision work.

It was some kind of fabric! Artfully disguised to look like a block of concrete. That steel bar that was exposed when it moved … that was a rifle barrel.

'Another hostile,' he said hoarsely in his radio, 'at our ten, next to that pillar.'

Thermal, which had proven to be unreliable, had missed the shooter's presence. His men scanned the street again, looking again at every shadow, every building, every beam, and this time they identified more shooters.

A go from him that day would have resulted in an ambush.

He felt just like that day in Baghdad.

Marin's message had been good news. He had refrained from making any call to him, knowing the ISIL discussions needed all of the CEO's attention, and the sudden trill or vibration of a phone could be dangerous.

Hsu was also satisfied with progress. It looked like his killer had come out the loser against Carter. However, that wouldn't be a setback if Marin pulled off his deal.

Vaughan was annoyed that the president was now dragging his feet on his and the secretary of defense's Libya visit. 'That militia shootout in Sirte,' he grumbled. 'He's worried the security situation has worsened. Both McClellan and I have told him nothing has changed, but you know how he is.'

'In any case, we gotta wait,' Spears told him. 'Kanaan hasn't come back to Marin with the contract. Till then, you aren't going. Get your people to submit a report to the president. I can't see him calling off your visit.'

That feeling persisted when he hung up. He checked his meetings schedule. Nothing that couldn't be put off. A call with the Bolivian president. He was accused of corruption and was fearing for his safety. He had approached ShadowPoint for help, and Spears was happy to assist.

How about meeting him in person?

It helped that Spears had a secure villa in La Paz, the capital city.

He came to a sudden decision.

'Brody,' he called the head of his two-person security detail. 'Alert Jonas. Get the car ready. I'm coming down. Nope, we're going to Ronald Reagan Airport. Bolivia. Inform the jet. Yeah, right away.'

He hung up, told his EA to reschedule all his meetings, packed his briefcase and went to the private elevator.

There were several benefits to being single and having no family. Traveling at a moment's notice was one of them.

Lucky for me I was never into the wife, two kids, a

dog, white-picket-fence thing.

He strode into the parking lot and headed to his Merc. Black, gleaming, dark windows, armored body. It should have been the only vehicle in the lot, but there were two SUVs, neither of which he recognized. He opened his mouth in irritation, snapped it shut when it came to him.

Must be my team's rides.

'Brody, Jonas,' he snapped at his two men lounging against the wall. 'Move your asses. Let's get going.'

He opened the rear door, flung his briefcase inside and bent down to slide inside.

Chapter 102

Zeb stopped the briefcase's slide.

'Going somewhere?' he asked when Spears twisted his body to climb inside.

The CEO froze for a moment. He lowered his head to look inside the car. His eyes widened at Zeb's presence.

'You?' he whispered.

His right hand, which was reaching for the grab handle, straightened, and the concealed sleeve gun shot out like a striking snake, all in one smooth, practiced move.

Zeb was expecting it.

He snatched the briefcase and held it in front of his face just as Spears fired twice. The rounds flew out faster than the eye could see, slammed into the case, pierced through the leather surface and came to an abrupt halt when they struck the composite metal-foam panels inside.

He flung the case at the CEO, kicked him in the belly and sent him staggering back. Spears recovered fast. He recovered his balance and brought the sleeve gun up.

Zeb shot him in the left shoulder. Then the right. Leapt on him and whipped him across the face with the barrel of his

Glock, and when Spears fell, pounded his face on concrete.

'Hold up, fellas,' Bwana called out when Brody and Jonas started hurrying towards their boss.

He came from behind one of the SUVs and strolled towards the two men. Roger joined him. Both of them loose, ready, dynamite on legs.

'Who are you?' Brody asked, disconcerted by the sight of them, distracted by the shooting in the Merc.

'Me?' Bwana raised an eyebrow. 'I'm the one who can whoop your asses and not raise a sweat.'

There was some distance between him and Rog, enough that they could back each other up and yet not present a single target. Their hands were free, close to their bodies for a quick draw.

He eyed Brody and Jonas. No guns in their hands, but those bulges under their jackets were unmistakable.

He wasn't underestimating them. Beth had pulled their files. They had been special forces, too. Tours in 'Stan and Africa. But they had gone private several years ago and had been on this gig for a while now.

No recent field experience. That took the edge off an operative.

Nope, Bwana wasn't underestimating them. But he also knew what he and Rog could achieve.

'Let those two fight it out,' he said mildly, jerking his head at Spears and Zeb on the floor.

'Fight?' Roger exaggerated. 'Their boss isn't giving much of one, is he?'

'Who's he?' Jonas asked, sensing danger.

'Him? He can whip you too,' Bwana replied, 'but he'll

raise a sweat.'

'I will not!' Roger protested.

'You definitely will.

'Nope.'

'Only one way to find out.'

The protection detail had had enough of their act. Their hands flickered towards their guns.

Bwana was close enough to Brody that he didn't need to draw his Glock. He dropped his shoulder and charged.

His football tackle caught the man high on the shoulder and sent him backwards several steps. He grabbed the man's waist and threw him down in a judo-style move and smashed his face with a fist the size of a shovel.

Looked at his friend, who was trading punches with Jonas. Even as he watched, Roger dropped to the floor, pirouetted on one leg, extended the other in a balletic move and spun-kicked the security man's legs.

'Check your forehead,' he told his friend, who pounced on Jonas and rendered him immobile.

Roger wiped his brow, looked at the sheen of sweat on it and cursed.

'Told ya,' Bwana said triumphantly. He looked over at the Merc. His expression changed.

'Zeb! ZEB!' he yelled, 'we need him alive.'

Bwana's voice penetrated the red mist in Zeb's head. He let go of Spears's hair.

The ShadowPoint CEO's face was ruined. His nose was broken, his lips smashed; one eye was shut, the other barely visible through the blood.

He managed a laugh, which turned into a tortuous cough.

'You think,' he gasped, 'I haven't been through worse? You can torture me all you want; you won't get anything from me.'

'We know everything, dumbass,' Bwana said contemptuously as he hauled Zeb to his feet, began searching Spears and removed an ankle gun. 'Bob Marin—yeah, your man,' he chortled when the CEO stiffened, 'he didn't hold back. We want your phone and laptop access. Nothing more.'

Spears twisted his head to take them in. 'Marin—'

'Is dead,' Zeb said shortly. 'He confessed. You, Vaughan, Hsu, we know it all.'

The CEO coughed blood and groaned. 'Why am I alive, in that case?'

'I want to rip you apart,' Zeb said bitterly. 'But Bwana's right.'

'You want only my cell phone and laptop passwords?'

'You heard us the first time,' Roger sighed.

'What do I get in return?'

'Your freedom,' Bwana growled. 'In a prison cell,' he added.

'Why should I believe you?'

'Why wouldn't you? You think we can't hack you? How do you think we got here? However, it takes time. You could save us that by cooperating.'

'You would be dead by now if we wanted to kill you,' Roger said, wiping his forehead again. No, it must be the heat. He wasn't sweating from his fight with the bodyguard. The heat and the air-restricting clothing he wore.

Spears's visible eye blinked as he considered their offer. He craned his head to look at Brody and Jonas, both of them secured with zip-ties.

'Alright,' he said, and when Roger took his phone, he

guided him to unlock it. 'Similar sequence for my laptop,' he said.

'You sure?' Bwana asked him.

'Yeah.'

Bwana shot him in the forehead.

'I lied,' he said, when Roger looked at him in that amused way the Texan had perfected. 'What's he going to do? Sue me?'

President Morgan made the call to Prime Minister Sabbagh in Clare's presence.

The two leaders exchanged pleasantries, and then the president got down to it.

'I have a delicate matter to discuss, sir,' he told the Libyan leader.

'Anything, Mr. President. If I can help, I will.'

'Sir, I understand there's a file circulating in your cabinet. It might have come to you as well. It's about a contract between NOC and a large, prominent US oil company.'

He looked up to check if the Agency director had heard the prime minister's sharp intake of breath.

'I am not aware of such a contract, Mr. President,' Sabbagh said, hiding his reaction smoothly. 'In any case, NOC's an independent company. They have many contracts with many companies.'

'This one is very different, sir. It has come to our knowledge that the US firm has broken several laws to secure this contract. I wanted you to know that the company is under investigation. That this contract will never be honored.'

A long silence.

'Mr. President,' Sabbagh began after a while, 'I was under

the impression US presidents don't interfere in the runnings of American firms.'

'They absolutely do, sir, when our national security is at stake and when significant federal laws are broken. Sir, I would also appreciate if no one knows of our conversation. Not at this moment.'

'Mr. President, you want me to keep knowledge of a contract, of which I know nothing, to myself?' Sabbagh asked sarcastically.

'Yes, sir, and when this file comes to you or when you become aware of it, I would like you to reject it. This contract cannot go ahead, sir.'

'I don't know what to say, Mr. President.'

'The US government will be most grateful, sir.'

We'll increase trade with them, the President mouthed to Clare, who nodded.

'I think it would be good if you made a state visit to DC, sir,' he said, adding another sweetener. 'The world will know how strong our relationship is. Please bring your family, too. We'll be delighted to host them.'

'I'll make note of that, Mr. President,' Sabbagh said, warming. 'And this file, I will do what I can.'

'Thank you, Mr. Prime Minister. Like I said before, please keep this conversation to yourself.'

Which meant, *I'll know who the leak was if it goes public.*

Chapter 103

⎯⎯⎯∞⎯⎯⎯

Paul Vaughan took the rooftop elevator in his bathrobe.

He had swum fifteen laps in the pool and was feeling pleasantly buzzed. Who the heck was going to object if he wandered around in his robe? It was his home!

He padded across the warm, concrete floor and reached the table. On it was a bottle of fine cognac brandy, a snifter and nibbles. His butler had laid them out for him and had made himself scarce.

He reached for the bottle and twisted it open. Huh? He could have sworn this was a new bottle, since he had finished the previous one a while back. Never mind. He poured himself a generous shot, swirled it around in the glass and went to the parapet.

Four-story, luxury house in McLean. Indoor swimming pool, private theater, huge front and rear gardens ... Vaughan had splurged on the house when he had been appointed as secretary of state. What else could he spend his money on? He was divorced and dated occasionally but had no partner. The house, which had been featured in a few architecture journals, went well with his image and his ambitions.

'Fine night,' a voice said.

He shrieked in alarm and jumped back when a figure appeared next to him. A woman. Tall. Light hair. Green eyes, from what he could make out.

'Who are you?' he said, recovering. 'You're trespassing. You need to leave immediately.'

He darted to the table and picked up a phone.

'It's dead,' another voice said.

He spun around—wait, how did she get *there*? No, this one was different. They were twins!

They faced him, arms crossed, backs to the parapet. No weapons in their hands, he noticed.

'Who the hell are you?' he roared. 'Do you know who I am? How dare you—'

'He doesn't know us,' one twin said to the other.

'Why would he? He's the secretary of state. An important person. Very Important. He knows people like Hazim Kattan and Nashaat Munjid Kanaan.'

Vaughan stared at them.

'Don't forget Nasir Fakhir Almasi.'

His insides turned to jelly. Did they know? No, that couldn't be possible. No one knew.

He strode towards them, his hands reaching out to drag them towards the elevator.

'Touching us will be harmful to you.'

'You won't live,' the other added said softly, with such confidence that he knew they weren't lying.

'I don't know who you think you are,' he bellowed, 'but you need to leave. I'll call my security—'

'They won't respond.'

He ran to the elevator, reached inside for the wall-mounted

phone, started shouting in it before he realized it was dead, too.

He hung up and took them in with his gaze. He was a cabinet secretary. One of the most powerful people in the world. He had been a warrior once. He could deal with a couple of intruders.

'What is this?' he said, laughing scornfully as he tried to hide his fear. Drank from his snifter to get some liquid courage. 'A robbery? Some extortion scheme?'

'You read about any twins recently?'

'What?'

They kept silent.

'I don't keep any money with me—'

Wait, stop talking, his lizard brain warned him. *What did she say? Did I read something about twins?*

He wracked his memory as he looked at them. He hadn't met them before, he was sure of that. It was his job to remember faces, and these two were strangers.

Something about their comport, their quietness, unnerved him. What they had said scared him. These weren't petty burglars or a home invasion team.

And then he got it.

The Agency! Carter's team had a pair of sisters in it.

'My God,' he breathed as his snifter slipped from his fingers and crashed to the floor. 'You're with him.'

'Now, he remembers,' one twin said, drolly.

'Zeb Carter?' the other said. 'Yeah, we are with him.'

'What are you doing here?' he shouted. 'Shouldn't you be hunting him?'

'We found him.'

'He's dead?'

'Shhh … we came to show you a movie. Oh no, none of those dirty ones. You'll enjoy this.'

She removed a tablet from her jacket, swiped on it and turned it around for him.

'GET OUT OF MY HOUSE …' he trailed off when he saw Marin in the video.

'It was Paul Vaughan's idea,' the Saharol CEO was saying.

'Paul Vaughan, the US secretary of state?' an offscreen voice asked.

'Yeah, him. He and Randy Spears roped me in. Jian Hsu joined us.'

'LIES,' Vaughan thundered. 'WHO'S THAT MAN?'

'Get equity in NOC … frame Carter … threat as long as he was alive …'

'ENOUGH OF THAT,' he gesticulated angrily. 'Some stranger says that and you believe him?'

'Randy Spears implicated you as well. Earlier today. You want to hear his confession?'

Vaughan swayed as if he had been hit. Marin and Spears. What else did they say?

'Everything,' one of them said. They looked at him with contempt and disgust.

'Why did you do it?'

He licked his lips, looked behind him to check if the FBI were there. No. Then he remembered Carter's exploits. His missions didn't end in arrests.

'It isn't what it looks like,' he began, fear filling him, sweat breaking out.

They weren't listening.

'What you have,' her sister gestured at his fancy house, 'wasn't enough? You wanted more?'

'He did, and don't forget the presidential run.'

'Money and power, yeah. The oldest two motives.'

An inarticulate sound escaped him. He could convince them. Offer them millions. Only if he could get himself to speak. But he was paralyzed. His body couldn't move. His limbs felt heavy. His robe was sticking to his back. His entire body was perspiring. His mind—there was nothing wrong with it. He heard and watched and understood what they were saying.

'Funny, it would have worked.'

'Yeah,' the other agreed. 'You made one mistake.'

They approached him. He feet felt leaden as they responded with difficulty, taking him backwards. They kept coming until he was jammed against the elevator wall.

'Three of them.'

'You're right. First, you picked on the wrong man. Zeb Carter.'

It felt dreamlike, the way they twined their arms with his and led him back to the parapet. He tried to say something, but the words stuck in his throat. He tried to resist, but, a firm tug and his feet followed them. That, or he would be dragged, and he didn't want that. He, the secretary of state, wasn't going to be dragged anywhere.

'The second, you underestimated Zeb. He doesn't die easily.'

'Third, he has friends. Us.'

Vaughan didn't know who pushed him. Maybe it was both of them. All he knew he was flying through the air, screaming for help, his garden approaching fast.

Then he felt nothing.

'You think he's dead?' Beth asked dispassionately.

'If that fall didn't finish him, that chemical concoction in his brandy will,' Meghan replied. 'Let's go.'

They scaled down the house, ran across the garden, climbed up the compound wall and continued running to their vehicle.

Meghan slid behind the wheel and tore away the moment Beth joined her.

The shadow moved when their lights were distant. It came out on the road and watched until they disappeared. It entered Vaughan's house the same way they had exited it.

It bent over the secretary of state and confirmed he was dead.

Zeb smiled grimly when he straightened.

They knew I would head here. They wanted to finish him before I did.

He went through the house, checked that the twins had left no trace.

They hadn't.

The home's security system would turn back on after a period of time, its phones would resume. The cops would be puzzled why everything was down for a while. There would be a rigorous investigation, but they would find nothing. They wouldn't find anything in his body, either.

He drank too much. Lost his balance and fell.

That would be their verdict.

Those sisters, Zeb shook his head ruefully in the darkness, *I'm glad they're on my team.*

Chapter 104

DC commentators noticed that President Morgan didn't eulogize former Secretary of State Paul Vaughan, nor did he attend his funeral. He didn't mention him in any speech, either.

The White House released a bland statement expressing regret at his accidental death, conveyed condolences to his kin. Nothing more.

The media went to town. TV channels speculated why the president was so cold towards the secretary who had been a presidential hopeful.

The White House press secretary didn't take any questions on the subject. Told the journalists to respect Vaughan's family and give them space.

In the furor, little attention was paid to two news items. One was the killing of Bob Marin, Saharol's CEO, in a home invasion. Libyan police attributed it to a militia group that was demanding extortion, safety money, from the oil company.

The other was the abrupt disappearance of ShadowPoint's CEO, Randy Spears. He had been in Bolivia and was feared kidnapped and killed by terrorists.

Vaughan, Marin, Spears and the DOJ's announced opening

of an investigation into Saharol were forgotten when the president announced, a week later, the appointment of Miriam Chambers as the new secretary of state. Chambers, a former ambassador to the European Union, commanded the respect of world leaders, and her appointment was widely welcomed.

The public never came to know about a CIA report that concluded Zeb Carter had been set up, that the videos implicating him were fake, and that most likely a foreign nation was behind it.

That report went out to all home and allied agencies. Following that, a meeting of the kill committee was called and the termination order formally revoked.

The president had to wait for this due process to be completed before he quietly announced the reinstatement of the Agency and that Clare would resume as its director.

'This is Miriam's first cabinet meeting,' President Morgan announced as he surveyed his team in the White House. He paused for the applause to die down, introduced her to every other member, some of whom she had already met, and started discussing various agenda items both domestic and international.

Later, he put down his reading glasses. 'Two more matters,' he said. 'ShadowPoint. Catlyn isn't happy with them. Nor are DSS, Defense and many other intelligence agencies. A multi-agency team— CIA, FBI, NSA, a few others—will be investigating that firm for how it handles classified intel and how it operates. Needless to say, we have terminated all ShadowPoint contracts. That leads me to my main point. I don't like it that we're working with so many private contractors. Why do we need them? Why can't we grow numbers in our military?'

No one answered his rhetorical question.

'Lester,' he looked at his defense secretary, 'I need you to form a team. Catlyn should be in it; you can decide who else. I want a plan from you. ASAP. On reducing our dependency on contractors. The billions of dollars we spend on them … I would rather spend on our own personnel. Any questions?'

No one spoke.

'A final point. Catlyn?'

The CIA director passed a set of envelopes, which were circulated around the table.

'Open those.'

He grinned broadly when gasps broke out.

'Yes, that is Nasir Fakhir Almasi and his deputy, Abu Bakhtar. They are dead. A CIA operation supported by an unnamed agency. We have dealt a major blow to ISIL.'

He let the cheers and clapping go on for a long while, turning his eyes to Clare, who smiled briefly.

It had been her idea that the CIA should get credit. Feder had argued vehemently against it, but the Agency head got her way.

'We work in the dark,' Clare had explained. 'We've had too much attention of late. I want the spotlight removed.'

'Your team did this. Carter, he's responsible,' Catlyn said.

'Yes, but they don't want credit. It's how we work.'

'Catlyn,' the president had intervened, 'listen to her.' And that was the end of the argument.

'I want to discuss these kill orders,' the president said after the cabinet meeting ended. He was addressing Catlyn Feder,

Clare, Lester McClellan and Lizzie Kahn, whom he had asked to stay back.

'I don't like that we have them.' He raised a hand when Kahn and McClellan began protesting. 'I *understand* why they're necessary on certain occasions,' he clarified. 'What happened with Carter'—everyone in the room knew all the details beyond the CIA report— 'shouldn't have happened. I want to make some changes.'

'Sir,' McClellan objected, 'you shouldn't be involved with the details.'

'I am not going to be, Lester. From now, only three people will decide on whether such an order is to be issued. Those two will bring in more people in the decision-making if they see fit: Clare, Catlyn and Lizzie. They have to be unanimous, otherwise no kill order is issued.

'Sir—'

'Lester, this isn't up for discussion. I am confident they will act as checks and balances on one another. The current twenty-person committee is too cumbersome—'

'Sir, the more people we have, the fairer the decision.'

'The more people we have,' the president shot back, 'the more opportunity for politicking. Lester,' he said in a conciliatory tone, 'let's try this out my way. I am happy to review it. What I don't want is another incident like Carter's.'

'I like the president's idea,' Kahn said, joining in support. 'Clare and Catlyn will work like counterweights. They'll provide balance. I suspect you want me to do the refereeing, sir.'

'You read my mind, Lizzie. Lester,' the president turned to his defense secretary, knowing he had to soothe him. 'When are you going to Libya?'

'Sir?' McClellan stammered, 'I thought that visit was canceled, what with Paul's death.'

'It got delayed, that's all. You are going. By yourself.' He smiled when McClellan's face brightened. *He'll love that. All the limelight to himself.*

'You're going to Beijing?' he asked Clare when they were heading out.

'Tonight, sir.'

'Bring them home, Clare.'

'We will, sir. If they want to come.'

He winked when Feder, Kahn, and McClellan looked on in confusion.

'You'll hear about it in a few days.'

Chapter 105

Beijing

Mulan Yuan Chia packed her bag listlessly and went to the bathroom. She washed her face, wiped it, and inspected herself in the mirror.

She looked tired. New wrinkles at the corners of her mouth and eyes. Her dark eyes, which had once been sparkly, were dull.

She had been different when Shaming Chia, her husband, had been around. Sure, he worked long hours and often came home when she was asleep. But he was there. She had a life with him. She had laughter and joy in her house.

Now?

She lived only for her daughter. Eight-year-old Zhao Jilin. For whom she had to continue working, even though she didn't enjoy it anymore.

Mulan was an English teacher in the British International School in downtown Beijing. She was the only Chinese woman who taught that language in her school. She had been proud of that fact when Shaming was around.

Her face crumpled when she thought of him. She grabbed a paper towel and dabbed at the tears flowing down her face.

He had just disappeared. He was there one day. He kissed her and Zhao, and went to his office.

He never returned.

The days that followed were horrifying. MSS officers, hooligans really, trashing their apartment, taking away all his files. Not answering any questions. Ignoring her screams and Zhao Jilin's crying.

She called MSS got no response. Wrote letters, didn't get a reply.

One evening, an officer came to her and said her husband was a traitor and that she should stop pestering the agency. She was lucky to be alive, he sneered.

The next day she and her daughter were turfed out of their government apartment. All the benefits they had enjoyed from his employment, his pension, subsidized bus and train tickets, everything stopped.

Thankfully, they had set aside some money. That, and her parents' help, had allowed her to rent an apartment in Shijing-shan. It was small, stuffy, and the roof leaked, but it was all she could afford.

She kept her job. The school didn't seem to know of what had happened to her husband, and her service continued. She was eternally grateful for that.

They killed him.

She knew that with a deep certainty.

Probably tortured him as well. She knew of the MSS's reputation and what it did to traitors.

She shivered. Her Shaming was a traitor? No, that couldn't be possible. He was proud of his country. Sure, he didn't think much of the government, but he wouldn't betray them.

But, who could she turn to for help?

She straightened when the door opened and another teacher entered. She washed her face again, straightened her hair and made small talk with an effort.

'I have to pick my daughter up,' she said, glancing at her watch, and hurried out.

Pick Zhao up from her nearby school, make the hour drive back to Shijingshan, cook dinner, spend some time with her daughter, help her with her homework, watch some TV, get her to bed, repeat the routine the next day.

She had become a machine, with no feelings left.

She drove like a robot to Zhao's school. Collected her from the school gate and seated her in the rear.

She headed home, absentmindedly listening to her daughter chatter about her day.

Later, she would know the accident would have happened even if she hadn't been robotic.

Chapter 106

⸺⸻⸺

The van crashed into the side of her vehicle and drew her off Golou Street.

It happened so fast, she couldn't react. She sat in stunned silence as steam hissed from the front of her car.

Then she screamed. Looked back to see Zhao was crying. She scrambled back, shouting hoarsely, praying as she unbuckled the girl and held her and found she was unhurt—not even a scratch. And Mulan then realized she, too, was unhurt.

She was sobbing, however, holding her baby to her chest, crying, and thought was beyond her. So, when the door opened and three EMS workers helped her out, she didn't question them.

She was vaguely aware one of them was a woman and the other two men, all three taller than her.

'We'll take you to the hospital,' the woman said.

Mulan nodded, still crying, shivering, and shaking with shock, and let them guide her into the ambulance. It sped down the streets of Beijing.

Awareness returned when she realized the emergency vehicle was taking a long time to get to the hospital. She frowned and peered out of the window. They were going northeast. Well away from the nearest medical center, which had been just a few minutes from the crash. On top of that, she was alone in the back, with Zhao. That was strange. Didn't EMS workers get in the back, along with the victims?

MSS! They kidnapped me and Zhao.

'STOP!' She hammered the glass partition, through which she could see the driver and the three workers.

'STOP!' she repeated when they didn't look back.

She kept pounding the partition until her wristwatch broke and Zhao resumed crying. Her voice turned hoarse and only then, with fear spreading through her, did she stop and pick up her daughter.

She slid on the leather seat when they halted abruptly.

She lashed out with her foot when the door opened.

The tall man avoided the kick.

He stood aside and a woman approached her.

'Mrs. Chia,' the woman said in Mandarin. 'I'm sorry for that accident. We took great care to make sure you and Zhao weren't hurt, but still, I know it must have been frightening.'

Mulan stared at her, the words registering. She started noticing details. The woman wasn't Chinese. Her eyes were grey. Her skin tone ... she was a Westerner for sure, yet she spoke like a native.

The men with her ... the driver had green eyes. The two others—one looked older than the second, and that one, oh my, he was like a model. None carried weapons. None seemed aggressive. All of them were waiting for her to answer.

They were in some kind of concrete bunker ... no, it was a parking lot, but the ambulance was the only vehicle.

'Mrs. Chia?' the woman asked. 'Did you hear me?'

'Who … are you?' Mulan climbed out carefully, hugging Zhao. She shied when the handsome man offered to help. He dropped his hand immediately and stepped back.

No, this wasn't MSS behavior.

'My name is Clare. I am the director of strategy at the White House.'

'White … House?' Mulan asked dumbly.

'Yes, Mrs. Chia. The US White House. I report to the President of the United States. He's my boss.'

This couldn't be real. She must have fallen asleep at the wheel.

'Mrs. Chia,' the driver said in Mandarin, 'this isn't a dream, ma'am. The accident happened. We *rescued* you and brought you here.'

Mulan looked around her. She saw a sign *Terminals* with an arrow pointing the way. Smaller letters beneath it. She squinted and read: *Beijing Capital International Airport.*

'Airport?'

'Yes, Mrs. Chia, we're there,' the woman, Clare, replied. She removed a visiting card from the inside of her suit and presented it.

Mulan took it with shaking fingers. She recognized the double-headed eagle from countless Hollywood movies. Her trembling increased when she read the woman's name and her title.

'I don't understand,' she whispered.

'It's a long story,' the American replied. Those cool eyes turned distant. Something flashed in them. 'I am responsible for your husband's death. In a way.'

The card slipped from Mulan's hand.

The handsome man picked it up and handed it to the woman.

Seconds ticked. They felt like hours. Mulan's heart thudded so loudly she felt it would burst from her chest and spring out of her body.

'You killed him?' her voice shook.

'No, Mrs. Chia. He was helping us, but MSS found out about it and they killed him.'

Mulan didn't know she was crying until the driver handed her a paper towel. She shifted Zhao to her other arm and dabbed at her eyes.

'You're going to kill me?'

'What? No, Mrs. Chia. Here, this might help you understand.' The woman removed an envelope and presented it to her. Saw that Mulan's hands were busy and slit the envelope with a nail.

'It's from President Morgan,' she said. She removed the letter and held it for Mulan to read.

Dear Mrs. Chia, the letter began.

Her head swam as she took it in. ... *deeply regret what happened to your husband ... a grateful United States ... fast-track citizenship ... a new life ... the very least that our country can do for you.*

'You want me to come to America?' She was proud that her voice was steady.

'Yes, Mrs. Chia. We have some idea of what you've gone through. As the president said, we owe you. We can't bring your husband back, but we can offer you and Zhao a new life, a new start. Freedom.'

Freedom.

The word echoed in Mulan's mind.

'When?' she croaked.

'Right now,' Clare replied. 'There's a jet waiting for us.'

'My school … apartment … Zhao's –'

'Mrs. Chia, we'll take care of it. You have my word.'

'You want me to leave my life, just like that, and go with you?'

'Yes.'

Clare came forward. Gripped her shoulders and looked in her eyes. 'I never knew Shaming Chia, but I think he would have asked you to come with us. He was a brave man who did what he did for China. He wanted a better world for you and Zhao.'

Mulan broke down. She leaned into Clare and bawled on her shoulder; her daughter crushed between them. She didn't care that she was crying unashamedly, on a stranger, on a foreigner; it felt right, and when she felt the American's arms go around her, she knew it *was* right.

The bike entered the parking lot as she and Zhao were being led to the terminal, to the waiting aircraft. Clare was in the front of the group, the driver with her. Mulan and Zhao were behind them, and the remaining two men at the rear.

Clare stopped. Looked at the rider, who removed his helmet. Brown-haired man. Lean. Tall. Relaxed. Looking at Mulan and Zhao intensely.

'All okay?' she asked him.

'Yes, ma'am,' he replied.

Clare resumed walking.

'He's one of yours?' Mulan asked him when they turned a corner.

'Yes, Mrs. Chia.'

'He isn't coming with us?'

'He's got some unfinished business.'

Chapter 107

———— ∞∞∞ ————

Jian Hsu finished a meeting and headed to his office.

It was on a high floor in a skyscraper in Beijing's Central Business District. This was one of many MSS offices from which he worked. He changed his location each week as part of his elaborate security precautions.

He closed the glass door to his office and sat down in his chair, glaring at a flunky who dared to look up from his screen at the MSS head. The worker straightened and bent over his keyboard.

Discipline. It was necessary. It had to be enforced. That was the only way China would progress.

He drank some water, wiped his lips and prepared to address his files. He had to demonstrate that he could put in long hours, like his underlings.

What? No files. His desk was bare, except for a white envelope.

That secretary of his was slacking. He needed to be threatened.

He opened the envelope and removed the sheet of paper inside it. Glanced at it impatiently.

There was just one sentence on it.

Shaming Chia says hello.

Handwritten. Neat lettering.

Hsu felt like he had been punched. He stared at it dumbly. Got up so rapidly that his chair went hurtling backwards.

He spun towards the window, half-expecting to see a missile streaking towards him.

Nothing.

He found his voice as he ran out of his office.

'WHO PUT THAT ENVELOPE ON MY TABLE? GET SECURITY TO CHECK MY OFFICE FOR BOMBS. CHECK IT FOR POISON. MOVE.'

Poison!

He raced to the bathroom as the office exploded with commotion, his staff jumping at his commands. He rushed to the sink and soaped his hands. Scrubbed them. Applied soap again and washed them some more. Repeated three more times.

He noticed he was trembling. When he returned to the office hallway, he masked it with a show of anger, directing his people here, there, everywhere.

He was back at his desk several hours later.

No bomb. No poison. No virus in their computers. No stranger captured on the cameras. Nothing. Everything normal.

Finally, he was alone, his security detail outside his office. He had sent everyone else home.

His eyes went involuntarily to the letter that lay on the table. To that single line.

And one of the most powerful men in the country started

shivering. He clenched his fists. That didn't work. He rubbed his jade ring furiously. That didn't help.

Someone had hacked into their systems and enabled the entry of a messenger so well-disguised that no one noticed him. That man had placed the letter on his desk and had disappeared.

Jian Hsu trembled.

There were a few organizations out there who could hack into the MSS systems, but he instinctively knew who was responsible.

The Agency.

There were a few men who were bold enough to carry out the deed. He knew who it had to be.

Zeb Carter.

Jian Hsu also knew what that line meant.

The American wanted him to spend the rest of his life looking over his shoulder, jumping at the slightest sound, fearing every shadow.

Zeb Carter wanted him to wake up every morning thinking it would be his last day on Earth.

Jian Hsu had poked the beast.

The beast was coming.

Bonus Chapter from *Zeb Carter*

'I have a particular talent.' The speaker was young, in his mid-twenties. He was dark-haired, brown-eyed and stood ramrod straight.

He was casually dressed—shirt tucked into a pair of jeans, belt around his waist—as he stood in the room in front of five seated men in suits. All of them had a presence.

The speaker guessed they were men who decided on war; how it was fought and where. He knew he was looking at military men. That had been made clear before the interview. Now, on observing them, he guessed they were three- or four-star generals, or their equivalents from the Navy or Air Force.

No names had been exchanged when he entered the room, in an anonymous-looking building in DC.

He had looked it up. It was occupied by various private companies and also rented out rooms by the hour.

'What talent is that?' said a balding man, as he removed his glasses and rubbed his eyes.

It had been a long day and they seemed to be nowhere near making a decision. That's what it felt like to the speaker.

'Finding people, sir.'

Several suits snorted.

'The military has enough of such soldiers, son,' a silver-haired man spoke. 'We don't need another one.'

'And killing them, sir. Killing those who are threats to us.'

That stopped them.

Those who were good in the killing arts weren't uncommon in the military, either. Or on the outside, in the private-sector world.

But the way the young man had spoken struck them.

He was utterly confident, without being arrogant. He was calm, his voice so soft they almost had to strain to hear him.

It was rare for men of their seniority to come together and interview candidates. Most men or women would have felt intimidated by them, even without knowing who they were, what rank they held.

Yet, the man facing them seemed unaffected.

He stood, arms crossed behind his back, legs spread apart slightly and looked them in the eye.

No hesitation. No fidgeting.

Many of the previous candidates had been arrogant. One had boasted about the kills he had made. The panel had shown him out quickly.

A squat, suited man picked up the speaker's folder and rifled through it. Somalia. Iraq. Lebanon. Israel. Greece. London. Belfast. Several redacted portions, to which they had access.

The current candidate had been to several of the hot spots of the world.

He had led units. He had worked independently. He had been in hostile country, undercover for months.

He spoke several languages fluently.

A superior had jotted a comment. *Has an ear for languages.*

In just a few weeks, in a new country, can speak well enough to get by.

He was a master sniper. He had won several unarmed-combat trophies. Those who knew him, respected him.

The man lingered in the last country the candidate had been to while in the military.

Afghanistan.

He whispered to his peers. The file was passed around.

'We didn't know we had Superman in our ranks,' Silver Hair said sarcastically.

The candidate's reaction astounded them.

He unbuttoned his shirt, all the while looking at them.

'What? What are you doing?' the suit roared.

The candidate didn't stop.

He removed his shirt. Removed his vest.

And then pointed to a badly healed wound just below his heart.

'I don't think Superman has such a scar.'

'You think this is a joke?' Silver Hair rose. 'Do you know who we are? Just because you aren't in the military, you think you can get away with such behavior? You are walking that close to the edge, young man.'

The speaker finished dressing and stood smartly, waiting for the outburst to finish.

'Yes, sir. And I apologize for offending you. I meant no disrespect. Way I figure, you have been sitting there all day, listening to other candidates like me. You are trying to decide who's the best person for the job. You made a comment. I do not know if you were serious. I could have said something. Lots of words, but I thought you probably have had enough of words, and hence my action.'

He paused a beat. 'I will understand if I am not selected. For whatever you have in mind.'

The suits did the bent-heads-whispering-furiously thing again.

'You are not afraid?' the balding man asked him.

'Yes, sir. I am.'

'I don't mean that stunt you pulled off,' the man waved. 'I mean in the field.'

'I am often afraid, sir.'

'And yet you came here.'

'I was told it would be a good idea to offer my services to my country,' the candidate said, smiling sardonically.

'You know you won't get paid?'

'Yes, sir.'

'Driven by noble intentions, no doubt,' Silver Hair said sarcastically.

The candidate didn't rise to the bait.

'You know what this is about?' The balding general threw an irritated glance at the interruption.

'I can make a guess. You are looking for an outside contractor. That means whatever you are planning is high-risk and has to be deniable. I was told your candidate should speak Pashtun. Right now, Afghanistan is our hottest spot. Maybe you're thinking of rescuing those three Delta operators. Using someone like me?'

Silence in the room.

'You are still bound by the declarations and non-disclosures you signed,' Silver Hair barked.

'Sir,' the speaker said, smiling fully, 'I am sure you vetted all the candidates before interviewing them. None of us would have been in this room if we were in the habit of running to the nearest newspaper, TV channel, or website.'

More silence.

'That's the most hostile terrain in the world,' squat suit said, shifting in his metal chair. 'The most dangerous fighters out there.'

'Yes, sir. I have been there. I have fought them.'

'Indeed, you have. And you still want to go back? Assuming that's the operation. You could die.'

'I don't mind dying, sir.'

'Let me get this straight,' Silver Hair said brusquely. 'You are willing to go on something that's pretty much a suicide mission. Involves no payment, no fame, no movie or book deal out of it. Why? Love of country?'

'I was Delta. Those men are Delta, sir,' the speaker said, as if that explained it all.

'You could be tortured.'

'I have been tortured, sir. Quite a few times.'

Silence.

The men stared at him.

He held their eyes.

'You like killing?' Silver Hair said, no inflection in his voice.

'No, sir.'

'What do you like?'

'Saving people, sir.'

A clock ticked somewhere. A chair scraped.

Outside the small room, faint voices could be heard.

The bald man spoke finally. 'Someone will let you know.'

'Yes, sir,' he squared his shoulders and turned to leave.

'A moment?'

'Sir?'

'Why did you leave Delta?'

'I was getting promoted, sir. That meant a desk job.'

'You don't like management? The administration side of operations?'

'I do, sir. But not if it's what I have to do all day.'

'You like the money as a private military contractor?'

'I am a mercenary, sir,' a smile ghosted over his lips and disappeared quickly. 'There's no need to use fancy words. To answer your question, I do, but I don't do it just for the money.'

'What's your name? All the folders are anonymous.'

'You don't have to share it, if you don't want to,' he added quickly.

'Zebadiah Carter, sir.'

'Zebadiah. That's quite a mouthful, son.'

'Everyone calls me Zeb, sir.'

And Zeb Carter left the room.

Author's Message

———∞∞∞———

Thank you for taking the time to read *Traitor*. If you enjoyed it, please consider telling your friends and posting a short review.

Sign up to Ty Patterson's mailing list (www.typatterson.com/subscribe) and get *The Watcher*, a Zeb Carter novella, exclusive to newsletter subscribers. Join Ty Patterson's Facebook Readers Group, at www.facebook.com/groups/324440917903074.

Check out Ty on Amazon, iTunes, Kobo, Nook, and on his website www.typatterson.com.

Books by Ty Patterson

Warriors Series Shorts
This is a series of novellas that link to the Warriors Series thrillers

Zulu Hour, Book 1
The Shadow, Book 2
The Man From Congo, Book 3
The Texan, Book 4
The Heavies, Book 5
The Cab Driver, Book 6
Warriors Series Shorts, Boxset I, Books 1-3
Warriors Series Shorts, Boxset II, Books 4-6

Gemini Series

Dividing Zero, Book 1
Defending Cain, Book 2
I Am Missing, Book 3
Wrecking Team, Book 4

Cade Stryker Series

The Last Gunfighter of Space, Book 1
The Thief Who Stole A Planet, Book 2

Warriors Series

The Warrior, Book 1
The Reluctant Warrior, Book 2
The Warrior Code, Book 3
The Warrior's Debt, Book 4
Flay, Book 5
Behind You, Book 6
Hunting You, Book 7
Zero, Book 8
Death Club, Book 9
Trigger Break, Book 10
Scorched Earth, Book 11
RUN!, Book 12
Warriors series Boxset, Books 1-4
Warriors series Boxset II, Books 5-8
Warriors series Boxset III, Books 1-8

Zeb Carter Series

Zeb Carter, Book 1
The Peace Killers, Book 2
Burn Rate, Book 3
Terror, Book 4
Traitor, Book 5
Zero Dark, Book 6

Sign up to Ty Patterson's mailing list and get *The Watcher*, a Zeb Carter novella, exclusive to newsletter subscribers. Join Ty Patterson's Facebook group of readers, at www.facebook.com/groups/324440917903074.

Check out Ty on Amazon, iTunes, Kobo, Nook and on his website www.typatterson.com.

About the Author

Ty has been a trench digger, loose tea vendor, leather goods salesman, marine lubricants salesman, diesel engine mechanic, and is now an action thriller author.

Ty is privileged that thriller readers love his books. 'Unputdownable,' 'Turbocharged,' 'Ty sets the standard in thriller writing,' are some of the reviews for his books.

Ty lives with his wife and son, who humor his ridiculous belief that he's in charge.

Connect with Ty:
Twitter: @pattersonty67
Facebook: www.facebook.com/AuthorTyPatterson
Website: www.typatterson.com
Mailing list: www.typatterson.com/subscribe

Made in the USA
Las Vegas, NV
07 March 2022

45210165R00343